Toy
Soldier

Toy
Soldier

R P Salmon

The Book Guild Ltd

First published in Great Britain in 2022 by
The Book Guild Ltd
Unit E2 Airfield Business Park,
Harrison Road, Market Harborough,
Leicestershire. LE16 7UL
Tel: 0116 2792299
www.bookguild.co.uk
Email: info@bookguild.co.uk
Twitter: @bookguild

Typeset in 11pt Adobe Garamond Pro Pro

Printed on FSC accredited paper
Printed and bound in Great Britain by 4edge Limited

ISBN 978 1915122 766

British Library Cataloguing in Publication Data.
A catalogue record for this book is available from the British Library.

For Cos

PART ONE

Rhianne

Eithan padded into the kitchen, rubbing a large black hand over a stubbly chin.

'Oh, I didn't mean to wake you,' lamented Rhianne, knowing how little sleep he was likely to get in the coming days and months.

'You didn't wake me. I came looking for that beautiful babe who deserted mi bed. Well truthfully, I came looking for a cuppa,' he added with a mischievous grin.

'Have mine. I can make another.'

'I knew there was a reason I married you,' he said, shamelessly accepting the proffered mug. Eyeing its pinkness and its *Girl Boss* slogan, he shrugged his shoulders in mock trepidation. 'Guess my manhood can survive a few slurps behind closed doors.'

Rhianne's weak smile was not lost on him. 'What's up babe?'

'I'm shit scared, Eithan.'

'You mustn't worry, Rhianne, I'm a sapper. I'll be on reconstruction work, bridge repairs, road maintenance, that sort of stuff. I won't be in the heat of the action.'

'But it's Basra not Belfast.'

'I'll keep myself safe, I promise. There's something else, isn't there?' he added, nodding to the letter lying on the kitchen table. 'I presume it's from Saint Ciara.'

3

'A job's come up, not far from her. I wish you'd stop calling her *Saint* Ciara. One of these days it'll slip out in her hearing. She'd be hurt.'

Eithan howled with laughter almost spilling his tea. 'Saint Ciara *wounded!* That sister of yours has the hide of a rhino.'

'You're truly awful, Eithan McArthur. Truly AWFUL. She's been so good to me and after you the person I love most in the whole wide world.'

Eithan could see Rhianne was upset so pulled her onto his knee. 'I'm sorry babe. Forgive mi rough sapper ways. I'm only teasing.' He squeezed her hand and kissed the end of her nose encouragingly.

'Come on Mrs McArthur, spill the beans. I shan't let you go till you tell me what's going on in that dreamy head of yours.'

'Now I've finished my catering course, I'll be kicking my heels for six months until you get back…' Eithan's playful expression dissolved instantly. The dark shadows were never far away. Now, they seized their opportunity to swoop back in, dulling his eyes and stiffening the faint laughter lines on his youthful jaw. Rhianne cursed her clumsiness. Those six months would have been given over to getting everything ready for the baby. The loss had knocked him sideways, punched another hole in his colander of grief.

'I didn't mean it to come out like that,' she moaned, burying her head in his chest. 'I—'

'It's okay, Rhianne. You don't need to tiptoe round me all the time.'

'Let's just forget it…'

'*Tell* me, Rhianne,' he insisted, 'and spare me the tiptoes.'

She pulled the advert out of the envelope and pushed it towards him.

Trainee pâtissier required for Beth's Bakery and tea shop. Applicants must have basic catering skills. Experience of special occasion cake making an advantage, but not essential as full training will be provided. The successful applicant will be required to carry out general duties in the bakery and tea shop alongside his or her training. Permanent appointment is conditional upon successful completion of six months' probation. Live in or out. Letters of application with two references to the proprietor Mrs Beth Brennan.

'What do you think?' she asked him nervously.

'Sounds intriguing. What have you got to lose?'

'My pride I suppose – if I get rejected. I thought you would hate the idea,' she said quietly.

'Rhianne, when have I ever hated any crack-brained notion of yours?'

'You think it's crack-brained?'

'No, you daft apeth, I think it's a swell idea. But you'd better get your skates on, the closing date's in six days' time.'

'I love you, Eithan McArthur,' she said, throwing hers arms around his neck, slopping what was left of his tea onto his boxer shorts. 'You're thoughtful and caring... and sensitive... and—'

'Hey, don't forget handsome and ripped...' he added, pointing to his torso in a fruitless attempt to regain the playful mood of earlier. She caressed his six-pack and then snuggled into him.

'... And I don't deserve you.'

'No, you bloody don't when a guy can't even get a decent breakfast round here.'

She smiled at him tenderly, understanding his pain and his hollow attempt to throw off the suffocating blanket that periodically enveloped him. She pulled his face into her hands and kissed him, long and hard. 'I SO love you,' she murmured, 'and breakfast will have to wait until you've taken me back to bed.'

*

Ten days later Rhianne's mobile rang. She rushed to pick up hoping it might be Eithan.

'Hi Sis.'

'Oh, Ciara,' came the deflated response. 'I thought it might be Eithan. You okay?'

'Yes, I'm good. Just in from school and checking the post. There's a letter come for you.'

It could only be from Beth's Bakery. Rhianne had been too cowardly to put the barracks address on her application, fearful of how it might be interpreted.

'You'd better open it and see what it says.'

'Okey doke, here goes:

Dear Ms McArthur,

*With regard to your recent trainee application, please attend for interview on Monday 27*th *March at 4pm at the address on the letter head.*

Yours sincerely,

Mrs Beth Brennan, Proprietor.'

'Is that it? Is that all it says?'

'Yep, that's your lot. Doesn't mince her words does she, our Mrs Brennan! What's with the Ms – something you're not telling me?'

'I just thought Mrs might not go down too well for a trainee post.' Another little white lie she had hidden behind. As the impact of the letter sunk in, Rhianne suddenly let out a squeal of delight. 'I've got an interview for my first *proper* job.'

The emphasis on 'proper' was not lost on Ciara but she chose not to react. Rhianne was in raptures. 'This is so exciting. Oh God, it's Thursday already…'

'Yeah, well she thinks you live thirty miles up the road not a couple of hundred down south. So, get your butt here pdq. I'll shoot out of school as early as I can tomorrow, but I'll leave a key in the usual place just in case you get there before me. Make yourself at home. Have to go now, pile of marking.'

Rhianne's excitement only momentarily lifted the anxiety that plagued her waking hours. The lump in the pit of her stomach refused to soften. She still had not heard from Eithan. *No news is good news*, everyone kept telling her. The two tours in Belfast had been nervous times but communication had been much easier. Basra was a whole different, chilling ball game. She tried to avoid watching the news when Iraq was featured but found herself drawn to it inexorably. The images made her blood run cold.

*

Ciara was still on the drive unpacking her school paraphernalia when Rhianne pulled up behind her. In seconds they were hugging each other.

'Hello, Sis,' beamed Ciara. Rhianne clung to her, not wanting to let go. 'Come on, let's go inside. You must be exhausted. I don't think you've ever done that journey by yourself. I'll put the kettle on. How's Eithan?'

'I don't know. Complete radio silence, so far.'

'But he's okay isn't he. I mean you would have heard something if he wasn't?'

'Oh yes. That's about the *only* news I can be sure of getting – if he's injured or captured… or killed,' she added quietly.

'Let's banish those thoughts right away. Nothing's going to happen to him. He's a walking four-leaf clover that guy. And you're going to get this job – and we're going to see lots of each other. And you'll have lots more babies and—'

'He took it so hard, Ciara,' interrupted Rhianne. 'His dad, his mum and then the baby,' she wept.

'I know, I know.' Ciara's tone softened, her habitual breeziness yielding to the higher demands of sisterly comfort. 'You'll get through this. It's going to be okay. We'll get through it together.' Rhianne just nodded, weeping silently into the folds of Ciara's cardigan.

'How's Dad?' asked Rhianne, lifting her head from a soggy woollen patch.

'Oh, much the same, you know. In good health but his world is very small these days. He's collapsing into himself.'

'Does he ever ask about me?'

Ciara said nothing, just shook her head resignedly. 'What you need is lots of TLC,' she said, attempting to lighten the mood. 'I'm officially designating myself Eithan's deputy for the weekend. So, you go and unpack, have a long soak in the bath and then we'll head out for the evening. Forget your fancy catering. You could do with some good old-fashioned comfort food. I'm taking you to the Seven Stars tonight. My treat. It's a bit of a drive, but worth it.'

*

That evening, the two sisters left early. Ciara was hoping for an opportunity to chat with the landlord before it got too busy. Jack Spedding knew everybody and everything hereabouts and she was anticipating fleecing him for some information about Beth's Bakery. The pub was characterful and inviting. There was a roaring log fire that Jack insisted on lighting every night, rain or shine, from October until Easter Day. Scratched, wonky tables and chairs with faded tapestry seat pads were strewn about under low oak beams that would have seen Eithan doubled over.

'Aiya Ciara, long time no see. What'll it be?' asked a beaming Jack Spedding.

'A large glass of chardonnay and a lager shandy. I'm driving!' she added, pulling a face.

'How've yer bin? And who's this beauty?'

'This, Jack Spedding, is my younger sister, Rhianne. A very respectable married lady, so you watch your Ps and Qs.'

'You can allers trust a teacher t' give yer a put down,' he mocked. 'Just visitin' yer bossy sister, Rhianne, or 'ere on business?' he asked.

'I've got an interview at Beth's Bakery in Silecroft on Monday – as a trainee pâtissier.'

'What's that when it's at 'ome?'

'*Pâtisserie* is the art of cake making, Jack,' replied Ciara, archly.

'Trust Beth Brennan to invent a posh name for bakin' buns.'

'She didn't invent it, Jack, the French did.'

'Hhmmp.'

'What can you tell us about Beth's Bakery?'

Jack warmed instantly to his gossipy task. 'It's got a good reputation. Even bin knoan t'order an odd occasion cake from 'er meself. Yeah, she runs a pop'lar tea shop. 'Twasn't allers like that mind. Built it up from nowt. Just a tiny little bread shop as once was.'

'And what about Mrs Brennan herself? What's she like?' pressed Ciara.

'Can't say as I know 'er personal like – she's not the sort to cum gallivan'ing out to a country pub. But Hilda and me, we goes way back.'

'Hilda?' queried Ciara.

'Hilda works in the bakery kitchen – so I knoas sommat about Mrs B that way.'

'And…?' asked the older sister, a little impatiently.

'There's no flies on Mrs B is what Hilda sez. Keeps 'erself to 'erself. Bit of a mystery woman. Nobody quite knoas when she cum 'ere or wheer she 'ailed from. She started out as t' kitchen assistant in t' bread shop as was owned by t' Cartwrights afore they retired. But she must've 'ad money behind 'er cos she bought t' shop outright when they left. If yer believe t' rumours, she's worth a bob or two – 'as an 'andful of rental properties an' all.'

'I knew you'd have the low down on this one, Jack. Thanks. What's on special tonight?'

'Steak an' kidney pud wi' mushy peas.'

'Wicked!' exclaimed Ciara. 'You have to taste Jack's steak and kidney pud, Rhianne. It's legendary in these parts. But you'll never finish it. Even Eithan might struggle to finish a whole one.'

'Eithan?' inquired Jack.

'Eithan's her husband, Jack, he's six foot four and a soldier so you watch your step,' replied Ciara. 'Let's have one pud special and one sausage and mash, that way we might finish them between us.'

'Okay, bossy britches. Cumin' up ladies. Yer must bring that there 'usband of yers 'ere one day an' we'll see if 'e can finish a pud all by 'imself.' Rhianne laughed along with the other two although she secretly thought Eithan more than up to the challenge.

*

'I've got cereal, toast, eggs – or we could be really naughty and have bacon butties,' announced Ciara next morning as she pushed a steaming mug of tea into her sister's hands.

'I'm still full from last night,' puffed Rhianne, 'just tea is fine honestly.' She was used to Ciara organising her. It had been so ever since they were kids, and it was oddly comforting. Ciara the no-nonsense go getter who never saw problems, only challenges and goals. They were chalk and cheese. Hardly credible they came from the same stable.

'I thought I'd check out the tea shop this afternoon, see if I can pick up any useful info,' she proclaimed with her usual clipped efficiency. 'Best if you stay here, of course – wouldn't do to be spotted casing the joint. You could have a mosey round the shops, or there's a pile of DVDs on the shelf by the TV if you want a cosy afternoon in.'

'I'll be fine, Ciara. I could do with the time to go over some of my college notes and reorganise my portfolio to frontload more pastry dishes.'

It was almost five o'clock before Rhianne realised she hadn't thought about Eithan all day. She felt a mixture of guilt and relief. Today had felt different. She had been busy and focused – animated even. She packed away her portfolio and wandered over to the bookcase to browse Ciara's DVD collection. On the shelf above was an array of family photographs. She fingered, lovingly, the one of herself and Eithan on their wedding day, smiled at a comical image of her and Ciara nose-deep in ice cream cones and took a deep intake of breath as she picked up a photo of her parents. The gentle eyes of her mother smiled out at her, in stark contrast to the severe expression habitually worn by her father. She winced, trying to quell the emotions, staunch the memories that flooded in.

*

She had been an eternal disappointment to her father. He perpetually berated her lack of ambition, her feeble sporting prowess, her inferior school grades and maintained she used her dyslexia as an excuse for laziness. The evening she was confirming her A level choices, he stood over her, his impatience menacingly palpable in the stale air between them.

'Geography, yes,' he said, 'but Art and Cooking, give me strength!'

'It's not Cooking, it's Food Technology, Dad. I got an A* and I got Bs in Art and Geography. They were my best grades and the subjects I like most.'

'Art and Cooking aren't proper subjects,' he added derisively. 'What about Maths and Combined Science?'

'I was lucky to scrape Cs – I'd never manage A level. Look, Dad, I know you're disappointed I failed three GCEs outright, but why can't you be pleased I did well in the others?'

'You need to make *wise* choices, Rhianne, with *proper* career prospects. I'll get you some extra tuition for the maths and science. You could major in Geography at teaching college and the maths and science would get you into a good primary school.'

'But I don't WANT to be a teacher,' interrupted Rhianne angrily.

'Teaching's a great career. It's been good for your mother and me, fitting the hours around raising a family. It paid for this house.'

'Didn't stop her DYING though did it!'

Her outburst silenced him mid flow. He slapped her face, something he had never done before. She ran to her room, barricaded the door, crept under her duvet and sobbed till she thought her heart would break. If Ciara had been there, she would have made it alright. But she was far away at teaching college doing those things that made their father proud. Later, she had gone to him to apologise. But there had been no forgiving nod. He had been frosty and stiff. He stopped badgering her, seemingly accepting the indignity of a Head of Humanities' daughter wasting her education on 'cooking and painting'.

*

For the next year they danced gingerly around each other. She spent more and more time away from the house. The fragile peace was shattered when Mr Atkinson discovered his daughter was not out with her girlfriends but holed up with a boy on 'that sink estate', in a house of blacks. It led to an almighty row.

'You take the biscuit, Rhianne, you really do. I'm only glad your mother never lived to see this day. You're not pregnant, are you? God preserve me from brown babies.'

'You fucking hypocrite!' she had screamed at him. Never in her life had she used the f-word to anyone, least of all her father, and never had she spoken with such venom. 'You pretend to be such an upright citizen. *Everyone, no matter their race or creed should have the same educational opportunities dah de dah,*' she taunted him, mimicking the posh teacher voice he could put on at will. 'You stinking fraud! Just empty words from a black heart. All nicey-nice as long as it's not in your own back yard.' Her voice had reached screeching pitch. 'As long as they don't bed your daughters, or thrust brown babies under your nose.'

'How dare you speak to me like that—'

But Rhianne was not to be deflected. 'And I'm NOT pregnant. Eithan's very proper and gentle. He knows I'm not ready yet. He respects that. Not that it's any business of yours. I'm seventeen. I can do what I like with my own body.'

She had paused to draw breath and he had rounded on her, his icy words freezing the hot air that steamed between them. He spoke slowly, enunciating the ends of each word with exaggerated superiority. 'Not under my roof, you ungrateful little vixen! My house, my rules. I always knew you'd amount to nothing. Well now you can fester in your putrid nothingness. You've had all the help you're ever going to get from me. If you want to carry on seeing this wastrel, you can pack your things and leave this house. Take your filthy mouth over to that sink estate and see what it really means to live on the wrong side of the tracks. And don't think you can come crawling back. If you leave this house, you're as good as dead to me.'

As desperate as she was to be out of his sight, she was determined to have the last word. 'You're right about one thing. I'm glad Mum *isn't* alive to see this. She'd be appalled at your bigotry. And she'd never give up on me. Never, EVER.'

'I think I knew my wife better than you knew your mother. She would have stood with me on this.'

'You know nothing! *Nothing! Yours* is the stench of nothingness. Stinking, lonely nothingness.'

They had not spoken since.

*

Ciara breezed in. 'Hi Sis – you been okay?'

'Yes, absolutely fine, thanks. Do tell me what it was like. I'm dying to know.'

Ciara threw her fleece over the back of the sofa and flopped into its soft cushions. 'It's bigger than I thought it would be. I counted thirty-six covers.'

'Was it busy?'

'Busy! It was heaving. It was already full when I got there. I had to hang around outside for twenty minutes before a table came free.'

'What was the food like?'

'I had a scone with all the trimmings and a slice of orange and passion fruit cake. Both delicious. Nice china cups, tablecloths – proper napkins. All very tasteful but not pretentious. Just quality. Quaint but not too twee. I think it might become a new favourite of mine, despite the distance.'

'Mrs Brennan was there?'

'Yes, she was there, doing a bit of everything. Doesn't seem too stuck up to wait on tables. But she kept flitting in and out, keeping an eye on the kitchen staff and the shop. Which reminds me I bought a Victoria sponge and some peanut butter cookies so you can sample—'

'What was she like, Mrs Brennan?' pressed Rhianne.

'Poker-faced, no-nonsense type. Mid-fifties, plainly dressed, no make-up, blonde hair, greying a little at the temples and…' Ciara hesitated.

'And what?' pressed Rhianne.

'And she had this huge ugly scar splodged across one side of her face. Looked like some kind of a burn. Perhaps she'd been in a fire.'

'Maybe it was a kitchen fire,' shuddered Rhianne.

'Shame, 'cos in profile – you know just looking from the other side – she had quite a striking face. Beautiful even.'

'So, you think she'll be a stickler of a boss?'

'I didn't hear her shout at the staff or anything. She was efficient and professional. Courteous with the customers – but she was quite austere. Never smiled!'

'Oh well, I'll meet her on Monday. At least now I know it's not some two-bit grease shack. Were there any speciality cakes in the shop?'

'No, I think they are special order, but there were a couple of photos of them in the window. They did look amazing.'

'What are the premises like?'

'I had plenty of time to size it up while I was hanging around outside waiting for a table. It's in a terrace of three cottages named – unimaginatively – East, Middle and West. Quite big cottages, three-storeyed with dormer attic windows. The tea shop is located on the ground floor of East Cottage and spreads out into a pretty garden area at the back. The bread shop is in what would have been the front room of Middle Cottage and I assume the bakery kitchen is behind it. I don't know if Mrs Brennan owns West Cottage but if she's as well-heeled as Jack thinks then I imagine she does. All rather picturesque. I can see why it's popular. It's in the most idyllic location. A bit windy, but a stone's throw from a fabulous beach that stretches for miles.'

'Wow, you have been thorough,' remarked Rhianne. 'Sounds like I could learn a lot from Mrs Brennan. Might be a good role model for me. Eithan always says I'm too much of a softie.'

'Fingers crossed for Monday then.'

*

The interview was not going well. Beth Brennan was a difficult woman to impress.

'You're the last one,' she pronounced officiously, as she waved her to an uncomfortable-looking chair. Mrs Brennan flicked through Rhianne's application as if to remind herself of its contents, when, in fact, she knew them backwards. It was a ploy she had used with all the applicants to unsettle them. Rhianne's nerves got the better of her. She started to fill the oppressive silence with banal witterings. Her mouth took on a life of its own completely detached from her brain.

'My tutor said my chocolate and almond marble was the best she'd tasted,' she volunteered, her voice sounding small and girlish. She hated herself for not being more self-assured, relieved Eithan was not here to witness this feeble effort. 'And I have some new ideas for green tea loaves,' she added nervously. 'Oh – and my tutor suggested I might enter the national student baker competition but I er... I er...'

'Didn't? Is that the word you're looking for? I don't want to know about things you DIDN'T do. And I'm not interested in your hallowed tutor or your blessed green tea loaves. I have cake specialities coming out of my ears. At Beth's Bakery, *I* decide recipes. It's a privilege that comes with ownership. I'm looking for a trainee to learn the ropes, not a wannabe Pierre Hermé. What I *am* interested in, is why you want this job?' At that point, she put down the application form and peered intently at her interviewee, waiting for an earth-shattering response.

It didn't come.

It was all going downhill very fast. Rhianne's carefully prepared statements that she had practised with Ciara deserted her.

'I, er I... want to get some experience, give baking a go, see if I want to specialise in it.'

'Give baking a go!' mocked Mrs Brennan who started to put Rhianne's application back in its envelope and dumped the notes she had been making into the waste bin. It had been a long day and she had hoped for better. Despite a promising application, this last one was no better than the rest. She tossed the application onto the desk, indicating with an exasperated wave of her index finger for Rhianne to take it back.

'Clearly you're not right for this position. Thank—' She didn't get to finish the exit niceties because the girl suddenly jumped up from her chair in some distress.

'You don't understand. I really want this... *need*... this job. My husband's a soldier in Iraq. I promised him I would use the time he was away to make a new start for us. He'll be out at the end of the year. This is his last tour of duty. It's so nice here. The air's so fresh – no stench of death. It's exactly the kind of place we were hoping to put roots down. I... I ...know I've completely messed up. I was nervous, you see... but I'm a hard worker and a good learner. I... I...' The verbal diarrhoea had kicked in big time. Despair, loneliness and pent-up anguish had all spewed out in one undignified rant. Her humiliation was complete. Her father had been right. She really was a waste of space.

'Your husband's a soldier?' Beth interjected. Her tone had changed. It was softer now, no longer dismissive, not even business-like.

'Yes, he's a sapper with the Royal Engineers,' she answered meekly. 'He joined up when he left school' she replied, a little astonished at the gentler approach from this formidable woman.

'So, is it Ms or Mrs McArthur?'

'Mrs,' came the embarrassed response.

'How old is he?'

'Twenty-three.' Rhianne misread the anguish she saw flicker across Beth's face. 'You mustn't think him young or unreliable. You grow up fast in the Forces. He'll have good skills and an engineering HND when he comes out so I'm sure he'll find work. It wouldn't interfere with my duties. And I know he would love it here,' Rhianne added almost inaudibly, her cheeks hot with shame. She had finally run out of steam.

Beth Brennan had gone very quiet. Rhianne took this to mean that she was dismissed. She returned her unopened portfolio to her rucksack and picked up the discarded application form. What on earth had possessed her to blab like that? The woman must think her a complete lame brain. 'Thank you for your time,' she said, trying to rescue a morsel of dignity as she edged towards the door. She wanted to run now, far away from this embarrassing scene.

'Wait a moment, Mrs McArthur – Rhianne – sit down again would you please.'

Rhianne did not want to sit down again. Her cheeks were burning. The urge to run was threatening her last embers of pride. Unaccountably, she found herself doing as she was bid. She sat down again in that stifling office waiting timidly for this fearsome woman to speak.

'You're not from these parts then?'

Rhianne's blushes deepened.

'No, I'm visiting with my sister – at the address on my application form,' she confessed. 'I didn't like to put the barracks' address, thought it might count against me.'

'I realise you've come a very long way and that you were nervous. I'm willing to make some allowances on that count. Your references are impressive. Let's have a look at that portfolio of yours, shall we?'

Rhianne was astonished. Mechanically she retrieved the folder. Unaware of the excitement that crept into her voice, she talked through the photos, the recipes, the creative achievements and challenges. She even flicked to the page with her green tea loaf, the mention of which had drawn such a cruel barb from the woman who now fingered the pages with growing respect.

'I'm willing to take you on a six months' trial,' announced Mrs Brennan, closing the portfolio and handing it back to Rhianne. 'Though I'm warning you – there'll be no time for daydreaming here. It's hard work and long hours. I'll teach you everything I know but I expect loyalty and commitment in return and above all, respect for my privacy. I've built this business up from nothing. I won't brook tittle tattle.'

'No, of course not. I know how to be discreet. You have to be if you're married to the army.'

'Good, then we understand each other. Tuesdays and Wednesdays will be your regular days off but every third week you get to swap them for a Saturday and Sunday. It won't always be pâtisserie. I'll need you to help out in the shop and the tearoom at busy times. There's a room I can let you have unless you want to get up before four every morning to commute from your sister's.'

'A room?'

'Yes, the attic room on the floor above us,' she said pointing to the ceiling. 'It's where I stayed when I first came here twenty years ago. There's a bathroom on this floor next to the storeroom.'

'How much would the rent be?' asked Rhianne.

'There's no charge. I don't rent it out commercially these days, not since we've modernised the bakery kitchen. The bigger machines are noisier and few paying residents would relish being woken at five in the morning. When would you be able to start?' enquired Mrs Brennan.

'Thank you, that's very generous. Oh, thank you so much. I'll work so hard for you, I—'

'Yes, yes,' she said a little impatiently, 'but when would you be able to start?'

'Just as soon as I can collect my things from the barracks. A few days at most is all I need.'

'In that case, you can start on Friday. It will give you a day to get the hang of things before the busy weekend. Now, I'll show you round and then take you up to have a look at that attic room.'

'Do you own all three cottages?' asked Rhianne conversationally as they climbed up to Middle Cottage attic.

'Yes. I live in West Cottage. That's out of bounds to staff,' she said firmly. 'As I said, I value my privacy.'

'Yes, of course,' nodded Rhianne.

The attic room was larger than Rhianne had expected. She was instantly drawn to look out of the dormer window where she was rewarded with an exquisite view of a huge beach bordered on one side by Black Combe Fell.

'It's so beautiful,' she whispered, quite mesmerised. Her wide-eyed amazement almost drew a smile from Mrs Brennan, but it was gone instantly. The glacial veil settled itself back into its customary home amid the wrinkled creases of her pale skin. The brusque, business-like tone had been re-set too.

*

Rhianne left her proprietor an hour later having signed a contract and accepted the offer of the attic room, which was more than adequate for her needs. It would save over-imposing on Ciara, and she could still spend her weekends off with her. Rhianne could not quite believe Mrs Brennan's astonishing change of heart. Either she had felt sorry for her or been impressed by her portfolio. She hoped it was the latter. It was a mystery but not one she needed to solve. She had her first proper job; that was all that mattered. She was going to become an accomplished pâtissier. She *was* going to amount to something. Her father would have to eat his words.

It was after seven when she got back to Ciara's. Her sister already had dinner underway and a bottle of wine chilling. Ciara reckoned alcohol would be needed whichever way it had gone. Rhianne was tempted to blag it and pretend she had walked the interview, wowing Mrs Brennan with her green tea loaf. But this was Ciara. There would be no fooling Big Sis.

'Who'd have thought it?' said Ciara. 'The old battle axe has a heart after all.'

'I wish you'd told me she was a battle axe *before* I went for the interview. I might not have made such an ass of myself.'

'*Mea culpa*, kitten, but you were nervous enough without me putting the skids under you.'

'I can't wait to get started,' said Rhianne excitedly. 'I'm going back to Swinton tomorrow to get my things. It won't take long to pack up a few bits and pieces. I'll be living in one room for the next five months until Eithan gets home, and then we'll look for a place of our own.'

'You know you can stay here for as long as you need to.'

'Yes, I know, Ciara. But Eithan will likely need the car and I can't get to work for 5am from here without it. Besides, we need to put some roots down.'

'There's plenty of work going at Sellafield if he can't find anything better.'

'One step at a time, eh, Sis.'

'Ooh – listen to you, our kid, quite the grown-up pragmatist all of a sudden. Amazing what transformation a job offer can make. You'll be getting to be a *reet cocky sprog* soon,' she teased.

'I need to make this work, Ciara,' Rhianne replied, suddenly serious. 'For Eithan's sake, I need to make it work. He deserves some happiness. So much pain and sorrow – you don't know the half of it. He's been through so much.'

'So have you kitten, so have you,' came the soft response from the older woman.

Eithan

Basra, March 2003

Eithan took refuge from the searing heat in the tent that housed four makeshift bunks. It had been another exhausting day carrying out repairs to the OSF oil pipeline. The work was slow because of the landmine sweeps on every foray. He was missing Rhianne. It was three weeks now. The longest they had gone without contact since they had been seventeen. Sarge had promised there would be a secure line in place by tonight and they would be able to make a short call home. He pulled out her photo and stared longingly at the freckly face smiling at him. A case of oil and water if ever there was one, he thought, gazing at the dark skin on his arm.

*

Their paths had not really crossed until sixth form. The Atkinson girls lived on The Redlands, where the houses had double garages and en suites. Eithan did not mix much with The Redlands lot. Their designer keks and high-tech game consoles were out of his league and made him feel uncomfortable. He lived on a council estate across the other side of town: just him and his mam and dad. A loving, untroubled childhood. No racism to speak of beyond a few ignorant monkey grunts in primary school. There was still a sizeable Jamaican contingent on the estate but these days it was a racial melting pot, and everyone got along. He liked school and had done well. His parents hoped he would be the first in their family to go to university. His dad was never out of work, a succession of low-paid labouring jobs. Whatever he could find. Llanso McArthur would have swept streets before he would go on the dole. His mam had a part time cleaning job at the hospital.

It was in the second term of lower sixth when it happened. A car mounted the pavement where his dad was waiting for his bus. They operated on him for three hours but could not save him. Eithan stood with his mother looking incredulously at a corpse that had once been his father. In a few short hours their whole world had fallen apart. Some of the basketball team parents left flowers at the school gates. Lots of teachers and pupils sent their condolences and gave him sympathy cards. Cards with pictures of white lilies, or prayer books or crosses and neatly scripted messages. Well-meaning. Sterile. Futile. It all felt futile. Dad was dead. Nothing could change that. Eithan did not believe in a hereafter. This was the end of the line.

It was the action of Rhianne Atkinson he remembered vividly from that time. She had crept up to him during Geography and slipped an envelope onto his desk, too shy to stay and talk. To be polite, he opened it expecting another white lily or Bible or some such crass inanity. The card inside was handmade. She had drawn a globe on the front and inside she had written:

It must feel like your wurld has stopd turnin
I am so sorry

Rhianne.

There was another envelope labelled 'Mrs MacArther'. She had spelt it wrongly, but he was touched by the thought. Later that afternoon, he presented it to his mother.

'One of the girls in my Geography group gave me this for you. Don't take it wrong if there are any spelling mistakes. It's not disrespectful, she's dyslexic. She made a card for me too.' He showed her his card and Mrs McArthur nodded appreciatively. Opening her own, she found another handmade card. On the front was a picture of a heart with a crack in it and inside were the simple words:

> Your haerrt must be broakn
> I am so sorry
> I hope it will mend
>
> *Rhianne Atkinson, Year 12 Oakvale.*

His mother ran her finger down the card. 'I think maybe your friend's nursing a broken heart too. Make sure you thank her for me. Perhaps you should ask her round for tea some time.'

*

Eithan made a point of seeking Rhianne out in the common room at first break. 'Mi mam said to say thank you for the card. She was very touched. It was a sweet thing to do.' Rhianne flushed with embarrassment. She had not expected any thanks. She liked Eithan but was unsure how to act around him. She was not sporty or clever and did not know what to say that would be vaguely of interest to him. Eithan felt compelled to plug the awkward silence.

'Mi mam said she thought you might be nursing a broken heart too.' He had no idea what on earth had possessed him to say that. Her eyes filled up and he thought she was about to turn and run so he had added quickly, 'She said perhaps you'd like to come for tea some time.' He must need his head looking at! He had just made it ten times worse. Why had he extended an invitation to her of all people. She was from The Redlands and had probably never been inside a council house in her life. But those doe-like eyes welling up with tears had tugged at something inside him.

'My mum died when I was fourteen – cancer,' she blurted out. And in an instant, he felt her pain.

'I'm sorry, Rhianne. I had no idea. Listen, do you want to bring your packed lunch up to the oak tree at the corner of the sports field? I eat mine there sometimes when I want to be quiet. You could tell me a bit more about your mum and I could tell you about mi dad.'

*

And so, it had begun. They met more and more often at the oak tree. Her shyness disappeared and he found he liked the simple, authentic girl he discovered underneath. He felt sorry for her, not in a pitying sort of way but sorry that few people seemed to value her or appreciate her many talents. She might not be gifted academically but she was very creative. Brilliant at food technology, a good artist, and when you could persuade her to sing, she had a beautiful voice. Most of all, she was warm and caring – and sensitive. Having initially bonded over a dead parent, they were to cement their friendship through the bonding with a living one: his mother. Rhianne spent more and more time at the McArthur house as the relationship with her own father deteriorated. Eithan helped her with Geography, and she helped in the house because his mother was now doing extra shifts. Eithan wanted to leave school and get a job, but Jenna would not hear of it, saying Llanso would turn in his grave if he thought his boy would not finish school for the sake of cleaning a few extra floors. Eithan secured a Saturday job at Asda and they got by. Rhianne often kept Jenna company on his late shift. Her father thought she went dancing with her frivolous girlfriends, oblivious to the deepening relationship his youngest daughter was developing with a boy from 'the wrong side of the tracks'.

Eithan marvelled at the new lease of life Rhianne bestowed on his mother. She brought joy back into those sad eyes and lifted her out of the profound grief that had threatened to engulf her first Christmas in widowhood. On the anniversary of her husband's death, Jenna stood next to her son at the graveside. 'Llanso would've loved a babby girl, but I couldn't have no more after you. He'd have liked Rhianne. She's real special that girl. Has a gift for mending hearts. Fragile though, Eithan. She's fragile. Don't you go breaking *her* heart, now.'

He would never forget the day Rhianne turned up on their doorstep having struggled onto a number 9 bus with a suitcase in one hand, holdall in the other and a rucksack on her back. Eithan was eating an early tea before his Asda shift. It was Jenna who spotted her wobbling up the front path.

'What in the world... oh my Lord, it's Rhianne. Eithan, come quick. It's Rhianne.'

He had rushed out just in time to catch her from falling as she dropped her bags with exhaustion.

'What's happened?' he cried out.

'I'm so sorry, Jenna,' she said to his mother, 'I didn't know where else to go. I've left home.'

'Grab her bags, Eithan, C'mon lass, let's get you inside. Now don't you mither about nothing, you hear? It's gonna be okay, Rhianne,' she said soothingly. 'Don't you worry, lass.'

Once inside with a strong cup of cup of tea in her hand, she told them what had happened. Eithan paced up and down while she spoke. 'Fucking bastard!' he mouthed under his breath. 'If he weren't such an old geezer, I'd go round there and punch his lights out,' he said more audibly, not realising Rhianne had heard him.

'Please don't, Eithan. It's over. It's done. He's a sad, lonely old man. Let's just leave it behind us now.'

He nodded and came to sit beside her. Then he smiled. Amid the ugliness of it all he could see so many positives peeping out. 'So, the mouse finally roared,' he declared. 'And you used the f word! I hope that isn't going to become a habit, Miss Atkinson. Wouldn't want you leading mi mam astray now, would we?'

She smiled shyly and Jenna breathed a sigh of relief. It was all going to work out. They would muddle through just fine.

*

Despite excellent A level grades, especially in Maths and Physics, and the frustrated attempts of his teachers, Eithan refused to go to university. His mother was distraught, but Eithan was adamant.

'I can't afford three years of debt. I need to earn enough so she can cut her hours. Preferably pack in altogether,' he had told Rhianne, resolutely. 'Her angina is much worse. She tries to hide it. I've seen her stopping up Primrose Hill pretending to look in a shop window or coo at a babby, when all the time it's a ruse to catch her breath.'

'I could stay here. Get a job. Look after her while you're at uni – and you'd have your Asda shifts in the holidays.'

'No, Rhianne. I won't have you sacrifice your future on my account. You said you wanted to go to college and re-take your Geography. You only missed it by a smidgen, and they are much better geared up for dyslexic support there. Anyway, you couldn't earn enough to cover the rent and our keep.'

'But couldn't she apply for social or get housing benefit?'

Eithan turned on her furiously. He rarely lost his temper, usually so gentle and kind. 'Over my dead body! No McArthur will ever live off benefit. It was mi dad's way. It's always been the McArthur way. I won't betray his memory. I don't ever want to hear you talk about welfare again, Rhianne. Do you understand me?' he yelled.

She nodded assent, fighting back the tears that were pricking the back of her eyes. He pulled her to him and hugged her. 'I'm sorry, babe. I didn't mean to shout. I know you were only trying to help.'

'What are you going to do then?'

'I'm going to join up. I've looked into it. I can get some qualifications while I serve. Maybe even a degree.'

'But you'd have to do active service. They might send you anywhere – Oh, Eithan, you might get wounded or… or… killed!'

'The odds are in my favour.' It was the mathematician talking now. 'Injury or death is very low risk.'

'Oh Eithan, please don't do this. There must be another way. It feels so drastic – and I would miss you so much.'

'I'll be fine. Saint Ciara says I'm a walking four-leaf clover...
you'd wait for me? If I join up?' he said more seriously. 'I'd be out
in five years with good prospects, and we could set up a nice home
together, you, me and mi mam.'

'Don't think you can get rid of me that easy, Eithan McArthur.
I'm like a piece of pesky chuddy you can't get off your shoe.'

He laughed at her attempted mimicry. She had picked up a few
choice phrases from the estate that she trotted out proudly every
now and then.

'Which force are you thinking of?'

'I want to make the most of mi Maths. I'm thinking of the
Royal Engineers, if they'll take me.'

'They'd need their heads looking at if they turned you down!
Three A levels with top grade in Maths and Physics, prefect,
basketball captain. Fit, strong – and I know you won't mind me
saying this but for once it might be an advantage – you being black.'

'I'd had the same thought, Rhianne. It's a whole different world
from when mi granddad first came across on the *Windrush*.'

*

Rhianne had been right. The Royal Engineers were keen to take
Eithan. He sailed through his training. In January 1999 he signed
up for five years and settled quickly into the disciplined routine
of army life. He was popular with the basketball team who were
delighted to have someone of his calibre in their crew, but his
popularity did not extend much further. He rarely joined in the
off-duty revelries that most of the sappers engaged in, preferring
to send his pay back to his mother. It earned him a reputation
for being a bit tight and a tad dull. Nonetheless, he liked his
life as a sapper. The first six months were mainly taken up with
airfield construction and repair. Then came the preparation for
his first active tour of duty in Belfast: two months learning about
explosives, bomb disposal and defence fortifications. His first
tour in Northern Ireland was uneventful and it earned him a long

chunk of leave. That was a magical time. Rhianne had passed her Geography and had stayed on at college to start a catering course. Jenna spent more time with her feet up because the money Eithan sent back had enabled her to reduce her hours significantly. The only dark cloud was the all too brief periods of his leave. But they made the most of the precious moments they had and Jenna, astute enough to know the youngsters needed time on their own, developed a convenient interest in bingo and an overpowering urge to join the WI.

*

Two years in, Eithan was a seasoned sapper and Rhianne was approaching the end of the first year of her catering course. There was no warning, and the impact was devastating. Walking home from her cleaning shift, Jenna had suffered a heart attack. She had died in the street despite an ambulance being minutes away in a hospital parking bay. Eithan was given compassionate leave. The news nearly broke him, coming so soon after the death of his father. Jenna was only fifty-four. Eithan thought she would have the joy of grandchildren, perhaps even great grandchildren. He blamed himself for not being able to provide well enough for her to drop her shifts altogether.

'I don't think it was the cleaning, Eithan, really I don't,' said Rhianne, trying to rouse him from the crushing gloom engulfing him. 'They said it could have happened any time. None of us knew how bad her heart was. Please, Eithan, she wouldn't want you to blame yourself. She wouldn't want to see you despair like this. She was so proud of you, believed you had a great future ahead of you. You owe it to her memory to prove her right, Eithan.'

Her words seemed to stir him out of his stupor. He pulled himself together but overnight he had aged ten years.

*

After the funeral, he sat Rhianne down at the kitchen table. 'There's something we need to talk about, Rhianne, and I don't think it can wait until my next leave.'

'Okay,' she replied, giving him her full attention.

'There are other consequences of mi mam dying. The tenancy for this house was in mi mam and dad's name. I'm a single man with no dependents, and I have accommodation at the barracks, so I will be very low priority with the council. This is a three-bedroomed house and there's a long waiting list for families with babbies living in bedsits desperate for a house like this. They would have a much stronger claim, and to be honest, it's only right that they should. It don't make no odds to me 'cos I can bunk at the barracks but you will be homeless, Rhianne. You can't go back to your dad. Even if he would take you, I wouldn't let you go back there.'

'I could go to Ciara,' Rhianne interjected. 'I could see about transferring my catering course up there.'

'No, babe,' he said, taking her hand, 'I want us to get married. That way I could apply for married quarters, and we could be together. I've over three years to serve yet and I can't afford to buy myself out. I know it's not the fairy tale wedding you might have hoped for, but I'll be a good husband, I promise, and you'll never want for anything once I get on mi feet. I don't have a ring nor nothing, but I'll get one pdq if you say yes.'

Rhianne was very quiet. Deep in thought.

'What do you think?' he pressed, suddenly nervous.

'I think,' she began slowly and deliberately, 'I think I'd be the luckiest girl on the planet to be your wife, but I can't have you feeling trapped into marrying me. You don't have to marry me, Eithan. I can find a way through this. It's you who taught me to be strong and to believe in myself.'

'But I WANT to marry you, Rhianne. I'm not doing this because I feel sorry for you. I'm being selfish. I want this for ME.'

'In that case, yes! Oh yes please! Of course, I'll marry you, Eithan McArthur.'

*

Under the heavy black stubble, Eithan was blushing. That had to have been the least romantic marriage proposal ever. One day when he was properly on his feet, he would make it up to her. She could have a proper honeymoon somewhere exotic. He did not deserve her. Jenna had been right, she was special, his girl. Real special. His thoughts were interrupted by Pete dashing into the tent. 'C'mon guys, the secure line is up. Sarge says we can phone home. Quick, let's get in the queue.'

'Hello?' came a small, nervous voice from the other end of a crackly line.

'I love you Mrs McArthur,' were the first words out of Eithan's mouth.

'Eithan! Oh Eithan! – is it really you! I'd almost given up hope! Are you okay? Are you safe?'

'Yes. I've only got five minutes. There's a long line of sappers wanting to phone home but next time I'll get longer.'

'What's it like, Eithan? Is it very horrid?'

'Not really. The heat's very sapping...' and then he laughed realising he'd made a pun. Her stomach flipped over at the sound of him laughing.

'Oh, Eithan, I miss you so much.'

'Miss you too, babe.'

'Is it very dangerous out there?'

'Nah – I've been working on fixing an oil pipeline. Then we're moving onto repairing damaged water pipes in the outlying villages. They've not had clean water in over a month. Our American friends seem to have some odd priorities about which pipelines to fix first.' He omitted to mention the daily landmine sweepings. Best not to scare her with the bad bits. In the three weeks he had been out there, he had quickly learned that army personnel kept a tight ship. They did not burden their loved ones with the everyday horrors. They offloaded to each other. Supported each other. What happened in the desert, stayed in the desert. That way there was more chance of them leaving it behind them and picking up a normal life back home. He was already bonding with the squaddies far better than he ever had at the barracks. Sarge warned them about getting too close. They weren't all going to make it. The stronger the friendship, the harder to cope if your mate takes a hit. Nonetheless, firm friendships were forged, especially with tent mates. He had already formed a close bond with Pete. Pete was like the best big brother a man could wish for.

'Oh, that must be terrible for them,' said Rhianne in a small voice. 'But I'm glad you're away from the front-line action. On the news it was predicting the Allied forces are planning to take Basra.'

'I've only a few more minutes, Rhianne, tell me about you,' he said, skilfully steering her away from any discussion of the big push that was coming soon.

'Well, Mr McArthur, you are talking to the new trainee pâtissier at Beth's Bakery.'

'Wow, babe, that's fantastic. You did it. Knew you would! What's it like?'

'It's heavenly. You'd love it here, Eithan. It's a beautiful, sleepy backwater of a place with a huge sandy shoreline. A bit windy and it rains more than down south, but it's magical.'

'What's your boss like?'

'Quite severe but fair. She's an astute businesswoman. I can learn a lot from her. She's letting me have a room for free which is a godsend because I start work at five in the morning.'

'And how's Saint Ciara?'

'*Ciara* is fine. She's been wonderful as always.'

'I'm gonna have to go, babe. There's a long queue behind me. Talk soon. Keep your mobile with you all the time 'cos I'm not sure when it might be. They only set a line up when they're certain it's safe. So, it might be a bit hit and miss. But Sarge says we should get a call home every couple of weeks or so. I love you, Rhianne.'

'Love you too. Stay safe.'

That night, Eithan slept more soundly than he had since he left home. He was proud of Rhianne. She had the talent; all she needed was confidence. It sounded like this set up in Silecroft was a good opportunity for her. Perhaps there would be something for him too. It all felt very promising.

*

The weeks ticked over and Eithan was pulled off the oil pipe repair taskforce. All sappers were needed to clear the route ahead of the advance on Basra. They spent their days painstakingly sweeping for landmines on the dirt track with the tanks of the Royal Scots Dragoon Guards following in their wake. It was dangerous work. American squaddies went with them, their eyes peeled for snipers whom they shot on sight, as they did any armed Saddam loyalists lurking in deserted buildings of the shanty towns that lined the route. As they neared the outskirts of the city, the Allied air force stepped up their raids. Hundreds of laser-guided bombs were dropped, clouds of smoke constantly rising from sites all over Basra. Eithan could only imagine what damage was being wreaked on civilian quarters. By 6th April the Allied forces had taken the city. Some civilians came out on the streets to hail them, others spat in the dirt as they passed by.

The months ahead were harrowing for Eithan. More used to infrastructure repair than combat, he was sickened by the whole campaign. The smash-and-grab raids were brutal. Grenades through windows first, then smash the door in. Shoot first or be shot. Too often there would be no insurgents inside, just women and children cowering against the walls, loved ones bleeding in the dirt. Their homes, already bomb damaged, reduced to squalid crumbling wrecks. Each side upped the ante. The Allied forces resorted to cluster bombs; the insurgents to more sophisticated booby traps, car bombs and snipers. Eithan was spared much of it. When not on bomb detection and disposal duty he was busy repairing infrastructure in Allied-friendly quarters. Some Iraqis even began to trust him and no longer hid their children away behind closed doors. Eithan liked to see the kids playing out, a morsel of hope in that God-forsaken place. Only boys of course, never girls. But he sometimes saw the girls peeping out at him through curtained windows as he kicked a few stones around with their brothers. He set up make-shift goals for them and hoops to throw through, even brought them a gift of a ball from camp.

*

By June he had stopped interacting with the kids. If any came out on the streets to play, he shooed them back into their houses. He blamed himself. He should never have given those kids that ball from base and encouraged them to throw it around rugby-style. One of them found a dud from a cluster bomb raid. He shouted to his playmates that he had found a good 'rugger' as they liked to call the English rugby ball. Eithan watched in horror as it blew up in the boy's face. Brains and guts spilled out into the dirt. Wailing women poured out of the surrounding houses. Men appeared from nowhere, some carrying guns. Pete grabbed hold of Eithan and pulled him into the truck. 'Gotta get out of here, Eithan. This is gonna get ugly.' Pete drove at breakneck speed back to the safety of the camp while Eithan sat motionless next to him. Back in their tent, Pete, still a little shaken himself, tried to comfort Eithan. 'It wasn't your fault, Eithan. It wasn't anyone's fault. It's shitty, I know, but you couldn't have seen that one coming.'

'Of course it was my fault,' snapped Eithan angrily. 'I gave them a ball. I encouraged them to throw it around rugby-style. He's dead because of me. A little kid! Couldn't have been more than seven. His guts spewed all over the sand. A little kid!'

'Look Eithan, don't do this to yourself. It'll eat you up. If it's anyone's fault it's the bastards authorising the cluster bombs. They're evil things. Too many civilians get killed or maimed. I'm gonna campaign when I get back to have them banned.'

'Don't let Sarge hear you talk like that, he'll have you up on a charge,' replied Eithan, 'but you can count me in.'

*

June passed into July. More of the same. Day in day out, the heat, the dust, the black smoke from burning oilfields, the gunfire, the smash-and-grab raids, the killing, the maiming. Eithan's calls with Rhianne got shorter. He could not raise himself to think up more fabrications to tell her of what he was doing so he said nothing, just listened to her news. Sometimes he even passed up the opportunity altogether, let another sapper have a longer chat with his girl. Rhianne would never know.

One more month to endure and then he could escape this hell on earth. He was looking at the empty bunk across the tent where Steve usually slept. Steve had been taken out by a sniper while fixing an electricity line in one of the outlying villages. He was trying to help them, for God's sake, get their lights and televisions back on and some fucking bastard shot him dead. Even Pete was quiet these days. Their trips out to civilian quarters were often done in silence.

Sarge asked Eithan and Pete to come with him to check out a suspicious dwelling. Intelligence had come in that it was holding a stash of arms, likely booby trapped so they needed sappers to detect and defuse. It was a classic sting. They had seen the like many times in their training briefings. The property was cleverly disguised, set a little apart but nevertheless mixed in with other houses to look like any normal domestic dwelling. There was a goat tethered round the back, a rake and hoe leaning against the front wall, a rug was slung across a makeshift line, a beater on the floor beneath. To the side of the front door was a pram, its raised hood an effective sun shield.

'Okay lads,' whispered their sergeant, 'let's take this one real gentle. We'll sweep as we go. My guts tell me this one is booby trapped. I bet it'll be that pram. There won't be any baby in it. Intel said the place was empty, nothing coming up on the body thermal maps. Keep your eyes peeled for stray wires, recently raked sand and the like.'

As they edged gingerly forwards, sweeping their detectors before them, they heard a cry from the pram.

'Christ, there really is a babby in there,' said Eithan.

'Stay back,' shouted Sergeant Brentford. 'We'll have to send the robot in.'

'But the babby!' screamed Eithan. 'You can't send the robot in till we've got the babby out. It could set it off!'

'There's no baby, Eithan, it's a trick,' said Pete.

'But I heard it cry,' insisted Eithan.

'Pete's right, Eithan. It's a trick. Intel say the place is empty.'

'But what if they're wrong! What if there really is a babby and there's a mam and a gran inside somewhere. What if they're wrong!' he repeated at the top of his voice. 'They've been wrong before.'

'I think you'd best go and wait in the truck, Eithan,' said Sarge firmly. 'Me and Pete have got this one.'

'No!' shouted Eithan. 'I've got to save the babby!' Before Sarge could stop him, he was down on his belly crawling along the sand, distributing his weight as evenly as possible so as not to set off any land mines. He was crossing terrain they had not swept yet. Pete and the sergeant looked on desperately.

'Come back, Eithan,' shouted Pete. 'It's a trick. It's not safe. You have to wait for the robot.' But Eithan would not be deterred. He crawled as far as the pram. The baby was still crying. Carefully he stood up and reached out to pull the hood down.

The blast threw him several feet in the air and ripped his arm clean off.

'Eithan!' shouted Pete, distraught. This time it was Pete who ignored his sergeant's command to stay put. He ran towards the burnt-out pram to pull his friend clear. It was a bigger blast this time. Pete stepped on a land mine. It killed him instantly.

Beth

Beth removed her reading glasses and closed the book, rubbing her
eyes mechanically. She was tired. The new girl started tomorrow,
and she would need to be on top of her game. She knew it had been
unwise to read that extra chapter but had wanted to know if Milly
Theale was going to die soon or whether the author would keep the
reader dangling a little longer. Beth had come to Henry James late
in life and now could not get enough of him. Books and walking
were her only two hobbies. She eschewed company. Off duty, Beth
Brennan was the epitome of a recluse. Her home was her castle
and staff knew it was out of bounds. If not at West Cottage, she
would likely be found at the library in Millom or walking. She
walked for miles across the beach, toes digging into the squelchy
sand. The locals might complain about the wind, but she liked to
feel it whistling through her uncapped hair, pinking her one good
cheek. She never tired of the sea, of embracing its great expanse,
of probing its secrets, its mysteries. Those walks were when she felt
most alive, most free. Her imagination was her companion. Beth
lived inside her head: a pulsating cauldron of creations, memories,
songs and dreams.

Beth rose from her armchair, emptied the ashtray, swilled it
under the tap and headed up to bed. She had two hobbies but

only once vice – cigarettes – unless you counted the occasional Irish whiskey now and then. As she lay waiting for sleep to come, she wondered if she had done the right thing. She had taken a big risk with the newspaper advert. She had never advertised for staff before. The maintenance workmen were from round about and could probably have walked to work if they did not need their trucks to carry materials. She paid good wages and always settled on time so never found herself short of a plumber or electrician when she needed one. As well as the bakery complex, she had three rental properties, all with long-term tenants although the occupants of Briar Cottage had recently given notice. There would be no need to advertise for a new tenant. Word had got around and a couple of families had already approached her. She would take her time deciding whether to re-let it straight away or do some refurbishments. It was not as if she needed the money. Her businesses were thriving. The bakery reputation had been built by word of mouth and she had more than enough regular customers without the need to advertise. Special orders came in by phone or in person at the shop counter. Beth was nervous of the internet, of opening up her safe haven to the unknown masses and had stalwartly refused to set up a website. A one-line entry in Yellow Pages was as far as she was prepared to push her exposure to the anonymous enquirer.

The girl clearly had talent, it leapt off every page of her portfolio, but was Rhianne McArthur mentally and emotionally tough enough? Did she have grit? Beth wanted more than a trainee, she needed to find someone who might eventually become a partner. She splayed her hands out in front of her. The fingers were long and slender, two of them nicotine-stained, the sort of fingers that sparked pianist envy. She scrutinised the hardening distal joints. An expert eye would spot the early signs of arthritis Beth already knew was approaching. Five years, if she was lucky, before she would have to hang up her icing tools. She was pinning her hopes on this girl. If she was wrong, she would have to start afresh and was nervous of advertising again. Rhianne had been canny. If she had put her barracks address, Beth would not have touched her with a barge pole. Indeed, she was alarmed that a small advert in the local paper had reached so far south. The sister must have sent it to her. Other sisters, mothers, grannies might have seen that advert and passed it on? She had no way of knowing how many, or where, or when. Beth did not trust interlopers. She kept to a small local radius, a safe bubble she could control.

*

Rhianne arrived in the bakery kitchen at ten minutes to five. 'Good morning, Mrs Brennan,' she said, more breezily than she felt.

'Good morning, Rhianne. You'd better start calling me Beth. We can hardly work together with you Mrs Brennan-ing me all day long.' It was said drily and matter of fact, careful to ensure Rhianne did not over-read the invitation. She was still her trainee and there were professional boundaries that came with that relationship. 'Hilda will be here in a few minutes. She will get the basic bloomers on the go, then the speciality loaves, then pastries and scones, finishing with sponges and cookies. Once she gets to the end of the cycle, she goes through it all one more time. The shop opens at eight and the first batches will start flying off the shelves, so the second batch needs to be ready by eleven. Meanwhile I get on with the cupcakes, pre-orders and speciality bakes. Normally that's the range you would help me with, but I want you to get the hang of the basics first, so you'll work with Hilda for now. There's an apron and cap on the worktop over there.'

Rhianne nodded, listening carefully and taking everything in. She was secretly relieved to discover she would not be in the kitchen on her own with Beth. The woman still scared her witless. At five o'clock on the dot, Hilda turned up. She must have been six feet tall with an Amazonian frame to match. 'Mornin' Mrs B,' she chirruped brightly, as she pushed her mousy grey hair into a clean cap. 'Aiya. You must be Rhianne,' she said, extending an enormous frying pan-sized hand, 'I'm Hilda,' and to Rhianne's utter delight – she winked at her!

Rhianne got the hang of the basics very quickly. If Beth was impressed, she did not let on. Her customary glacial countenance never slipped. Rhianne saw no more signs of the compassion shown in that extraordinary Damascus moment of her interview.

'Don't let the boss scarze yer,' said Hilda. ''Er bark's wurse than 'er bite. Pussy cat 'iding in there someweer,' pointing knowingly to her large nose, and winked again.

By the end of her first week, Rhianne was exhausted. Never in her life had she worked so hard. But she was happy. She had been so preoccupied there had been no time to fret about Eithan. She soon adopted Hilda's tack of turning up on the dot of five. Those extra few minutes in bed were precious. She and Hilda got on like a house on fire. Rhianne marvelled at how she could knock dough into loaves two at a time, one with each hand. For her part, Hilda marvelled at how quickly Rhianne learnt the ropes.

'Yer too good at this,' Hilda declared. 'You'll 'ave me owt of me job afore long.'

'Oh no, she won't,' snapped Beth sharply. 'She's not here to do your menial stuff. She's training to be a proper pâtissier. I'll need her to do more and more of my work in time.'

Rhianne felt hurt for Hilda. It had been such a cutting put-down. But Hilda did not seem the least perturbed. She gave Rhianne one of her wicked winks and said under her breath, 'Water off a duck's back, luv, water off a duck's back.'

Beth Brennan was certainly a virtuoso pâtissier. Rhianne gazed in awe at her creations and her speed – with both hands – and decided her employer must be ambidextrous. They settled into a steady routine and although Beth's countenance rarely thawed, it betrayed all the signs of a growing respect for the younger woman's talent. On her weekends off, Rhianne stayed with Ciara. There was a new man in Ciara's life, an engineer at the Thermal Oxide Reprocessing Plant at Sellafield, so she was careful not to overplay the gooseberry. She hoped this one would work out. She would love to see her sister settle down with a few kids of her own. She suspected it was all bravado on Ciara's part. 'Who needs any more kids when I have thirty of them mithering the life out of me,' she would say. Matt had a good job, he was a project manager at THORP, and a big brain – he'd specialised in Nuclear Physics at university. Good enough prospects for her ambitious sister, decided Rhianne.

*

Beth was a creature of habit. Her life had a strict routine even on a Monday, which was her habitual day off. Monday mornings would typically begin with a long hike, a visit to Millom library and then snuggling down with a good book in the afternoon. On summer days she sometimes took a book with her and stayed out all day. June 9th was different. It was Rhianne's twenty-third birthday. Her protégé had been rather subdued of late. The calls from her soldier husband had been drying up and it was too much to hope that fortune would favour a birthday call. She remembered Rhianne had told her Eithan was the pragmatist, she the dreamer. Castles in the air. Yes, that was what she had said. Eithan liked to tease her about her pink castles. Uncharacteristically, Beth decided to abandon her morning hike and headed into West Cottage kitchen.

Rhianne's low mood had not escaped Hilda. 'You okay?' asked the older woman at the end of their first shift. 'Yer look a bit peaky.'

'I'm fine, thanks, Hilda. Just worried about Eithan. It's been a while since I've heard from him. I hope he's alright.'

'You'd 'av 'eard if 'e weren't,' she replied. 'Look, Ruth an' me 'av got this covered. Why don't yer bunk off the second shift. Yer could drive up to that sister o' yers an' spend t' evening with 'er. Mek a nice change. Mrs B nivver cums near on a Monday. She's not t' knoa. An' if she did, I cud say yer wasn't feeling well.'

'I could never do that!' said Rhianne, aghast. 'Besides, I'm better working. Keeps my mind occupied.'

It was at that moment that Beth walked into the kitchen. Hilda's jaw almost dropped to the floor. It must be ten years since she had seen sight of her boss on a Monday. Rhianne blushed, hoping her employer had not overheard Hilda. Beth was carrying a beautiful cake in the shape of a castle, covered all over in pale pink icing.

'Happy Birthday, Rhianne,' announced Beth, dusting off a rare smile.

'But how did you know it was my birthday?' asked Rhianne, astonished. 'I never told anyone.'

'Little things like your driving licence proof of ID. I make a habit of remembering these things.'

'Ah,' nodded Rhianne. 'Thank you, this is so nice. Gosh, what an amazing cake! I'll have to take a photo of it so I can show Eithan when he gets home.'

'You'd better be quick then, because we're all going to have a piece of it right now,' said Beth.

'Why didn' yer say sommat, lass. I'd 'av brung yer a card an' sum flowers,' said Hilda a little peeved.

'Yeah, me too,' joined in Ruth, 'yer should 'av sed.'

'Well, you know now, so you'll have no excuses next year,' said Beth to the two Silecroft women.

'Next year?' breathed Rhianne, almost inaudibly. It was the first indication from her employer that she might get through her probation.

Rhianne's spirits improved as the four of them tucked into slices of the pink masterpiece. Beth missed nothing. She could see the girl was still edgy, constantly glancing at her mobile as if willing it to ring.

'I'll cover your second shift if you'd like to spend the rest of your birthday with your sister,' she offered, looking pointedly at Hilda as she spoke.

Rhianne blushed a deeper pink than the cake.

'That's kind, thank you but I'd rather work. In any case Ciara has a school club on a Monday so she'd be home late. We've agreed

I'll go up tomorrow and stay over so we can go to the Seven Stars together.'

'Well, I can't have you sitting in that attic room all on your own on your birthday,' said Beth. 'You must pop into West Cottage. We'll have supper together and finish off this cake with some bubbly.'

Hilda's jaw fell open again, so wide this time it could have caught a dozen flies.

'Blimey!' she whispered to Rhianne. 'That's a furst! Nivver knoawn 'er invite a living soul into that fortress of 'ers. *Pop* down she sez! Like as if it were t' most reg'lar thing in t' world!'

*

West Cottage was not at all how Rhianne had imagined it would be. The olde-worlde exterior belied a very modern interior. She was shown into the front room. No exposed stonework, just clean plastered walls painted a dove grey with a couple of pieces of modern art on display. The open fireplace and hearth had been replaced by a contemporary electric fire, the sort that had leaping flames coming out of artificial logs. The furniture was modern too. One cream armchair, a matching two-seater sofa, a coffee table and one stylish sideboard were the only pieces in the room. It felt very minimalist. There were no fussy ornaments or knick knacks, just an ashtray and a few books on the coffee table. So, Rhianne noticed the two framed photographs straight away, positioned on the top of the sideboard. A small one of a little boy, not much more than a toddler, with what looked like a toy soldier at his feet. The other photo depicted an adult soldier in full combat gear, rifle slung across his body in sentinel pose.

Beth saw where Rhianne's gaze was resting. 'My son, Sidney,' she said proudly. 'He served with the British Army in Belfast. He was killed in a roadside bomb. Blown into so many pieces they could only identify him by his dog tag.' Rhianne was horrified by the revelation. Beth spoke fondly but mechanically: a learned emotionless patter, carved out of an eternity of grief. 'This is my favourite photo of him as a child and that was his favourite toy,' she said, pointing to the little wooden soldier at his feet. 'It seems he was always destined to become a soldier.' She opened the top drawer of the sideboard a fraction and pulled out a tiny wooden figure, its paint long since faded and one arm broken off at the elbow. Rhianne recognised it as the toy soldier in the photograph.

'How old was he when… when it happened?'

'Twenty-two.'

Rhianne gasped. Almost the same age as Eithan! In a flash, it all made sense. The extraordinary job interview, the sudden change in Beth's manner when she had told him her husband was a soldier.

'Oh God! That's why I got the job!' she blurted out. 'You felt sorry for me having a husband on active tour, he was even a similar age to your son. I got the job because you felt sorry for me…'

'Not exactly. But perhaps it did influence me to give you a second chance. And you've proved you're up to it, Rhianne. So, in a way, Sidney did me a favour that day. I've ended up getting the kind of trainee I was hoping for. Someone with talent – and passion. You can't do this kind of work long term unless you have a real passion for making cakes.'

'So, you think I'm doing okay then? You're pleased with me?'

'I'm *very* pleased Rhianne. You're more than I hoped for. I think we could agree to abandon the rest of the six months' probation, don't you? I wouldn't want you to start applying for other jobs and lose you.'

It was the best birthday present anyone could have given Rhianne. 'Oh, thank you! Thank you so much,' she said, curbing an overwhelming temptation to fling her arms round her boss. 'Do you have any other children?' she asked, politely, attempting to regain the respectful footing expected of an employer-employee relationship.

'Only Sidney. His father and I divorced a very long time ago.'

'I lost a child too – last year,' she volunteered. 'Nothing like your loss. I can't imagine what that must have been like. Mine was a miscarriage. The midwife said not to worry, we would still be able to have other babies. She was trying to be kind, said it was "Nature's way", but it didn't feel kind to me. I wanted to kick Nature's teeth in. Eithan took it very badly. He had wanted that baby so desperately. New life to quench the heavy toll of death.'

It was a relief to tell someone, at last. The tears came. Little sobs at first, but when Beth took her into her arms, the tears flowed unchecked down her cheeks. Wordlessly, Beth held her close until the sobs abated. 'Let it go, Rhianne,' she said soothingly. 'Let it go. I'm here. I can take this for you, but you have to want to let it go.'

She told Beth everything. About her mum dying, about her overbearing dad, about her dyslexia, about Llanso and Jenna, about her great love for Eithan and her fears for his safety. In the telling, Rhianne felt much of her pain drain away. Beth soaked it up. Only the stillness, the gentlest pressure on the young hand clasped in hers and the unblinking eyes betrayed the heaviness of Beth's sorrow. From that day, the relationship between the two women changed forever. The younger became less like an employee and more like a daughter. Hilda, basking in the balmier environment of the bakery kitchen, watched their relationship blossom. 'Told yer there were a pussy cat in there sumweer,' she winked gleefully.

*

Rhianne and Beth spent most evenings together now. They took turns to cook for each other, swapping recipes and experimenting with new desserts.

'Only five weeks to go before Eithan will be home, so we should talk about where you will live,' said Beth.

'Yes, I've been looking in the local paper at what's around to rent. Ciara says there's work going at Sellafield if he can't get anything better. He'll need the car so it would be best if we could live near enough for me to walk to work.'

'The tenant of Briar Cottage is leaving soon. You and Eithan can have the use of it for as long as you need. It's got three bedrooms and a sizeable garden. I'll ask the Simpsons to show you round.'

'That would be amazing. How much is the rent?'

'I won't hear of you paying rent. Not until you're on your feet at least. It won't be easy, those first few months.'

'But… but—'

'It's not up for discussion, Rhianne. It's yours if you want it and there's an end to it.'

Rhianne threw her arms round Beth. 'I can't wait to tell Eithan. You're so good to me. I really don't deserve this.'

'You deserve a lot more than I can ever give you, Rhianne.'

*

It was mid-July and Rhianne had not heard from Eithan for five weeks. She was dying to tell him about Briar Cottage. It was better than anything she could have hoped for. She was so worried about him. His calls had got shorter and shorter. He always sounded subdued. He hardly told her anything beyond that he was safe. She did all the talking. He just kept asking her to tell him about her pink castles. Well, this was a castle fit for a prince. If only he would call.

Beth tried to reassure her. 'Try not to worry. They are probably in transit. He'll call soon. And it's only four weeks to his homecoming. The weeks will fly by.' Rhianne did not have to wait four weeks. Two days later she learned Eithan was coming home. Not to the barracks. He was being flown to the Royal Centre for Defence Medicine at Queen Elizabeth Hospital, Birmingham.

Theo

Birmingham, August 2003

Dr Theodore Kendrick was just leaving his office when the phone rang.

'Hi Charlie, what can I do for you? I'm in a bit of a rush. I've got a Skype call with Mia and want to be able to take it from home.'

'I'll cut straight to the chase then. I'm ringing to ask a favour.'

'Thought it might be,' he sighed.

'Theo, look, I know you're winding down ahead of your sabbatical, but will you take one last case for me? It's a tough one and I need the best man I can get.'

'Flattery will get you everywhere, old friend.'

'Seriously, this poor bastard's in a bad way. We've patched him up as best we can but it's his mind, Theo. He hasn't spoken a word. Not a word.'

'How old?'

'Twenty-three, going on twenty-four.'

'Family?'

'Just a wife. Lovely young thing, visits every day. Even she can't get a peep out of him. Thing is, Theo, he doesn't need our specialist care anymore and he's blocking a bed. I don't want to discharge him home without PTSD support. Could you see your way to taking him on?'

'Such a smooth talker as always, Charlie. Okay. But this is absolutely the only one or I'll never get the book started. Email me his notes so I can look at them later. Have to dash now.'

'Thanks, mate, I owe you one.'

'How many times have I heard that one. Hang on a minute, Charlie – which barracks is he based at?'

'Ah, I was afraid you might ask that. Er, we'll be discharging him into his wife's care – she's in West Cumbria…'

'Bloody hell, Charlie! That must be two hundred miles away. How do you expect me—'

'You're breaking up Theo… have to go… I'll email you the notes.'

Theo picked up his car keys, shaking his head and muttering what a prize sucker he was. Deep down he knew he would have taken the case even if it had been John O'Groats. Charlie would not have asked if this one had not been critical. He supposed he could always catch up with Matt while he was in that neck of the woods. He had not seen his nephew since he had taken the job at Sellafield. Theo needed some peace and quiet to kick-start his new book. A sleepy backwater in West Cumbria might be as good a place as any. By the time he pulled onto his drive in a leafy avenue of Solihull, Theo was completely reconciled to the prospect.

Once inside, Theo hastily fired up Skype on his laptop. The screen flickered and minutes later she was there.

'Hi Mia. How are you? How's the case going?'

'The prosecution folded. We won hands down!'

'Atta girl! I knew you'd do it. Your first case in Strasbourg! How do you feel?'

'It feels fantastic, Theo. That poor guy went through hell. He should never have had to take it this far to get justice. Theo, I know we had this Skype call booked, but as the case has finished earlier than expected the team are going out to celebrate and although I'm just the junior they've invited me along. So, can we postpone our catch up till I'm back? We could have dinner together if you like. Guita and Nasim would gladly put you up for the night.'

'Sure, no problem. You get yourself out there and celebrate. This is amazing. I'll book us a table for the day after tomorrow. I'll text you the restaurant details. Seven-thirty, okay?'

'Perfect.'

'This really is amazing, Mia. I'm so proud of you.'

'Thanks, Theo. Bye for now.'

Smiling broadly, Theo made himself a light supper and then settled down to study the case notes Charlie had sent through.

*

Theodore Kendrick's route into clinical psychology had been a convoluted one. The son of a Scottish RAF reconnaissance pilot and a Lebanese mother, he grew up bi-lingual. Given his fluency in Arabic, and aptitude for languages, his teachers thought he would study some branch of Linguistics at university and were surprised that he chose Psychology. Having graduated with first-class honours, he decided he did not want to be a psychologist after all, much to the exasperation of his tutors. The editorial work he had done on the student rag had given him a taste for journalism. So Theo joined a long line of idealistic, callow graduates heading for Fleet Street where he cut his teeth on metropolitan small beer before getting his first break: a posting to Belfast as a junior reporter.

In the years he spent covering The Troubles in Northern Ireland, Theo earned his spurs with fearless undercover reporting: gritty, uncompromising. There was precious little he did not know about Operation Banner. He would have been a shoe-in for a senior correspondent role but after six years, he opted to take a junior position in Palestine. Some colleagues thought he was playing the long game. His Arabic would ensure rapid preferment in that part of the world. Those who understood him better knew why he wanted to get as far away from Belfast as he could.

While his fluency in Arabic and disdain for his own safety got him into places other journalists would not risk, it was not the X factor responsible for his rapid success in the Middle East. It was his soft, Scottish accent and striking eyes that made him an obvious choice to put in front of a camera. Liquid brown eyes pooling under a fringe of dark lashes, intense, unsmiling, emulating the grim solemnity of his reports. His voice, a comforting shield deflecting the starkness of the words, cocooned the listener. Within a year he had been offered a contract as a Middle Eastern correspondent with the BBC. Within two he was fast becoming a household name. Several years later, when the Americans invaded Iraq in 1990, Theo was an obvious correspondent choice. He flew to Iraq without a moment's hesitation. Belfast, Gaza, Baghdad: what did it matter to a man who valued his life so cheaply? Harrowing as the grubby underworld of Belfast and the brutalising years on Gaza Strip had been, they had not prepared him for the unimaginable horrors awaiting him in Iraq. Some too disturbing to report for fear of traumatising viewers, some that are difficult for him to recount even to this day.

The year in Iraq rocked his moral compass. It shook his faith in humanity. It was the year he found Mia. She was his salvation.

*

Theo unhooked his reading glasses, closed the lid on his laptop and sat digesting what he had read. The field operational report had been very detailed. The guy was a sapper in the Royal Engineers on his third tour of duty. Previously he had been stationed in Belfast, which was where he gained his bomb disposal experience. It would appear he was very near the end of his last six-month stretch. Unlucky sod! This was going to be a complex case. There was something more to it than he could glean from the notes. He could not put his finger on it. Was it really a naïve mistake? This was no rookie sapper. Five years in, third tour of duty, what was he thinking? Maybe he was not thinking. Maybe his nerves were so shot he had lost the ability to think straight altogether. The injuries were life limiting but not life-threatening. The burns to the right side of his face and upper body were not too severe and had responded well to skin grafts. The vocal cords were not damaged. His good arm had been torn off at the shoulder, but the other limbs were intact and in time he could learn to use his left hand. If Theo could help him through the PTSD, the guy might be able to salvage a decent existence. He would check him out tomorrow but now sleep beckoned. By choice Theo was a lark, not an owl.

*

Theo strode into the RCDM Unit at Queen Elizabeth Hospital next morning. He was a regular there and popular with the female staff. At fifty-four he could have passed for ten years younger on a good day. His hair had no hint of grey. His frame, half an inch shy of six foot, was lean and wiry. His deep brown eyes under long lashes were an instant draw although it was his voice that had the real swoon factor: velvet and granite rolled into one, a hint of his Scottish heritage evident in the warm, musical intonation. His voice, a great asset as a reporter, was even more of an asset in early rapport building with vulnerable patients. They responded to the calm vibe and soft, muted tones. If a tinge of arrogance permeated through, it merely gave them confidence that Doc knew what he was doing. His male medical colleagues, irked by having to compete with his dulcet tones, also had to suffer a cocky bastard who thought himself some kind of walking PTSD god. So, what if the guy was a leading light in PTSD? They were leading lights in their fields too. They would like to see him rebuild a face with third-degree burns or fit a prosthetic onto a mangled arm. They would have welcomed a bit more respect from Theodore Kendrick, not the dismissive superiority thinly disguised with a veneer of comradery. They need not have worried on one count. Adulation was lost on Theo. He was singularly disinterested in anything other than his work and his precious Mia.

*

He found his new client in the day room. A young woman, presumably the wife, was sitting next to him, trying to interest him in a buttered muffin.

'Good morning, Lance Corporal. Good morning, er... Mrs McArthur?' She nodded by way of acknowledgement. 'My name is Dr Kendrick. Colonel Walton asked me to help with your husband's recuperation. I'm a clinical psychologist specialising in post traumatic stress disorders.'

'Pleased to meet you,' said Rhianne, offering her hand to him. 'Thank you for taking an interest in Eithan. I hope you will be able to help him get back to his old self again.'

'That's what I intend to do,' replied Theo confidently. 'How are you feeling today, Eithan?' he asked, not expecting a response but needing to assess how deep the mutism went. 'Muffins not a favourite of yours I see.' There was nothing, not a flicker. 'Have you had any other visitors besides this lovely wife of yours?'

'Perhaps I could talk to you for a few minutes please, Dr Kendrick,' interrupted Rhianne rather anxiously.

'Of course, let's go and find somewhere quiet.'

Rhianne kissed Eithan tenderly on the good side of his face. 'I'll be back soon,' she said. Theo was impressed by her attentive gentleness. She would be easy to work with, he thought, even if the husband was going to be testing.

Rhianne needed no invitation to unburden herself. Her words tumbled out like a burst bag of rice. 'He's been through so much, you see. It's not just what happened in Iraq, it's everything that led up to it.'

'I have plenty of time, Mrs McArthur,' he reassured her, 'why don't you start at the beginning.'

'Eithan's an only child. He lost his dad in a freak road accident when he was seventeen.'

'Was Eithan involved?'

'No, no, he was at school. It was a pedestrian accident, Llanso – that's his dad – was hit by a car when he was waiting at a bus stop.'

'I see,' said Theo.

'Eithan's very clever. Amazing at Maths. He should have gone to university, but he refused to go, said he didn't want to take on debt and wanted to earn enough so his mum could stop work. She was a cleaner at the hospital. She had angina.'

Theo nodded, encouragingly.

'He joined the Royal Engineers hoping they might put him through some qualifications.'

'And did they?'

'Yes, he's already got his HND in engineering and hopes to get chartered status eventually. Joining up, missing uni – it was all for nothing. His mum died of a heart attack two years later. She was only fifty-four. The Council gave him notice on his parents' house and that's when we got hitched. His sergeant got us married quarters. I've recently finished a catering course. The post in Silecroft is my first proper job.'

'How did Eithan get on with his army buddies?' asked Theo patiently. He was used to this kind of disjointed outpouring.

'He was never overly matey with the sappers at Swinton, just the basketball team. So, I was really pleased to see how well he had bonded with Pete – the soldier who died. Pete was a quite a bit older. He was like a big brother looking out for him. Eithan talked about him all the time in our phone calls in those first few months. Not so much the last few months. Latterly, he hardly talked about anything to do with Iraq. Just wanted me to chatter away about pink castles.'

'Pink castles?'

'Oh, it was just something he used to tease me about,' she said, blushing. 'I'm a bit of a dreamer, you see. Always making plans.'

'You said Pete was like a big brother to him?'

'Yes, that's the way it came across anyhow.'

'More "family" taken from him,' said Theo, thoughtfully.

'Yes… and… and…' Rhianne hesitated.

'And?' pressed Theo gently. 'There's something else, isn't there.'

Rhianne nodded, fighting back the tears. 'We were planning to have a baby. Eithan had lost all his family and he wanted to start

Theo

a new one of his own. We had timed it so that the baby would be born after his last tour of duty. He was so happy about it. *Really* happy. Happy in a way he'd not been since before his dad died. And... and I... I miscarried. Eithan took it so hard.'

'I understand,' said Theo softly. 'How much have they told you about what happened when he was injured?'

'They told me he was on a bomb detection and disabling mission. I didn't even know he was doing that kind of work. He only told me about the oil pipelines and the road repairs and stuff like that. They said there was a landmine that killed Pete and injured Eithan.'

'I see,' said Theo again. 'Mrs McArthur...'

'Oh please call me Rhianne, everyone does.'

'Rhianne, you and I will need to work together if we are to get Eithan back to his old self. Upsetting as it will be to hear, I think you need to know what really happened on that day. Do you want me to tell you?'

'Yes,' she replied quietly. 'I'll do anything you ask. Anything to get him better in his head. He's such a wonderful person with a big heart. Too wonderful to be imprisoned, locked in like this.'

'We'll get him better, Rhianne. I promise. The bomb that injured your husband was a booby trap device. It was located in a pram. It had a motion sensor, which set off the recording of a baby crying. When Eithan heard the baby crying he rushed in thinking there was a real baby in imminent danger. Pete tried to stop him, he knew it was a booby trap. Eithan should have known, he's an experienced sapper. That's what's been puzzling me, but now you've told me about your miscarriage I understand. Already traumatised by his experiences in the desert, the thought of a helpless baby in that pram must have blown his mind. He acted out of pure instinct. When he pushed the hood of the pram down, the device detonated. The blast ripped his arm off and threw him up in the air. Pete could see his friend was injured and in great danger. The whole place might go up at any moment. Pete ran in to pull Eithan clear but stepped on a landmine and was killed instantly.'

There was no intake of breath, no gasp, no 'Oh my God' reaction from Rhianne, just a sad nod of the head and a stray tear escaping which trickled down the side of her nose.

'Thank you,' she said a little unsteadily. 'I'm glad you told me.'

'Trust me, Rhianne. I've been doing this a lot of years. I know how to help Eithan. We'll get him talking again soon. He's going to need some intensive PTSD therapy but he's going to be okay. I'll go with you back to Silecroft when they discharge him. I'm starting an extended period of leave to write a book so I can be on hand in Cumbria for as long as it takes.'

'Thank you,' breathed Rhianne. 'I'm so grateful. And I *do* trust you.' She returned to tend to Eithan and the now discarded muffin. Theo watched her go, gangly, inelegant, more girl than woman. 'I'd like to know your story too, Mrs McArthur,' he said to himself. 'You're stronger than you look. Bamboo strong. Not as heralded, or as expensive, as steel but the first choice of Asian scaffold workers when they know their lives depend on it. I'd put money on you being bamboo strong, Mrs McArthur.'

Mia

Mia was nine when her whole life imploded. It was at the height of the 1990–91 invasion of the country of her birth, Iraq. Her family lived in a farming village three hours on foot from Basra. The day had started like any other, no hint of the cataclysmic events that were to unfold. It was the back end of summer, dry and dusty. The ground was parched, and cracks had started to appear in the walls of their clay houses. Mia's family were farmers. In the desert scrubland you were a farmer if you had a few chickens, skeletal goats and some vegetable crops. Her village had grown up around a well that irrigated the crops and provided their household water. But it often ran dry by late summer. There was a small school with two rooms: little school and big school. Mia had moved up to big school because she was nine and liked it much better. In little school you only got to see the teacher once a week. On other days, the teacher set work to be overseen by two of the village mothers. The lessons were simple, and Mia was often bored. Big school was much more interesting.

Mia was trying to put off beating the rugs as the dust from them always hurt her eyes. That and fetching water were the two chores she had to do before school. She decided to skip off and get the water first, hoping that by the time she returned one of her sisters might have done the rugs in her stead. Normally, it was not very far to go for water, but today it would be much further as the well in the centre of the village had run dry. Water treks to the second well were always frightening because of the infidel helicopters patrolling overhead. The loud, menacing roar of their blades scared her. Her father insisted she was quite safe. They would not be interested in their few 'mud huts', as the infidels called their houses. The noise overhead was getting deafening, it didn't sound like helicopters. She could see two infidel planes hurtling across the sky. They were not heading for the city; they were heading in her direction. Terrified, she quickened her step and then started to run. The planes were getting nearer. She abandoned the heavy water cans and ran as fast as she could, trying to reach the safety of home. She was almost there.

*

Mia did not know how long she lay on the ground. Her arm felt like it was on fire and her leg hurt so badly she could not get up. All she could see was fire and smoke around her. She cried out for her mother, but no one came. The sun was hot; she was so thirsty. She heard trucks arriving and lots of shouting. She could hear heavy boots marching around, getting nearer and nearer. Through the smoke Mia saw four infidel soldiers coming towards her. Terrified, she cried out for her mother again. One of the soldiers stood over her, so close she could see the sweat beads rolling down the side of his face. He spat some words at her that she did not understand. He pointed the rifle at her face. One of the other soldiers wrestled him to the ground, shouting at him and beating him with his fists. Another soldier grabbed his rifle. The fourth soldier moved towards her, slowly, with both hands outstretched, palms open. He was not shouting. He was saying some words that she did not understand but they sounded kind. He picked her up and carried her to the infidel truck. She had stopped screaming but was still sobbing and moaning for her mother. The kind soldier carried her into their medical tent and lay her gently on a bed. All the time he talked to her, softly, quietly. She did not understand any of the words, but they sounded soothing. Before she realised what was happening, someone stuck a needle in her good arm and then everything went black.

*

When she awoke, Mia cried out for her mother again. A nurse tried to calm her unsuccessfully, so brought back an older man who spoke some rudimentary Arabic. Mia struggled with his pronunciation of her language but managed to assemble enough of what he told her to understand that her mother was dead. They were all dead. Mia pieced it together and filled in the gaps his inadequate tongue failed to describe. The infidels had obliterated her village. All seventeen houses were blown to pieces. Every man, woman and child in the community where she had grown up had been killed. Her mother, father, two sisters and three brothers and all her neighbours – senselessly, barbarically mown down. Mad with grief, she divided her waking hours in those first two days between planning how to escape and how to make the infidels pay for what they had done. She hissed and spat at anyone who came near her and refused to eat their infidel food. With her good arm, she threw a jug of water at one of them. That's when they chained her to the bed.

*

It was the third day when Theo arrived. She spat at him too and invoked Allah to curse him and his children and his children's children. To her surprise he spoke back to her in fluent Arabic. She was so startled she stopped ranting.

'Tell Allah he's too late. I'm already cursed. My parents, my sister, my wife and unborn child are all dead. So, you see, we're not so different, little one.' While keeping a safe distance to avoid being spat at again, he explained that he was not a soldier and he was not a doctor; he was a journalist. Journalists were interested in truth and justice. He said he could help her, but she had to eat first. He had brought a dish of rice and corn. She could smell the spices were ones she liked. He ate some himself first to show her it was not poisoned and then helped her take her first mouthful.

'What do I call you?' he asked.

'My name is Amira Saleem,' she announced proudly, 'but my family call me... called me... Mia.'

'Then, little one, may I call you Mia?'

She nodded, still a little unsure of him.

'My name is Theodore Kendrick, but my family called me Theo, so why don't you call me Theo too.'

She nodded silently.

'You are going to have to trust me, Mia, if I am going to help you. And I will trust you. See, I am going to unfasten this chain because I trust you are not going to attack me.'

*

Mia did not attack him or anyone else after that. Theo did not treat her like a child. He explained everything to her and although she could never forgive the atrocity the infidels had inflicted on her village, he helped her to some degree of acceptance. It had been a terrible mistake, he had said, a terrible accident. Flawed intelligence had resulted in the Allied forces bombing what they thought to be a concealed armoury in the well and surrounding houses. When the soldiers went in afterwards to clean up, they found nothing but charred civilians and scorched, emaciated carcasses of their livestock. Theo said there would be an inquiry to uncover all the facts and make sure accidents like that could never happen again. Much later, Mia was to learn that 'accidents' like that did happen again. Many times. She also realised how lucky she had been to escape alive: the only survivor, the only Iraqi witness, to an Allied operation that had gone badly wrong.

*

After a few days, she trusted Theo enough to tell him about the soldier who was going to shoot her and how terrified she had been. She suspected he already knew but he did not let on. Theo asked her to try not to be bitter, that the soldier who did that was very wrong but that he was not a bad man. He was ill. His mind had become sick with the horror of the war. He had been sent home. Theo came every day for five weeks and talked to her in her own language. He translated what the doctors said about her arm, which was not broken but needed skin grafts. The burns on her leg were much less severe and would heal on their own although she would always have the scars. The same went for the burns on one side of her face. Theo said her lovely long black hair would probably cover most of it when it grew back.

They talked and talked and talked. She told him about her brothers and sisters, about the nanny goat that used to butt her when she was little, about the food she ate, the rugs and baskets they weaved and the occasional trips to Basra that her older brothers undertook to sell their wares and bring back supplies. It would take them the whole day. If the sales were good, they might bring home some carp so mother could cook *masgouf*. And when it was someone's birthday there would always be dates. Dates were Mia's absolute favourite food. She had had nine birthdays. It would be her tenth birthday in a few months but there would be no dates to look forward to this time. Theo talked with her as if she were a grown up, like an equal, not a dirty little Arab kid. He told her about his parents, his Scottish father and his Lebanese mother. He showed her a worn photo of them. The other photo he showed her was of his wife, Josie. She was not a striking dark-haired beauty like his mother. She was a smaller woman with unruly blonde hair and pale, laughing eyes, visibly pregnant with a huge camera slung around her neck. He clammed up if she asked about her and the unborn child.

'They died and part of me died with them. That's all you need to know, Mia.'

*

Mia was eating properly now and getting stronger. Theo had left instructions about the kind of food that was familiar to her and how to cook it. After five weeks, he had to leave. There was an Allied coalition summit to report on but he hoped only to be away one week. That same week, Mia was discharged to an Iraqi orphanage. The food at the orphanage was scant and the beds were dirty. Good as it was to be with her own people and some children of her own age, it was a frightening place. Some girls who did not have injuries or ugly scars like the ones she had, disappeared without warning, mysteriously taken in the night never to be seen again.

*

Theo's assignment kept him away for two weeks and it was another two before he had tracked Mia to the orphanage. He was appalled at the conditions he found her in and when she told him about the children who mysteriously disappeared in the night, he picked her up there and then and strode out of the orphanage with her in his arms. No one dared to challenge him. Theo would not let Mia out of his sight after that. There was no turning back. He had abducted a nine-year-old girl and would have to see this through. He had little appetite for a return to England now his parents and sister were dead, but his sights were set on a safe haven for Mia. A life chance for a disfigured orphan; an innocent victim of a world on fire.

'Mia, I want you to come back to England with me where you will be safe,' he said. 'I understand how frightening it must feel to have to go to a strange country with a strange language, but I can't bear to leave you behind, abandon you to another hideous orphanage. I will help you learn English. I will get you into a good school and find a kind Iraqi family to look after you.'

'I won't be scared as long as I'm with you,' she replied. 'But I must live with you. You are my family now.'

'It won't be possible, Mia. It won't be allowed. It wouldn't be proper. You're almost ten and I'm a single man. I have no wife to be a mother to you.'

'Then I will not go. You cannot make me.'

Theo dropped his head into his hands, and for the first time since Josie died, he wept. Mia had never seen a man cry, only her brothers before they grew too big. It was a strange, noiseless weeping, not like the women's wailing she was used to. Tears rolled silently down his cheeks. All the horror, the despair, the grief had finally vanquished him. 'I can't lose you as well as them,' he whimpered. Mia knew instinctively that he was talking about his dead wife and child. She flung her arms around his neck and hugged him, clinging fast to him as if the tighter she held him the more she could ease his pain.

'Please don't cry any more, Theo. I won't leave you. I will go with you to your England.'

*

They left Iraq a week later. Theo was well respected at the British base. He was a responsible journalist who did not need to be schooled in the importance of keeping a lid on what had happened at Mia's village until an inquiry could establish the full facts. There were all sorts of conspiracy theories swirling around. A lesser man would have made a grab for a scoop, but not Theo Kendrick. He had been very understanding about the solider who had lost it big time, seemed to have an empathy for sickness in the head, and he had helped them out of a tight spot with the wild cat girl. So, it was not difficult for Theo to cadge a ride for himself and Mia on a Hercules flight heading back to RAF Fairford.

Before he left, Theo contacted an Iraqi refugee couple he had helped escape to England. Nasim Azizi was a university professor and political activist who found himself on Saddam's wanted list. Theo had helped him seek asylum in England with his wife Guita and their two teenage children, Farid and Lina. They readily agreed to take Mia. Theo and Mia arrived at Nasim's in the early evening of a cold, dark winter day. When Theo saw how tenderly Guita embraced the little orphan, how softly she spoke to her, how gently she stroked her hair and how Mia melted into those maternal arms he realised how crushingly she must be feeling the death of her mother.

*

Next morning, Theo wasted no time. He knew what he had to do. He called the Home Office. 'Theodore Kendrick for the Home Secretary,' was his insistent command. He was a well-known figure in the media world, so he was confident the receptionist would know who he was.

'I'm sorry Mr Kendrick, you of all people must know I can't connect you directly with the minister. You have to go through Media Liaison. Would you like me to transfer you?'

'Screw ML. Tell the Home Secretary I want a meeting with him within twenty-four hours or I go public with a news report about the WWO atrocity. He's best pals with the Defence Secretary so he'll know exactly what I'm referring to. Don't try and fob me off with any of his monkeys, I'm only prepared to talk to the organ grinder about this.'

At 11.30am, Theo's mobile rang.

'Mr Kendrick, the Home Secretary will see you at seven-thirty this evening. Come via the security checkpoint at Queen Anne's Gate.' Theo smiled wryly. He knew the drill: evening meeting squirrelled away in some back room. It would be just the two of them so the minister could deny the meeting ever took place. That suited Theo just fine. It meant he could go in with the gloves off.

*

When Theo had been scanned and frisked by security to make sure he was not carrying any recording device and had surrendered his mobile phone, he was taken to a back meeting room where the Home Secretary was already seated.

'What the hell's going on, Kendrick?'

'I'm not prepared to be messed around, so you'd better listen good.'

'I'm listening,' came the icy response.

'I've brought a nine-year-old girl back with me from Iraq. She is the only survivor of that almighty water well fuck up.'

'Now hold on – the Defence Secretary hasn't concluded the internal on that yet and there is speculation that our guys might not have been at fault. It's possible the flawed intelligence was planted by Saddam loyalists. They're not above killing their own people to discredit us – you've been out there long enough to know that.'

'I don't give a toss about your conspiracy theories, whether it's our almighty fuck up or an enemy sting is immaterial to me. My concern is an innocent child who's been orphaned, disfigured, not to mention traumatised by having a British soldier try to blow her brains out at point-blank range. *We've* done this to her, *we* have a responsibility to make it right. There's no way I was leaving her in that hell hole of an orphanage she'd been dumped in.'

'It's war, Kendrick, shit happens.'

'I'll try and forget you said that. I just fucking hope this kind of shit never rains down on your own family.'

'What do you want, Kendrick?'

'I have a shopping list.'

'I'm warning you, Kendrick, I'm in no mood to barter with journalists.'

'Don't worry, there'll be no call for bartering, I'm not prepared to compromise. First up, I have an ideal Iraqi family lined up ready to foster her. I want your assurance they'll be allowed to take her.'

'Look Kendrick, there are procedures to be gone through, asylum holding centres, child safeguarding issues, vetting fostering processes—'

'There'll be no asylum detention camp for her, not after what she's been through. *I've* vetted this family and told you they're ideal. I'm sure social services will come to the same view. I just don't want you putting any obstacles in the way. As for child safeguarding! Don't make me laugh!! Bit late wouldn't you say? Where in your fucking safeguarding manual does it mention protecting a child from an L85 rifle spraying her brains across the desert? She remembers every detail of what happened, you know. It haunts her waking – and sleeping – hours.'

'Look Kendrick, I feel for the kid, obviously I do, but you can't just tear up the rule book.'

'I haven't finished my shopping list yet.'

'God Almighty, Kendrick. This is insane.'

'I want a passport and British citizenship fast tracked for her – you can do it speedily enough for Olympic medal hopefuls and oil-rich donors, so don't give me any bullshit about rule books and procedures. Plus, I want the Government to pick up the tab for international school fees, it's the only sensible educational option.'

'Are you done?'

'Not quite. We both know this *internal* inquiry will be a whitewash. It'll all be hushed up. She'll never see a penny of compensation for what we did to her. So, the Government is going to top up the fostering allowance by five hundred pounds a month until she turns twenty-one.'

'And what if I won't play ball?'

'Then be prepared for a colossal stink you and your lofty political ambitions won't be able to shake off. I have graphic footage of the carnage inflicted, the dozens of charred civilian bodies, interviews with two of the soldiers involved and testimony from a nine-year-old surviving victim. It's all there in my report – which of course also refers to the lengths you've taken to hush it up.'

'This is blackmail, Kendrick, reckless, irresponsible blackmail.'

'You can call it what you like. I call it justice, retribution, honour. And don't get any ideas about setting your MI5 muppets onto me to arrange a convenient accident. If anything happens to me, or Mia, or the Azizis, I have lodged copies of my report with a few loyal friends who know what to do with it.'

'How do I know you won't publish anyway once I've given you everything you ask for?'

'Because I'm a man of my word, not a shithead politician. Honour and integrity still mean something to me.'

'And what if the girl blabs—'

'She's a bright kid. She knows that keeping schtum is her best chance of a decent life.'

'You're finished as a journalist after this, Kendrick. I'll make damned sure of that!'

'Be my guest. I'm quitting anyway. There's only so much putrid humanity a man can stomach.'

His heart hammering, Theo strode out with a deliberate step, resisting the temptation to hurry or to slam the door. It was important he left behind an impression of an arctic, ruthlessly determined foe in case the Home Secretary had second thoughts. Having collected his mobile phone, he marched out into the welcome relief of the London drizzle, which cooled the adrenalin pumping round his veins.

*

By the time he was back at the Azizi house it was after nine. Mia was still up. Guita instinctively knew she would want to stay up until Theo returned. Only then could she surrender her fears of abandonment to the restorative realms of sleep. Lina had been keeping her entertained, showing her what her karaoke machine could do. Mia hugged Theo goodnight and allowed the mother figure to take her to bed. Guita stayed with her until the child fell asleep.

'Did it go as you'd hoped, my friend?' Nasim asked Theo.

'He knows which side his bread's buttered, so yes, I think we'll get what we need for Mia. I was so scared I wouldn't be able to pull it off. It's the toughest hand of poker I've ever had to play.'

'Would you have gone through with it if he had refused?'

Theo ran his hand through his damp hair. 'You know I couldn't do that, Nasim. There's an imperative to protect Mia but I couldn't unleash that kind of information until we have a better understanding of what really happened there. It would be dynamite in the wrong hands. And I couldn't bring myself to destroy an already traumatised soldier. He would be the one they would scapegoat if they were forced into a corner. He's in a bad way, poor sod, needs helping not throwing to the wolves. I'm just glad it didn't come to it, Nasim. I was banking on his ego and ambition to carry this off. I didn't have a plan B.'

'What will you do with your report?'

'There is no report, it was one unholy bluff. I do have some footage locked away and the information is all carefully logged in my head. Perhaps one day it will need to come out, but only when it's safe. When the world is in a frame of mind to learn from this, not fuel more hatred, more carnage.'

'What will you do now, my friend?'

'I've got plenty of savings so I'm going to take some time out. Retrain. Go back to my psychology roots and do a conversion to clinical. I'd like to try my hand at healing people rather than hounding them.'

*

Theo stayed with the Azizis for a month, during which time he explored options for clinical conversion courses. Once Mia's passport and citizenship came through, he breathed more easily knowing the Home Secretary had not had second thoughts. He felt it would be safe, now, to contact social services about formalising a fostering arrangement. His instinct had been spot-on. Mia settled very quickly into the Azizi household. Lina had her mother's nature and delighted in the prospect of having a little sister to indulge. If the only danger Theo foresaw was of Mia being thoroughly spoiled, it was a small enough trade off.

*

Mia struggled at first with her schooling, having virtually no English but she got lots of help from her foster family and soon caught up.

She proved to have an aptitude for languages, French in particular. By the age of nineteen, with perseverance, an innate love of learning and endless help from Nasim, she had secured a university place to read French and Law. As Theo predicted, her lustrous dark locks covered most of the disfigurement on the affected side of her face. She did not attempt to hide the scars on her arm and leg – they were part of her heritage, they were a constant reminder of love and loss, of conflict and devotion.

*

'Sorry, Mia!' said Theo, leaning over to kiss her, as he draped his coat over the chair. 'I hope you haven't been waiting long.'

'I was lost in thought and reminiscence so hadn't noticed you were late,' she fibbed. For Theo's benefit, they always spoke Arabic when they met or talked on the phone. Mia had ample opportunities to speak her mother tongue with her foster family but since Theo was no longer based in the Middle East, he had much fewer.

'I want to hear all about Strasbourg. I can hardly credit it, this spitting fireball I picked up in Iraq is now fighting cases at the European Court of Human Rights!'

'Hardly, Theo – I was the most junior member of the team. But I learned a lot and I think I was useful. I did a lot of the backroom research. I think I have an aptitude for digging up skeletons.'

'Is human rights where you're going to specialise?'

'Definitely. I don't think I ever really doubted it but this experience in Strasbourg has made me more determined than ever.'

'You were never short on determination, Mia. Have you ordered?'

'No, I was waiting for you.'

'Let's have a look at this menu then, see if there's any rabbit food that's edible.'

'At least my rabbit food is helping save the planet, unlike you and your cannibal friends. One day, Theo Kendrick, one day you'll see the light.'

'How are Nasim and Guita?'

'As lovely as ever, if feeling their age. Guita's arthritis is much worse and Nasim's macular degeneration is pretty severe now. I think he'll lose his sight eventually. Guita has finally persuaded him to retire. They are giving him an Emeritus Professorship.'

'And so they should! Took them long enough to give him his professorship, even though he was a respected professor in Iraq long before he came here.'

Theo tucked into his surprisingly tasty vegetable lasagne. 'I'm so very proud of you, Mia,' he grinned at her.

'None of it could have happened without you,' she answered softly.

Ciara

Whitehaven, July 2003

Ciara was in the supermarket when she took the call. School had just broken up for the summer. Matt was coming over that evening and she was browsing the shelves for a good bottle of red to go with the steak sitting in her basket. Her mobile phone vibrated in her pocket.

'Hi Sis, I'm just in the supermarket, I'll ring you back in ten.'

'No don't hang up, Ciara,' came the frantic response.

'What's wrong Rhianne?'

'It's Eithan! He's been injured. He's been flown to the Royal Centre for Defence Medicine at Queen Elizabeth Hospital in Birmingham.'

'Oh my God! Oh God, Rhianne. *How* bad?'

'I don't know for sure, but it must be pretty bad if they've sent him there.'

'Sit tight, kitten. I'm on my way. I'll be with you in less than an hour.' Ciara hastily replaced the steak, abandoned the empty basket in the aisle and dashed to the car park texting Matt on the way. No point ringing him, he was bound to be in a meeting. She drove home and packed a few things into a holdall. Best to be prepared just in case she needed to drive to Birmingham. The next few days could be a little uncertain. She found Rhianne in West

Cottage kitchen with Beth. The older woman was standing by the wall-mounted land line, pad and pencil in hand ready to take notes. Rhianne was sitting at the dining table still in shock. The two sisters hugged each other silently.

Beth covered the handset and addressed her visitor. 'Hello, Ciara, I'm on hold waiting to speak to someone at the hospital.'

The two sisters sat motionless at the table, fingers tightly entwined.

'Yes, yes, I'm still here,' said Beth. 'Yes, Lance Corporal Eithan McArthur. He was admitted earlier today. I have his wife here wanting to know what's happening. All she's been told is that he's injured.' Beth covered the mouthpiece again and addressed the sisters. 'She's gone to get someone.' The wait was only a few minutes, but it felt like hours.

'Mrs McArthur?' inquired a different voice.

'One moment, please. I have her right here.'

Beth beckoned to Rhianne to come to the phone, and she jumped up as if she had been shot.

'Hello, this is Mrs McArthur.'

Beth sat down opposite Ciara waiting patiently until Rhianne came off the phone. There was an uncomfortable atmosphere between the two seated women. They were too alike. Both professional, efficient, stony. Ciara was jealous of the nurturing role Beth had adopted with Rhianne. That was *her* role. She was the older sister. She had looked out for Rhianne ever since their mum died. This baker woman acted like some substitute mother. No one could replace their mum. No one. Yes, she felt sorry that she had lost her son in some horrific roadside bomb, but it did not mean she could muscle her way into the Atkinson nest.

'How bad is it?' asked Ciara nervously, as Rhianne returned to sit next to her.

'He's got some burns to his face and upper chest, and he's lost one arm. Torn off at the shoulder.'

'Which arm?' asked Ciara nervously.

'His good one.'

Ciara bowed her head, unable to say more. It was Beth who piped up, 'But he's alive, Rhianne. That's what you've got to focus on. He's alive and he's home. And he's got *you*. You'll get through this together and we'll all help.'

Ciara wished she had been the one to say those comforting words.

'They said I can go down there. They'll put me up in the visitors' quarters. I'm going to go and pack. I'm sorry to leave you in the lurch, Beth, but I have to be with Eithan. He needs me.'

'Of course, you must! Don't give it a second thought. We'll manage fine.'

'I'll drive you,' announced Ciara. 'I threw a few things in a holdall just in case. I don't want you driving, not after a shock like this.' She had recovered her composure. Big Sis was ready to take charge again. At least this was something Beth could not muscle in on. She did not have a car and probably could not even drive.

'Your sister's right, Rhianne,' said Beth. 'And you need your family with you at a time like this.'

Ciara felt somewhat chastened by the older woman's remark and the sincerity with which it had been said. Perhaps she should make a bit more effort to like her.

While Rhianne packed a bag, Beth went off to check on the shop and Ciara checked her phone. There was a nice text from Matt.

Sorry to hear about your brother-in-law. No worries about tonight. We can rearrange when the picture's clearer. Take as long as you need. I'll be here when you get back. Please give your sister my best wishes. I hope things go well for her. x

She sent him a warm text back. It was early days, but she had not felt this good about a guy in a long time.

Hilda bustled out just as the two sisters were getting into Ciara's car.

'Here, Rhianne. I've put yer up sum ginger parkin an' there's a flask o' te.' Her ample cheeks were blotchy red from crying. 'Go kerful now won't yer.' Rhianne dropped her suitcase and ran to give the large woman a hug. 'It ain't reght. It ain't fur. What 'arm 'av you ever dun t'anyone. Why did it 'av t'appen to yuse. It ain't reght.'

'You go in now, Hilda. I'll be okay – and I'll be bringing Eithan back with me. That's what we must hold onto. He's coming home.'

*

The journey took them nearly four hours. No jarring radio, the two young women were lost in their own tense, silent thoughts. They spoke with the doctor first. He needed to prepare Rhianne for what she would see. 'Eithan will be heavily bandaged and sedated so don't be upset if you get no reaction from him. It's going to take a while.' Rhianne nodded gently.

'He's going to pull through though, isn't he?' asked Ciara much less gently.

'Yes, his injuries are not life threatening. I'm afraid we won't be able to fit a prosthetic arm. There's not enough of the shoulder joint left to attach anything to. The burns should heal well enough. We are confident the skin grafts will take.'

Ciara winced. Rhianne merely nodded gently again.

When they went onto the ward Ciara hung back. Rhianne stood by the bed looking tenderly at her husband. 'You're safe now Eithan,' she whispered. 'I'm here. Everything's going to be fine. I have the most splendid pink castle waiting for you when you're allowed home. I can't wait to show it to you.'

*

Ciara stayed in Birmingham for five days. Rhianne had been given a bed in the visitors' quarters and Ciara booked herself into a nearby Travelodge. In that time, Eithan's physical recovery progressed well. The doctors were pleased with how the skin grafts were taking. He was given morphine for the pain, which made him sleepy and unresponsive much of the time. Rhianne spent two hours by his bedside each morning and two hours each afternoon. She read to him and she sang to him. No matter that after five days she still had no response, patiently, gently, she persisted.

'Ciara, I think you should go home now,' she had said. 'There's nothing more you can do, and I'm well catered for here in the unit. This has already eaten into your summer holiday, and you've left that lovely new man of yours kicking his heels.'

'I can't leave you here, alone, Sis.'

'I'm not alone, Ciara, I'm with Eithan. I *want* you to go back now, Ciara.'

'If that's what you want, then yes of course I'll go,' she replied, a little hurt. Suddenly it felt like the Big Sis/Baby Sis table had flipped. Ciara did not feel needed. It felt strange, like experiencing sea sickness for the first time.

*

Ciara checked out early next morning and headed up the M6. She had decided she would call in on Dad on the way. She normally visited him once a month, did a bit of housework for him, topped up his food store and generally checked he was not letting himself go. It was over five weeks, and he would be fretting. 'It's me, Dad,' she shouted as she made her way down the garden into the greenhouse where she knew she would find him. It was a large greenhouse with three beds, one for tomatoes, one for gourds and one for orchids. He was tending the flower bed.

'Hello, love. It's been a while.'

'Yes, sorry, Dad, but a lot has happened in the last few weeks. Let's go in and I'll make us a cuppa. I've brought some Eccles cakes, your favourite.'

*

'I need to talk to you about Rhianne,' said Ciara as they sipped their tea.

'If it's about your sister, I don't want to know. She made her bed so she can lie in it. I've told you umpteen times. She's dead to me now.'

'Well, you're going to listen whether you like it or not,' scolded Ciara.

Mr Atkinson shrugged his shoulders and slurped his tea noisily.

'Her husband—'

'I don't want to hear anything about that husband of hers either,' he interrupted.

'As I said. You're going to listen whether you like it or not. It's high time. This has gone on long enough.'

Mr Atkinson shrugged again and overfilled his mouth with Eccles cake so that the currants protruded from his lips and patting them back into his mouth gave him an excuse to ignore this remark.

'As you know – or as I've told you – Eithan is a Lance Corporal in the Royal Engineers. He's just been flown home from Iraq, badly injured.'

'What's that to me?' he snarled.

'He's a fine man, a wonderful husband and a brave soldier. It's time you found it in your heart to acknowledge him as your son-in-law.'

'Never,' came the firm response.

'Rhianne is going to need all the help she can get over the coming months and it would be a great comfort to her to know her father had her back.'

'Who?' he asked.

'Rhianne!'

'Who's this Rhianne you keep talking about? I don't know any Rhianne.'

Ciara sat back in her chair, utterly shocked at the callousness of the man who had sired her. She got up and left the room. She did not go and clean the bathroom, tidy the kitchen or put away the shopping she had brought him. She simply walked out of the front door, got in the car and drove away. It was the first time she had left without kissing him goodbye. It was a nauseating end to a sickening few weeks.

*

Ciara rang Rhianne every day for an update. It was always the same. The burns were healing, the shoulder stump had stabilised and he was comfortable – and quiet. Rhianne did not tell her that Eithan had not said a single word since being admitted. She did not want to burden Ciara with the worry of it. There would be time enough for that when he was cleared for discharge. Ciara was embarking on a new relationship with someone she finally seemed keen on. That was what she must focus on right now. Eithan's state of mind could wait. The only person Rhianne did confide in was Beth. She spoke to Beth every day on the phone too. And every day she poured her heart out to the baker woman.

*

Ciara lay awake, her thoughts too frenzied to give in to sleep. She watched Matt as he lay peacefully beside her. It was the first time he had stayed over. She had not expected things to progress so quickly, but everything had felt right. *He* felt right. He was different. Comfortable in his own skin, not eager to impress or hen pecked like the others. She must be careful not to lose him. She had a talent for scaring men away. The normality of school routine was firmly re-established. So much so she could hardly believe the tortuous events of the summer had really happened. Ciara was still fretting over the phone call from Rhianne that she was bringing Eithan home in the next few days. Any joy she might have felt was blunted by the information her kid sister had imparted. Eithan had made a good physical recovery, but his mind was not right. Apparently, he was in some kind of catatonic state. Had not spoken a single word. Why had Rhianne not told her earlier? It was as if she was trying to protect her. But this was

all the wrong way round. It was Ciara who should be protecting
Rhianne.

*

Over breakfast, Matt could see Ciara was exhausted.

'You look like you haven't slept. Perhaps I shouldn't have stayed.
You're not used to a hairy beast sharing your bed.'

'No, no. It's not you. No! Last night was wonderful. Well, for
me anyway.'

'Me too,' he smiled at her. 'If it's not my snoring or my sweaty
body keeping you awake—'

'You don't snore, Matt…'

'Well, whatever. If it's not me keeping you awake what is? You
can tell me.'

'Rhianne's husband is going to be discharged in the next few
days, but she's only just told me that his mind's not right. All this
time. All these weeks and she said nothing. It's like she only told
me when she absolutely had to. As if she's trying to protect me. But
that's *my* job. I'm the one who's supposed to protect *her*.'

'Hey,' he said soothingly, pulling her towards him. 'She's a
grown woman with a husband. It's not your job anymore. You
can't spend the rest of your life compensating for the sins of your
father – or the death of your mother,' he added gently. It had been
a bonding experience when they had swapped stories about their
mothers. It had moved their relationship onto another level. Not
that Matt remembered anything of his. She had died when he was
a toddler, but he remembered what it was like growing up without
a mother.

'She said he hasn't spoken. Not a word in seven weeks. He's
trapped in some kind of catatonic state. Suspended shock or
something.'

'Sounds like PTSD,' interjected Matt. 'Post traumatic stress
disorder,' he qualified. 'Look, I don't want to stick my nose in
where I'm not wanted. It's your family but if it's any help I could

give my uncle a ring. He's a PTSD specialist. Best in his field. He has a leave of absence coming up so might be able to give us some time.'

Ciara liked the 'us' he had slipped into the conversation. It boded well. She desperately wanted this relationship to work out.

'That sounds wonderful, Matt. Thank you.'

'No time like the present,' he said, reaching for his mobile. That was another thing she liked about him. He was a doer, not a procrastinator. She felt even more included when he put his mobile on speaker.

'Matt! Lovely to hear from you,' came the reply. 'Great minds think alike. I was going to give you a ring later today. Looks like I might get to see you pretty soon.'

'That's great Uncle Theo but before you say anything else, you're on speakerphone. I have my girlfriend here.'

'Girlfriend?' said Theo, intrigued. 'Must be serious. Don't recall ever sharing a call with one of your girlfriends before.'

'It *is* serious, Uncle Theo, so don't go embarrassing me with any salacious stories about my mis-spent youth.'

'I promise to be on my best behaviour. Does she have a name, this special lady of yours?'

'Ciara. She's called Ciara.'

'Hello, Ciara – pleased to meet you. Don't believe a word he tells you. I'm not the wicked uncle he pretends I am.'

'Pleased to meet you,' replied Ciara laughing. She liked him already – and what a gorgeous voice he had.

'Uncle Theo. I have a favour to ask. Ciara's brother-in-law's a soldier who was injured in Iraq. He's being discharged from QE in a few days, and it sounds like he's got a pretty serious case of PTSD. As you've got your leave of absence, I was wondering if you might be able to take a look at him. You could—'

'His name's not Eithan McArthur by any chance?' interrupted Theo. 'A Lance Corporal with the Royal Engineers?'

'Yes!' squealed Ciara. 'That's him! How did you know his name?'

'I've just agreed to take his case. Charlie rang me about it. That's what I was going to call you about later – to tell you I'm heading up your way and… well, I never! What a small world it is.'

'You can stay with me for as long as you want,' said Matt, 'although it's a fair way from Silecroft.'

'Sounds great. I'll definitely come and stay for a few nights till I find somewhere a bit more local. Let's get the lie of the land first before we get ahead of ourselves.'

'Oh thank you so much er…' Ciara hesitated, not sure what she should call him. It seemed very forward to call him Theo and overly familiar to call him *Uncle* Theo. 'Er Mr, Dr, er…'

'Theo, please. Or Uncle Theo if you prefer. I like being an uncle. Makes me feel I still belong to the human race. If you don't think I'm human enough, you can always resort to Dr Kendrick.'

'Thank you very much, *Uncle* Theo,' repeated Ciara, laughing. 'I can't wait to meet you.'

*

Ciara would have volunteered to drive Rhianne and Eithan home, but it was a school day. Matt kindly offered to go in her place. It was another brick in the wall for Ciara – Matt getting involved like this. He had a much bigger vehicle and she had to remember Eithan was six feet four. As soon as she could see her Year 6 pupils safely off the premises, she drove herself to Silecroft. The hospital party had already arrived at Briar Cottage and Rhianne was making teas and coffees for them all.

'Thanks for doing this,' she whispered to Matt as she slid her hand into his.

'My pleasure. Glad to be able to help. Your sister's nice.'

'Yes, she's a lovely kitten.'

'More of a lioness, I would have said, the way she managed her husband into the car. Talked and sang to him most of the journey. Seems to have natural empathy for situations.'

Ciara felt that lurching hurt again and instantly felt ashamed. She should feel pleased for Rhianne that she was growing into a capable, accomplished woman. She could not baby her forever.

*

Eithan was slumped in an armchair to the side of the unlit fire. One sleeve of his hoodie hung limply. The right side of his face was badly scarred. She shuddered involuntarily. Matt felt it and squeezed her hand more tightly. Ciara knew she was not good with disfigurement. It made her feel uncomfortable. She never knew what to say or where to look. Hers was a perfect world. Neat. Ordered. She took shelter in the distraction of Dr Kendrick being there. He had followed in his own car. It would not have been appropriate for him to drive the McArthurs. He had to develop the right client-doctor relationship with Eithan.

'*Uncle* Theo,' she said breezily, 'we meet at last.'

He smiled briefly and shook her hand but did not speak. He was watching Eithan intently. Observing his every movement – or lack of it. She had misjudged the mood. Rhianne came to her rescue.

'Ciara, could you help me in the kitchen. Beth has left a box of cakes and cookies and I need to plate them up.' Matt was right. Her sister did seem to have a natural empathy for situations. So, the baker woman was not there. At least that was something. Perhaps she shied away from disfigurement too. But Ciara knew she was clutching at straws. The woman lived every waking moment with that huge scar on her cheek! No, she had to grudgingly admit that her absence was more likely due to sensibility.

Eithan nibbled at a cookie and slopped his tea. He never lifted his head nor looked around at his new surroundings. As they drained their cups, Theo was the first to make a move.

'Matt, I think we should leave the family to get settled. Let's head up to yours. You lead, I'll follow.'

'Sure,' replied Matt. He pecked Ciara on the cheek. 'I'll ring you tonight, sweetheart.' And before she could collect her wits to make an appropriately warm response, they were gone. She was left alone with her sister and a corpse-like soldier. She went to Rhianne to give her a hug and the two sisters clung to each other. It re-set Ciara's compass. She felted needed again.

PART TWO

Briar Cottage

Beth missed the company of the young woman who had become like a daughter to her. She had never met Eithan but felt she knew him already from all Rhianne's downloads. That was the old Eithan of course; she had no idea what the new Eithan would be like. He had obviously been through some horrific experience that had left his body maimed and his mind traumatised. Apparently, some shrink was journeying with them. She had no time for head doctors. Theory-loving idiots who thought they could heal pain. They knew nothing about pain, not real pain. Satisfied that everything was as ready as it could be, she locked up Briar Cottage and returned to her own home, a brisk five-minute walk away. She had filled the fridge, arranged some flowers in a vase, left a box of provisions on the worktop and a welcome home card. She would ring Rhianne this evening but would not go round for a few days. They would need their space. It would be strange for Eithan and it sounded like he was in a very bad way. Rhianne knew she could ring for anything she needed.

In her own front room, she lit a cigarette and stood by the window watching for passing cars on the high street. It was foolish because she did not know what kind of car Ciara's boyfriend drove, but it passed the time. She was too agitated to go back to her baking. She just needed to know they had got home safely. She wandered across to the sideboard and picked up the smaller of the two photographs, the one of Sidney when he was a toddler. He had been such a sweet child. She hoped Eithan's injuries would not preclude them having children. Rhianne would make a wonderful mother. She opened the top drawer of the sideboard and fingered a few of its treasures: Sid's christening gown, his dungarees, the stack of birthday cards and Mother's Day cards, the soldier's beret. She reached for the small wooden toy soldier and placed it between the two photo frames: the man and the boy. 'You can stand guard until they are home safely,' she said aloud, fingering its faded painted face fondly.

*

It was a little after eight when Rhianne phoned her.

'Thank you for the flowers and all the provisions,' she said.

'You're home safely. Thank God,' breathed Beth.

'Eithan's very tired from the journey so he's gone to bed. I won't be long after him. I'm exhausted too.'

'He managed the journey alright then?'

'Yes. Matt's a good driver and his car eats up the miles.'

'Any change?' asked Beth.

'No. He didn't even look out of the window when we were driving here. He just sits. That's all he does all day. He just sits.'

'It'll take time but now he's home he'll get better. And you're both young. You have your whole lives ahead of you. Your whole lives for those pink castles.'

'Yes. I can wait, Beth. I'll wait as long as it takes.'

'I won't come over for a couple of days. You both need time to adjust but you know where I am. Just pick up the phone if you need anything.'

'Thanks, Beth. Goodnight.'

'Goodnight, Rhianne. Sweet dreams.'

Beth heaved a sigh of relief. They were home. They were safe. She picked up the little soldier and put him back in the sideboard drawer. 'Job well done, Sid,' she smiled to the wooden toy, 'you kept them safe.' She lit another cigarette and poured a whiskey. She rarely indulged, but their safe homecoming felt like the right occasion for a small tot.

*

It was the third day when Beth ventured over to Briar Cottage armed with freshly baked bread and some cookies. Rhianne had mentioned Eithan was content to nibble on the cookies. Rhianne must have spied her coming because she met her halfway up the path that led to the front door. The two women hugged each other as if they had been parted years, not weeks.

'Any change?' asked Beth.

Rhianne shook her head. 'Come on in. I'm dying for you to meet him.'

Beth followed Rhianne into the front room. She spotted Eithan straight away. He was in an armchair by the fireplace. You could not really miss him. Even hunched in a chair he was a giant of a man.

'Eithan, this is my very good friend and employer, Beth Brennan. Remember, I told you lots about her.' If Eithan heard his wife, he showed no sign. 'I'll make us a pot of tea,' said Rhianne unfazed. 'Thank you for these. Eithan likes the cookies. Look, Eithan, Beth has brought us some home-baked cookies.'

Ten minutes later, Rhianne returned with the tea things. She stopped in her tracks almost dropping the tray. Not only had Eithan lifted his head from its customary sag, but his one arm was wrapped around Beth. She was cradling him, rocking him gently. Her good cheek pressed against his good cheek. Quiet soothing noises were escaping from her lips – and Eithan was… yes Eithan was crying. Slow silent tears were trickling down his cheeks. It was the first response of any kind Rhianne had seen in weeks. She wanted to yelp with delight but kept her composure, careful not to break the spell – or spill the tea tray. She stood for a long time transfixed, watching the extraordinary scene in front of her. Fortunately, she heard his car pull up. It was Dr Kendrick. He had visited yesterday and the day before that, just to watch and observe. She liked him. He seemed to have heaps of patience. Softly she crept out of the room and ran into the street to caution him.

'Rhianne!' said Theo, a little surprised to be greeted at the roadside. Rhianne put her finger to her lips and then whispered to him.

'You must come and see! You *have* to come and see! But you'll need to be quiet as a mouse.'

Theo duly followed her instructions and the two of them peeped through the window of Briar Cottage from the garden path. The scene had not changed. Rhianne's eyes glistened with happiness. 'It's the first response I've seen of any kind,' she whispered. Theo watched on thoughtfully, quietly nodding his head and then whispered back, as much to himself as to his young companion, 'Mother and child! Of course!'

'Mother and child?'

'The Madonna factor. I don't think Eithan has ever really got over the death of his mother. What he craves more than anything in this trauma is the love and security of a mother. Your employer has unwittingly provided a mother figure.'

'I don't know about unwittingly. She did something similar for me when I broke down – and yes, come to think of it, it *did* feel like it was my mother hugging me. Oh, Dr Kendrick, do you think he will get better now?' she asked excitedly.

'I'm sure of it. This was the breakthrough we needed. It will be a long haul, but he will get better now. I think we should go in, don't you?'

'But is it safe to break the spell?'

'Perfectly safe and it would be good for me to be able to work with Eithan while he is in this heightened state of emotion.' He spoke with natural authority, used to having to convince people. It was not needed here. Rhianne already trusted him.

Beth pulled away from Eithan as soon as she realised there was a stranger in the room. 'Beth, this is Dr Kendrick,' said Rhianne, a little sad to see the magic moment slip away.

'Ah! The quack they've sent up from Birmingham,' she said, eyeing him frostily.

'Theodore Kendrick,' he replied, 'most people call me Theo. Pleased to meet you. And you would be?'

'Mrs Brennan.'

'Ah, yes, of Beth's Bakery. Rhianne did tell me. She thinks the world of you.'

'And I of her, not that it's any business of yours, Dr Kendrick.'

'Theo, please,' he added pleasantly. 'Perhaps we could talk in the kitchen,' he said a little too firmly, ensuring she saw that his gaze was pointing warningly to Eithan.

Without speaking, Beth stepped resolutely into the kitchen where Theo closed the door behind them. It was the doctor who spoke first.

'Mrs Brennan, I'm sure you are going to be a very important part of Eithan's recovery, but I would be grateful if you did not undermine me in his hearing. It's vital I gain the confidence of my client.'

'*Your* client. What gives you the right to come here interfering?' She spat the words out between tight lips.

'I'm a specialist in PTSD – post traumatic stress disorder—'

'I know what PTSD is – don't treat me like a five-year-old,' she snapped sharply.

'I didn't mean any offence,' he apologised stiffly.

'Can't see what good you'll be. It's love and understanding he's going to need not some quack wading in with crack-brained theories. Can't you leave him in peace.'

'I can see you don't have much time for—' began Theo.

'You're damned right I don't have time for you lot,' she interrupted. 'You're all the same. Lame-brained know-it-alls. It's grief! Are you blind as well as lame-brained? It's grief!'

'I'm well aware of that Mrs Brennan, but it's layered over with PTSD, it's complex…'

Beth was not listening. She was already heading out of the kitchen.

'Ring me if you need anything, Rhianne,' she shouted through the closed front room door as she headed out of the house.

Theo formed his mouth into a silent whistle. *Someone must have rattled her cage, big time,* he thought to himself, a look of amusement on his face. *Or perhaps it's grief too, Beth Brennan,* he wondered, concern suddenly crowding out the wry smile.

Theo returned to the front room where he was pleased to see Eithan was now clinging to Rhianne, their heads bent together. He had something to work with at last.

'Has Beth gone?' asked Rhianne, getting up from the floor where she had been kneeling. 'I'm just going to make a fresh pot of tea, Eithan. I let this one get cold. Be back in a mo.'

'I don't think your employer and I got off on the best footing,' replied Theo, following her into the kitchen.

'She can be a bit prickly, but she has a heart of gold underneath. It must be hard for her too – all this. Her son was a soldier too, you see. He was killed by a car bomb in Belfast. Beth said they could only identify him from his dog tag. He was twenty-two. Even younger than Eithan.'

'Ahh,' was the light bulb response that came from Theo's lips.

Theo stayed another hour to kick-start the building of rapport with his client. He could not risk starting any therapy until he was confident he had Eithan's trust. 'I'll come by again tomorrow. Is the same time alright for you?'

'Oh yes, any time, Dr Kendrick. Any time is good for us.'

'Don't get disheartened if progress is slow. We have to take this at Eithan's pace. His PTSD goes very deep – it's not just what happened in Iraq, it's the cumulative effect of losing his father, his mother, his unborn child and his close friend in rapid succession. He hasn't had time to grieve properly. We have to proceed very gently, very carefully. As delicately as an archaeologist on a dig.'

'I can wait, Dr Kendrick. I can wait till the end of time for Eithan.'

'Good girl! And don't you think it's about time you started calling me Theo.'

'See you tomorrow, then... Theo... And thank you!'

*

Theo came every morning for two weeks. Eithan was responding well. His progress was palpable.

'I think two short rather than one long session would be better for Eithan,' he said to Rhianne. 'Could you stand me disrupting your afternoons as well as your mornings? It would be just for a few weeks and then I would start to space them out.'

'Of course, Theo. Anything that will help Eithan is fine by me, but you can't do that trip twice a day! It's a fifty-mile round trip from Matt's as it is and it's eating into the time you have set aside for your writing. You could hang out here with pleasure, or even stay over if you wish. There are three bedrooms here.'

'It's a kind offer, Rhianne, but it wouldn't be right. It would be too confusing for Eithan. I wouldn't want him to start thinking of me as anything other than his therapist. Not after what happened to Pete. Besides, you two need your own space. I need my own space – and Matt needs his space too, he can't always be going over to Ciara's. Sometimes he will want her to come to him. No, Rhianne, I've been mulling this over and the best solution is for me to get a room at the Red Lion in Millom. As long as there's good internet, I'll be able to crack on with my work.'

'But it's a pub. It will be noisy, especially at night. And you told me you were a lark, not an owl.'

'It will be fine, Rhianne. Don't worry on my account. You have enough to worry about with Eithan.'

*

The other daily visitor to Briar Cottage was Beth. She came late afternoons after the tea shop closed when she knew she would not bump into the quack. She did not like to think of herself as one prong in what Dr Kendrick called Eithan's three-pronged recovery plan: the love and devotion of Rhianne restoring his self-worth, Beth's maternal tenderness soothing his troubled spirit and Theo's psychotherapy sessions seeking out and quelling his demons. What she did was instinctive. It was what any mother would do. She did not need a shrink to draw her a diagram. In the kitchen, away from Eithan's hearing, the two women swapped notes.

'He's getting much stronger – physically,' began Rhianne. 'We walked two miles today and he's eating so much better. He gets frustrated that he's so clumsy with his left hand and he still has the nightmares, but less often. I wouldn't wish him back in that catatonic state, but it did at least protect him from the nightmares. Theo says it will be a long time before they go, if ever. Beth...' Rhianne hesitated. She already felt indebted to her employer on so many fronts and she was about to ask for more. 'Beth, there's something I wanted to ask... a favour.'

'Yes?' said Beth encouragingly.

'Theo wants to move Eithan's therapy to the next level, two short sessions a day rather than one longer one. He already does a fifty-mile round trip from Matt's. It must be eating into his writing time. He said he's going to get a room at the Red Lion in Millom. But I think it will be horrid for him, so noisy. They're revelling until after midnight some nights. I offered to put him up at Briar Cottage, but he wouldn't hear of it. Said it would confuse Eithan. I was wondering... well I was wondering whether he might be able to stay in the room I had in Middle Cottage? He's an early riser. I think he runs most mornings so I don't think the noise of the machines would trouble him. And it would only be for a few weeks. Theo said he would start to space the sessions out after that.'

'But it doesn't have an en suite, Rhianne. He would have to use the bathroom on the floor below.'

'Oh, he's not precious about creature comforts – he used to be a journalist, you know, in the Middle East... and Iraq,' she added quietly. 'He's roughed it in a tent many a year.'

'Sounds like you know a lot about him.'

'Well, we talk most days over a cuppa. I like him a lot.'

Beth sniffed a little dismissively. 'I've read his book,' she announced.

'You've read his book!' exclaimed Rhianne in surprise. 'The famous one – the PTSD one?'

'Yes, got it out from the library. It's better than I expected. Quite good in parts. I think there's a whole dimension missing from it which I hope he'll address in his new book, but I have to admit it was a good thing he did: getting it out there: getting the world to wake up to the fate of our traumatised soldiers and how to help them. And the accounts he included, from those men, from all those different wars. He captured their authentic voices very powerfully.'

'Beth, I know you and he didn't hit it off when you first met but when you get to know him, he's really nice. I think you would like him if you gave him half a chance.'

'He's an arrogant prig but if it will help you and Eithan then I'll make the offer. Can't see him accepting, mind, but I'll make the offer.'

Beth was rewarded for this concession by an enormous hug from her young protégé. 'You're the best, Beth. You're the best ever. Thank you!'

Beth did not relish the prospect of Dr Kendrick as a near neighbour but would make good on her promise.

*

'Beth asked if you might pop over to the bakery before you leave,' said Rhianne to Theo the next day. 'She has a suggestion she wants to put to you.'

'I'm intrigued,' replied Theo. 'I can't imagine what Mrs Brennan might want to *suggest* to me unless it's to remove myself from her sight.'

'You should give her a chance. She's very kind when you get to know her. She may surprise you.'

'Says Little Miss Harmony,' he teased, 'always wanting everyone to get along. Somehow I don't think you'll succeed in this instance.'

'I didn't succeed with my dad. He hates my guts. He disowned me when I was seventeen.'

'Well, that *does* surprise me. What a prize idiot he must be.'

*

Theo walked into the tea shop later that day. It was near closing time and the last couple were just finishing off their afternoon tea. He had seen it from Main Street several times as he drove past but never entered before. It was larger, and classier, than he expected. He spotted the proprietor at the till cashing up.

'Mrs Brennan!' he beamed, as he approached her. 'I am here, as summoned.'

'Dr Kendrick,' she replied rather stiffly. 'Thank you for coming. Can I get you a tea or a coffee? A cake perhaps? On the house.'

'Well, given what everyone says about your cakes Mrs Brennan, how could I refuse? And a white tea, no sugar, would be nice, thank you.'

She put her head round the door to the kitchen and Theo heard her say, 'Before you go, Ruth, could you bring Dr Kendrick a cream tea please. We will be sitting at the table by the window.'

She showed him to a large table that could have seated six. Clearly, she wanted to keep a safe distance from the 'quack', mused Theo.

'Rhianne tells me Eithan is making good progress.'

'Yes, better than I could have hoped. Rhianne tells *me* you have read my book.' It was a direct challenge said in a level tone with his gaze fixed unwaveringly on her face.

Despite her frostiness, Beth felt herself blush. She hated to blush because only her good cheek reddened, and she felt it made her look ridiculous. This infuriating man had already got her on the back foot.

'I thought I should see how much of a quack we were dealing with,' she retaliated, archly.

'And?' he demanded, his gaze not faltering.

She shifted uncomfortably, not able to hold his piercing stare and dropped her eyes.

'It was missing a whole dimension,' she said, turning to look out of the window to avoid his gaze, 'but apart from that I thought it was interesting and well researched. It had journalistic flair as well as scientific rigour. I accept it was an important text, given the time it was written.' The words had been squeezed out grudgingly, but Theo felt a slight thaw in her voice. Her scarred cheek was turned to the window, and he was studying her in profile. She must have been stunning in her youth. He had seen enough burn scars in his career to know this one had been inflicted on an adult face. He guessed she was about his age, mid fiftyish, tall and willowy, her blonde hair fashioned for convenience rather than style. She wore no make-up and had striking hazel eyes. On this good side, Theo could see the skin was slightly leathery and he did not need the evidence of nicotine-stained fingers to conclude she was a smoker.

'Yes, even its third edition is a little dated now – that's why I'm writing a new book. Should have done it years ago but I'm always too busy with clients and students.'

'But you have a leave of absence to do it in now, is that correct?'

'Yes, a book contract and a sabbatical from my university. I have a locum covering my clinic work.'

'How are you managing to write with the demands of Eithan's case?'

'I manage.'

'That's what I wanted to talk to you about. Rhianne told me you're going to give Eithan two daily sessions now and that you're going to get a room at the Red Lion in Millom to cut down the travel.'

'You're remarkably well informed, Mrs Brennan.'

He was not making this easy for her. God dammit, *she* was the one about to do *him* a favour. Why did he make her feel as if it were the other way around? Ruth's arrival with the cream tea tray was fortuitous timing and enabled her to regain her composure.

'My goodness!' he exclaimed graciously. 'This is a veritable feast.' He poured himself tea from the pot and began to butter a scone. 'Are you going to join me, Mrs Brennan, there's enough here for three people.'

She was tempted to say that he had a head big enough for three people but resisted. 'I won't, thank you, Dr Kendrick.'

As Theo tucked into his cream tea, she dived into her spiel. She would have the advantage of him if his mouth was full of clotted cream. He was bound to refuse, so this could all be over in a matter of minutes. 'It's probably far too lowly for a man of your eminence,' she began, 'but if it's of any use, there's an attic room above the bakery – Middle Cottage,' she amplified, 'that I could let you have. It doesn't have en suite facilities but there is a bathroom on the floor below. That floor also houses my office, the storerooms and a separate toilet that the staff use.'

Theo was genuinely surprised – and touched – by the offer but before he could respond she was continuing.

'Of course, the reason I don't rent it out anymore is that the new machines are noisier and would wake up tenants at five in the morning. Rhianne was the last person to use it before she moved into Briar Cottage. She had to get up for a five o'clock shift so it made no odds to her. I'm sure it would be *singularly* uncomfortable for you, but I thought I should make the offer.'

These words tarnished the good opinion of her he had been forming. She had clearly had her arm twisted. By Little Miss Harmony. The cynic in him got the upper hand. Instead of thanking her graciously, as he had intended to, he taunted her. 'But we would be neighbours, Mrs Brennan. How would you sleep at night with a quack next door?'

'I'd *manage*,' she replied, loftily, as loftily as he had used the phrase to her earlier. 'West Cottage is out of bounds to staff. It would be out of bounds to you, also, Dr Kendrick, so I'd *manage* just fine.'

'In that case, I'll take it.'

'But I haven't even shown it to you yet! And the five o'clock machines and the—'

'I'm sure it's far superior to anything I'd get at the Red Lion. And I'm rather partial to the world at five in the morning. It's when I do my best work. When can I move in? And would you like some rent in advance?'

'I don't want any rent. I told you, I don't rent it out because of the—'

'But you have to accept some rent, Mrs Brennan. I can't take it on any other basis.'

It was her way out. She could have grasped it with both hands, she could have told him to stuff his rent and had him out of her hair. Inexplicably, she did no such thing. Goaded by this maddening individual, she found herself retorting, 'Very well, if you insist – put twenty pounds each week in the tip box on the counter of the tea shop. Hilda shares it out among the staff. I don't touch it. It will cover a continental breakfast in the bakery kitchen if you choose to take it.' Theo threw his head back and howled with laughter at being out manoeuvred by this feisty woman.

'My compliments, Mrs Brennan. Remind me never to play you at chess.' He pulled a £20 note from his wallet and walked across to the counter where he deposited it in the tip box. 'You'd better show me this garret then, now I've paid my dues,' he said, still chortling.

*

'The bathroom is here,' she said, opening the door so he could peep in. It was a modern, four-piece bathroom with a separate shower cubicle. All sparkling clean. 'This is the staff toilet,' she said pointing to the door next to it but not opening it. She wanted him to know it was off limits to him. 'Here are the storerooms – and that's my office,' she said pointing to a fourth door. 'I keep it locked when I'm not using it,' she added pointedly. They ascended a second flight of stairs which brought them up into a large attic room, much larger than he was expecting. It had a double bed, a wardrobe, an armchair and a small table and chair that could function as a desk or dressing table. Like Rhianne, he was drawn immediately to the pretty dormer window from where you could see the shoreline and Black Combe Fell.

'It's beautiful. It's perfect!' he breathed. 'I assure you, Mrs Brennan, I will be *singularly* comfortable here.'

The Seven Stars

Leaves were falling and nights were closing in. The glorious Silecroft autumn would soon give way to winter. The new tenant of Middle Cottage attic was an instant hit with the bakery staff. Ruth swooned over his velvet voice and Hilda spoiled him as only a mother could. It was the same with the part-timers and the weekend temps; they all fell for his charm. Beth did her best to level the playing field, sharply reprimanding them if she thought they were giving him special favours, but it was a losing battle. As soon as her back was turned they would pamper him shamelessly. She saw through him, of course, saw that he turned it on like a tap. Beneath the thin, captivating veneer there was a layer of cold, hard rock. No one would get through that. She knew because she had the same granite strata running through her, compressed out of bitterness and grief. They were both closed books, chains and padlocks guarding the secrets hidden in their pages. Such irony, she ruminated, choosing to spend his days exhuming layers and layers of human trauma and his nights pushing his own deeper into their igneous pit.

Beth was wrong on one count; there was another who already had the measure of Dr Kendrick and that was Hilda. She was third generation Silecroft, born and bred. There were no flies on Hilda. She knew everything about everyone hereabouts. So seamlessly was she sewn into the landscape you forgot she was there. Yes, she saw through Theo's top layer, but it did not stop her enjoying his banter and his charisma. Unlike Beth, she did not shy away from the granite strata beneath. It intrigued and saddened her. The other staff were too young, but she remembered Theodore Kendrick from the telly. He was the dishy Middle Eastern correspondent who disappeared from their screens in a cloud of mystery. You could not forget a voice like his. She liked Dr Kendrick. But for all his genial magnetism, his arrogant confidence, it was the little boy lost she was most drawn to.

*

Theo had settled into an enjoyable routine. He got up at five each morning, put his headphones on and wrote productively for two hours. The first of three daily stints. The book was going well. He was ahead of schedule. At seven he would go for a run along the splendid beach that stretched for miles or up Black Combe Fell where the autumn colours were magnificent in the early light. Back at Middle Cottage he would shower before going down to the bakery kitchen for his continental breakfast: a coffee and a pastry – or two, if Hilda could press him to take a second. When he 'accidentally' let slip how fond of porridge he was, he found a steaming bowl of oats waiting for him ever after.

'Mrs B didn't specify what continen'al brekkie was to contain so I reck'n we can consider oats continen'al. They're Scottish after all!' she said, favouring him with one of her legendary winks. He adored Hilda. He timed his kitchen visits to coincide with the staff breakfast, partly for the company and partly because Beth always absented herself at that time to do some paperwork in the office.

Theo would make himself a sandwich for lunch or occasionally treat himself to a cream tea. He had to go into the tea shop every now and then. How else would he put his rent into the tip box? Ciara and Matt had him over for dinner once a week and on other nights he either took a boxed salad back to his room or sampled the local hostelries round about. Each day he did two short therapy sessions with Eithan. These were working out even better than he hoped. In a couple of weeks, he would start to stretch them out. By Christmas, Eithan would probably only need one session a week and that could feasibly be by telephone or at his clinic so he should really be starting to plan his withdrawal.

Eithan's splendid progress was not lost on Beth either. She was seeing more and more of the sharp brain Rhianne spoke of, and seeds of possibility had been germinating in her fizzing head. After she cashed up, she wandered over to Briar Cottage.

'Hi Beth, Rhianne's not back yet, you must have missed each other,' said Eithan.

'Rhianne's still in the bakery kitchen finishing off a speciality cake, it's you I came to talk to, Eithan.'

'Oh?' he replied, a little warily. 'If it's about the cottage, I've told Rhianne we should be paying you a proper rent by now. I still have my army pay until the end of the year and I'm due some injury compensation.'

'No, no, it's nothing like that. I don't want any rent, not until you're both properly settled, and you have a job.'

'That's very decent of you, Beth. Matt's looking out for something for me. I could do a desk job, even if I can't… you know… physically do the hands-on engineering.'

She could see how much it saddened him to utter the word 'hands' and it wrenched her guts.

'It's all grown too big for me, Eithan. I've long needed a business manager for the property side but haven't been brave enough to go there. I don't like advertising and I'm nervous of strangers. I need a business manager I can trust. East Cottage maisonette has been lying empty for two months now and I still can't decide what to do with it, whether to let it out again or expand the tea shop. My accountant keeps telling me I have more than enough to invest in another cottage, but I don't have the time to think about it and if I'm honest I don't have the drive anymore. Rhianne has revived my enthusiasm for the bakery side, and it got me thinking that the right person might do the same for the property side. I think the right person is you, Eithan, I want you to become my business manager.'

'But I don't have any business management experience and I'm still a bit ham-fisted with my one hand.'

'It's not your hand I'm interested in, it's your brain, Eithan. Anyway, if a business management qualification is important to you, there are oodles you can do, many of them distance learning. I did my own degree that way, through the Open University.' It was the first time she had mentioned anything from her past other than Sid, and realised she must be careful not to leave any doors open. 'We can start gently and build up gradually to you taking charge of the portfolio. It would be well paid, including a profit-sharing scheme. I won't be offended, if you try it and don't like it or a better job comes along. It's not going to affect my friendship for Rhianne or her position at the bakery.'

'Are you doing this because you feel sorry for me?' he challenged, 'I don't want your pity, Beth.'

'You couldn't be more wrong, Eithan. I absolutely *don't* pity you. I rejoice that you survived.'

He was looking at her now, seeing the pain in her eyes and understanding the pain was not for him. It was for a dead soldier who had *not* survived.

'I'd be honoured, Beth, truly honoured.'

The pain eased in her eyes, liquid pride displacing it. 'I'll have a contract drawn up. Perhaps you could start by giving some thought to what we might do with East Cottage maisonette.'

*

Theo and Beth kept a polite distance but there was a growing respect between them for the part they each played in Eithan's recovery. His landlady occupied much of Theo's free-thinking time. The psychologist was fascinated by her. How had she got that scar? Why was she so closed? What had her marriage been like? Rhianne had let slip she was divorced many years ago. What other grief might have befallen her besides the death of her son? How could such a cold woman be so warm with the McArthurs? She was a total enigma. Try as he might, he could not get her out of his head. His instinct told him something else had happened to Beth Brennan besides the loss of her son, something bad. The dormant journalist in him could not let it go. He was determined to root it out.

*

It was the Friday of his third week in residence at Middle Cottage when Theo surprised Hilda at breakfast that morning.

'Hilda, put your glad rags on when you go home, I'm taking you out tonight. You must have a favourite pub you like to frequent. I'm in need of company and a good chinwag. You're the fount of all knowledge around here, so best to go straight to the horse's mouth.'

'An' what meks yer think I'm not washin' me 'air t'neght, Doc?'

'Aww, come on, Hilda. Don't play hard to get. I know you go home and sit in front of that telly of yours all evening.'

'So wud you, if yer'd bin on yer pins all day in an 'ot kitchen.'

'Come on, Hilda. How often does a handsome beau shout you a meal?'

'Yer too full o' yersel' by 'alf, Doc Kendrick. But I s'ppose I cud wash me 'air anuther neght.'

'Seven o'clock okay for you?'

'Good as any time I re'kon.'

'Where shall I book a table?'

'T' Seven Stars. That's me fav'rite. The landlord's an old pal o' mine. We waz at school t'gether.'

'It's a date, Hilda. Glad rags, don't forget.'

'Well, yer'd berra smar'en up an' all. I'm not walkin' int' Seven Stars wi no slouch.'

Theo decided to take Hilda at her word. He put on the suit he had not worn in months and dug out a tie from a pile that still lay untouched in his suitcase.

'Yer punch'al, Doc,' said Hilda as she came out through her front door, 'an' yer spruce up nice.'

'So do you,' he said handing her an enormous bunch of flowers.

'My, my, Doc – yer'll have the neighb'rs yakkin'' she grinned, clearly delighted.

Theo held the car door open for her and she eased her large frame into the front seat.

'Thought yer'd 've 'ad a posher motor 'n this,' she sniffed.

'I'm not into material possessions, Hilda. This is a trusty workhorse that does me just fine.'

Hilda marched into the Seven Stars beaming. Jack Spedding spotted her straight away and came over.

'Nice t' see yer, Hilda. It's bin a while.' It was then he noticed her handsome companion standing behind her.

'This 'ere is Doc Kendrick, new tenan' in Middle Cottage.'

'Doc,' nodded Jack, a little surprised and not a little put out.

'I have a table booked for seven-thirty, I believe,' was the only answer he got from a diffident Theo.

'Yeah. Table by t' winder, Hilda,' he said pointing the way and then scurrying back to the bar.

'This is nice,' said Theo approvingly as they perused the menu. Hilda was enjoying herself enormously. She had not seen Jack Spedding so put out in many a year.

'I'm gonna 'av t' steak an' kidney pud. Yer'll 'av t' 'elp me finish it, Doc. It cums hooge.'

'In which case I'd better stick with something lighter, the salmon, I think. What would you like to drink Hilda?'

'Pint o' mild – in a streght glass, mind.'

While they waited for their food, Theo made polite conversation. 'Do you have kids, Hilda? Grandkids?'

'One kid, three gran'kids an' they run me ragged I can tell yer.'

'How old?'

'The kid or the gran'kids?'

'All of them, I guess.'

'The youngest gal is seven goin' on thirteen, the two lads is nine and eleven, both goin' on six and the big gal is thirty-seven but she'll tell yer she's twenty-five.'

Theo laughed out loud. 'You crease me up, Hilda, you really do.'

Jack Spedding heard the laughter and looked over sharply from the bar. Hilda spotted him and raised her pint glass to him with a mischievous nod.

'There must have been a Mr Hilda once upon a time?'

'Once upon a *long* time ago. Waste o' space 'e were. Cleared off when t' bairn waz still in nappies. 'E's probly six feet under be now for all I knoas.'

'I'm sorry,' said Theo, more seriously, 'it must have been hard for you.'

'I can fend fer mesel'. Get by alreght. Mrs B pays me a good wage an' she's set aside a pension fer me fer when I duz decide to 'ang up me pinny.'

'Can't imagine you retired Hilda. You're part of the fabric of the bakery. It would fall apart without you.'

'Get away wi' yer,' she replied. 'Anyways, it gets me owt o' gran'ma duties which is 'arder than bakin' a few loaves o' bread, I can tell yer.'

Theo was not surprised to see Hilda down a pint of mild with ease and ordered her another, just as her humungous steak pudding arrived.

'So, Doc, what's t' real reason yer wanted a chinwag then. Spit it owt.'

Theo laughed again. Hilda was nothing if not direct.

'I want to know everything you can tell me about your employer. I need to find a way to get to know her better, thaw the ice a bit...'

'Yer mean, get 'er to like yer,' she levelled at him sternly.

He could see there was going to be no fooling Hilda. 'Well, yes, I suppose I would like her to like me. She fascinates me.'

'Don't surprise me a jot. Yer too alike, you two. Yer like two magnets both pointing north, repelling t' other on sight. One o' yer's gonna 'av to turn yer south end round if yer ever gonna get on.'

'Tell me about her,' pleaded Theo, more earnestly. 'I have this feeling that something bad has happened to her – more than her son dying – something bad in her past that makes her the way she is.'

'Like the bad thing that's 'appened to you,' she challenged him, 'in *your* past.' It was not a question, it was a statement, and it threw Theo completely.

'I don't know what you mean, Hilda.'

'Yer know *precisely* what I mean but I don't reck'n yer gonna tell me, just as she ain't nivver gonna say nowt to me neether. It ain't natrel, keepin' bad stuff burrid like tha'. It'll eat yer up evencherly.'

Theo rarely suffered with flushes of embarrassment. He was normally too cocksure of himself, but Hilda's words had made him blush and he dropped his gaze to the table.

'One day, Hilda, maybe one day. I'm just not ready. I don't think I'm strong enough. Not yet.'

Hilda knew better than to push him, so she just nodded. 'Mrs B then – what d'yer wanna knoa?'

'Start at the beginning, Hilda.'

'I can't start there, I only knoas 'er from when she came 'ere.'

'Start there then, Hilda… please,' he added softly.

'She came 'ere twenty year ago. Noabody knew though. Noabody really knew she were 'ere til she tuk o'er t'bakery. I knew t' Cartwrights as 'ad the bakery afore 'er so I'd 'eard they'd tak'n on a kitchen assistant. But yer nivver caught sight of 'er, she were allers in t' back kitchen. The Cartwrights waz getting' on be then. Sounds like Beth did everythin' save serve in t' shop. It were a tiny shop an' a tiny bakery back then. The Cartwrights just did bread. They lived on t' furst floor and Beth 'ad the attic room. It weren't nice like you 'ave it now, very basic, more like a prison cell, if y'ask me but it must 'ave suited 'er 'cos she lived in it for three year. The Cartwrights let 'er stay there in exchange for doing their 'ousework. She must 'av worked like a slave those furst few year, doing all the bakin' 'erself and cleaning t' place top t' bottom an' all. The Cartwrights waz onto a good thing there alreght. Then it all 'appened so quick. Suddenly the Carwrights waz retiring t' Seascale an' the business 'ad bin sold. It were just Middle Cottage in them days. It nivver cum on t' market. Beth must 'av med 'em an offer they cudn' refoose. She must 'av 'ad money behind 'er 'cos I think it were a cash sale. Any'ow, once she owned t' business, she started selling cakes an' pastries as well as bread an' the little business tuk off. She's canny is Mrs B. She got in on t' American cupcake craze real early. Money fer ol' rope is cupcakes. That's when she tuk me on. She were expanding t' cake side an' needed a body to keep t' bread side going. When East Cottage cum up for sale, she bought it wi' a loan from t' bank. That's when she opened the tea shop on t' ground floor an' rented owt the two floors above as an 'oliday let. She must 'av bin rakin' it in be then 'cos she bought West Cottage when that cum up for sale an' rumour 'as it she bought it wi' no mor'gage. She rented that out fer 'oliday lets for a while an all.'

'Did she still live in the attic?'

'No. When I started workin' fer 'er she 'ad the living quarters the Cartwrights 'ad 'ad. T' business were a goldmine. She started takin' pre-orders fer cupcakes an' special occasion cakes. Folks ordered bi phone an' collected from t' shop. T' profits enabled 'er t' buy a rental cottage t' let. She tuk more staff on – all local. She nivver needed t' advertise. She were a tuff boss but fair an' she allers paid on time. Ten year later she 'ad three rental cottages plus t' bakery. That's when she stopped expandin' an' she moved int' West Cottage. She didn' wan' t' tek on more staff and she must 'av 'ad had money cumin owt 'er ears. Sum got ploughed back int' business but she must 'av a fair sum stashed away be now. I don't think she's even int'ressed in t' money, it were more that she wanted to prove she cud do it.'

'What about now, Hilda? What's she like now?'

'A creature of 'abit an' routine. Yer can set yer watch by 'er. Very private. Dun't socialize nor nuthin'. Books is 'er thing.'

'Books?' asked Theo, surprised.

'She thinks I don't knoa wot she gits up t' on 'er day off but I 'as a friend at t' libr'y in Millom,' she said, tapping her nose with her finger.

'Is there anywhere roundabout you don't *'av a friend?*' he mimicked, smilingly.

'Me friend at t' libr'y says she teks out four books a for'nigh'. Reg'lar as clockwork. 'As dun these twenty year. Yeah, books an' walkin', that's Mrs B.'

'Walking?'

'Long treks along t' beach or up Combe Fell. Mostly she walks t' Millom tho she meight tek the bus if she'as shopping. Allers the bus, you'll never get 'er in a taxi. Gets her books from t'library, bit of shopping, bank, that sort of thing. I knows 'cos—'

''Cos you 'av a friend!' finished Theo and they both laughed.

'As I sed, walks everyweer. Don't think she likes cars. Must be fit as a fiddle.'

'Not for much longer. Not unless she gives up the fags,' interrupted Theo. 'It catches you up in the end.' It had been said with a bitterness that startled Hilda, but she ploughed on.

'Well, I don't knoa 'bou' tha'. As I sed, walks everyweer. She could afford a fleet o' cars but she won't 'av one. I don't think she can drive. She'll take a bus from Millom, but yer won't ever git 'er in a taxi.'

'Friends – does she have friends?'

'Rhianne's t'only one I'd say waz a friend as such. She's t'only one she 'as in West Cottage.'

'What's it like – West Cottage?'

'I've nivver bin inside meself as I told yer but Rhianne tells me it's very modern an' minimal like.'

'Not very homely then,' commented Theo.

'As 'omely as a nun's cell, if yer ask me. But each to 'er own.'

'What about her son and her divorced husband?'

'That's weer I can't 'elp yer. I knoa nowt about them. She clams up if yer ask anything about 'er past. Sez she's only int'ressed in t' present and t' future. Flatly refuses t' talk about anything from 'er past other than that soldier boy of 'ers as got killed. That's all I knoa about 'er afore she cum to Silecroft. He were a soldier who were killed be a bomb in Belfast. Young lad, only twenty-two. Sidney 'e were called. If you were t' ask me that's the root o' it all. She luvs kids yer see. Must 'av 'it 'er real 'ard losing that lad.'

'Yes, Rhianne told me about that. You say she loves kids?'

'Yeah. There were this time when she caught a young 'un stealing a cake from t' shop. It were one o' t' Dixon kids.'

'Ouch! I wouldn't have liked to have been in his shoes when Mrs Brennan got hold of him.'

'But that were t' thing yer see. She didn't knab 'im. She follered him back t' 'is 'ouse, probly to tear a strip off t'mother. I found owt later from a friend as lives that way that she'd bin so shocked when she saw 'ow little they 'ad she promised Ma Dixon two loaves a day until she got on 'er feet. She's on 'er tod yer see: three kids an' a bairn an' the dad long gone. Beth cum back an' told us there an' then we 'ad t' lay aside two bloomers each day for the Dixons until she sed oth'rwize. Those kids were miraculous turned out in no time an' it don't take a genius t' work owt who paid for their new kecks.'

'What's your advice then, Hilda? How do I break the ice with her? I don't have any threadbare urchins up my sleeve.'

'Walking an' books is weer I'd start. An' it wudn' do no 'arm t'eat some 'umble pie. But I'm warnin' yer, Doc. Much as I like yer, if yer meddlin' 'arms an 'air on 'er 'ead, yer'll 'av me t'anser t.'

'I don't mean her any harm, Hilda. I only want to help.'

'That's wha' wurries mi 'bowt you clever folks, yer don't allers knoa the difference.'

*

Theo's mind was buzzing that night. His mind would not focus on the writing stint he usually did before bed. It was filled with images of cupcakes, kitchen skivvies, burn scars, hungry urchins – and ghosts. Next morning, when he heard the sound of Beth's keys unlocking her office, he did not head down to the kitchen for his bakery breakfast. Instead, he knocked on her office door.

'Yes, come in, Hilda.'

'It's not Hilda,' said Theo taking a few steps onto the hallowed turf. 'It's me.'

'Dr Kendrick!' she said clearly surprised. 'Is anything wrong?' And then, more urgently, 'Nothing's wrong at Briar Cottage?'

'No, no, nothing like that. I was hoping we might call a truce.' He pulled a white handkerchief out of his pocket and waved it comically. Beth only just managed to quell the smile that was threatening to creep across the good half of her face but managed a brusque reply.

'I didn't know we needed a truce. Has there been a war, Dr Kendrick?'

'I just think we're on the same side, you know. Both trying to do the best for Eithan. Both sit in our lonely cells with our books. We could at least take a walk together occasionally or you could let me take you out for dinner, due compensation for the peppercorn rent you charge me.'

'Join a long line of your dinner guests, you mean. What number was Hilda?'

'Number one if you must know and it was so I could ask her advice.'

'Advice, Dr Kendrick! Since when did you need advice? I thought you had *all* the answers.'

'Since I wanted to find out how to get to know you better. How to get you to like me – a little,' he replied earnestly. 'I just want us to be friends.'

'Just friends?'

'Of course! What do you take me for? I'm not some kind of pervert preying on vulnerable, lonely women for Christ's sake.'

'I'm not vulnerable, and I'm not lonely,' she flung back at him.

'I didn't mean it like that. You know what I meant. Why are you making this so difficult for me? Anyone would think I was a monster with two heads!'

'Spare us, Dr Kendrick. Your one head is big enough already.'

'Okay, so you think I'm an arrogant shithead. Can we just change the record? Move on?'

'Very well. I usually take a walk on the beach at four forty-five. Join me if you wish.'

*

Later that morning, Theo drove to the library at Millom. 'I'm currently resident in Silecroft. May I take out a temporary membership?'

'Of course,' beamed the librarian, always keen to welcome a new member. She could have been a cartoon stereotype, mused Theo, sixtyish, short grey hair, round spectacles and neat plaid skirt.

'If you could just fill in this form, please, I will make you out a temporary membership card.' As she copied his details across, she exclaimed with delight, 'Oh you're staying at West Cottage. You must be a friend of Beth Brennan's.'

'Yes,' he replied. Well, it was almost true, he almost lived in West Cottage, and he hoped he would soon be her friend.

'Lovely lady is Beth. One of our most avid regulars. Must be twenty years she's been coming here. Takes out four books a fortnight. Regular as clockwork. And reads them cover to cover.'

Theo played his hand. 'Beth tells me she gets some great book recommendations from you.' It was a lucky guess.

'It's kind of her to say so but it's not difficult to make recommendations to someone with such eclectic taste.'

'No favourite genre then?'

'Oh yes, the novel. She always takes two novels. The other two loans could be anything from biography, poetry, history, philosophy or the like. As I said, very eclectic taste.'

'Any favourite novelists?'

'That's easy. English nineteenth century: Austen, Dickens, Trollope, Hardy, Eliot, all the classics. One of her two novels is always nineteenth century. The other is likely to be more contemporary. She often asks for a recommendation. And I know she reads it because we generally have a good discussion about it when she brings it back. Quite the literary critic is Beth. Very insightful lady.'

'Don't I know it,' said Theo pointedly.

He returned to the check-out desk ten minutes later with two books to take out. The librarian stamped them for him, making sure she looked at the titles first. She was curious to know about the reading tastes of Beth's gentleman beau. Her job was much duller these days. Fewer and fewer members. Only the old timers. Other than her monthly book club and Beth Brennan's fortnightly visit, she rarely got an opportunity to share her passion for books with like-minded enthusiasts, particularly rather dashing middle-aged gentlemen. *Wild Swans* by Jung Chang and *The Poetry of Yevgeny Yevtushenko*. She handed them to him with the sweetest smile she could muster.

'Do say hello to Beth for me Mr er…' she glanced down at the card she had filled in earlier, 'Mr Kendrick.'

'Of course. My pleasure. Oh – and Hilda says hello,' he added as he exited. No need for a lucky guess there. It was plain as a pike staff that this lady was Hilda's *friend a' t' libry'*.

'Kendrick. Kendrick. Now why is that name familiar?'

Fortunately, Theo was out of the door and heading to his car before the penny dropped.

*

Theo took himself down to the beach at four-thirty. He did not want to risk Beth getting there early and conveniently leaving without him. She turned up at four forty-five precisely.

'Good afternoon, Dr Kendrick,' she said coolly.

'Theo, please. I wish you'd call me Theo.'

'Very well – Theo.' She did not invite him to call her Beth.

They walked in silence for a few minutes. Beth took off her shoes and dug her toes into the sand. She did not see why she should change her habits just because he had forced his company on her. But even for Beth, the silence was uncomfortable, so it was she who broke it first.

'Do you have children, Dr Kendrick?' That was safe ground. Polite. Innocuous.

'No, sadly,' was the instant reply. 'I have a nephew – as you know – Matt. And I have someone I think of as a daughter, Mia, but she is not my biological child.'

Beth immediately took this to mean a stepdaughter. 'A wife? Ex-wife? Ex-*wives*?' The plural emphasis was not lost on Theo.

'No wife, singular or plural. I'm a widower.'

It was not the answer she was expecting, and she blushed, feeling embarrassed by her childish barb.

'I'm sorry,' she said simply, 'that was crass – and mean – of me.'

It was the first time he had ever heard her apologise for anything.

'You weren't to know,' he said, gently. 'How about you? Rhianne told me you're divorced, and you had a son, a soldier, who sadly died.'

'*Have* a son,' she butted in fiercely. 'Just because he's dead doesn't mean he's past tense. He will always be my son. I *have* a son.'

'Yes, of course. That was clumsy of me. I'm sorry.'

'Theo, can we agree not to talk about the past. If we are to be friends, we need to attend to the present. I don't like raking up the past.'

It was not what he had hoped for, but it was a start. She had called him Theo without prompting. 'If we are to attend to the present, may I call you Beth?'

She hesitated slightly before nodding her acquiescence.

'Hilda tells me you like books, so that's one thing we have in common. We could talk about books.'

'I don't think you would like my kind of books.'

'Try me.'

Although her favourite author was Henry James, she deliberately reeled off some female period authors to goad him. 'Jane Austen, George Eliot, Edith Wharton, Elizabeth Gaskell.'

'All great classical novelists,' he responded. 'Some of their lesser-known works don't get the acclaim they deserve. All the world is dotty about *Pride and Prejudice,* but I actually prefer *Sense and Sensibility.* And while Eliot will be forever synonymous with *Middlemarch,* agreeably a masterpiece, my favourite is *Silas Marner.*'

He would have gone on, but Beth interrupted him, unable to suppress her surprise. 'You've read them! Have you read them all?'

'Why should that surprise you?'

'But I thought they would appeal more to women.'

'Is that why you tried to catch me out? We'll never make it onto the friendship step if you keep trying to trip me up.'

Beth was blushing again. This was why she could not like him. He was a know-it-all who made her feel foolish.

'Why don't you tell me your real favourite?'

'Oh but I do like all of them, I wasn't fibbing.'

'I didn't say you were. But you still haven't told me who your real favourite author is.'

'Henry James,' she blurted out quickly. 'I adore Henry James.'

'Henry James!' he declared. 'Tell me what you like about Henry James and then I'll tell you what I like about Leo Tolstoy.'

'Tolstoy – is he your favourite novelist? He's Russian.'

'Well, James is American, we have to level the playing field,' he twinkled. 'But yes. Tolstoy is my all-time favourite novelist.'

*

They walked and talked animatedly until sunset. They did the same again the next day and the next. Hilda could have set her clock by it.

'There's something I need to ask you,' said Theo as they were heading back to Middle Cottage. They had been walking together most days for the past couple of weeks, adjusting the start time to accommodate the fading light. The tea shop closed earlier in the winter season.

'Yes?'

He paused momentarily, unsure of his ground, unsure if it was too early to make the request, but he had already dropped Eithan's sessions to twice a week. He was running out of time. It had to be now.

'Eithan's recovery is ahead of schedule.'

'Yes, he's done amazingly well.'

'I'm starting to stretch out the sessions. By Christmas it should be one a week and in truth, that could be done by telephone with just a monthly face to face at my clinic.' He'd slipped into professional communication mode. 'I really have to start thinking of withdrawing.'

'Oh…' she exclaimed, unable to hide the disappointment in her voice. 'Withdrawing back to Birmingham you mean?' The regret in her voice emboldened him.

'That's the thing. I still have nine months' leave of absence left. There's no requirement for me to go back to campus, and as I said I have a locum covering my clinic work. My new book is going well. I'm writing from case notes, not live interviews as I did for my other one, so I have everything I need here. I've found this environment very conducive to writing. I was wondering… I was wondering if I could stay on a while longer. I've grown very fond of my garret quarters.'

'I can't see why not, no one else uses the room.' She tried to adopt a business-like tone, but it barely disguised the relief she was feeling.

'I'd pay you a proper rent, of course.'

'I've told you before, Theo. I don't rent it out. It's not worth the tax complication.'

'Well, you must let me compensate you in other ways. The tip box hardly even covers my breakfasts. How about I take you out to dinner once a week. We both have to eat, and I don't think you ever treat yourself, do you?'

'I eat at Rhianne's quite often.'

'That's not what I mean, and you know it,' he replied.

'Alright then, if you insist. My day off is Monday so a Sunday evening would work best for me.'

'This Sunday, then. I'll call round at seven.'

*

As the Sunday hour approached, Beth became increasingly agitated. She was not sure this was a good idea after all. She enjoyed his company and they talked for England about every manner of thing, but she did not want him to start asking about her past. She still had to be careful. Even after twenty years she had to be careful. Once or twice he had gone there and she had steered him away. She was intrigued about *his* past but avoided asking anything in case it encouraged him to pursue hers again. Should she cry off with a headache? He would know she was shamming. That was cowardly. No, she must go through with it and be very firm about boundaries. Yes, she would be very firm about boundaries.

Theo was punctual and he brought flowers.

'Flowers, Theo. Whatever for? This is not a date you know.'

'If my flowers are good enough for Hilda, they should be good enough for her boss too,' came his reply.

'You bought Hilda flowers?'

'But of course. *I'm a gen'lman o' furst ord'r,*' he replied. She smiled appreciatively. She left Theo standing in the street while she put the flowers inside and locked up West Cottage. He had parked his car close by and opened the front passenger door for her just as he had for Hilda.

'Oh! Aren't we walking?'

'Walking? I'm taking you out to dinner, Beth, not scampi in the basket. Get in Mrs Brennan.'

'But I...' she began, backing away. 'I don't like cars... I'm a nervous passenger... can't we just go to the Green Man – please.'

'What is it, Beth?' asked Theo, suddenly concerned. Gently, he turned her to face him. 'Have you had a bad experience in a car? An accident?'

She nodded tearfully, trying to pull away.

'It's okay, Beth, I understand,' he said in his gentlest voice. 'It's okay. I'm no petrol head. I'm a very safe driver. No harm will come to you, I promise. You can do this. It's important you do this. You can't spend the rest of your life on foot because of a bad experience God knows how many years ago. Trust me – please.'

Reluctantly Beth got into the car. She sat woodenly, staring straight out in front of her. Theo had to reach over to pull the seatbelt round her.

'Oh,' she said, 'I forgot. The last time I was in a car we only had these in the driver's seat.'

'Christ, Beth, that's over thirty years ago.'

Theo fastened his own seat belt and then pulled away slowly. He talked her through what he was doing the whole time and kept his speed down to thirty even when they got on the open road. Beth said nothing, just sat rigid, clutching her handbag. When he helped her out of the car she was shaking.

'You were amazingly brave, Beth,' he said softly. 'It will get easier. Each time you do it, it will get easier. Let's walk up and down a few steps until you feel better.'

'Thank you. I need a cigarette,' she replied. 'Just a quick one. I've made us late already. I don't imagine you normally drive that slowly.'

'Take as long as you need, Beth. They'll hold the table. They know me here.'

When she had finished her cigarette, they went inside. Theo had been itching to say something about the cigarettes for a while but knew tonight was not the right time. A return car journey was going to be challenging enough for her without a lecture from him on the health hazards of smoking.

'Good evening, Dr Kendrick. We have your table ready for you if you'd like to follow me,' said a smiling waitress in a crisp white blouse and black skirt. Beth had put on her best pair of trousers and newest jumper, but she still felt under dressed.

It was all very tasteful: white linen napkins and shining crystal glasses.

'Did you bring Hilda here?' she asked when they were seated.

'No. We went to the Seven Stars. Her choice.'

Beth did not know why it mattered to her, but it did.

Beth, the pâtissier, was a good enough cook but no gourmet chef. That was more Rhianne's bag. The menu looked amazing.

'What would you like to drink, Beth? An aperitif, some wine?' he asked hoping she would indulge. A glass or two would relax her for the car journey home.

'I don't drink much beyond a tot of whiskey and the odd glass of fizz when there's a celebration.'

'Fizz, it is then.'

She chose a goat's cheese tartlet to start followed by the venison haunch. Theo waited for her to order and then ordered the same. 'And a glass of house champagne for the lady and a large bottle of sparkling water,' he added as he handed his menu back to the waitress. After her second glass of champagne, Beth was feeling much more relaxed. The food had been delicious. She declined a pudding but accepted a coffee and disappeared ostensibly to the ladies but in order to escape for another quick cigarette. It had been a wonderful evening. She could not remember another like it. Not ever. Not even before it happened. He was so interesting to talk to, knew so much about so many things. And she especially loved talking to him about books.

Theo drove back just as carefully and delivered her safely to the front door of West Cottage.

'Goodnight, Theo,' she said, 'and thank you. I had a wonderful time.'

'We'll do the same next Sunday. Same time. Different hostelry,' he replied.

She looked as if she was going to protest so he added, 'And no arguments. It's part of my rent, remember, and I always pay my dues.'

'Alright then but do we have to drive?'

'Yes, Beth, we have to drive. We are going to drive every Sunday until you can get in a car without shaking. Goodnight, Mrs Brennan. Sweet dreams.'

*

It happened exactly as he had said it would. Theo picked her up every Sunday at seven. Each week he chose a restaurant a little further so that the car journey was longer and by week four Beth had successfully negotiated a forty-minute drive each way. By then it was into December.

'What are your plans for Christmas?' Beth asked on one of their bracing walks.

'I always spend Christmas with Mia and my very good Iraqi friends who are her foster parents. Matt usually joins us, but I suspect he will have other priorities this year.' Theo had not spoken of Mia since that first walk on the beach when they had agreed not to talk about the past. Since coming to Cumbria, he had only visited Mia a couple of times in London, but he Skyped her regularly. He had hoped she would visit him in this quiet little enclave of paradise. She had not managed it so far. Mia had lived in England fifteen years now but had never ventured north of Birmingham. He wondered what his city girl would make of this tranquil haven.

'We close for Christmas at the end of the week. I give the staff two weeks' holiday. It's hardly worth staying open this time of year. I keep the special occasion orders going myself up to Christmas Eve but the staff aren't involved in those anyway so they might as well have the time off with their families. It will be easier for me this year as Rhianne is going to help me with some of the orders. She's back half time now.'

'And what about you? What do *you* do at Christmas?' he asked.

'Extra book time, that's my seasonal treat. It'll be different this year. Rhianne is determined to throw a big Christmas. Says she'll do all the catering. She's inviting Matt and Ciara. Ciara took some persuading because she always spends Christmas Day with her father – you know that there's a rift between Rhianne and her father…?'

Theo nodded. 'Yes she told me. Idiotic situation,' he added impatiently.

'Anyway, Ciara is going to see her father on Boxing Day instead and take Matt to meet him. First time.'

Good luck with that one, Matt, he thought to himself.

'I think Rhianne's hoping you will come?'

He shook his head. 'I always spend Christmas with Mia.'

'But she could come too!' said Beth. 'Matt will be here and they're close, aren't they?'

'Like brother and sister.'

'Well then…'

'I couldn't drag her away from Nasim and Guita and they have two grown-up children of their own, although their son is in America so won't be there, but Mia will want to see Lina.'

'It's all possible,' she announced firmly. 'Instead of Rhianne hosting at Briar Cottage we could have it in the tea shop with tables pushed together. Rhianne can do the catering from the bakery kitchen. Matt and Ciara could stay at Briar Cottage – they were planning to, anyway. Mia and Lina and Mr and Mrs…?'

'It's Professor and Mrs Azizi…'

'Yes, well, they could stay in the maisonette in East Cottage. It's empty. It's been standing empty pending discussions I want to have with Eithan about whether we expand the tea shop. I'll take you up and show you when we get back. Rhianne would be over the moon. She so wants to host a big Christmas.'

Theo's mind was racing. It had not occurred to him that he might stay at Silecroft for Christmas. The more he thought about it the more he loved the idea. It would be a nice change for Nasim and Guita and he would finally get Mia up to see this idyllic bolthole. 'I'll talk to Mia tonight and test the water,' he announced.

*

Mia was instantly sold on the idea. It was about time Nasim and Guita got waited on for a change. Most of all, she was intrigued to meet Theo's mysterious landlady. He said they were just friends, book pals and walking companions. Well, she would make her own mind up about that! It must be twenty years since Josie had died and in all that time, she had not known him show the slightest interest in another woman. To this day she had not been able to get him to talk about his dead wife. She resented being shut out. She wanted to rail at him, shake him. Theodore Kendrick, the great psychologist, who has healed so many but could not or would not heal himself.

Whiskey and Orchids

Rhianne's dreams of hosting a big Christmas were given a huge boost when Theo announced the Azizis had agreed to come. If spruce trees were not green, they surely would be pink! He decided to furlough his writing for a couple of weeks. There was too much excitement around him, and he had lots of extra present shopping to do. He was mulling over where to take Beth on the last Sunday before Christmas that would not be too crowded with seasonal parties when she surprised him with a suggestion of her own.

'You never get to drink when we go out for dinner as you're always driving. So why don't I cook for you on Sunday instead. It's going to be heaving just before Christmas, it will be rubbery turkey and watery sprouts everywhere.'

Theo was surprised and delighted by the invitation. She had never cooked for him before, not even breakfast in the bakery. And he had not put as much as a toe inside West Cottage. 'What a splendid idea!' he replied. 'I'll bring the wine – and the whiskey. You said you like a tot of whiskey occasionally.'

'Only if it's Irish.'

'Irish it is, then.'

*

Beth chose a simple menu. She did not want him to get the wrong idea if she pushed the boat out. She would do something en croute that would play to her strengths, a soup starter with olive and oregano granary rolls, and cheese to follow. He must get more than his fill of sweet cakes in the tea shop. When everything in the kitchen was as pre-prepared as she could manage, Beth went upstairs to shower and change. She fingered the one dress she possessed that had been hanging in her wardrobe for three years. She had bought it on impulse one Monday in Millom and never worn it. It was more suited to summer than winter. But it would be warm with the fire on. Quickly, she pulled it off the hanger and held it against herself. She looked at her reflection in the mirror. Then, just as quickly she put it back on the hanger. He might get the wrong idea. It was too risky. She liked his company but there could be no complications. These few weeks had been the happiest she could remember. She wanted everything to stay the same, safe in her bubble. It would burst if he knew about her past.

*

Theo was very complimentary about her salmon-en-croute. He had brought champagne and an Irish whiskey that she had never seen on a supermarket shelf. She suspected it was expensive. Conversation flowed easily, as it always did between them these days. He helped her with the dishes and then they retired to the front room to sample the whiskey he had brought. It was smoother than anything she had ever tasted. She took out a cigarette and was about to light up when she noticed him wince.

'I wish you would quit,' he said directly.

It was her turn to wince. 'Excuse me?' she said coldly.

'They're evil things, cigarettes. Death traps.'

'We're drinking whiskey, we've just shared a bottle of champagne. Isn't alcohol a death trap too?' The familiar frost was back.

'It's not the same, Beth. We can both take or leave alcohol. We're not addicted to it.'

'This is my house, my rules. I do as I choose in my own castle. Stop trying to control me.'

'I'm not! I'm trying to help you. I could help you quit, Beth. It's part of my day job.'

'What if I don't want to quit? What if I don't want to be helped? What if I don't want to be *healed*? That's what you do isn't it – go round *healing* people. Like some self-appointed god.'

Theo said nothing. He got up from the sofa. She thought for a moment that he was going to walk out but he just paced about the room, wrestling with something. She could not bear his silence so goaded him the more.

'What am I – a professional itch you have to scratch, another damaged creature you have to heal?'

'It's something in your past, isn't it Beth? Something in your past that makes you like this. Hell-bent on self-destruction.'

'I won't talk about the past, so don't go there, Theo. I'm only interested in the present and the future.'

'Why won't you talk about the past?' he persisted.

'Are you deaf, Theo or just thick? I said I *won't* talk about the past. This was a mistake. I should never have invited you.'

'Beth, please, no more questions, I promise.' He threw his hands in the air in an exasperated gesture before adding, 'My parents both died of lung cancer. Neither of them saw sixty. They died three months apart. Him first, then her. I don't want you to die young, Beth.'

She relented instantly, leapt up from her armchair and went to his side. 'I'm so sorry, Theo. I had no idea. But I'm not going to die. I'm as fit as a fiddle. I have the lungs of a whale.'

'You say that now, but it will catch up with you, Beth. And it's not just lung cancer that's the killer: heart disease, strokes, diabetes, any number of nasty things.'

'Alright. If it means that much to you, I'll quit.'

'You mean it?' he asked, astonished at her rapid response.

'I never say anything I don't mean,' she replied.

He pulled her to him, wrapping his arms around her in a silent hug. It was the first time he had touched her other than helping her in and out of the car. 'Thank you,' he whispered. 'Thank you.' His eyes filling up, he traced his finger tenderly over her scarred cheek – and then he left, left his unfinished whiskey, left her standing there, bewildered and breathless.

*

Beth ditched the functional artificial tree she put up each year in the tea shop and replaced it with a seven-foot spruce. Ciara took charge of the decorations and corralled Eithan to help her. He could fix up the lights as he was so tall and would not need a step ladder to put the fairy on the top of the tree. The Azizi party were to travel by train on Christmas Eve and Matt was charged with picking them up at the station. Rhianne and Beth were busy in their respective kitchens doing whatever prep they could. The only person who did not seem to be part of the action was Theo. He had kept a low profile since Sunday. In fact, he was nowhere to be seen on Christmas Eve. No one knew where he was, and his car was missing. Beth was uneasy. She was at a loss to understand why he had suddenly left her like that, the other night. It felt like something had frightened him, like he had seen a ghost. Was it his dead wife? Had he run back to Solihull? Not at Christmas, surely! Not when his good friends and his darling Mia were about to arrive. Where could he be?

*

If Theo was grappling with old ghosts, by Wednesday he had put them aside and recovered his equilibrium. He got into his car very early on Christmas Eve morning, typed a postcode into his sat nav and headed south, a determined expression fixed in the grooved lines of his face. The sat nav took him to number 27 Larch Grove on The Redlands estate, Samlesbury. It was 9.30am when he rang the doorbell.

'Yes?' came a grumpy inquiry from a half-open door.

'Mr Atkinson, my name is Dr Theodore Kendrick. I'm a clinical psychologist,' he announced showing him his card. 'I was hoping you would give me a few moments of your time.'

'What for? What would I want with a clinical psychologist? Do I know you? Your voice is familiar.'

'I used to be on TV, a long time ago, a war correspondent.'

'I don't have any time for journalists. Good day to you.'

'It's important, Mr Atkinson. It's about your daughters.'

'Daughters? I only have one daughter.'

'That's what we need to talk about.'

'Wait a minute – you said you were a doctor. Has anything happened to Ciara?'

'Let's go inside, shall we?' pressed Theo.

Reluctantly Mr Atkinson showed him into his lounge. Theo did not wait to be invited to sit down. He took up residence on the large three-seater sofa.

'What's this all about?' asked the older man.

'Ciara is dating my nephew. If it goes the way I think it will, you and I will be seeing a lot of each other in the future, so I thought we ought to get to know one other.'

'He's the reason she's not coming for Christmas, this nephew of yours,' he grumbled. 'Won't be coming until Boxing Day. First time ever she's not been here on Christmas Day.'

'Matt is not the reason. Rhianne is.'

'I don't know any Rhianne.'

'Rhianne is your youngest daughter. She is one of the sweetest, most talented and resilient women I have the pleasure to be acquainted with. I don't understand why you would not rejoice in your parenthood.'

'She chose her bed, now she has to lie in it.'

'What bed?'

'*His* bed. That guy from the wrong side of the tracks.'

'That *guy* happens to be an upstanding young man. Highly intelligent who sacrificed a university education to look after his widowed mother and your daughter. He's a Lance Corporal in the Royal Engineers, badly wounded on active service in Iraq. I count it an honour to have been asked to help with his recovery. He's already distinguished himself, but he will go far. He's got a very keen brain.'

'They're a bad lot, all of them from that sink estate.'

'All of whom?'

'All of them, you know…'

'No, I don't. Enlighten me.'

'They're different from us, they're—'

'You mean they're black.'

'I'm not racist. Whatever's she's told you I'm not racist. I don't wish them any harm, I just—'

'Don't want them in your back yard.' Theo finished his sentence for him. 'I'm half Lebanese. Matt is three quarters Lebanese and he'll likely marry your daughter. Do you have a problem with that?'

'No, of course not.'

'Because…?'

'Because… I don't know… just because…'

'Because I look and talk like you,' said Theo, finishing his sentence for him again. 'We're tribal by nature, Mr Atkinson. We're most comfortable with those who mirror ourselves. The further a stranger presents from that image the more cautious, the more fearful we become. Eithan is *Windrush* third generation. Jamaicans are a race that favour dark skin and dreadlocks. You're not racist, Mr Atkinson, you're fearful. You're fearful of the unfamiliar. You never met Eithan. You never got to know him. Your fear blocked any chance of the stranger becoming the friend. I will prove it to you. I will prove to you that you are not racist.'

'I don't need any proof. I told you I'm not racist,' insisted the older man.

'So you did, several times. You don't need to convince me, Mr Atkinson, it's you who needs the convincing. You're frightened that deep down in the depths of your soul, you *might* be racist, and you're scared to find out, so you avoid going there.'

Mr Atkinson had gone quiet, He seemed to be wrestling with his own thoughts, so Theo ploughed on. 'I am going to drive you to Cumbria today. You are going to spend Christmas with both your daughters – and your son-in-law. And I predict you will like him within a day of making his acquaintance. I would be surprised if you are not the best of friends within a week.'

'You're very cocksure full of yourself,' remarked Mr Atkinson.

'So people keep telling me. I'm not asking you to like me, Mr Atkinson. I'm asking you to trust my professional judgement.'

Patrick Atkinson shrank into his chair, the stuffing knocked out of him. 'It's too late. You might not think I'm racist, but I've done terrible things. I've cut my daughter off because she wanted to be with him.'

'No, Mr Atkinson, you cut your daughter off because she couldn't be like your wife. You wanted your wife to live on in her. You wanted Rhianne to be a teacher like her, marry a teacher like you. Be like Ciara, the clone you always wanted. You miss her, don't you?'

'Rhianne?'

'Your wife, Mr Atkinson, you miss your wife.'

'Every day,' he sobbed.

'That's why I know you're not racist. Grief unbalances us. Makes us bitter and angry. You didn't give Eithan a chance because you were not in the right state of mind to handle it. And you're a proud man, Mr Atkinson, I can see that. You're a proud man. Once you'd issued your decree you were not going to back down. I never knew your wife but from what your daughters tell me about her she must have been a wonderful lady. That's the cruellest irony in all this. And you can't see it. Grief has made you blind as well as deranged. Your daughters are steel and bamboo. Ciara takes after you, Mr Atkinson. I think you will find, upon reacquaintance, that it's Rhianne who is most like your wife.'

The older man nodded sadly, pulling a handkerchief from

his pocket to mop his cheeks. 'It's one of the last things we spoke about. I said I knew my wife better than she knew her mother. She told me I knew nothing.'

Theo put his hand on the older man's shoulder. 'You have a chance to put it right. Come with me to Cumbria. Let's make it a Christmas to remember – in honour of your wife.'

Mr Atkinson nodded and got up from the chair. 'I'll go and pack a few things. Would you like a cup of tea?'

'That would be very nice, thank you, but first I'd like a tour of this legendary greenhouse I keep hearing about.'

Mr Atkinson smiled for the first time since Theo's arrival.

*

'My goodness,' declared Theo, 'it's amazing!' He was standing in a large greenhouse that, even in late December, was heated to tropical temperatures. The electricity bills must have been astronomical. Well-tended beds bordered three sides. One had tomatoes – who grew tomatoes in December? A second had recently been seeded so Theo could not determine what it contained. The third boasted a superb display of orchids.

'These are exquisite,' said Theo. 'Rhianne would love them. Why don't you…?'

Mr Atkinson was already one step ahead of Theo. He had grabbed an empty pot and was carefully digging up one of the orchids and potting it into the container.

'It will make a nice peace offering,' he said wistfully.

*

It was two-thirty that afternoon when Theo's car pulled up outside Briar Cottage. He was glad the return journey had been straightforward. Undue delays might have meant he did not get back in time for the arrival of the Azizis. As it was, Matt had already left for the station and was expected back within the hour.

Theo knocked loudly on the front door of Briar Cottage and let himself in.

'It's only me, Rhianne.'

'I'm in the kitchen,' came the reply. 'Come through, Theo.'

Theo made his way into the kitchen where Rhianne was busy making a sauce to accompany the two geese she would cook tomorrow. Mr Atkinson hung back nervously.

'Oh Theo, what a relief! I've been so worried. No one knew where you were, and you've had your mobile turned off.'

'I hope you're making plenty of that sauce, Rhianne. We have an extra guest for Christmas dinner.'

'Hello Rhianne,' said her father, stepping into the kitchen from the hall.

'Dad?… Dad!'

'I brought this for you.' Hesitantly, plaintively, he held out the orchid.

It was all the invitation Rhianne needed. She ran across the kitchen to fling her arms round him, still holding a spoon dripping with prune and apple puree. Theo hastily grabbed the orchid before it fell to the floor, plucked the spoon from her grasp, laid them on the worktop and tiptoed out.

*

He headed across to the tea shop. 'Theo!' declared Ciara when she heard the ping of the tea shop door. 'Where on earth have you been? Well, now you're here you can help Eithan put up those lights across the windows. The Azizis are going to be here in half an hour and there's still the table to decorate.'

'You'll need to set an extra place. We have one more dinner guest.'

'Oh,' she said, rather startled, and not a little put out. 'I'm sure it won't be a problem, Rhianne always over-caters but I wish you'd said earlier that you were bringing a friend, Theo.'

'The friend happens to be your father.'

'Dad! How…? Oh my God, Rhianne! Where is he? Where's dad?'

'He's getting reacquainted with his youngest daughter as we speak – and she with an orchid he brought her.'

Ciara dropped the bauble she was holding, which had the audacity to smash on the tiled floor, and ran out of the tea shop.

Eithan had been listening to all that had gone on and now stared at Theo incredulously.

'I'd give them ten minutes, then go over,' said Theo. 'He's keen to meet you, Eithan. Give him a chance won't you. That wasn't the real Patrick Atkinson back then. He was unhinged with grief. He's still grieving. He's a sad, lonely old man.'

*

A little later, Eithan entered Briar Cottage to find his wife and sister-in-law in the front room, sitting on the sofa, heads bent either side of an older, greyer one. Rhianne jumped up when she saw him. 'Eithan, Eithan, isn't it wonderful. Dad has come to stay for Christmas!'

Eithan smiled at her and took her hand in his. Patrick Atkinson stood up and the two men eyed each other warily. Patrick was gazing at the sagging sleeve of Eithan's sweatshirt hanging limply from one shoulder and the scars down one side of his face. It was the younger man who made the first move.

'Eithan McArthur, sir' he said, holding out his only hand. Patrick did not know how to do a left-hand handshake, so he took it in both his own.

'I made a mess of things, Eithan,' he replied, 'but I want to put it right. If you'll give me a chance – I want to put it right.'

Eithan nodded stiffly, then turning to the plant pot already proudly displayed on the sideboard he said, 'Nice orchid. You'll have to teach me how to look after it. I want it to last a very long time.'

*

Theo had gone in search of Beth and found her in the bakery kitchen.

'Theo!' she exclaimed. 'Thank goodness! I'd started to worry. No one knew where you were.'

'I drove to Samlesbury.'

'Samlesbury! But isn't that where…? Theo! What have you done!'

'I took the liberty of inviting an extra guest for Christmas: Rhianne's father. He's at Briar Cottage just now getting acquainted with the McArthurs, but I'm sure you'll meet him soon enough. He brought them an orchid from his greenhouse.'

The significance of the orchid was not lost on Beth. She smiled contentedly. 'Well, I never! How lovely for Rhianne. Theodore Kendrick, you never cease to surprise me!'

'Looks like it's down to you and me to welcome the Azizis. They're a bit tied up at Briar Cottage.'

'Give me a few minutes to freshen up and then we'll go out onto the street to watch for them.'

*

It was a very happy party of twelve that gathered round the large table in the tea shop on Christmas day. Rhianne's geese were cooked to perfection and her cider-infused apple and prune sauce was almost as delightful as her plum pudding. Beth's Christmas cake was a triumph. It featured an intricate snow scene dotted with green spruce trees and decorated in the centre with a tiny marzipan replica of Briar Cottage. It stood out against the surrounding whiteness because she had coloured it pink.

*

The Azizis and Patrick stayed a week. It was an unforgettable occasion for all, balmy memories which would warm many a wintry night to come. Beth and Mia had shared an enlightening conversation. It was obvious both women were fishing.

'I can see you and Theo are very close. He thinks of you as a daughter,' was Beth's opening gambit, hoping to learn more about this intriguing man without having to ask him directly about his past. That would have been a breach of their hard-won agreement. For her part, Mia was trying to find out if there was anything more than friendship between this forceful individual and the father figure she adored. Mia recited the story of the water well atrocity and how Theo had rescued her from an uncertain fate in an Iraqi orphanage. In return, Beth told her about her long walks with Theo and their shared love of books.

'Does he ever talk about his dead wife?' asked Mia bluntly.

'No,' replied Beth, a little shocked at the directness of the question but keenly intrigued. 'We agreed we wouldn't talk about the past.'

'It's the only thing I know nothing about,' said Mia with a hint of resentment. 'Guita and Nasim and Matt neither. None of us know anything about his early life in Belfast or the time he was married to Josie. He simply refuses to go there. I thought perhaps he might have said something to you. You being such a *special* friend and both having lost a loved one there. He was killed in Belfast, that's right, isn't it, your son?' The question was rhetorical, unemotional. It was Mia the lawyer posing it, but it took Beth by surprise.

She nodded uncomfortably but did not elaborate, responding only to the earlier part of the enquiry. 'I know he's widowed, an orphan and that he has no biological children. Beyond that I know nothing of his early life. Perhaps we should respect his wish to leave the past in the past,' she added hastily.

'Well sooner or later he's going to have to tell someone. It's not healthy. Keeping all that locked up inside him, in some concrete cell.'

In spite of herself, Beth found herself blushing.

Old Ghosts

Before Christmas, Theo had started to accompany Beth on her Monday trips into Millom because the dark nights had scuppered their late afternoon walks. For her part, she had started to stay in the kitchen when he came down to breakfast rather than retreating to the office. That way they had managed to see each other most days. It was the Sunday dinner dates that Theo was eager to restore. On the second Monday of February, they took a trip into Millom together and Theo seized his opportunity. 'I must be several weeks behind on my rent by now.'

'Don't be ridiculous,' replied Beth, 'I'm well aware you put more than we agreed in the tip box each week.'

'But we also agreed I would take you out to dinner on a Sunday. How about we pick that up again? It was the highlight of my week. Shall I book somewhere for Sunday? Any preferences?'

'I rather liked it when you came to me that last time before Christmas. February is a dreary month to eat out. How about you come to me for the next few weeks and then we'll pick up the hostelry trail again in spring.'

'Sounds good to me. You must let me bring the wine and contribute something, even it's only a cheeseboard or a couple of steaks. Perhaps cook for you for a change. There is one condition though.'

'Oh – and what makes you think you have the right to impose conditions Dr Kendrick?'

'I don't want it to stop you getting in a car once a week. You were doing so well. I can't risk you going backwards. You'll have to let me take you out for a drive somewhere once a week.'

'You drive a hard bargain Dr Kendrick.'

'So do you, Mrs B, so do you.'

*

Theo brought steak and a salad and Beth let him cook them in her kitchen. Mellow from the red wine they had drunk, they retired to the front room. On the coffee table were a whiskey bottle and two glasses – and an impressively empty ashtray. Beth had been as good as her word about quitting. While Beth poured them both a tot of whiskey, Theo wandered across to the two framed photographs on her sideboard. He studied the smaller one. He was looking at a toddler with huge eyes, a milk toothy grin and neatly cut blond hair. The larger one was a grown soldier in fatigues, a rifle slung across his chest, a green beret perched on his shaven head. 'I'm guessing this is Sidney. You must be very proud of him,' he said. He knew he was on safe ground. Most of Silecroft knew about Sidney. Beth's pride in her son was the one thing that trumped her obduracy about her insulated past. She moved to stand beside him.

'Yes, this is my Sidney,' she said fondly.

'Rhianne said he was only twenty-two when he died.'

'He died tragically young,' she replied.

While he was scrutinising the larger photo more closely, she opened the top drawer of the sideboard just wide enough to slip her hard in and retrieve Sid's toy soldier to show him. It was hardly bigger than her thumb with half an arm missing and a helmet that looked like a bearskin that had lost its fur. The postbox-red uniform was long since faded. The facial features were all but worn away apart from the remains of what had once been a black moustache. Theo could see why it would have been a much-loved favourite toy for a toddler. It would have fitted perfectly into the hand of a small child.

'It's as if he was always destined to be a soldier,' she added sadly.

'A fine-looking soldier too,' he remarked pointing at the larger photo frame, hoping to draw Beth out. 'What regiment was he with?'

'First battalion Parachute regiment,' she replied proudly.

'I cut my journalistic teeth in Belfast. Terrible times. What year did Sidney die?'

Beth suddenly looked frightened. 'I don't like to talk about the past. Let's not spoil a lovely evening being morbid. A whiskey perhaps?' she said hurriedly. She stood the toy soldier between the two photos, seemingly unwilling to re-open the drawer to replace it.

*

Her reaction confirmed Theo's suspicion that there was something very odd about Sidney Brennan. The combat gear could have been almost any battalion, but the beret was definitely not the Parachutes. He had encyclopaedic knowledge of that period of history. He could have written a thesis on Operation Banner. He told himself not to be hasty. There could be a perfectly innocent explanation. Sidney might have swapped berets with a UDR soldier as a solidarity gesture, as a photography stunt or just plain larking around. The crest on the beret was the old Ulster Rifles badge, which was abandoned in 1970. The crown and harp had been retained for the newly formed UDR, but the Latin insignia had been dropped. It was definitely an Ulster Rifles crest. He was certain. What would Sidney be doing wearing a badge crest that had been taken out of circulation before he was even born? Theo was not going to press the point. He had learned when to keep his counsel with Beth. Her flustered response and hurried shutting of the sideboard drawer had deepened his suspicions. Sidney would have been with an English-based battalion. Yes, possibly the Parachutes. Well, that information would be easy to track down. The UDR made no sense unless Sidney had been born and brought up in Northern Ireland. The political reasoning behind the creation of the UDR was to populate it with Northern Ireland men, preferably a balanced demographic mix between Catholics and Protestants – which never happened of course, but let's leave that to the history books. Could it be that Beth Brennan grew up in Belfast? His linguist's ear had detected a Liverpool accent overlain with a kaleidoscopic mix typical of someone who had moved around but there was no hint of a Belfast intonation in there. Liverpool and Belfast were strongly connected of course. He himself had sailed to Belfast on the Liverpool ferry. Had Beth married a Belfast man? Brennan was a common Irish surname. Was her divorced husband a soldier? Perhaps the beret belonged to him or one of his relatives who had served in the Ulster Rifles. Perhaps Sidney was wearing it for sentimental reasons. It would not take Theo long to find out. His old investigative skills from his journalist days had never left him and he still had useful contacts. Despite his best efforts, the haunting memories of Belfast made him shudder involuntarily.

'Are you cold, Theo? Should I turn the fire up? Here, drink your whiskey.'

'I'm fine, really,' he replied curtly. 'I ought to be going. I promised you I wouldn't keep you late.'

'It's not late, Theo, not quite nine o'clock.' She sounded disappointed. 'If I were home alone, I'd be reading till eleven.'

'It's been lovely, Beth, really lovely. But I absolutely must be going.'

'Well, we'll do it again, another time,' she replied, rather stiffly. The substitution of 'another time' for 'next Sunday' was not lost on Theo but he made a hasty exit all the same.

*

Back in his room, Theo paced the floorboards. What must she think of him? That was the second time he had run out on her, but the memories of Belfast had unnerved him. He told himself he was being a hypocrite, trying to prise open Beth's former life while at the same time keeping his own firmly locked away. He knew the time was fast approaching when he must lay old ghosts to rest. But Mia must come first. She had been pressing him for more than a decade to tell her about Josie. He knew she resented him for shutting her out of that part of his life. He had not been strong enough to go there. He had convinced himself it was because it would be too harrowing for her to hear. That had been cowardly. Few women had lived through what she had. He should have told her years ago. He should have told Nazim. Maybe it would have given him closure, brought him peace.

*

Theo picked up his mobile. 'Mia, hope it's not too late to call you.'

'Hi Theo, lovely to hear from you. No, not late at all, it's only just nine. Do you want to Skype?'

'No, I… ' he hesitated momentarily, 'I have something to tell you and it might be easier by phone.'

'Okay' she said, a little concerned. 'You alright?'

'Kind of…'

'Kind of? Is this about Beth?'

'In a way… well maybe she was a trigger… but it's about Josie. I want to tell you about Josie, Mia. I think it's time I laid old ghosts to rest, and you should be the first to know about her.'

'High time, I'd say. I'm glad, Theo, even if it's the baker woman I have to thank, I'm glad. Are you sure you don't want to Skype? This could be a long call and I don't want you cutting corners. You must tell me everything, I need to know, I need to understand. Tell me everything.'

'Okay, I'll hang up and Skype.'

*

'Josie was a freelance photographer. Talented, vivacious, fearless and brave. She'd go to extraordinary lengths to get the right shot. A good photo was worth a thousand words, she always said. She wanted her photos to tell it as it was, trained her lens on the essence of what she saw, whether that was beauty, pathos, horror, pain – she could recreate an image that let people in – right in, deep to the core. Her work was mesmerising. *She* was mesmerising. I met her around that gut-wrenching time when my sister was killed in the plane crash. She helped me come to terms with that loss. I fell head over heels in love with her. It was easy to fall in love with Josie. She was spellbinding. Perhaps it was my highly emotional state or perhaps the journalist environment, but we seemed to function at a high-octane level. Within six months we were married. I didn't even go home to get wed: a registry office affair with a few of our media pals. It was such a whirlwind event, most of our friends suspected she must be pregnant. She wasn't of course, not then. We just knew we were right for each other and wanted to make the commitment. I got her plenty of assignments on the paper I worked for although she still did some other freelance pieces occasionally. We'd been married three years and Josie was five months' pregnant. We were planning to return to England before the baby was born and settle down to a less precarious existence. We had talked of her setting up her own studio and me doing local rag stuff. We'd backed ourselves to get plenty of work.

'Josie and I had a hot lead on paramilitary loyalist collusion with the British army. All the journalists suspected it was going on and that the Government knew about it, but nobody could get proof. Josie and I were getting really close to exposing a mole when he was *supposedly* blown to pieces in a roadside bomb. The charred remains could have been anyone, but it was his dog tag that was found at the scene. We suspected it was all an elaborate cover-up to get him out before he was exposed. It was also a neat way of disposing of the body of a sectarian execution. I used all my levers and contacts and traced him to a loyalist safe house. Josie was determined to get a photo of him because it was the proof that would validate our story. I didn't want her anywhere near that safe house. I regretted telling her I'd found it. It was too risky. We argued. I told her I was quite capable of taking a photo, it didn't need to be a work of art, just evidence. She got angry, accused me of devaluing her profession, of belittling pregnancy as if it were some kind of illness. She insisted she'd be safe with a long-range telephoto lens. Against all my better judgement, I gave in and took her with me. We kept a safe distance from the house. She had her lens trained on the door so she could snap anyone coming in or out. I thought we would pull it off. I really did. They must have had men patrolling a wide area because they caught us.

'They took Josie off somewhere. I got a heavy working over and they left me in a ditch. Someone must have found me because I came round in a hospital bed. I asked after Josie. She hadn't been admitted, so I discharged myself and hurried home in case she was there.'

'But she wasn't,' said Mia, ominously.

'No, she wasn't there. I was beside myself, Mia. My pregnant wife was with a bunch of brutal men who thought they had a God-given right to kill and maim at will. I didn't dare go to the RUC. If she was still alive that would be signing her death warrant. I knew all too well what long intelligence fingers were at work and you couldn't trust anyone in those murky times. Three days! Three agonising days where I virtually lived on coffee and painkillers. And then they dumped her in the street outside our block of flats. Bold as anything, in broad daylight, like as if they were untouchable. Oh God, Mia! Her clothes were all torn, she was battered, bruised and bleeding. And…' he hesitated.

'And?' pressed Mia.

'And they'd tarred and feathered her. It was a classic sting – Loyalist Paramilitaries passing it off as an IRA punishment beating. I'd seen pictures before – Josie had even taken photos once of a tarred and feathered woman tied to a lamp post. But in my darkest dreams I had never imagined it could happen to my own wife. Her broken camera was hanging round her neck with a message pinned to it, *"foto fucker"*.'

'But she wasn't dead,' said Mia, grimly.

'No. I got her to hospital. She lost our child that night. A baby girl – little Josie as she will always be to me.'

'There's worse to come, isn't there?' said Mia, her face set hard. The face of a woman who understood how deep the abysses of human depravity could be. She sat impassively. Waiting. Preparing herself for the inexorable manifestation of human cruelty that was coming.

'She recovered from the physical injuries, but she was broken, Mia. Mind and body crushed to a pulp. She'd been brutally raped, repeatedly, by the four men in the safe house. She couldn't bear me anywhere near her. She'd scream and hold her belly as if she were trying to protect little Josie. The medics said to be patient, that with gentleness and kindness she would get better in time. They'd misunderstood me. I'd have gladly settled for celibacy if she could just be well again.

'It was latish one evening. She'd been encouraging me to have another and another drink and once I'd had one too many asked me to go out and get her some cigarettes. I knew how dependent she'd become on the fags and that she would get hysterical if she ran out. I was over the limit so couldn't take the car. The shops were shut. It was a twenty-minute walk to the garage where I knew I could get some. When I got back, I found her in the bath fully clothed with her wrists slashed. She'd left a suicide note in her handbag next to a full packet of cigarettes. She'd planned it all, Mia. She'd planned to kill herself. She'd planned to leave me. I wasn't enough for her. I couldn't save her. I couldn't save our child.'

'Is that why you buried it all this time, because you blame yourself?'

'Of course I blame myself! It was my fault she went to that safe house in the first place. It was my fault we were still in Belfast. We should have left as soon as we found out she was pregnant. I should have been able to take better care of her and the baby. I failed her, Mia.'

'You didn't fail her, Theo, life failed her. She made her own choice. Yes, she was probably out of her mind with grief and trauma, but she made a choice, and you can't shackle yourself to it for the rest of your life. You have to let it go now.'

'I ran away to the desert. Took a posting that would get me far away. Palestine and then Iraq. I would probably still be there – or dead – if I hadn't found you.'

'Let her rest, Theo. That's what she wanted. That's why she did what she did. Perhaps she loved you more than you realise. Perhaps she wanted to set you free.'

'I didn't want to be set free. I wanted to be there for her, always.'

'And you still can be, but not locked away in the coffin with her. She wouldn't want that. Hold onto the good memories and leave the rest in the grave. That's what I've had to do with my sister, my brothers, my mother, my father. All of them. They would not have wanted me to bury myself in their winding sheets.'

'So young and yet so wise, Mia. And brave. Far braver than me.'

'Maybe brave, but not wise. It's Nazim who's the wise one. You should talk to Nazim, Theo. He would straighten you out.'

'Yes, I must visit soon.'

'And Beth. I think you need to talk to Beth. That's what this is really about isn't it? Liking her is making you feel guilty about Josie. I think you more than like her, Theo. You just won't admit it because there isn't room for three of you in that coffin. Every time you get close to Beth, Josie's ghost comes between you. Am I right?'

'I do like her, but I'm scared to go there. She's even more closed than I am. Point blank refuses to talk about the past. I think something bad has happened to her, something very bad, Mia.'

'There's certainly something very secretive and dark about her.'

'Frightened. I think she's frightened of something. I'm determined to find out what it is.'

'Go carefully, Theo. Some things are best left in the past. Be careful what you rake up.'

'I will. Goodnight, Mia – and thanks for being there.'

'Always, Theo, always. As you have always been for me. *Tasbah ola khayr.*'

West Cottage

Beth cried off their planned visit to Millom next morning and Theo suspected she was avoiding him. Hardly surprising after his ungallant exit the evening before. She was not in the kitchen when he breakfasted on Tuesday or Wednesday. So that evening he rang the doorbell of West Cottage. He got no reply although he felt certain she was there. Enough was enough. On Thursday, at a quarter to four, he strode into the tearoom where he knew she would be cashing up. The ambush was successful. Beth was not expecting him and could not escape.

'You okay for Sunday, Beth?' he said as nonchalantly as if they had just finished a coffee together. 'I've booked a seven-thirty table at the Dog and Partridge. We haven't been there in a while, and you said you liked their slow-cooked shin of beef.'

'That's very presumptuous of you, Theo. Isn't it polite to ask first?'

'Well, I'm asking now, damn it. And you've been rather elusive these past days.'

She was spared from answering by the door bursting open and four children charging into the tearoom.

'Are we too late? Are there any cakes left Mrs B?' asked one of the middle-sized boys breathlessly. Meanwhile the smallest – a girl who looked to be about three – had thrown her arms around Beth's knees and was hugging them. Beth's hand went instinctively to her head to stroke the little girl's hair while she addressed her brother. 'That would depend, Tommy.'

'I've bin good, 'onest I 'ave. Miss Swarbrick sed I've bin reght good at me sums t'day.'

'And have Sean and Kevin done their chores for Mummy?' she asked, shifting her gaze to the other two boys who both nodded obediently. 'Run along into the kitchen then. I think Ruth might have some cookies for you.'

'Cookies!' came a chorus of joy from the boys.

'Cookeez,' squealed the little girl with delight and toddled after her brothers.

Theo had been watching this pageant unfold with wry amusement. 'The Dixon kids, I presume?'

Beth was a little flustered. Whatever attempts she had been making to put a bit of distance between her and Theo since last Sunday had just been torpedoed by the spectacle he had witnessed. She shrugged her answer. 'It's only a few left-over cookies.'

'Left-over my eye!' he replied trying to keep a straight face. 'I've been very good today, Mrs B. I've done six hours of writing – does that earn me a dinner date at the Dog and Partridge?'

'Oh, very well,' she capitulated.

'And a drive in the car this evening?'

'As always, you drive a hard bargain, Dr Kendrick.'

*

Theo's antennae were twitching. It was a journalistic habit he could not kick where his thought processes invariably strayed to worst-case scenarios. He had seen enough ugliness in human nature to make him unduly suspicious. Beth had looked frightened when he mentioned he had worked as a journalist in Belfast. What was she afraid of? Was she protecting someone? What if Sidney had been implicated in some kind of army-loyalist paramilitary collusion? Or something on the other side? She said Sidney was always destined to become a soldier. What if she had meant a different kind of soldier? What if he was a soldier for the IRA? Was the oddity of the photograph part of some unholy cover-up? What if he was still alive? Lying low somewhere? Theo tried not to let his suspicions run away with him, reminding himself that he was less than objective after what happened to Josie. Surely his worst-case scenario was preposterous, absurd even? But the more he tussled with it the more it made sense. Hilda said no one knew where Beth hailed from, that she had kept a low profile in the bakery kitchen until the Cartwrights left and then she bought the place outright. Where would a kitchen maid get that kind of money? Theo berated himself for letting his thoughts stray down such grubby rat runs. This was Beth. The Beth who, against all the odds, stirred his restless soul.

*

For the first time in his life, Theo did not know what to do. It was disorientating – he had *always* known what to do. He was utterly conflicted, see-sawing from one side to the other. Mia's words plagued him like an earworm; *some things are best left in the past.* Should he leave well alone? Should he banish these suspicions to some cerebral vault and throw away the key? He was risking a friendship. He was jeopardising a comfortable happiness he had not felt in years. Perhaps something deeper. On the other hand, Beth might genuinely be in danger – possibly from her own son. He decided to put a toe in the water and at least find out whether Sidney Brennan might be an alias. Beth need never know. He searched all the British army deaths from Operation Banner. He could find no record of a Sidney Brennan killed in action. He could find no record of a Sidney Brennan ever having served in Belfast, nor could he find any record of a Sidney Brennan having served in the Parachutes. If Beth's son had been a soldier in the British Army, then Sidney Brennan was not his real name.

And what of Beth? Was Brennan her married name, her maiden name, her alias? Was Beth short for Elizabeth or Elisabeth or

Bethany? He had to start somewhere. He keyed Elizabeth Brennan into his birth registry database and it threw up over two thousand hits. He would have to repeat the process for Elisabeth, Bethany and Beth forenames. Given the vague parameters, this would not be a quick task. He decided to wait and see if he could draw Beth out, eek out some clue from her that would narrow the search.

*

Theo and Beth settled at their table at the Dog and Partridge. 'What have you been reading this week, Mrs Brennan?' he asked her jovially.

'Another Bill Bryson. *A Short History of Nearly Everything.* Science was never my best subject at school, so I thought I should give it a whirl – if anyone can make science accessible for dullards like me it's Bryson. He's such a fabulous writer.'

'Did you have boring science teachers at school?'

'They were okay, but the boys got all their attention.'

'Would you have liked to have been a scientist?'

'No, not a scientist. I wanted to be a...' She stopped abruptly realising they were straying into the past. 'I thought we'd agreed we weren't going to talk about the past, Theo,' she said firmly.

'Ah... sorry! It just slipped out,' he apologised, disappointed that his bait had not landed. 'Any re-reads at the moment? I'm always intrigued by the books people choose to re-read.'

'My guilty pleasure at present is a second outing for *Wuthering Heights.*'

'Oh, spare me! Wouldn't you know it! The rugged, brooding Heathcliff makes another female conquest. When will the rest of us chaps get a look-in?'

'I'm not a Heathcliff fan,' she said, a little indignantly. 'In fact, I regard him as a rather unpleasant protagonist. It's her writing I love – in parts her prose is like liquid poetry. And I'm re-reading *War and Peace.*'

'And?' he asked.

'I liked it the first time, but I've got so much more out of it on a second read. It's like there's a whole world bound between its cover, a philosophical interrogation of humanity. Class, power, free will, love, betrayal, identity, purpose – so many fascinating musings embodied in the characters, in the narrative, in the history.'

Beth spoke with passion and excitement. Theo had never seen her eyes more beautiful or shine more brilliantly. He leaned back in his chair, to better take in the whole of her animated vigour.

'You never cease to amaze me, Beth Brennan. Tolstoy would be flattered and the Existentialists among us would be impressed. Quite the literary critic as well as the cupcake queen.'

'Now you're making fun of me.'

'Not in the least!' he replied, earnestly. 'I love to hear you talk like this.'

'Well perhaps I did get a bit carried away.'

'Which translation did you read?'

'Which translation – you mean there's more than one?'

'Oh, several. The translator is in a privileged – and powerful position – entrusted with another's masterpiece. It's not just the language skills needed to deal with idiosyncrasies and colloquialisms, it's also about conveying the exact tone, atmosphere and emotion of the original. I've often reflected on how difficult it must be to translate poetry. In *War and Peace* there's the added challenge of some passages being in French.'

'In French?'

'Yes, in Tolstoy's original version.'

'You mean not all of it was written in Russian? But why?'

'French was widely spoken in those days. In Russia it was symbolic of class. The nobility spoke French, the peasants spoke Russian. And there are extensive war passages of course – the French army would not have spoken Russian. But Tolstoy agreed to his French passages being translated into Russian for the third edition. You can see how that could add additional complexity for any translator.'

'How come you're such an expert on *War and Peace*?' A note of pique had crept into the question. She resented him being such a know-it-all, forever sounding like he was giving a lecture.

'Because it happens to be my favourite book. And because I'm a bit of a linguist. My parents always expected I would read languages and were rather confounded when I chose psychology.'

'I've heard you speaking Arabic to Mia and the Azizis. How many other languages do you speak?' she half regretted asking – it would be another invitation for him to show off – but her curiosity had got the better of her.

'My mother was Lebanese. My sister and I grew up bilingual. Arabic was particularly advantageous during my time in the Middle East. I try to keep it up, I always speak to Mia and her foster parents in Arabic. I studied French and Russian at school. My French is better than my Russian – there are more opportunities to use it – but I could get myself around Russia if I had too. I read it better than I speak it. And I've got a rudimentary grasp of Spanish.'

'I bet you were one of those irritating swats at school. Good at everything. Real teacher's pet. Don't tell me – you were probably Head Boy!'

The note of sarcastic ridicule was poorly disguised, so Theo did not volunteer that he had indeed been Head Boy. 'I can't draw or paint or play a musical instrument. I wasn't even that good at sport. I don't think I'm any cleverer than your average grammar school boy. I just had an inquisitive nature, and I was lucky to have parents who didn't belittle a boy who would rather read poetry than chase after a football.'

The hurt in his voice was better disguised than Beth's sarcasm but she caught it all the same and felt wretched. It had been a mean, cheap innuendo. She should apologise but did not know how. Even with Theo – or perhaps, especially with Theo – she would not let her guard down. The armoury of stubbornness and stiffness that had carried her through these past twenty years had not rusted. There were times with Rhianne when it felt heavy, and she wished she could remove more than the helmet she laid aside with her. She made a clumsy attempt to change the subject.

'I like to read poetry too. Keats and Wordsworth – and the war poets, Wilfred Owen and Siegfried Sassoon. What about you?'

'Yes, I like them too. They are all English poets. Do you like any non-English poets?'

He hadn't meant it to sound condescending, but the remark made Beth feel small all the same and her riposte was a tad frosty. 'Didn't you say poetry was the hardest to translate, so wouldn't it be an inferior experience reading a poem in translation?'

'Yes, agreed, but a superior experience to missing out altogether. The emotion can be hard to capture but most of all it's the *sound* and the *rhythm* of the vernacular which is challenging to replicate. Some anthologies post the original beside the translation so even with a rudimentary grasp of the language you can *hear* it.'

'I did O level French at school. Are there any good French poets you would recommend?'

'If you like nineteenth-century poets you might try Paul Verlaine.'

'Who's your favourite poet?'

'Yevgeny Yevtushenko.'

She looked flummoxed, not sure whether she should be embarrassed she had never heard of him or irritated that yet again he had managed to make her feel small.

'He's a Russian poet,' he offered.

'And which of his is your favourite poem?'

'It's actually one of his shorter ones, *Colours*.'

'What kind of poem is it?'

'A love poem,' he replied with no hint of embarrassment.

'Oh...' said Beth, trying not to blush.

'It's about love breathing colour into a grey world and the fear of losing the colour when love expires.'

She knew instantly that he was thinking of his dead wife and was unsure how to respond.

'Perhaps I'll read it to you one day – in Russian – as Yevtushenko intended it to be heard.'

'Why not next Sunday? We said we would eat in more during the winter weeks. I'll cook a beef wellington.'

Theo was delighted with the suggestion. It was a sign they were regaining the ground they had lost. 'I'll bring a good bottle of red.'

'Would you mind if we made it a half bottle – unless you can drink most of it. Half a bottle is too much for me with a whiskey to follow.' The significance was not lost on Theo. It had been his refusal to stay for a whiskey last Sunday that had triggered the onset of the frost.

'A good half bottle it is.'

Beth beamed too, glad to be back on an even keel. She had had a scare but would be much more watchful in future. She could manage this. She could keep him at bay if she kept her wits about her.

*

Theo turned up at West Cottage on the following Sunday with a half bottle of shiraz and a new copy of Yevtushenko's poetry with each poem set in both Russian and English. He wanted to make her a present of this and had made a special trip to Lancaster to get it. It would help set the tone. This was the night he was going to tell her about Josie. The meal was delicious, as he knew it would be. Any dish that involved pastry would be sensational if Beth was cooking. He offered to help with the dishes, but she would not hear of it.

'Let's retire to the front room and have a whiskey. I just need to give Rhianne a quick ring about a specialist order that has to go out tomorrow. You go on through and pour the whiskies. It's all out on the coffee table. I'll be with you shortly.'

Theo knew this was a golden opportunity. The doors were open so he could hear Beth's voice and would know when she got off the phone. Quickly he poured out the whiskies and then strode across to the sideboard. He pulled open the top drawer. Its contents were laid out like a shrine. On the left a christening robe, some dungarees, a pair of tiny shoes, in the middle the toy soldier. Next to him were two neat piles, each with a dozen or so cards: one of birthday cards, the other of Mothers' Day cards. Deftly, he flipped open a few in each pile. They were all fall from Sid. On the right was a green beret. He recognised it immediately. It was the one from the photograph. And yes, it was definitely an Ulster Rifles cap badge; he could pick out the Latin *QUIS SEPARABIT* motto underneath the harp. Not wanting to take any further risks, he closed the drawer softly and was flicking through the pages of Yevtushenko by the time Beth bustled in.

'All done,' she said. 'Rhianne will sort it.'

'It's a gift,' he announced, offering her the book.

'Oh…' she said hesitantly, flushing with delight. 'Yevtushenko!'

'I didn't bring flowers. This will last longer. It's an edition set to both the Russian and English.'

'Thank you,' she breathed, taking the book from him and fingering its pages.

'Are you going to read *Colours* to me in Russian then?'

'Yes, if you like.'

'I would like that very much.'

*

When he closed the book and placed it on the coffee table Beth's cheeks were damp from soft tears that had broken free from their hazel prisons. She got up from her armchair and went to him. He took her in his arms. There were no words, no kiss, just the deepest, most tender of embraces. They clung to each other for a long time, feeling the colour seep into their monochrome lives.

Theo seized on the intimacy of the moment. It was the perfect time to tell her about Josie, but some lemming urge took him to Sid.

'Beth, I know you don't like to talk about the past, but I wish you would confide in me. I'm convinced something very bad must have happened to you.' He noticed her stiffen and pull away from him, but he ploughed on. 'You'll say it's none of my business, but I want to make it my business. I want to help you,' he said picking up the larger photo frame. 'This is very troubling. The crest on the beret is of the Ulster Rifles but that crest was discontinued in 1970 so I don't know how Sidney came to be wearing it. I spent years as a conflict correspondent in Belfast. I know my Irish history and I know my way around the British Army. I can't find any record of Sidney's service in any British regiment let alone the Parachutes.' She had grown pale, so he hurriedly blurted out, 'Are you hiding something Beth? Is Brennan your real name? Is it Sidney's? Is he actually dead? Are you protecting him?' He realised how stark the questions sounded and saw her face cloud over with anger and distress. He carried on regardless.

'During my Belfast years, I saw more than I would have liked. I saw too many atrocities on both sides. And I'm not just talking punishment beatings and sectarian executions. I knew of collusion and double dealing. A bomb blast is a convenient means of disposing of a troublesome sectarian corpse especially if you want to fake the death of a soldier who needs to go underground. I knew all about undercover agents operating on both sides. I knew of men in hiding and men on the run. If Sidney is still alive, he might be lying low somewhere, he might be traumatised – you might be protecting him, *you* might be in danger—'

At first, Beth had been too shell-shocked to speak but now the fury kicked in. 'How dare you!' she exploded. 'How dare you suggest such a vile thing. Isn't it enough that my son had to die without you besmirching his memory, making him out to be some sort of traitor. What gives you the right! What gives you the fucking right! How dare you come trampling over my life like it's some fucking jigsaw puzzle. You sanctimonious, arrogant, know-it-all prick! You think you're God's gift. You think you know how to heal people! You know nothing. NOTHING, do you hear me!'

'But was his body formally identified, did you actually—'

'My God, You're the fucking limit! It was all a ruse wasn't it, you bastard – the meals out, the walks, the fucking poetry! Once a journalist, always a journalist. How could I have been such a dolt to be taken in by a silver-tongued snake like you. Get out of my house,' she screamed at him. 'Get out of my house. Don't ever set foot in here again. If you have ends to tie up with Eithan do it at Briar Cottage but don't show your miserable face in here again. I want you out of Middle Cottage by noon tomorrow.'

'Beth, please… you've got me all wrong, I never meant any—'

'It's *you* who's got it all wrong, you lowlife scum.' With that she held open the sitting room door and stood by it until he had no choice but to go.

'I'm sorry, Beth, it came out all wrong, I—'

'Get out!' she yelled.

Shaking his head resignedly, he got up to leave.

'And take your precious Yevtushenko with you,' she snarled, nodding towards the volume on the coffee table.

He stood up to his full height before shaking his head, defiantly this time. 'Yevtushenko was a gift, Beth.' And he strode out without a backward glance.

Beth picked up the bottle of whiskey and flung it at the wall where it smashed into pieces, its contents trickling down onto the cream carpet. The two glasses went the same way. She picked up the poetry anthology ready to throw that too but instead she held it fast to her chest and wept bitterly.

*

Theo was dismayed by his misjudgement and botched efforts. He paced the attic floor churning it over, trying to make sense of Beth's ferocious reaction. He knew she could be fierce when riled but he had never heard her use language like that before. He was hurt by her mistrust, but mostly he was furious with himself. Furious that he had ruined such a precious moment. No words had been said when they embraced but a deep connection had been forged. Every fibre in his body told him Beth was in a deep hole she could not dig herself out of.

*

It took him five hours to get there, but eventually he found what he was looking for. A birth entry on the registry database for an Elizabeth Margaret Brennan, born 21st March 1947 in Prescot, Liverpool. The father was a Sean Michael Brennan, Customs Officer. Once he found her birth registration it was an easier search to find her marriage register. Elizabeth Margaret Brennan had married George Andrew Sherwin at St John the Baptist Church, Barlaston on 16th April 1970. The groom's occupation was detailed as ceramic artist; the bride's was school teacher. *So, you were a teacher once upon a time, Beth! That fits. I've found you Beth and now I'm going to find your son.* He keyed Sidney Sherwin into the birth registry database. There were only a couple of dozen hits. None of them fitted with the time scales. He went through each one meticulously and neither did any of them have a father named George Andrew Sherwin. Finding Sid was not going to be as simple as he had first thought.

Theo snatched a couple of hours' sleep and got up before staff started arriving at the bakery. After one last lingering look around the room and across to the beach from the dormer window, he placed the room key on the bedside cabinet and left.

*

Beth left at first light to lose herself in the vastness of Silecroft beach. After a sleepless night, lingering sadness had finally cooled the heat of her anger. Why did he have to turn out to be a snake? Was he really a snake? Had she misjudged him? Would it have ended this way if she had trusted him with her past? Would he really have run a mile, as she had so often told herself he would? Well, it was too late now. She wandered wearily back home taking a detour via the side street where she knew he parked his car. But it was gone. *He* was gone.

*

Hilda was surprised to hear her boss come in through the bakery shop entrance on a Monday and assumed she was going up to

Middle Cottage attic to see Doc K. Theo had been a no-show for breakfast and Beth's slow, heavy tread on the stairs told Hilda something was wrong. 'Hold t' fort a mo, Ruth. I'm jus' gonna check on Mrs B.' She went up to the office and knocked on the door. No answer, it was locked. She puffed her way up the attic stairs where she found Theo's door wide open and Beth standing by the window looking out to sea. The room was bare.

'He's gone, Hilda. I sent him away. I let him get too close. He tricked me. He was pumping me for information. Once a journalist, always a journalist. But I liked him, Hilda. I more than liked him.'

The larger woman moved towards the window and Beth took refuge in the comfort of her Amazonian shoulder. 'Shush, now, it'll all be alreght. It'll cum owt reght enuf int' wash. 'E'll be back.'

Beth shook her head. 'No, he won't. I told him never to set foot here again. I called him a sanctimonious, arrogant, know-it-all prick.'

That's nowt to what I'll call 'im when I gits me 'ands on 'im,' muttered Hilda under her breath. 'You'll get o'er 'im, lass. Shush now.'

Sidney

Theo resisted the temptation to drive straight to Barlaston. He needed to get home, put his life back in order and wait a while in case Beth had a change of heart and contacted him. After two weeks he had to accept that was an idle dream. Nonetheless, he could not let it go. He could not move on, not until he found out the truth. Not until he knew for sure she would be safe. So, after two weeks in limbo, he headed to Stoke-on Trent library. He searched through the microfilm of all the local papers. The *Sentinel* had covered their wedding and featured a picture of the bride, Elizabeth Margaret Brennan and groom, George Andrew Sherwin. He could not take his eyes off her. She was stunning – and no scar. The groom looked to be a good ten years older and was a couple of inches shorter. He was wearing round metal-rimmed spectacles. The caption read '*Popular local teacher marries Wedgwood artist*'. A short report described the bride's gown and her bouquet of yellow roses. Children from Barlaston First School had sung at the St John the Baptist church ceremony and showered their teacher with confetti they had made themselves in the shape of paper hearts. Next, Theo searched the phone directories going back thirty years. He found an entry for a G.A. Sherwin every year at Sycamore Lodge, Fern Lane, Barlaston. Apparently. G.A. Sherwin still lived at this same address. If his estimate was right, George Sherwin

155

would be mid to late sixties by now. Perhaps the entry had been allowed to fall dormant as sometimes happened or perhaps he really did still live there. Well, there was only one way to find out. Theo was resourceful enough to come up with a ruse for knocking on his door.

*

Theo's route took him down a narrow lane bordering the old Wedgwood estate to a large detached Victorian house with beautifully manicured gardens. He walked up the impressive driveway lined with hundreds of daffodils, resplendent in early March, and rang the doorbell. He was prepared for anything behind the door. A different family altogether. George himself? A younger wife? A teenager? Even a housekeeper, given how grand the property was. But nothing could have prepared him for the vision that stood before him as the door opened. Theo thought he was hallucinating. The likeness was uncanny. The woman was the same height as Beth and a similar age. She had the same willowy figure, the same huge hazel eyes, the same captivating elfin face although the hair was a deeper, chemical blond and stylishly coiffured. His gaze went instantly to the familiar high cheek bones looking for a scar which was not there and in place of Beth's leathery, tobacco-damaged skin was a soft, flawless complexion with forgiving wrinkles that fanned out from her eyes and flickered at the corners of her mouth as she spoke.

'Yes, can I help you?' the hallucination enquired. It even spoke with Beth's voice! Mechanically he held up his lanyard ID but found nothing more than an involuntary gasp would escape from his lips.

'Can I help you?' she repeated more insistently.

'I... I...' but still the words wouldn't come.

The polite smile faded from her lips as she eyed him more warily. 'This is private property. Please state your business or leave.'

Theo's brain finally kicked into gear. Beth must have an identical twin! It was the only possible explanation. 'No please, don't be alarmed, I...' he started desperately. 'I'm here about your sister,' he blurted out.

'Meg?' she shrieked. 'Oh, please tell me she's not dead!' Her hands rushed to her face, and she momentarily lost her balance. Theo reached out to steady her. It helped him recover his own composure.

'Your sister is fine, I promise you,' he reassured her in a calm, curative voice he used with clients.

Her crumpled face brightened, her beautiful wrinkly eyes fixed themselves intently on Theo's face. 'Have you found my sister?' she asked, more quietly now, visibly holding her breath. 'Please, I beg you, if you've found Meg you must tell me where she is. It's been more than twenty years...'

Theo was touched by her desperate, almost girlish supplication. But he was confused. She had called Beth, Meg?

'I'm sorry, I didn't mean to shock you. I had planned to tell you more gently. Oh, and I should have introduced myself. My name is Dr Theodore Kendrick and I'm a clinical psychologist.'

'So I can see,' she said looking at the raised lanyard he was still gripping tightly.

'I had no idea Beth was a twin. I came here looking for George Sherwin.'

'My husband died five years ago. But what would you want with George?'

'*Your* husband! I don't understand. Did he marry both of you?'

'You're not making any sense, Dr Kendrick. He's only ever been married to me. I'm Elizabeth Sherwin – Izzy. Now you really are starting to spook me. Why would you think he was married to Meg?'

'Who's Meg?'

'Meg is my twin sister, Margaret Dagnall.'

'But I know her as Beth – Beth Brennan.'

The penny suddenly dropped for Izzy. 'Ah... now I understand...'

'Well, I wish you'd share your enlightenment with me, I'm mightily confused.'

'If you promise me faithfully that Meg is well and not in any danger, and that I don't need to get in my car right this minute to go to her, then I think you should come inside and let me explain. It's a long story.'

'Beth… er… Meg… is perfectly fine, Mrs Sherwin. I'm sorry I spooked you. I thought I was hallucinating.'

*

Izzy showed him into her sitting room and disappeared into the kitchen where she made tea in a china pot and put out some Battenburg cake and a handful of custard creams on a matching plate. Theo's practised eye scanned his surroundings. The room was large and bright with high ceilings and French windows opening out onto a palatial rear garden with intricate box hedging and pruned rose beds. The room was spotlessly clean and housed some expensive-looking furniture. A vase of yellow roses graced a polished side table. His memory flashed to the newspaper report of her wedding bouquet. A dozen or more framed family photographs adorned the sideboard. He homed in on a cute one of the twins in school uniform. They looked to be about nine or ten. Next to the sideboard was a glass cabinet filled with some exquisite Wedgwood pieces.

'Before I fill you in on our family history, let's get a few things out of the way first.' She spoke with determination, almost severely. 'Are you treating my sister? Is she ill? Has she had a breakdown? Is she your patient? Please don't keep anything from me. I need to know everything, Dr Kendrick, even the bad bits.'

Theo resisted the urge to smile for fear of appearing impolite but the notion of Beth accepting treatment from anyone, least of all him, was so far from the mark as to be comical.

'I am definitely NOT your sister's psychologist – and I wish you would call me Theo. I think you'd see her walk over hot coals first. She's a *tour de force* is Beth, fiercely independent, doesn't suffer fools gladly. She runs a successful bakery and property business. No! As far as Beth's concerned, I'm a prize twally.'

Perhaps it was the Scottish colloquialism or the slightly more pronounced lilt on the word 'twally' that triggered something in Izzy's memory. 'Do I know you from somewhere?' she mused. 'It's just that your voice seems familiar.'

'I used to work for television many moons ago,' he replied, more embarrassed than gratified.

'Of course!' she said triumphantly. 'You were that Middle Eastern correspondent, the one who disappeared mysteriously from our screens. Quite the desert darling! You wouldn't believe the conspiracy theories swirling around at the time: that you'd been taken hostage, been discovered in an illicit affair, criticised the Americans once too often...'

'Nothing quite so colourful,' he said ruefully. 'I merely quit. Anyway, we are here to talk about your sister, not me. And I need you to explain something that is confusing the hell out of me. How come I know her as Beth, and you call her Meg? Which one of you is Elizabeth?'

'We both are,' she replied enigmatically.

'Now you've completely lost me!'

'My mother was old when she had us. I think they'd all but given up hope of any children and then she fell pregnant aged forty.'

'Yes,' interjected Theo mechanically, 'sometimes it's the release of stress when you believe you can no longer conceive. Sometimes it's pre-menopausal erratic ovulation.'

'Whatever. Anyway, they were old in every sense of the word. Very traditional, very proper. We always had bonnets at Easter and had to learn to dance around a maypole. All that old Englishness. Mum was obsessed with the royal family. The Queen Mother was her idol. I don't think any daughter of hers was ever going to escape being called Elizabeth. If I had been a boy, I would have been called George of course. Twins took her completely by surprise. I was the elder by four minutes, so she named me Elizabeth. When my sister popped out Mum said she got two princesses for the price of one, so she called my twin sister Margaret. To acknowledge our twinness and to accentuate the royal connection, she went further and christened me Elizabeth Margaret and my twin, Margaret Elizabeth. Can you imagine being saddled with that! We hated all that pretentious royalty stuff. From an early age, we rebelled and called each other the least royal version of our names we could think of – hence Izzy and Meg. Mum detested the names, precisely because they were so unroyal. She insisted on calling us Elizabeth and Margaret her entire life. Made a real fuss with the teachers at our schools about it.'

'But why would Meg call herself Beth Brennan? I don't follow.'

'She reverted to her maiden name when she divorced. Meg got it into her head that she needed to disappear so I can see that she might want to take a diminutive of her middle name. Maybe it will make sense if you tell me everything you know. Every little detail, every scrap. I have missed so much – lost so much.'

'Beth lives in a small coastal town, Silecroft, on the western edge of the Lake District. It's a beautiful spot, a bit windy but there's a long stretch of unspoilt beach and it's rather quaint. Years ago, it would have been off the beaten track but it's getting more popular with tourists now, especially walkers and bird watchers.'

'Off the beaten track – yes, that figures,' nodded Izzy gravely.

'From what I have been able to piece together she arrived there about twenty years ago. No one seems to know much about her from that time. It's like she appeared from nowhere. But in the last decade she's become better known – quite the entrepreneur, your sister, Izzy.'

'Really!' exclaimed Izzy, delighted. 'Oh, do tell me more.'

'She's the proprietor of Beth's Bakery, a very successful bakery, tea shop and bespoke patisserie. She also has a few rental properties that bring in a good income. I don't know all the ins and outs. Hilda could probably quote you chapter and verse.'

'Hilda?'

'Hilda is the kitchen assistant she hired when she wanted to expand the bakery.'

*

As the light began to fade, Theo shared with Izzy all that he had learned from Hilda about Mrs B.

'Is Hilda still there – I'd love to talk to her.'

'Yes. She's stayed with Beth ever since the early days.'

'That says a lot,' nodded Izzy approvingly, 'that Meg could instil that kind of loyalty.'

Theo looked troubled. 'You need to prepare yourself, Izzy. I don't think Beth is the sister you remember. She's hardnosed, Izzy. She's closed, stern – grim almost. I've always had the feeling that something very bad must have happened to her to make her so sour. She's not unkind. In fact, if you dig deep enough there are lots of examples of her generosity. She's been amazingly kind to an injured veteran I've been treating and his wife, and she has taken a destitute family of kids under her wing. I like your sister, Izzy. I duped myself into thinking I was melting that armour of ice she wears but I blew it big time. She balled me out.'

Izzy put her hand on his arm at that point, as if to stop him saying any more. 'Don't judge her too harshly. When it's my turn to share, when you know about Meg's early life, you'll understand why she is like that. Please tell me some more about her. Did she marry again? Does she have children? Is she *happy*?'

'I don't think Beth knows how to be happy. She won't *let* herself be happy. I don't think she re-married. She refuses to talk about the past. Only ever mentions one child, Sidney, a soldier who died in Belfast.'

Izzy was looking bewildered, a fearful expression spreading across her face. 'I don't understand. Sid loved to play with his toy soldier but how could he be a real solider when he died as a child.'

'WHAT?' exclaimed Theo in disbelief. 'But Beth said Sidney died aged twenty-two, a roadside bomb in Belfast, that he—'

'He died aged twenty-two *months*,' interrupted Izzy, shuddering as she uttered the words. The significance of what Theo had divulged was just sinking in. Both hands flew to her face. 'She hasn't just kept Sid's memory alive – she's… she's—'

'Now it's me that doesn't understand…' interrupted Theo. And then, as if someone had just released the pause button in his brain, it all clicked into place. His head flopped back against the sofa. 'Christ Almighty! What have I done!'

'What is it, Theo? Please tell me.'

'You've no idea what I've done. I've done the most terrible thing. I've made the situation worse not better. I've been such an arrogant prick – just like she said – a sanctimonious, arrogant, know-it-all prick.'

'Now it's you who's not making any sense, Theo. What is it you've done?'

'It smelt all wrong. Her soldier photo of him was wearing an obsolete cap badge and I couldn't find any record of Sidney's death or service in the army archives. I was a journalist in Belfast for many years, you see. I know the history intimately. I began to suspect he might not be dead at all, but in hiding – perhaps a paramilitary mole or even an IRA soldier. I knew of other cases like that when I was covering The Troubles. My own wife…' Theo hesitated momentarily. After unburdening himself to Mia, it felt easier to talk about Josie, so he continued, 'My wife… died a terrible death at their hands. We were trying to uncover a British army mole, prove the Government knew about the collusion that was going on. She was beaten and raped and… tarred and feathered… and she miscarried our child… and because she couldn't live with the trauma of it, she killed herself.' There. He'd said it. After almost twenty years he had told a complete stranger about Josie and little Josie and the sky had not fallen in.

'I'm so sorry, Theo,' said Izzy. 'Is that why you became a PTSD specialist?'

'No, I was a coward. I ran away to the Middle East.'

'Yes, of course, you were on our screens for many years as the Middle Eastern correspondent.'

'I retrained as a clinical psychologist after my experiences in Iraq. That's another story for another time.'

'There's a lot to tell on both sides. I think it's my turn to fill in some of the blanks.'

*

As the darkness descended, Izzy took Theo step by step through her twin sister's early life. 'We grew up in a suburb of Liverpool. Dad was a customs officer at the docks. We were inseparable as children. Yes, we squabbled now and then but if the other were attacked we defended her fiercely. Mum was a bit of a pillock about the royal family – you can imagine how she reacted when her Elizabeth married a George. Of all the names in the kingdom, I had to fall in love with a George! Otherwise, we had quite a privileged childhood. We weren't rich but we weren't poor. We both did well at school and we both had ambitions to become teachers. There was this wonderful teacher called Miss Evans at junior school who gave us our love of books and stories – and drama. We loved acting and would make up plays at home. We each had our dalliances with local boys. Nothing serious. Quite innocent I guess by modern times. Innocent, that is, until Meg started going around with Bruce Dagnall. He was different. He was much older – twenty-nine and Meg was only seventeen. He was a motor mechanic and a bit of a petrol head. Always had plenty of ready cash – he had packed in his job at the garage to work at the Vauxhall plant but still did up motors in his spare time. He had his own place and earned extra cash renting out a spare room to one of his drinking pals. She found it exhilarating to ride pillion on his motorbike. It was the first time in our lives that we didn't do everything together. Bruce didn't like me hanging around. She was infatuated with him. He'd really got his hooks into her. He worked alternate shifts, earlies and lates – six till two and two till ten. She started bunking off school when he was on lates. I tried to reason with her, but she wouldn't listen, said I was jealous that she had a proper grown-up boyfriend. But I wasn't that petty. I didn't like him because he was all wrong for her: arrogant, controlling and he was leading her astray. He was too old for her. He drank a lot too. If he wasn't charging around on this bike, his idea of a good time was getting pie-eyed in the pub, playing darts with his mates. He had an older brother he idolised who was a bad influence on him. The brother lived in Staffordshire. He worked at the Michelin tyre factory. Despite the distance, Bruce went over there a lot at the weekends on his motorbike. Increasingly, with Meg. She started to fall behind at school – and then she got pregnant. She was still only seventeen. Mum and Dad were stoic about it but insisted they got married. I was devastated for her, but she seemed ecstatic to be marrying Bruce. She had to leave school without taking her A levels. The baby was born in April of our upper year. They called her Charlotte, after his mother.'

'A girl!' interrupted Theo. 'So not Sidney?'

'No, Sid came later.'

'What happened to Charlotte?'

'I'll come to that in due course. Our parents moved away as soon as I'd finished my A levels. Dad was retired by then. I don't think they could cope with the shame Meg had heaped on them, especially Mum – royal princesses and all that. I started at teacher training college and tried to see as much of Meg as I could. Charlotte was the light of her life. Meg doted on her and surprised us all by how easily she took to motherhood. Anyway, events took a different turn when Bruce got laid off at the Vauxhall plant. He was out of work for a few weeks until his brother persuaded him to take a job at the Michelin factory where he worked. It meant they had to up sticks and move. The money was good, and Bruce still did up motors in his spare time, so they were able to get a nice semi-detached house with a garage and a garden not far from his brother's. She wanted to finish her A levels and was pinning her hopes on being able to go to the local college once Charlotte started school. I was glad she was thinking like that, it was a travesty to waste a brain like hers. The mistake she made was in signposting it to Bruce. That's when things started to go badly wrong for her. Bruce wanted a stay-at-home wife who had his tea on the table when he came home, kept his house tidy and his bed warm. The idea of Meg going to college grated with him. They rowed about it. Bruce became more controlling, went to the pub more…'

'Was he violent?'

'I don't think so. At heart he was a coward. His older brother was the one handy with his fists. Poor Jacky must have had a rough time of it. I was in my final year of teacher training, so I applied for jobs near to Meg. The Potteries turned out to be a good location for me. I got a post in a lovely village school – and it's where I met my wonderful George. He was a ceramic artist and assistant manager at Wedgwood. I was crazy about him, still am even though he's been dead five years. He was a wonderful husband and father.'

'How many children do you have, Izzy?'

'Just one girl, Shelley. Grown up now, of course, with her own life. She has her own pottery shop down in Cornwall with its own little gallery. Has her first exhibition coming up soon.'

'You said Mr Sherwin died five years ago?'

'Yes. Heart attack. He was ten years older than me. Ironic isn't it that both princess twins went for older men. I was the only one to get a prince though. She got the frog. Bruce found the contraception pills Meg had been hiding and flushed them down the toilet. He made sure she got pregnant again just before Charlotte started school, so that put paid to any college plans. Meg capitulated, stopped challenging him and resigned herself to the hand she had been dealt. Things got better for a while when Sid was born. Bruce was ecstatic to have a son. Carrying on the blood line, his namesake, all that crap – excuse my French,' she half apologised with a tinge of embarrassment. Theo smiled, 'crap' sounded incongruous coming from the mouth of this polished lady, immaculately turned out in her powder blue cashmere sweater.

'Don't apologise on my account. "Crap" all you like…' And then they both laughed when they realised what he had said.

'Sidney was a family name. Both his father, and Rob as the elder brother, had Sidney as a middle name. Eldest boy thing. Meg hated all that bloodline...' she hesitated momentarily and then before she could continue, he jumped in to fill the gap.

'Crap, Mrs Sherwin?'

'*Crap,*' she repeated, emphasizing the word for effect and grinning broadly. 'What Bruce didn't know was that Meg had this massive crush on Sidney Poitier, so she was secretly keen on the name. Bruce was surprised, and delighted, when she suggested they reverse the order and go with Sidney Ian, not just because it gave the male family name more prominence but, as Meg took pains to point out, the initials spelt out SID – Sidney Ian Dagnall – so he was Sid twice over. Bruce loved it.

'He was besotted with his son. The little lad was very physical, walked at ten months and had amazing ball skills for one so young. On Saturday mornings Bruce was often doing up motors or lying in before going to the pub so he didn't mind Meg spending time with me and George as long as she took the kids with her. I would collect them and bring them to our place. We didn't live far away – fifteen minutes by car. It always had to be me, or both of us. Bruce didn't like George picking Meg up on his own. He was incredibly possessive, had a hang up about Meg being alone with any man, even her brother-in-law. But we were happy to play by his rules because it gave us precious time together. I always had to get Meg home before Bruce got back from the pub. Life settled into a tolerable routine and things had improved so much that Meg asked Bruce about having driving lessons. Bruce's Ford Anglia was redundant most of the week – he always took his motorbike to work. Meg tried to persuade him that it was a waste having the car standing in the garage all day. He was furious. Refused point blank. Meg's sudden interest in learning to drive had made him suspicious. He became more controlling, more possessive, always imagining anything in trousers wanted to get into bed with his wife. He had convinced himself there must be a man sniffing around.

'It was an uncomfortable passage of time: Meg walking on eggshells trying not to rile him and Charlotte like a rabbit in headlights, not able to do right for doing wrong, poor lamb. As Sid's star shone ever brighter with his father, Charlotte's waned. If Sid got upset, it was always Charlotte's fault. If Sid wanted a biscuit, Charlotte must go and get it. And yet she adored her little charge. We all did. He was a very lovable little boy despite Bruce's excesses with him. A relative peace descended on the Dagnall household, and it emboldened me and George. Knowing how disappointed Meg was about the driving, we bought some lessons for her, arranging for the instructor to pick her up from our house on a Saturday morning. She had to apply for a provisional licence, but we calculated it was very low risk that Bruce would discover it. He was never around when the post came and she could leave it with us for safe keeping.' Izzy stopped at that point, as if she couldn't go on. She looked up at Theo, her beautiful, dancing eyes had misted over. They were Beth's eyes now, numbed by pain.

'We thought we were helping her,' she continued, hardly above a whisper. 'We thought we'd been so clever outmanoeuvring that brute of a husband. But it was the most disastrous thing we could have done. Unknowingly we catapulted Meg into a living hell. There's not a day goes by I don't reproach myself for my stupidity.'

'Is it too painful to go on, Izzy? Would you rather stop?'

She shook her head. 'No, I want you to know it all. It was the Saturday of her third lesson. Everything was going like clockwork. We made sure the kids were happily occupied so they wouldn't notice the hour their mother was missing. We didn't want any unconscious slips to Bruce about what Mummy was doing. If they happened to ask after her, I would just say she was doing an errand for Aunt Izzy. That evening two police officers knocked on our door. They demanded to know if we were holding a provisional driving licence for a Margaret Elizabeth Dagnall.

'I asked why they needed it – they said it was evidence as Meg had been in a car accident with her two children. She was driving. They told me all three were being treated in hospital. I explained that they must be wrong about her driving, that she'd only had three lessons and her husband didn't let her touch the car. He would have been driving for sure. "Mr Dagnall wasn't there," they told me. "He was at his brother's. It was Mrs Dagnall at the wheel, she was still in the driving seat when we got there."

I couldn't take it in – it was like stumbling into an alien world where the walls turn black and close in to crush you. George took me in his arms. I couldn't feel anything. I couldn't breathe. I couldn't speak.'

'It was the shock,' Theo said comfortingly.

'Yes, I was in total shock. It was George who took charge. He asked which hospital they had been taken to, they told us it was the North Staffs Royal Infirmary, but said they doubted we would be allowed to see Meg, not until they had finished questioning her. They told us Meg had regained consciousness when the paramedics pulled her from the car, but they wouldn't tell us any more about the children – they said we had to ask the medical team. By the time we got to the hospital the worst had already happened. Sid had died from a bleed on the brain. The police would not let us near my sister or my niece.

'George said that if Meg had been driving that car, uninsured, unsupervised on a provisional licence she was going to need a good solicitor, the best we could afford. I couldn't believe she would be so reckless. She would never put her kids in danger. They were everything to her. They were the reason she stayed with that beast she was married to. George said we shouldn't jump to conclusions until we talked to Meg. She would tell us what happened. There could be a simple explanation that might have been overlooked. He was going to look for a good solicitor straight away.

'Charlotte was unhurt and was discharged into her father's care. The next day we went round to see what we could find out and if Bruce needed any help. I wasn't sure if he would even let us through the door, but he was surprisingly decent to us, thanked us for coming but said there was nothing we could help with. His brother and sister-in-law, Rob and Jacky, were there for Charlotte.

She was sitting on the floor at the back of the room. Not playing, not reading, not watching TV, not doing anything – just sitting. I smiled at her and asked her gently if she was alright, if there was anything she would like us to bring for her? She lifted her head but didn't answer. Bruce appeared broken. I'd never seen him unshaven before, he always prided himself on his appearance. He didn't rant at me about Meg, just sat in the chair staring at the wall. I found myself feeling sorry for him, this cruel man who had tormented my sister. If I'd known then what I knew later, I don't think I could have left without scratching his eyes out. It was monstrous what he did. Monstrous.

'Meg was discharged from hospital into police custody. George engaged a solicitor, Raymond Braithwaite. After he'd spoken with Meg, he felt confident he could get her released on bail into our keeping if we could put up the bail bond. It took all our savings, but Raymond accomplished what he'd promised. Meg came to us on bail. It was the first time we'd seen her since the accident. She looked ashen when she arrived, crushed under the weight of grief and injustice. First up she wanted to know about Charlotte. They wouldn't let Meg see her and she was desperate to know how she was. Raymond explained she wasn't hurt but was suffering from shock. I said Charlotte was physically fine, just needed time to get over the shock – she hadn't spoken since the accident. I was trying to disguise my own anxiety about Charlotte.

'Meg was adamant. "I didn't do it. What they are saying I did – I *wasn't* driving, *HE* was." She told us that Bruce must have placed her behind the wheel while she was unconscious and fled the scene. The police didn't believe her. Bruce had got his weasel of a brother to give him a false alibi. We were sure the truth would out. Rob might sell his own grandmother down the river, but Jacky wouldn't lie, surely? Not under oath? And Charlotte would be able to tell the police what really happened once she recovered from the shock.'

Theo interrupted at this point. With his clinical training, he could see exactly how this was unfolding. 'She didn't though, did she?'

In response, Izzy shook her head slowly.

'Elective mutism – is that what they told you?'

'Yes, how did you know? Oh, of course, I forgot. You're one of those psychologists like the one they took her to.'

Theo nodded without speaking.

'Raymond Braithwaite tried his best but all he had to work with was Meg's courtroom testimony and it was not enough to convince a jury in the face of two fabricated alibis – Jacky lied too, that's what did for Meg. The jury verdict was unanimous. Meg protested her innocence throughout. She might have got a lighter sentence if she'd pleaded guilty, pleaded temporary insanity, pleaded PMT, depression – anything that might reduce it to involuntary manslaughter. The judge saw no remorse, no mitigating circumstances. He threw the book at her. Gross negligent manslaughter and he added on time for driving without a licence and insurance. She got eighteen years. Eighteen years!'

'Eighteen years!' repeated Theo incredulously.

'But it's worse, Theo – far worse.' He said nothing, just closed his eyes and took a long, deep breath in preparation for what he knew was going to be a painful revelation.

'Bruce divorced her with unseemly haste and secured sole custody rights over Charlotte. He never let me near my niece – I think he was always afraid of what she would say once her speech returned. I was friendly with one of the teachers at her primary school so got to hear bits and pieces which I could pass on to Meg. I got a prison visit once a month. First up she would ask after Charlotte. By then she knew about the elective mutism. Then she would ask about me and George. I could rarely get her to talk about herself. She just said she was managing okay and not to worry. On my fourth prison visit she didn't turn up. I couldn't find out anything other than that she was in hospital. It was to be another two months before I got to see her again. I'll never forget that day. She walked into the visiting quarters with her right arm in a sling and her face – Oh Theo, half her beautiful face was covered by an ugly scar. She wouldn't tell me what had happened, just that there had been an accident in the laundry room. I knew a burn when I saw one and I knew it was no accident. It made telling her about Charlotte all the harder. I nearly wimped out, thought about lying to her, making something up about her school progress. But I had never lied to Meg in our whole lives, never once.

'When I told her Bruce had taken Charlotte to Canada two weeks before, she didn't weep, she didn't yell or scream – not even a moan. She just nodded. Then she got up from the visit table – we still had twenty minutes left but she got up to leave all the same. She said that I mustn't come again. That there were bad people in there and they had contacts outside. I looked too much like her and she didn't want anyone to see me visiting her. She didn't want anyone to know she had a twin sister. She said Charlotte would be safe in Canada and it was probably all for the best. I tried to argue, I said it was insane, that me and George were all she had, but she just asked me to keep her things safe for when she got out.

'And she limped away. She turned to look at me briefly before she passed through the security door. I felt it, Theo. I felt it, as I know she did. After twenty-five years, I felt our shared heart splintering.'

Izzy dropped her head and Theo knew he needed to give her a few moments to compose herself. Platitudes were futile in the face of such pain. After a while he spoke, gently, neutrally, changing direction to try and diffuse the emotion.

'What things were they that she asked you to keep safe?' asked Theo.

'When Raymond got Meg out on bail, he invoked her right to claim her personal belongings from the marital home. He even went with her to ensure everything was done by the book. Bruce, ever the coward, didn't want to face Meg. He was absent. It was Jacky who let them in. A condition of the bail was that Meg couldn't be alone with Charlotte before the trial because of potential witness contamination but Meg had hoped she'd at least get to see her, even if it was in the presence of others. There's no way that bastard was going to give Meg even the chance of a snatched conversation with her daughter, so he kept her away. By absenting himself, Bruce had forfeited his opportunity to object to anything she chose to take. And Jacky wasn't going to challenge her. So, she filled two suitcases with all the things she wanted, and I kept them safe for her while she was in prison.

'I went to the prison on my next three visit dates, but she never came. In the end, I had to give up. I wrote to her once a month instead. After a while she started to write back. Short notes that said very little other than she was coping well, and I hadn't to worry. She told me she had started an Open University course called Introduction to the Humanities. She kept up her study – did a full degree in the end. After ten years, her parole board came up – I was so excited. She was a model prisoner, I really believed she would get out, that we were going to be together again, that she would come and live with me and George, that we would help her rebuild her life. She was a young woman still, only thirty-four...' Izzy paused, let out a sigh and threw her hands up in the air in a gesture of despair.

'Something tells me, it didn't work out the way you hoped,' said Theo apprehensively.

'It all went swimmingly except for Meg refusing to accept her guilt. She doggedly protested her innocence. The parole board concluded that until she accepted her guilt, she could not show true remorse, so she was not ready to be released on licence.'

On hearing this, Theo's patient listening poise finally gave way. 'What the hell were they playing at! For pity's sake! Hadn't the woman been through enough! God Almighty, didn't they even have the decency to think about balancing the scales, compensating her for *their* fuck up. It was in *their* care she was assaulted and maimed. They *owed* her – irrespective of any original miscarriage of justice. They *owed* her for fuck's sake.'

'At the parole board the following year the same thing happened.' By this point, Theo was up on his feet, pacing around the room. 'Unbelievable!! Fucking unbelievable!'

'And the board the following year,' added Izzy. 'It was like some ghastly groundhog day.'

'Please don't tell me she had to serve the maximum eighteen years?' he asked, astonished.

'She served twelve. Two years more than the minimum. She still protested her innocence but by then prisons were getting overcrowded and she had accrued so many good behaviour credits that they finally agreed to release her.'

'I hope they can sleep at night,' said Theo, sitting down again.

'George and I met her at the prison gates and brought her home with us. She stayed one night. One measly night was all I had with her after twelve years! George had invested the money from her half of the sale of their house in a high interest bond. It was worth a tidy sum by then. He cashed in the bond when he knew she was being released and put the money in a building society account for her. She took the bank book and a few things from the suitcases we had kept for her, and she was gone before we were up next morning. She left a thank you note on the kitchen table, telling us not to worry, that she knew how to look after herself – prison had at least taught her that. But we must forget her now. It was safer this way, safer for everyone she loved. And I've never seen or heard from her since until you rang my doorbell. She never wrote, she never phoned. I didn't even know if she was alive or dead. I tried every avenue I could to track her down, but she had just disappeared into thin air.'

Theo ran his hands through his hair, a restless hangover habit from the days when it was much longer. 'There's so much I just don't understand! Why would she talk about Sidney openly, with sadness and pride – yes pride, all that pretend soldier stuff. Why would she do that and not volunteer she had a daughter? Surely she wouldn't disown Charlotte because her father took her to Canada?'

Izzy was way ahead of him. 'Stop thinking like a psychologist and think like a mother, Theo. What does a mother do first and foremost for her children?'

'Love them?'

She shook her head. 'No. First and foremost a mother *protects* her child. Sid is dead. She can't protect him anymore, only his reputation and his memory. Charlotte is still alive. I don't know what went on in prison, but Meg obviously considers herself toxic so the best way she can protect Charlotte is to give her up. She's kept her love for Charlotte secret, her memories hidden.'

Theo nodded soberly. 'What happened to Charlotte in the end?' he asked suddenly, realising that part of the story was still untold.

'I don't know. I couldn't discover where they'd gone. I tried to find out. I called on Jacky when Rob was at work to beg her for a contact address. I think she knew where they were, but she didn't let on. She was scared stiff of Rob. I had to give it up, it was making me ill. I had to let Charlotte go and hope she made a good life for herself. I can't imagine what it must have been like for a mute eight-year-old who'd lost her brother, her mother and then her teachers and school friends trying to make her way in a new country, but children are remarkably resilient.'

'Yes, especially if she inherited it from her mother.'

'As a psychologist, where do you stand on all that nature-nurture debate? I've always wondered about it.'

'It's a bit of both but I lean more to the nurture side.'

'That's bad news for Charlotte then, holed up with that reprobate of a father.'

'You're forgetting that she had the first seven years with her mother. They're the formative years. Charlotte may surprise all of us.'

'If we ever find her.'

'I'll find her Izzy. I owe Beth that much. I've piled more misery onto her with my conceited meddling, my preposterous theories. I found you, didn't I? I can find Charlotte. Just another needle in a bigger haystack.'

'Stop right there, Theo Kendrick,' said Izzy sharply. 'It's not your decision to make. It's Meg's. Don't go wading in until you know what *she* wants.'

'Yes, you're right, of course. Me and my meddling again.'

'Could you give me Meg's address please, I'm going to drive up there first thing tomorrow.'

Theo wrote it down and gave her a card with his own details. 'There's only a landline for her cottage. Beth doesn't have a mobile, says she's no use for one. Stubborn as a mule sometimes, your sister.'

'I'm not going to risk phoning. I don't want her to do a runner again. I intend to turn up unannounced.'

'And I should be getting on the road. Back home to Solihull. It's been a great privilege to meet you, Izzy,' he said, proffering his hand. 'Let me know how it all goes.'

'You're not driving anywhere tonight. Not after the day you've had. There are five bedrooms in this house. You can take your pick from four of them. You need a good night's sleep and a proper meal.'

Theo started to protest.

'No arguments. You'll do as you're told for once. I suspect it's a novel experience for you, Dr Kendrick,' she insisted, her hazel eyes twinkling.

'I give in,' he said, raising his hands in a gesture of capitulation.

As they headed up to their respective bedrooms, Izzy asked, 'Are you sure you won't come with me tomorrow, Theo?'

'No. I'm the last person Beth would want to see. Anyway, she's banned me from setting foot on her property ever again.'

'Sounds complicated, Dr Kendrick.'

'Believe me, complicated doesn't come close.'

'Well don't stray too far. I'd lay money on you being summoned back to Silecroft. We princess twins aren't big on banishments – beheading's much more our style!'

Confessions

Theo had sent an explanatory text to Rhianne when he left Silecroft assuring her he would continue Eithan's sessions by Skype and organise a face-to-face appointment in about a month's time, but that it would need to be at his clinic in Birmingham. Rhianne had immediately gone over to West Cottage to find out what on earth had gone on. She found Beth in a miserable state.

'I said some terrible things to him Rhianne, mean things.'

'I don't think he meant to be hurtful, Beth. Sounds like he got things tangled up because of his Belfast years but I honestly don't think he meant to be hurtful.'

'I can't forgive him, Rhianne. He – he all but accused my son of being a traitor.'

'I think you've had a big shock and you need to rest. I've spoken with Eithan and we've both agreed that from tomorrow I'm going to come back full time. You need to take a couple of weeks off. You're emotionally spent, Beth. You need time to recuperate. I can pick up the special orders and we'll manage just fine. Then when you feel rested, we should talk about how we can change the work patterns with me taking on more responsibility. Now Eithan has recovered so well, it's you we need to focus on. Getting *you* back on an even keel. No arguments, Beth. You've to take a couple of weeks off. It will be a good test. You like to test people. It will be a test of my management abilities. I'll come in at the end of each day and give you a full report.'

To her surprise, Rhianne got no arguments, just a weak thank you and a pat of her hand.

*

Beth's mind was too agitated to read but she dozed fitfully in her armchair in between bouts of self-doubt and self-loathing. She should have told him! Why could she not confess everything to him? Was she more afraid of his disapproval than the shadows of her past? He would have walked. If she had told him her story, he would have walked. She had just cut out the middleman. That was all she had done – cut out the middleman. There was no point in moping over the spilt milk. She had to get used to the idea that he was gone from her life forever. It had been a brief enchanting interlude, a fairy-tale, a dream. But it was over.

*

On the Saturday of the second week, she woke in much the same mood. She felt desperate for a cigarette but would not succumb. She had told him she would quit and was determined to do it. The discomfort was a fitting punishment for the lies she had told. It was early afternoon when she heard her doorbell ring. It would be Rhianne checking up on her. Sure enough, the chimes were followed by the usual 'It's only me, Beth,' as she let herself in. Rhianne put her head round the front room door. Her cheeks were flushed and her eyes bright. 'Someone came into the tea shop asking for you.'

'I'm not in the mood for visitors, Rhianne. You handle it please.'

'I think you'll want to see this one, Beth,' replied Rhianne, opening the door more widely to reveal a tall woman standing behind her.

'Hello Meg,' said the woman, as she stepped into the room.

'Izzy? Izzy!' The twins stared at each other for a microsecond before running into each other's arms, clasped in an embrace neither of them wanted to be released from. Rhianne, grinning from ear to ear, skipped back to the bakery.

*

Seated in Beth's front room, with a pot of tea and a supply of cakes to hand, they talked long into the afternoon.

'How did you find me?' came the first breathless question.

'It was Dr Kendrick, your psychologist friend who tracked me down.'

'He's no friend of mine. He's a conceited, meddling pri… louse.'

'Perhaps he is,' replied Izzy, inwardly smiling at Meg's attempt to avoid shocking her with her choice of language. In good time, she could assure Meg she had heard men called far worse than prick. 'But his intentions were honourable, Meg, and he went to extraordinary lengths to track me down. It couldn't have been easy. I've been trying to find you for twenty years and never managed it. I may never have done, if it hadn't been for him. I've a lot to thank him for.'

Beth nodded her assent, if a little grudgingly.

'Why didn't you write, Meg? I would have come. I would have gone to the ends of the earth to see you.'

'It had to be this way, Izzy. It wasn't safe. You don't understand how evil some people are. What lengths they will go to hurt you – to hurt people you love.'

'For God's sake – it's been twenty years, Meg! Okay, so life is never completely risk free, but it must be minimal risk by now. Whoever this person – these people – are you're afraid of might be dead, might be back in prison. Any which way they'll have much bigger fish to fry than you. You're just a minnow in their world. If you want to live, Meg, really live – not just exist – you have to accept an element of risk.'

'Is that what you think I've done – just exist?' she asked meekly.

'No, Meg, I don't think that. You've survived, that's different. Look around you, look at this successful business you've built – that's not existing. But I'm not sure it's living either – a life without love.' As soon as the unguarded words were uttered, she wished them unsaid. 'I'm sorry, Meg – I didn't mean it to come out like that – it's just that more than anything I always hoped you would find some love in your life, some happiness...'

'How do you know it's been a life without love. I might be married; I might have children. A lot can happen in twenty years,' she replied defensively.

'I know because he told me.'

'He?'

'Theo. Theo told me all about how you are with people.'

'That interfering toad, how dare he, what right has he to judge me—'

'He wasn't judging, Meg – he was trying to help. He was convinced something very bad had happened to you and wanted to help.'

'He thinks he can fix everyone, heal everyone. He believes he knows everything, and he knows nothing. Nothing! He's the most conceited man I ever met. Well, he can't heal me, no one can!' It was said with a venom that gave Izzy a glimpse of the sister she did not know and cautioned her to tread carefully. She did not want to spoil their first few hours together, so she steered her questions onto safer ground, trying to avoid any painful triggers. There would be time enough for that in the coming days, when Meg was ready to let her sister back in.

'Enough of Theo and his theories. I want to hear all about you and this amazing bakery of yours. You've done so well Meg. I'm really proud of you – must I call you Beth now?'

'We will always be Meg and Izzy. Perhaps it can still be like that just for us, like it was when we were kids. But I've been known as Beth here for twenty years so it might be less confusing if you refer to me as Beth to other people. It's not a falsehood...'

'Of course it's not,' interrupted Izzy, reassuringly. 'You've just reverted to your maiden name and chosen a diminutive of your middle name. Perfectly legal – and sensible in the circumstances. It made it harder for me to find you though,' she scolded.

'That was kind of the point. But please keep calling me Meg when we are alone. It reminds me of happier times. Tell me how you've been, Izzy. How's George? How's Shelley?'

'George died, Meg – five years ago. A heart attack. He was sixty-one. No age really, these days. It was a terrible shock when it happened, and I miss him like crazy. I wish he could have lived to see this, to see you so settled and so successful. He'd have been immensely proud of you.'

'I'm so sorry, Izzy. George gone! I can hardly believe it. He was so good to me – and such a good husband to you.' It was said without bitterness, without envy but it prompted her to add, 'I wonder if Bruce is still alive, he would be sixty-eight now.'

'Shelley's doing really well,' put in Izzy quickly, eager to turn the conversation. 'She takes after George. Gentle, kind, very artistic. She has her own pottery studio down in Cornwall with a little gallery.'

'Any grandchildren?'

'Not yet, but I'm hopeful. She and her partner, Carole, just have to decide which one of them will have the babies, or whether perhaps they might have one each.'

'Is Carole an artist too?'

'No. She's in hospitality – that's how they met. Carole was working in the local hotel. Shelley invited her to set up a café inside the gallery and it went from strength to strength, the café – and their relationship. The business is very tying so they can't get up to Barlaston very often. That's partly why I decided to retire early. The school terms were very limiting. I couldn't get down to Cornwall as often as I wanted to. I love my visits there. I like being by the sea. I'm planning to re-locate down there.'

'Oh, no! That's *so* far away.'

'There are motorways and trains, you know – you can even fly from Newquay.'

'I'm glad for her, Izzy. Glad she's found love. After what you and George had she must have wanted something special. I'm sure we'd get on famously.'

'Yes, she definitely struck gold with Carole. They are really good together.'

'I can't promise you real Cornish cream teas and smuggler coastlines but if Beth's scones and a windswept beach will suffice, you'll get plenty of that here.'

'I'm looking forward to exploring hereabouts.'

Beth insisted Izzy must stay with her. She would be her first-ever house guest. Before retiring to bed Izzy went to look at the photo of little Sid on the sideboard. It stood alone now. After Theo's accusations, Beth had taken the other one down. She came over to stand beside her sister. 'There's so much I have to tell you, about what I did to survive. You'll think me a very wicked sister.'

'I could never think that Meg. I'm not going anywhere fast. There's time enough for you to tell me when you're ready.'

*

Beth was ready sooner than Izzy anticipated. She slept late and awoke next morning with a clear sense of needing to make a clean breast of everything to her twin sister. That afternoon, they sat by the fire and Beth replayed the thirty years of her life that Izzy had missed. Izzy did not interrupt. She just listened, absorbing this alien world her twin had inhabited for three decades. When all was told, she took Beth's hands in hers, addressing her gently, but firmly.

'Meg, you are brave, you are strong, and you have borne more suffering than most of us could even conceive of, but all this has to stop now. You *have* to start living in the real world again. And you *have* to tell Theo.'

'I can't, Izzy. I'd be too ashamed. He wouldn't want to know me if he knew the truth. It's best I try and forget him.'

'You're wrong, Meg. I've only known the man for a few hours, but I know you've got this one badly wrong. He wasn't chasing a story. He was chasing you! He cares deeply for you, Meg. And if you knew what had happened to his wife, you would understood why he over-reacted about Sid.'

'Why? What happened to his wife?'

'It's not my place to tell you. Only Theo can do that.'

'I don't have a contact number for him. I've never needed one with him staying next door. Rhianne will have his mobile number—'

'I have it,' interrupted Izzy, fishing out a business card from her purse.

'Would you ring him for me?' asked Beth timidly.

'No, Meg. I will not.'

*

At four forty-five, Beth rang Theo. It was a time when they had taken so many walks together and she thought the memory would give her courage. Izzy had tactfully taken the opportunity to walk over to Briar Cottage and introduce herself to Eithan. She dialled the number.

'Theo Kendrick,' came the business-like response.

On hearing his voice, Beth almost lost her nerve. 'Theo, it's Beth,' she said uncertainly.

'Beth!'

'I'm sorry, Theo. I was wrong to have said those mean things to you.'

'No, no. It's me who got it wrong. If I'd known about Sidney, I would never have suggested for a moment—'

'You weren't to know. You acted in good faith. You have nothing to apologise for. I lied to you, Theo. I've lied to everyone. I've been living a lie for thirty years. If you can find it in your heart to forgive me, please would you come back so that I can explain everything to you. I owe you that even if it means you despise me once you know it all.'

'I couldn't despise you, Beth. No matter what you've done. I couldn't despise you. I'll leave first thing tomorrow.'

'I'll be waiting in West Cottage. I'm not working. Rhianne is in charge.'

*

When Theo rang her doorbell, it was a different Beth who answered, not the brusque woman he had grown used to. There was an awkwardness, almost a shyness in her greeting.

'Hello Theo, please come in.'

She turned to lead the way when he put his hand out to halt her. 'Beth,' he began, hesitantly, 'I'm sorry. I was wrong about everything, so wrong...'

'I was more wrong.' She lifted her head briefly, beautiful hazel eyes, soft and moist, pleading forgiveness.

As he entered the front room, he noticed it straight away: the photo of the grown-up solider had been removed from the sideboard. In its place was one of Izzy and George on their wedding day. He recognised the bespectacled groom from the newspaper cutting and the bouquet of roses, which he could see now in their full yellow glory. Sid's toy solider stood guard between the two picture frames.

When he was seated with tea and snacks, Beth said, 'I need to tell you everything, Theo. It's not pretty listening, and my shame knows no bounds, but we can't move forward until I can be honest with you.'

'Please let me go first, Beth. I have been wanting to tell you about Josie ever since that night at the Dog and Partridge. It's intricately connected with how I reacted about Sid so might make yours the easier to tell.'

'Of course,' said Beth, relieved she was going to find out about Josie at last, but a little thrown. She had been ready to make her confession, now she would have to psyche herself up again and hoped her courage would not fail her.

*

Theo paced the room in the telling of his story, but Beth sat perfectly still. Impassive, armoured, a seasoned combatant in the trenches of human suffering.

'She'd planned it, Beth,' he said eventually. 'She sent me on a fool's errand to get me out of the way. She'd planned it meticulously. She *wanted* to die. She *wanted* to leave me.'

Only at this point did Beth get up from her chair and go to him. She pulled him into her arms, embracing him silently. Soaking up his pain.

'I couldn't save our child and I couldn't save her,' he wept.

'And you've been punishing yourself ever since. You've worn your grief like a hair shirt.'

'Mia told me the same.'

'Then she has a wise head on her young shoulders. None of us can ever really know another's pain, Theo. Josie's must have been unbearable. She chose to end her pain. She wouldn't have wanted you to carry it forward to *your* grave.'

'That's why I got it wrong about Sid because I was so hung up on what had happened to Josie. It clouded my thinking.'

'You don't need to explain, Theo, I understand – I understand it all.' She kissed him softly on the lips.

*

It was Beth's turn, and her courage did not fail her. 'In the beginning it was something to help me get through the recovery period after the prison attack. Something to lose myself in, and then it became a sort of addiction I couldn't kick. I didn't think I was doing anything wrong. I wasn't hurting anyone. It was just something I made up in my head. A fantasy that kept me going, helped me survive. But it grew and grew, it lived with me day and night until the boundary between fantasy and reality started to blur. I think there was a point where I started to believe he really was still alive, that it had been a horrible nightmare I would wake up from.'

'What happened in the prison attack, Beth?' asked Theo, trying to steer her to a natural starting point.

'I was so pathetically green in those days. Yes, Bruce had been very jealous of me, very possessive of me with other men but it never occurred to me that how I looked could be a problem – or a threat – to other women. Well to one woman, a self-anointed queen among the prisoners. And a queen has to be much more beautiful than her commoners. I was too naïve to realise that none of the women around her were glamorous. Whether by accident or design, they all managed to look plain. She decided I was too pretty. It rankled with her. Two of them cornered me in the laundry. Two of her hench-bitches. She was very powerful, Becca. Had powerful friends on the outside. There were always plenty of hench-bitches lining up to do her bidding. She had some of the prison guards in her pocket too. I'm not sure if the laundry prison guard was in on it or not but they had arranged a disturbance to kick off, so the guard was distracted. She was only absent five minutes but that was more than enough time for what they intended to do.

'"If you think you're gonna topple Becca... think again, you little vixen," they said. "We know your game – wheedle your way into those guard dyke knickers so you can whore your way to the top of the hive. There can only be one queen around here and it's not going to be you." They threw me against the wall and then stamped on my arm when I was on the floor. One of them held me down while the other put a hot iron to my cheek. "Squeal and we'll make sure that cute little girl of yours gets a face ironing too – Charlotte, isn't it? We know where she lives, we know what school she goes to, and we know people who can fix it for us – people who aren't as gentle as us." They pressed the iron harder into my flesh. It was agony. I passed out.

'My right arm was broken in three places. It took a long time to heal so I learned to write with my left hand. I was hopeless initially, worse than any kid trying to wield a pencil for the first time. My attempts looked like something a five-year-old would bring home for a mother to pin on the fridge. That's when I got the idea. I started to pretend I really was five – a five-year-old Sid learning to write and draw for the first time. I folded a piece of paper and made a paper birthday card, "To Mummy, Happy Birthday, Love from Sid xx" and I drew stick figures: a boy giving a flower to his mummy.

'As the weeks went by I gradually improved. I drew a picture with crayons – the sort mothers proudly display on their kitchen walls. It was just about recognisable as a house with a smoking chimney, two windows, a door – and some flowers in the garden. I made another birthday card, another picture, and then another card and another picture. I did the same with Mother's Day cards. Each one just a little more skilled than the last, mimicking a child's developing drawing skills. I imagined each one was done by Sid. I got better and better at using my left hand. So even when my right arm was mended and I could write perfectly well with it, I kept up my daily left-hand practice. I got competent enough to produce birthday cards from Charlotte, simple ones at first to match her age and then more elaborate ones. As the years went by, I even made the later ones with my right hand because I thought she would probably be as good, if not better than me by then.'

'You never mentioned Charlotte. I had no idea you had a daughter.'

'I couldn't risk anyone knowing about her. I couldn't risk anyone harming her. You've no idea what long fingers these people have. How evil they are. I was in prison for twelve years. When I was released, I kept twelve birthday cards, twelve pictures and twelve Mother's Day cards and threw the others away.' She opened the top sideboard drawer to show him the Sidney cards.

'What about Charlotte's?' asked Theo.

'I keep those in my bedroom. I will show you those in a little while. It kept me going – I could lose myself in the fantasy of being a mother, of Sid still being alive and Charlotte not lost to me. I got carried away and couldn't stop at drawings. I invented a persona for Sid, what he might have become, how he might have looked. On my release, he would have been fourteen and

I daydreamed about an acne-peppered teenager, a very physical, outdoorsy type – football mad. And of course, I remembered how obsessed he was with his toy soldier. So, I began to imagine that he might have grown up wanting to be a soldier. During the three years I spent as the Cartwrights' kitchen assistant, the fantasy kept on growing. Sid was seventeen. I had him join the army. I had little experience of the forces, didn't know what kind of soldier he would have been, what regiment he would have joined, where he would have been based and where he would have served. It all came together for me when I was on one of my shopping trips to Millom. I spotted the framed photo in a bric-a-brac shop. It was of a young soldier in fatigues and next to it was the beret and cap badge from his picture. It was a moment of madness, I suppose, but I bought them both. The fiction took on a new and exciting reality. In my head, Sid became a real soldier. Of course he was a real soldier – I had a photo of him in uniform and I had his beret. I could make him anything I wanted. I could make him a hero. It was all in my head, so I believed it was harmless. The Troubles in Northern Ireland dominated the news at that time. In my fantasy, I decided Sid should be deployed to Belfast. I went to the library to try and find out what kind of regiment he might have been in. I liked the idea of the Parachutes, it sounded romantic and exciting, so I placed him in the Parachute battalion. If I'd researched more thoroughly, I would have discovered my schoolgirl error – you spotted it straight away, Theo – that the cap badge on the beret wasn't the Parachute battalion, it wasn't even from the right time period. But even if I had realised my mistake, I don't think it would have mattered because it was all a fantasy, the photo and the beret were just fantasy props.

'I got carried away. My three years as a drudge for the Cartwrights were hard. I worked all hours, and I kept my head down, hidden away in the bakery kitchen. I stayed away from people, I wanted to be anonymous. I wanted to be safe. I wanted Izzy to be safe. In some ways those three years were like an extension of prison. And just like in prison when my imaginary drawings took on a life of their own, soldier Sid grew and grew. I listened to all the news reports from Belfast on my radio so I could breathe life into my burgeoning fantasy. I kept the photo and beret on the bedside table in the attic room. No one ever went up there. It was my private sanctuary, and it was where I indulged my make-believe.'

'Did you create a persona for Charlotte as well?' asked Theo.

'Not in the same way as Sid. I didn't need to make her real. She already was real. She hadn't died, she was just lost to me. But I didn't want anyone knowing about Charlotte – just in case. So even in my head, I kept her locked away. Yes, sometimes I did wonder about her life in Canada, hoping she was happy – perhaps married with children of her own – but it was just idle wondering. When I took over the bakery from the Cartwrights and started to build my business, it became more complicated. I moved down from the attic to the first-floor rooms they had occupied. I never invited anyone into my private space, so Sid was safe. But as the business expanded and I started to take on staff and deal with more suppliers and tradesmen, I couldn't be the anonymous kitchen maid anymore. People noticed me and started to talk about me. Early on, I decided I wanted to be *Mrs* Brennan. It felt more solid, more sober – would command more respect than Miss Brennan. And I had to be a mother. There was just something that wouldn't let me deny my motherhood. But I couldn't be a mother of living children. There would be too many questions, too many risks. So that's when I decided soldier Sid had to die. My fantasy world gave him a hero's death. Killed in action – a roadside bomb. Hilda was the first person I shared the information with and Hilda being the gossip she is, soon did the rest for me. I didn't need to explain anything. Osmosis-like, Sid, the hero soldier, killed on active duty, just became a part of my new world. But once I'd told Hilda, I crossed the line from fantasy to falsehood. I felt guilty but I couldn't turn back, I had to keep up the lie. It wasn't difficult. I kept people at a distance. Rhianne was the first person to see his photo other than workmen.'

'And Charlotte?' he asked.

'I never mentioned Charlotte to anyone, not even to Rhianne. She was never part of my new world. I kept her in my heart and in the keepsakes in my bedroom. But she's thousands of miles away and lost to me for ever.' At this point, Beth's composure broke. 'I'm not proud of me. I'm a fantasist and a liar. I'm a sour, hard woman who could have been kinder,' she sobbed.

Theo took her in his arms. 'First and foremost, you're a survivor, Beth. What you describe are things you did to survive. And you're not fooling anyone with this sour, hard-skinned veneer. Look at what you've done for Rhianne and Eithan. Ask the Dixon kids. And as for Hilda – the woman adores you! Why else do you think she gets up before dawn to come and toil in a hot kitchen when she could be putting her feet up with her grandchildren? She comes out of loyalty, out of respect, out of love for you. Ask *me*, Beth Brennan, ask *me* what I think of you.'

Beth looked up at him, trying to take in all he was saying. Unsure of what to make of it all, what to make of him.

'What should I ask you Theo?' came the childlike response.

'Ask me why I stayed here long after Eithan was on the road to recovery. Long after he really needed me.'

'But I thought you stayed to finish your book.'

'At first, perhaps, but I could have written my book anywhere. I have a home. I have an office.'

'I... I...' she began in confusion.

'I stayed because I liked you. I wanted to be near you. To be your friend. To get to know you better. I wanted to help—'

'You mean, you wanted to heal me,' she interjected hotly. 'Another lame duck to add to your collection.'

'That's unfair, Beth and you know it!' he retorted angrily.

'Yes, that was unfair,' she conceded. 'You see, there's no hope for me. I'm bitter to the core.'

'Let's not fight about this. Not now, Beth. Not now we've come so far.'

She nodded quietly.

'Tell me about Charlotte.'

'You will need to come upstairs. I keep Charlotte locked away in my bedroom. She's safer that way.'

Theo followed Beth upstairs. He had often wondered what her bedroom was like. It was even more austere than her front room. A single, metal-framed bed, a chair, a wardrobe, a bedside cabinet and a chest of drawers were the only pieces of furniture. The curtains and duvet were a plain grey colour. It felt like a nun's cell, a prison cell. There was a framed photo of Charlotte on her bedside table, a pretty little girl with shoulder length dark hair in pigtails. Beth opened her chest of drawers and pulled out the cards she had spoken of earlier, some toys and some photos. Photos of Charlotte alone, Charlotte with Beth, Charlotte and Sid together. In another drawer were photos of Beth with Izzy and Izzy with George – and all the letters that Izzy had written to her in prison.

'I have to keep them hidden up here. It's how I've kept them all safe.'

Theo had not noticed it at first because it was lying on her pillow, not on the cabinet with the photo. He was looking at the Yevtushenko anthology he had given her. Beth saw where his eyes were resting. She stepped towards him. He took her in his arms and held her. It was as if time had stood still, and they were locked in that first embrace when colour had flooded into both their hearts. This time he did kiss her. A long, slow kiss. It all felt right. Wonderfully right.

'It's been two decades since I did this,' he said as he lifted her onto the bed.

'And even longer for me!'

'We'll figure it out.'

*

That night, Beth cooked for Theo and Izzy in West Cottage. Izzy chose her moment carefully. Once the dishes were cleared away, she swooped. 'You have an important decision to make, Meg... sorry... Beth.'

'What kind of decision, Izzy?' asked her sister.

'Charlotte,' came the simple but direct reply.

'Charlotte?'

'You have to decide if you want to see Charlotte again. Theo has offered to try and find her. He's good at finding needles in haystacks.'

Beth looked shocked. The blood drained from her face. 'Even if you found her, she might not want to see me. I'm a convicted criminal. I'd be an embarrassment to her. She's been damaged enough, she may still be mute, I can't risk bringing her any more pain.'

'She will almost certainly have regained her speech,' said Theo confidently. 'And you are speculating about her pain – you could just as easily speculate the opposite: that being reunited with her mother would be restorative. I know you hate me talking about healing, but it might give her some kind of closure. You were torn from her, her brother was torn from her, cruelly, abruptly, it's beyond traumatic. Admittedly, she may not want to resurrect the past. But can you live with not knowing, Beth? Don't you think she deserves to make the choice for herself?'

'But don't you see,' replied Beth with renewed bitterness, 'having to choose *IS* the pain. She was seven and a half. Old enough to be afraid of the police, old enough to fear the wrath of her father, old enough to understand his threats – pleas even. The truth would put her father in prison, a lie would put her mother in prison. It was an impossible choice for any child to make, let alone a grieving child whose only sibling had just died almost in front of her eyes. She took refuge in mutism. Can you imagine what *pain* she must have endured to drive her to that? There is no way on God's earth I am going to be the cause of any more pain for her. No more about choices and choosing. Let sleeping dogs lie. It's better this way.'

It was Izzy who spoke up then. 'Charlotte's not a child anymore, she's a grown woman of thirty-eight. You can't deny her the opportunity to see her mother again, if she chooses to. You're not asking a child to make a choice; you're asking a mature adult.'

'Please trust me, Beth,' said Theo. 'I know you don't have much time for head shrinks as you call us, but if I find her, I will handle the situation sensitively. I promise no harm to Charlotte. If I thought there was any risk of harm, I would pull back. I'm not going to go wading in with size thirteen boots.'

Izzy spoke up again. 'You've carried this for thirty years, Meg, let someone else take the load now. It's not a weakness to accept help.'

'And you really think you could find her? After all these years. Thousands of miles away…' asked Beth of Theo.

'If she's alive, I'll find her. I won't rest until I find her. Even if it turns out better to leave her in judicious ignorance, at least I can come back and update you on the woman she's grown into. If she's married, if she has children, what kind of house she lives in, whether she has a career – surely you would want to know how she's turned out? If she's happy?'

'Yes, yes – oh yes, of course! I would treasure every little nugget about her,' replied Beth, her face softening as she began to believe the unimaginable might be possible.

'Then let me do this for you, Beth,' he responded, taking both her hands in his.

'You promise zero harm…?'

'I promise zero harm,' came the earnest reply.

'Then yes,' she said, more animatedly, lifting her head to look at him and nodding as she spoke, 'yes.'

'I'll get started in the morning. Izzy, is there anything you can remember at all? Anything that would shrink the haystack?'

'When they first left, I remember Jacky talking about Edmonton,' replied Izzy. 'But it was thirty years ago, they might have gone anywhere since then.'

'At least it's a start. Would Jacky talk to me, do you think? She might even know where they are currently living.'

Izzy shook her head. 'I could never get a peep out of her. I wanted to be able to correspond with Charlotte. At least keep the door open for the future. Jacky feigned ignorance. She's terrified of Rob. And they both perjured themselves, remember, so they would be very tight about it all. I've had no contact with her for nearly thirty years. She may not even live in the same house anymore.'

'Let me have the address anyway, Izzy. I can track her from that, and I might be able to prize a lead out of her.'

'You'd have to get her on her own, she'd never talk to you with Rob there.'

'Don't worry, Izzy. I know what I'm doing. My years as an investigative journalist weren't wasted. I'm good at this.'

Theo left after breakfast. Beth found it a bitter-sweet departure. She was happy at the prospect that he might find Charlotte but sad to be losing him just as their relationship had taken off.

*

Theo found the address Izzy had given him without any trouble. An elderly woman opened the door only as far as the safety chain would allow.

'Mrs Dagnall?' he enquired, through the small gap.

'What do you want?'

'My name is Dr Theo Kendrick,' and he passed his card to her through the gap. 'I'm hoping you can help me find your niece, Charlotte Dagnall.'

'Get lost,' she replied curtly and was about to slam the door, but Theo jammed it with his foot.

'Please hear me out, Mrs Dagnall. This is a very sad case. She's your niece, you must care about her.'

'She was a sweet kid, but it's a long time ago.'

'I want to find her and give her the opportunity to choose if she wants to be reunited with her family, that includes you and your husband of course.'

'Rob's been dead these two years.'

'I'm very sorry to hear that,' he said, all the while thinking this might make his task a whole lot easier.

'I lost touch with Bruce after Rob died. Don't know if he's still in the same place.'

'If you happen to have the last address for him, it would be a big help.'

She looked at him long and hard and pulled her thin shawl closer around her shoulders.

'Wait there,' she instructed. She checked the chain lock was securely in place and then shuffled off into the house. When she returned, she poked a piece of paper through the gap in the door on which Theo could see she had written an address.

'Thank you, Mrs Dagnall. You've done a great kindness today.' He'd taken five steps when she called after him, releasing the chain lock and opening the door as if she would pursue him.

'Wait!' she cried, taking a few steps towards him. 'If you do find Charlotte, tell her Auntie Jacky sends her love... and... and just say she's real sorry for everything. She'll understand.'

'Any message for Bruce?'

'No,' she replied, bitterly. 'Hell could freeze over before I'd have owt to say to him. Charlotte, though, Charlotte was a sweet kid. And Sid was a cutie, bless his little soul. Tragic it was, tragic. Couldn't have any of me own. Lost five trying. Sweet kids both of them, yeah, sweet kids.'

Standing outside her front door, Theo was seeing her properly for the first time. She was very frail. Her slippers were worn and her shawl almost threadbare.

'Forgive the impertinence, Mrs Dagnall, I suspect you've had a very hard life, I hope the remainder is easier – and happier. As I said, you've done a great kindness today and I thank you.'

She nodded listlessly and then went inside, bolting the door behind her.

*

Theo looked at the address written neatly on the paper. It was in a place called Beaumont, Edmonton. This was a better start than he could have hoped for. If Bruce was still around Edmonton only two years ago it was likely he had put down roots there when they first emigrated. Charlotte, at thirty-eight, was unlikely to be still living with her father. Bruce would be unwilling to disclose his daughter's whereabouts, so he was going to have to use stealth. Theo had no compunction about resorting to deception. He had done it many times in his journalist days and Bruce was hardly innocent prey. He would need warm clothing. Alberta would be chilly in early April.

PART THREE

Charlotte

Beaumont, Canada, March 2004

The funeral had gone off well enough, a few close friends, Zac and the boys of course, but now that her father was cold in the ground, Charlotte felt numb. Her body had gone on strike, unable to cope with so many conflicting emotions swirling around.

'Penny for them,' said Zac, pulling her into his arms as they stood in their kitchen looking at the debris from the simple wake they had laid on for well-wishers.

'A thousand pennies wouldn't be enough, Zac. I don't know how I feel, or what I think, there's just this great emptiness.'

'He was a huge part of your life, there's bound to be a big hole. Give yourself time, go gently. It will all come right soon enough.'

'I loved him, of course I did, he was my dad, and he was good to me once we moved to Canada – indulged me even. But there's a part of me that hated him too. Hated his cowardice and his treachery, hated how he hid behind the skirts of a seven-year-old girl. He stole my childhood, Zac. He wrenched me from my family, killed my brother and betrayed my mother. And he trapped me. How could I choose? It was an impossible choice. I ought to loathe him, yet I still loved him.'

'It's only natural you loved him, honey, he was your father. Apart from me and the kids he was the only family you've had these past thirty years.'

'It's just that… just…'

'Just what, honey?'

'Just that I hoped he would confess at the end, when he knew he was dying, when he knew they couldn't touch him. I thought at least he would admit what he'd done. Perhaps even ask my forgiveness, but he died the way he'd lived: looking after number one.'

'In his own way, I think he did try to make amends, just not brave enough to do the right thing.'

'It completely broke him, losing Sid. He gave up drinking. Never touched a drop after the accident. Every penny he earned he set aside for me. Anything I wanted, a pony, a car. And he was a better man for being away from Uncle Rob. I never liked Uncle Rob, he frightened me. I know Auntie Jacky was terrified of him, I used to see her shrink when he shouted at her. I feel so conflicted, Zac. I despised him but felt sorry for him all at the same time, if that's possible.'

'Of course it's possible. Emotions aren't black and white, and you've certainly had a colourful cocktail. Give yourself time, Charlotte. You need time to grieve. Don't try and square off all the circles until you've had time to get around them. And before you accuse me of being a medical pedant, that's not the GP talking, that's your husband who loves you more than anything in the world.' He pulled her closer and kissed her gently.

'I'm so lucky to have found you, Zac Adams.'

'Not half so lucky as me to have found you.'

'No time for canoodling when there's all this to clear up. And there'll be Dad's stuff to sort out up at his place.'

'Take it slow, whizz kid. There'll be time enough for all that when you've got your head straight.'

'We're a head doctor now, are we?' she teased him.

'Leave it till the weekend at least.'

'I just feel guilty being on compassionate leave and not making a start.'

'But you've only one more day before you go back. Have that day to yourself.'

'Alright. But this lot can't wait till the weekend – I'll wash, you dry, Dr Adams,' she said, throwing him a teacloth.

*

Charlotte heeded Zac's advice and did not go up to her father's house until the weekend. The house was adjacent to his garage business – repairs and used motor sales. It would all have to be sold. Hopefully someone would want the house and business together. Bruce would have liked his grandchildren to carry on the business but Anna, now sixteen, wanted to become an actress, or a model or a pop star – or possibly all three – and Jarrad, aged fourteen, was showing early signs of wanting to follow his father into the medical profession.

Charlotte wandered aimlessly through the rooms of the house she had grown up in but not lived in since her marriage to Zac, seventeen years ago. The house had been empty for almost a month. She went from room to room opening windows and paused in his bedroom. This was the last part of the house he had occupied before his transfer to the hospice. She sat on the bed and smoothed her hand across his pillow where he had lain his head, waiting to die. Pancreatic cancer was a killer. Zac had told her there would be no hope and they had not hidden the truth from him. He had known he was dying which made it harder to forgive his unwillingness to show any remorse for the cowardly betrayal of his wife. She thought she might as well start in this room as any. She pulled three black refuse sacks from her holdall: one for the charity store, one for garbage and one for any memorabilia she might want to keep.

She sorted through his chest of drawers. There were a few bits and pieces that could go to the charity store, but it would mostly have to be binned. In the bottom drawer was a shoe box. There were no shoes in it, just a lot of cards. They seemed to be birthday cards. She sat on the bed and tipped them out in case there were any she would like to keep. She recognised some of the ones she had given him as a child. She put a few of these to one side. Perhaps she would keep them. They represented the happiest part of her time with her father. The other birthday cards had pictures of beer glasses and footballs, cars and sordid cartoons. Before she opened them, she knew they must be from Uncle Rob. Two cards stood out because of their large forty and fifty numerals. She opened the first. Inside, Rob had scrawled, *The big 4-0 little bro. Can't see my way to getting out to see you anytime soon but me and the lads will raise a glass to you in the Plough tonight. Twin bitch has been sniffing around again, whining about wanting to send stuff out for Charlotte but Jacky knows to keep it zipped. Have a good one!*

Charlotte felt sick. She worked out she would have been ten on his fortieth and they would have been in Canada almost two years. Two years! Two years Aunt Izzy had been trying to reach her. How could he have been so cruel as to deny her access to Aunt Izzy – and lovely Uncle George. Perhaps her mother had been trying to find her also? Hastily she opened the fiftieth card. *Old man of 50 now, bro. Got laid off from Michelin, bit short of the readies, so if you can spare a few quid to tide me over that would be neat. Have a good one!*

She sifted through the rest of the cards and right at the bottom was a thin paper pamphlet. It was a copy of Rob's funeral service dated 2001. Inside was a note on a small piece of paper written in neat handwriting.

Rob passed away. It was a perforated ulcer. There's no call for you and me to have anything to do with each other now. Don't worry, I'll keep your grubby secret. I'm not doing time for nobody, least of all you. I'm guessing Rob never told you she had to serve 12 years in the end. I hope you rot in hell.

Jacky

Charlotte gasped as the note slipped from her fingers. She paced the room, hot with anger then went to get a pair of scissors from the bathroom cabinet and set about the pillow she had so recently caressed, stabbing and slashing and shrieking until it lay in tiny pieces on the carpet.

'You fucking coward! Lily-livered fucking coward! I hope you ARE burning in hell! Do you hear me, Dad, I hope you ARE burning in hell!'

Hoarse from shouting, she piled the contents back into the box and carried it out to her car, leaving the half-full black sacks languishing on the carpet. On the short drive home, she thumped the steering wheel in fury. The kids were out, and Zac had just got back from his Saturday morning surgery. He saw her pull onto the drive, slam the car door and run into the house.

'Whoa, whoa – hey what's all this?!' he asked as she charged into the kitchen and threw her car keys and the box on the worktop.

'I hate him! I fucking hate him! I thought I loved him, but he was a monster. No one can love a monster.'

Zac took her in his arms and held her close. 'Tell me what's happened, honey.'

'I found some cards and some notes, Zac. The bastard told me my mother served eight months, but she did twelve years! TWELVE YEARS! Look here, look at this note I found from Auntie Jacky.'

Charlotte rooted out the note from the box to show to Zac and then dived back in to get the funeral pamphlet. 'He's a monster, Zac. A fucking monster. And all that time I thought she had abandoned me. God, Zac, I was twenty before she got out. I could have gone to England under my own steam if I'd known. And Aunt Izzy tried to write to me, but Uncle Rob wouldn't give her the address. Two years! Two years she kept trying to reach me. He lied to me. He was a liar and a thief. He stole my mother from me and Aunt Izzy and Uncle George. I can't forgive him Zac.' Her rant finally gave way to a torrent of tears as she buried her head in her husband's shirt.

'You will in time, honey. It's the shock. He was your dad. You'll find a way to forgive him. Give it time.'

As Charlotte wiped her face with a piece of kitchen roll, Zac filled the kettle. Tea was always good in moments of crisis.

'It's stirred it all up, Zac. Most of the time it's locked away in a forgotten past, a forgotten life. I can hardly remember what she looked like. I do remember I thought she was very pretty and wished I could have had blonde hair like hers.'

'I've always preferred brunettes,' he said gallantly and was rewarded with a faint, if distracted smile.

'I remember the smell of her and some little things like her putting my hair in pigtails and making me guess what colour ribbon it was going to be. And the hugs – so many hugs: bedtime hugs, school gate hugs – and storytime. I loved it when we read books together, but everything else is just a blur.'

'That's only natural, Charlotte. It's thirty years ago.'

'Aunt Izzy and Auntie Jacky are just hazy, ghostly images although I remember some things about them – like Auntie Jacky letting me play with her make-up and always buying me an ice cream when we heard the jingle in the street. She'd spoil me with sweets and cakes – iced donuts were my favourite and she used to put a chocolate flake in them like when we had the ice creams. And Aunt Izzy letting me play on her piano. And Uncle George, dear Uncle George, letting me use his paints and his easel. He made me feel so grown up. He was gentle and kind, like you Zac, just not as handsome.'

'It's good to have some nice memories, Charlotte, not just the bad stuff.'

'I can't get Mummy out of my head. She'll be fifty-six now. Who knows how much longer she might have – she might even be dead. What a horrible thought that your own mother might be dead, and you not even know it. It's my fault, you know. If I could have found my voice, I could have said something.'

'I wish you'd stop torturing yourself like this, Charlotte. You were a child, for God's sake. You have nothing to blame yourself for. You're a victim not a perpetrator.'

'I'm not sure there's a difference,' she replied.

*

It was three in the morning when Zac realised his wife was no longer in bed beside him. He went in search of her and found her sitting at the kitchen table staring at the contents of the box she had brought home.

'Hey, there,' he said gently. 'You need your sleep, Charlotte. Let this go, at least for tonight.'

Charlotte seemed lost in thought. 'It wasn't hidden on the top of the wardrobe, in a trunk in the attic or buried in that workshop of his. He left it in plain sight in his sock drawer. He *meant* me to find it, Zac. A man who is devious enough to frame his wife for a drink driving death is devious enough to hide or destroy anything incriminating. He *meant* me to find this. He wasn't man enough to tell me to my face. It was his confession. A coward's confession.'

Zac sat down next to her and took her hands in his. Words seemed inadequate.

'I want to find her, Zac. I have to find her.'

'I know you do, honey, and I understand.'

'She could have another thirty years in her yet. Thirty years to make up for the thirty I've already lost. If she's alive, I have to find her. And if she's dead, I have to visit her grave. You understand, don't you?'

He nodded sadly, knowing full well what was coming next.

'I'm thinking of asking for a career break, take a bit of time out. We can manage without my salary for a while. There's plenty of money from Dad's estate. I want to try and find her. I can't remember where Auntie Jacky lives but the name of the church was on the funeral pamphlet so I can start from there. You don't mind looking after the kids for a little while? They're old enough to sort themselves out, they just need someone to keep an eye on them. I'd be back within a month and if I find her, perhaps we could all go over there in the summer for a few weeks. I would want her to meet her grandchildren, Zac. You do understand, don't you?' she asked again.

'Yes, of course I understand, honey. But don't act too hastily, please. Take a couple of weeks before you burn any boats. You're in a highly emotional state. Best to make these kinds of momentous decisions in a rational frame of mind. There's no desperate hurry. The hospital would have you back like a shot so I'm sure a negotiated career break won't be an issue.'

'What *is* the issue then?' asked Charlotte, sensing there was something else.

'I just don't want you to get your hopes up too high. She may not be alive, you may not be able to find her, she may have remarried with a new family or, I'm sorry to have to be the one to say it, she may not want to see you, Charlotte. She may have grown very bitter over the years. Twelve years in prison, that's a pretty hard gig!'

'I could have spared her that, if I'd spoken up.'

'We've been through this endlessly, Charlotte. The only thing that could have saved her was a confession from your father.'

'I still want to make it right though, if I can.'

'Just don't get too keyed up, honey, I don't want you to get crushed by disappointment if it doesn't work out the way you want it to.'

She nodded her assent. 'I can do some prep on the internet before I leave. Try and find some court reports, see if I can get any clues as to where she might have gone when she was released. Aunt Izzy will know but I can't remember her address, it was somewhere near a pottery factory but in thirty years, she is likely to have moved on.'

'Try searching telephone directories...'

'I can't remember her surname, isn't that awful! I can only remember her as Aunt Izzy – Aunt Izzy and Uncle George.'

'You were only eight when you came to Canada, it's only to be expected...'

'They were so kind and nice, how could I have forgotten their name! Auntie Jacky was married to dad's brother so she will have the same surname, Dagnall. She's quite a bit older, but I could see if she's still in that area. Uncle Rob worked at the same factory as dad. I can't remember which one, but it wasn't a pottery factory.'

'You'll figure it out, honey. Go gently. Give yourself time.'

'Would you come up to his house with me? I don't want to go there on my own again, I'm scared of what I might find.'

'Of course I'll come with you, but not today, sweetheart. You've had enough of a shock. A nice long walk and then a Zac Sunday barbecue is in order I think.'

She smiled at him and hugged him. 'Don't ever change, Zac Adams, don't ever stop being so wonderful.'

*

After checking into a motel near the airport and a strong cup of coffee, Theo set to work, refusing to give in to the jet lag that was threatening to take its toll. He searched for Dagnall in the domestic and commercial telephone directories and found what he was looking for. An advert for Dagnall Motors in the commercial section. He cross-checked it with a B.A. Dagnall in the domestic section. That had to be him. He looked at the commercial advert:

All motor repairs undertaken,
Fast reliable service.
Vehicle roadworthy checks,
Exhausts, tyres, wheel balancing.
Used models for sale.
Vehicles bought for cash, any condition.

His eyes rested on 'used models for sale' and he visibly relaxed. He had found his entry path. All he needed now was a place to hole up, not too far from the garage. The map he had purchased showed the garage sited near an interchange of two highways.

*

Next morning, Theo checked out of the motel and rented a hire car. He toured the Beaumont area and was surprised at how attractive it was. From his French, he knew that *beau mont* meant *beautiful hill* and driving up the scenic hill with its picturesque church, he could understand why. He had never been to Canada before and was already fascinated by what he had seen. Theo drove past Dagnall's garage but did not stop. For now, he just needed a sighter. Small, local establishments were much better for picking up intelligence than international hotels, so he eschewed the Holiday Inn in favour of Maisie's Diner with Rooms, which was only a twenty-minute walk from Dagnall's place. He had expected a greasy transport café, so was pleasantly surprised by Maisie's Diner. The white plastic tables were functional, but neatly spaced out on a sparklingly clean floor. Low volume piped music was just audible above the noisy bustle. At eleven o'clock on a Sunday morning it was busy. He spied an empty table and made a swift beeline for it. He was equally surprised by the menu, which, in addition to the usual all-day breakfast, featured vegan dishes and 'calorie light' options. He chose smoked salmon and avocado on toasted sourdough bread. The smiley waitress was very young, fifteen or sixteen, he thought. When he paid the bill, he made sure to leave a large tip and asked whether there were any rooms vacant.

'I think there must be, but you'll need to talk to my mum. She's in the kitchen, I'll go and get her. Mum!' shouted Rosie above the noise of the blender. 'There's a man asking about a room. Seems nice. He left a huge tip – and I think he's from the UK.'

'Okay, I'm coming. Chalet number three's empty. Just let me finish this salsa dip and I'll be out.'

Rosie went back to Theo. 'Mum says she'll be out in a minute, if you don't mind hanging on. Would you like a free refill?'

'Yes, please that would be very nice. Is your mum Maisie?'

'Yes, and I'm Rosie. I'm still at school but I help out at the weekends.'

'Well, I'm pleased to meet you, Rosie,' he said proffering his hand. 'I'm Theo.'

'Are you from the UK?'

'Yes. First time in Canada. Love it already.'

'Have to get the next order in. But thanks for waiting.'

Rosie disappeared into the kitchen. 'He's *nice*, Mum!' she said dreamily, ever the hopeful matchmaker. 'So polite – and I just love his accent. A bit older than you, Mum, but looks in great shape.'

'Rosie!' scolded her mother. 'Behave yourself!'

Maisie had to agree with her daughter, Theo Kendrick did have a gorgeous voice and very polite manners. She showed him Chalet number 3 which he said was perfect and gave her a week's rent in advance. 'Is there anything else I can help you with, Dr Kendrick?' She'd noticed the 'Dr' on the driving licence he produced on registration.

'I'm in a rental just now, but if I'm going to be here a while, I was wondering about buying a second-hand car, I noticed there was a place selling used cars up the road. Do you know if it's a reliable garage? I don't want to get stung by a cowboy outfit.'

'That'll be Bruce's place. Dagnall Motors.'

'Yes, I think that was the name.'

'It's got a good reputation round here. I've always had my van serviced there and was planning to ask Bruce to look out for a little runabout for Rosie when she passes her test. But the old guy died a couple of weeks ago. I did the catering for the funeral. Not sure what's going to happen to the garage now. I expect Charlotte will sell it. She's handling everything. There were a few cars for sale on the forecourt last time I was over there so you might be lucky. I don't think Charlotte will have sent them to auction just yet. She would probably be glad to make a sale. You might get a good discount. Do you want me to ring Charlotte for you?'

'Sounds like you know Charlotte very well.'

'We go back a long way. Her daughter and my Rosie are best friends. In the same class at school.'

'Well, thank you, yes. That would be very kind of you. But I don't want to intrude on her grief if she's just buried her father.'

'You might be doing her a favour if you take a motor off her hands. Anyway, she can always say no, so what's the harm in asking?'

Theo thanked his host with a charming outward smile, a faint imitation of the inward beam spreading through his whole body. He couldn't believe his luck. Bruce was dead.

*

Charlotte and Zac had not long arrived at her father's house. 'Do you mind making a start on the loft while I finish clearing out the kitchen,' Charlotte said.

'Sure. Just shout me if anything spooks you,' replied Zac, as he heard Charlotte's mobile ringing.

'Hi Maisie, how goes it?' asked Charlotte.

'It's pretty busy over here so I can't be long, just thought you'd like to know I've let a chalet to a guy from England. Nice chap, a doctor. Says he wants to buy a used motor so I thought I should point him in your direction.'

'Thanks, Maisie. Zac and I are over at Dad's now, sorting stuff out, so today would be good if he wants to come over.'

'He was worried it would be an intrusion – hope you don't mind but I explained about your dad dying. He's that kind of a bloke, sensitive like.'

'No, it'll be fine, Maisie. Zac is here with me and to be honest I'd be glad to offload one of them. It would be one less to get to auction.'

'That's what I thought. Okay – must dash. Oh, nearly forgot. His name is Dr Kendrick. Theodore Kendrick. I've seen his driving licence ID so he's kosher.'

'Thanks, Maisie.' She put her phone away. 'Some English guy has checked into Maisie's place and might want to buy a used motor. I said he could come over to have a look at what we've got while we're here.'

'It would be good to offload one – but are you sure you're up to it, honey? Do you want me to see him?'

'I'll be fine, Zac. Besides, I know a lot more about cars than you. Dad made sure I grew up knowing my way round an engine.

I'll have to get the keys from his office in case he wants to take a test drive.'

'Are you sure he won't drive off in one?'

'I trust Maisie. She said he was kosher.'

'Okay – well keep your mobile handy. I'll be right here if you need me.'

*

At 1.45pm, Theo walked onto the garage forecourt of Dagnall Motors. A tall woman emerged from the office with a bunch of keys in her hand. Even with her dark hair he would have known her anywhere. She had a more athletic build than Beth and was a couple of inches taller, all of six feet he estimated, but she had the same hazel eyes and sculpted cheekbones.

'Dr Kendrick?' she enquired.

'Yes, Maisie recommended you. I'm interested in buying a second-hand car. Nothing too fancy, just something to tide me over while I decide whether I want to settle in Beaumont.'

'Maisie said you were from England. I would have guessed as much. Not many people would say "second-hand car" round here.'

'Yes. My first time in Canada. Loving it already,' came the practised patter.

'I'm from England originally,' she said, making polite conversation. 'Long time ago, I was only eight at the time, not been back since.'

'I was sorry to hear about your father. Please pass my condolences to your mother.'

He had played his gambit and held his breath.

She stopped in her tracks, keys jangling nervously in her hand. It was an innocent, polite remark. He was not to know but she was suddenly thrown.

'My mother didn't come with us. She... she got left behind. Now that Dad's dead, I'm planning a trip to England to see if I can find her.'

It was all he needed. He took three steps towards her and turned her to face him.

'I'm not here to buy a second-hand car, Charlotte. I'm here to help you find your mother. It's she who sent me.'

'What?' she said weakly. 'What did you say? My *mother* sent you. But... but—'

Just then Zac came running towards them. He had been watching warily from the house and on seeing Theo physically turn Charlotte to face him, had run out at full pelt. 'Take your hands off her, do you hear me! What the hell do you think you're playing at? Get out of here. We can do without your kind of custom.'

'He's come about my mother,' said Charlotte feebly. 'He's found her...' Zac got to her side just in time to catch her as she fainted.

'It's the shock,' said Theo, his regular authoritative manner taking over. 'Let's get her to a chair – and some water.'

'What the hell is going on?' snarled Zac, holding Charlotte protectively. 'Who the fuck do you think you are!'

Theo fished out some ID from his pocket. This time not the driving licence he had shown Maisie but his professional lanyard. 'My name is Dr Theodore Kendrick. I'm a clinical psychologist and a close friend of Charlotte's mother, Margaret Elizabeth Dagnall née Brennan.'

Charlotte was coming round. 'It's alright, Zac. Let's hear what he has to say.'

Zac still looked doubtful, but he allowed Theo to follow them to the kitchen where he sat his wife down and insisted she drank some water, not because Theo had advised it, but because he was a GP for God's sake and knew how to look after his own wife.

'I sincerely apologise for the initial deception, but I had to be sure that you would welcome news of your mother. She made me promise zero harm, that if I judged you would rather she were dead to you, I shouldn't volunteer her desire to be reunited with you.'

'Hardly zero harm,' growled Zac, still deeply suspicious.

'Please tell us what you know about my mother,' begged Charlotte.

*

Theo told them everything – even his own bumbling mistakes – and showed them photos on his mobile phone, including a recent one of Beth and Izzy together. Zac watched his wife's face as she took in the whole story, worried it would be too much for her on top of her recent bereavement and the discovery of her father's treachery.

'I'd only just found out about her being in prison for twelve years last weekend when I was going through Dad's things. He told me she served eight months! I thought she must have abandoned me. All those years I thought she must hate me because I never spoke up.'

'She loves you with every breath of her body, Charlotte. She didn't abandon you. She set you free to protect you. She's an amazing woman your mother, an amazing human being.'

'Are you married to my mother? Are you my stepfather?' It was a perfunctory question, asked without emotion, but it pitched Theo off balance. She was asking a question he had not even faced himself.

'No, I'm not your stepfather, though I'd be very proud to be. No, I'm not married to your mother. I'd like to be if she would have me, but I don't think she's ready for that kind of commitment. Look, it's nine-thirty in the UK at present, your mother will still be up. Would you like to speak to her?'

'I can speak to her! Right now – you mean, now, this minute?'

'This second even,' he said pulling out his mobile.

'Oh, yes, oh yes please…'

Theo dialled the number and then passed the phone to Charlotte.

'Theo – is that you. Hello? Theo?'

'It's me, Mummy – it's Charlotte. It's Charlotte.'

Shawls and Slippers

It was all arranged with lightning speed. Charlotte didn't let grass grow under her feet. As she had not been to England in thirty years, she thought it prudent to go back with Theo who was willing to wait while she served out her notice before taking an agreed career break. She finished clearing out her father's house, sent the cars to auction – minus two little runabouts she kept back, one for Anna and one for Rosie. She handed the keys for the house and garage to the estate agent and set about planning what she would pack for her trip to England. Back in the UK, Eithan showed Beth how to use Skype on his laptop so that she could speak to Charlotte and Theo most days. In the summer, Zac was to organise a locum so that the whole family could visit and Jarrad and Anna could meet their English grandmother. Anna was excited to be going to England and was already checking what shows were on in London's West End.

'Cumbria is a long way from London,' her father cautioned.

'There'll be trains, though, Dad, there's bound to be trains.'

Rosie did not know if she was more disappointed that her best friend was going to be missing the whole of the summer or that the fantasy of her mother marrying a charming English doctor was now in tatters. But the little blue motor Anna's mum had put aside for her would be an exciting diversion.

*

Beth, despite her eagerness to be reunited with her daughter, would not travel to the airport to meet her. Izzy had insisted it was all perfectly safe, but Beth still felt nervous about either her or Izzy being seen to be connected to Charlotte in such a public place as an airport.

'It's been thirty years for God's sake, Meg,' said an exasperated Izzy.

'I don't care. I want to know she is safe all the way up to Silecroft. I've waited over thirty years; I can wait a few hours longer.'

It was agreed that Matt would pick them up. Beth could not settle. She was up and down like a yo-yo.

'Shall I make us another cup of tea?' she asked Izzy.

'That would be the third in an hour, Meg. I don't think my bladder can cope. Try and relax, they'll be here very soon.'

Beth smoothed her hands across the dress she was wearing and patted her newly styled hair, which felt like it belonged to someone else. She'd gained a few pounds since giving up smoking but was still slender: slim rather than waif-like. It suited her.

'I'm so nervous. What if she doesn't like me when she sees me for real? What if this is too horrible for her to stomach?' she said, pawing at the scar on her cheek.

'It won't make a scrap of difference. She's coming to see her mum not some catwalk queen. Relax, Meg, it will be fine. Trust me. It will be better than fine.'

And then, all of a sudden they were there – earlier than expected. Beth rushed to open the front door as Charlotte jumped out of the car to what Theo would later describe as a mother-daughter Yevtushenko hug. Beth broke off from embracing her daughter to speak briefly to Theo. 'Thank you,' she whispered. 'Thank you from the bottom of my heart.'

'I'll be off then, you'll need some private time with Charlotte,' said Matt, ever the diplomat.

'Thanks again, Matt,' said Theo.

'Any time, Uncle Theo, any time.'

*

It had been agreed Izzy would stay with Rhianne and Eithan so that Beth and Charlotte could have uninterrupted time together in West Cottage. Theo planned to keep his distance for a couple of days to let mother and daughter get reacquainted and retired to Middle Cottage attic to put some serious writing time in. He popped down into the bakery kitchen in the morning, for old times' sake. Rhianne was running the show like she had been doing it all her life and Hilda was grinning from ear to ear, although when she spotted Theo, she pounced on him.

'Not an 'air on 'er 'ead, I sed, rememb'r! Proper lame-brain yer is. Just as well it worked owt. Yer'd 'av 'ad me to ansa t' if it 'adn't.'

Theo had the good grace to look chastened. 'I meant well, Hilda. The wires just got a bit tangled up.'

'That's what I sed abowt you clever folk. Don't allers knoa the diff'rence in yer wires. Don't yer go untanglin' no more, yer hear me!'

'I hear you, Hilda. Good and loud, I hear you.'

*

Theo was surprised that afternoon to hear a knock on his door and find Beth standing there. 'Beth! I hadn't expected to see you for a couple of days. I thought you and Charlotte would be inseparable.'

'We are – and it's wonderful, but I wanted to come and thank you properly.'

'Your smile is all the thanks I need. I'm glad it's worked out. Love the new hairstyle by the way – not that I didn't like the old one! Oh God, that came out all wrong. I'm such a clumsy oaf. You never have to dress up for me, Beth – or anyone else for that matter – you're beautiful to me inside and out.'

'I didn't do it for you, or for anyone else. Not even for Charlotte. I did it for me because I wanted to. I want to put the old life behind me. Make the best of what I can be – for *me*. It matters to *me*, Theo.'

'Then that's the best reason in the world, Beth.'

'Charlotte has gone over to visit Eithan. She thought he might be feeling lonely with Rhianne working long hours at present.'

'Looks like we've both got some time to kill. I wonder what we could get up to?'

*

Izzy announced she needed to go home for a couple of days to sort a few things out at Sycamore Lodge and offered to take Charlotte with her to revisit some of her childhood haunts and see her Auntie Jacky. The timing of this sudden decision had, of course, nothing to do with a new closeness she'd noticed between Beth and Theo and how much they might benefit from a few days to themselves. Charlotte remembered very little of Staffordshire. She was amazed at Aunt Izzy's magnificent home that had been transformed from the ramshackle house she thought she remembered. It had the feel of a renovated manor house. Her aunt attributed her good fortune to the senior management role Uncle George had enjoyed at Wedgwood. They visited Trentham Gardens and ate out in a quaint pub with a thatched roof. On the second day, they knocked on Jacky's door.

'Auntie Jacky, it's Charlotte,' the younger woman shouted through the safety-chained aperture. She heard the sound of chains being hastily unbolted. Charlotte didn't recognise the old, frail woman standing in the doorway, but Jacky would have known her niece anywhere.

'My goodness, what a fine young woman you turned into, duckie.'

Only Auntie Jacky had ever called her 'duckie', and on hearing this, Charlotte threw her arms round her and hugged her, exclaiming, 'Oh, it's so good to see you, Auntie Jacky. I've missed the donuts with the chocolate flakes,' – and Jacky burst into tears.

Izzy was still standing on the front path. She did not think she would be welcome in Jacky's house, so made an excuse to retire and collect Charlotte later but Jacky insisted she come in. 'If it weren't for you, Charlotte wouldn't be here now. I'm grateful to you, Elizabeth Sherwin. Let's have a cuppa all together, real civilised like.'

Once inside, both Charlotte and Izzy were shocked to see how emaciated Jacky was when the shawl slipped from her shoulders. They could not help but notice the single bed made up in the corner of the room. Jacky saw where their eyes fell. 'Not good with the stairs, these days. It's the old ticker, you know. Jeez, they must have big appetites in Canada, duckie. You must be full six feet tall, and what a swell Canadian twang you've picked up. Suits you.'

'Tall genes,' she replied, 'my two kids are tall too.'

'You've got kids!' she said excitedly. 'Oh do you have any photos? That'd be a sight for sore eyes after all this time.'

Charlotte dug a photo out of her bag. 'There's Anna on the left, she's sixteen. Wants to be a pop star or an actress or some such teenage dream. This is Jarrad, he's fourteen. He's the quiet one, wouldn't be surprised if he follows in his father's footsteps into medicine. That's his dad, Zac. He's a GP.'

'My he's a big un an' all – looks more like a rugby prop than a medic. You've done real well for yourself, Charlotte. Do you work as well as being a mum?'

'I'm a nurse – a theatre sister. Zac and I met when he was doing a hospital rotation before he decided to specialise as a GP.'

Jacky made them a pot of tea and dug out a few stale digestive biscuits.

'I see you've had a gas fire put in, Jacky, must be a lot easier for you than the open fire,' said Izzy conversationally.

'I s'ppose. Lot dearer though.'

Charlotte pitched in then. 'I was sorry to hear about Uncle Rob dying, you must miss him.'

'Was glad to see the back of him, if truth be told. He was a bad egg that one.'

'Dad died a month ago, did you know?'

'Nope, didn't know, don't care. Sorry, duckie, didn't mean no hurt by it. He was no favourite of mine, your dad.'

'I found out a lot of stuff after he died. He told me my mother got eight months. I only discovered she served twelve years when I found your note.'

It was Jacky's turn to look uncomfortable. Charlotte wanted to press the point, to ask her directly why she had perjured herself and let an innocent woman spend a dozen years in jail but thought better of it. Izzy had missed nothing and said breezily, 'I really must do that errand, Charlotte, shall I come back for you in a couple of hours?'

'Yes, that would be champion, thank you,' she said gratefully.

When Charlotte and Jacky were alone, they sat close together on the worn sofa. 'Are you alright for money?' Charlotte asked, fingering the tassels of the grubby shawl that had fallen onto her knee.

'I get by,' came the pained reply. 'After he lost his job at Michelin's he never really got a proper one again, just bits and pieces here and there. And when he was flush, he gambled on the dogs. He'd sell stuff to get by. There wasn't much left by the time he died, and I couldn't work with me ticker being the way it is.'

'How did he die?'

'He bled out. Right there in that chair over there. Perforated ulcer, they said, not surprising given how much he drank.'

'I'm sorry.'

'Don't be – I wasn't,' she said bitterly. 'How long did it take for the talking to come back, duckie?' she added, changing the subject.

'Soon after we got to Canada.'

'I figured as much,' she said ruefully. 'You saw what happened didn't you? You saw what he did.'

Charlotte nodded sadly. 'I remember everything. Other things are very hazy – I couldn't even remember Aunt Izzy's surname, but I remember the accident like it was yesterday. I had nightmares about it for years.'

'Do you want to tell me about it?' asked Jacky hesitantly.

When Charlotte had finished recounting her vivid memories of the day her brother died, Jacky bit her lip angrily. 'Bastard! Cowardly bastard!'

'He wasn't all bad. He was good to me in Canada, gave me everything I wanted. Spoilt me, even. And he never got over losing Sid. He stopped drinking, you know. Never touched a drop after the accident. He worked hard, too. Set up a lucrative garage business with a good reputation. The locals liked him.'

'Well that's summat, at least. But I can't forgive him for what he did. I suppose you can't forgive me for what I did neither.'

'You mean because you gave him an alibi.'

'Yeah, I'm not proud of that, Charlotte. But I was scared stiff of your Uncle Rob – he used to knock me about. It was good in the beginning. When I first met him, I was a typist at Bellinghams, had passed my shorthand exams, could have made it to secretary eventually, but he didn't like me working so I gave it up. He grew more and more bitter with time when I couldn't give him any kids – I had five miscarriages. He was jealous of your dad being so much younger and already having two kids. He drank heavy – a lot more than Bruce. Once I'd gone along with it, I couldn't go back on it – I'd have been done for perjury. I'm not proud of it, Charlotte. But you don't know what Rob was like.'

'I was frightened of him too,' said Charlotte. 'It's alright Auntie Jacky, I'm not blaming you, I just wanted to know what really happened, that was all. Did you know Mummy got assaulted in prison – had her arm broken and her face burned badly with a hot iron.'

At this, Jacky openly wept. 'I didn't know any of that. I knew she had to serve twelve years, which broke me up, but I didn't know any of that.'

'Like I said, I'm not blaming you. Auntie Jacky, I just think it's good that we can be honest with each other about what really happened.'

'But she's out now and... and they'd do me for perjury if I said owt now. Tell her I'm sorry, will you, when you go back to your mum. She must hate my guts but tell her I'm real sorry all the same.'

*

The time had flown by. Izzy arrived back with a couple of carrier bags of shopping. 'Got you a few bits and pieces while I was out, Jacky, save you a trip to the shops for a few days,' she announced casually, as if it was something she did every week.

'I don't want no charity from you Elizabeth Sherwin, nor no pity,' grunted Jacky at the sight of the overflowing bags.

Charlotte, touched by Izzy's thoughtfulness, didn't want her generosity to be wasted, so hurriedly jumped in. 'Oh no, you've got it wrong, Auntie Jacky. Izzy was doing an errand for me. They're from me, Auntie Jacky, they're from me. A thank you for all the lovely ice creams and donuts with chocolate flakes over the years.'

'In that case, thanks, duckie, real good of you.'

Charlotte was desperately trying to signal to Izzy not to betray her, but she need not have worried. Izzy had sized up the situation in seconds and needed no prompting.

'We'd better be going, Auntie Jacky, but I'll come again before I go back to Canada. And then we're all coming over for the summer. Zac and the kids. And I'll bring them to meet you.'

'I'd love that,' said Jacky, beaming, 'but don't worry about phoning. Mine's always on the blink these days. You can write me, if you've a mind.' The smile faded on her lips as she whispered, 'Don't forget to tell your mum what I said, duckie, will you?' and she hugged her niece one more time.

*

'If that phone's on the blink, I'm the Prime Minister,' asserted Izzy as they walked up the front path. 'It's disconnected. She can't pay the rent.'

'I thought the same,' said Charlotte. 'We'll find a way to get it fixed and I'll pay the bills. It can come out of dad's inheritance – he owes her that much at least.'

When Jacky unpacked the bags, she found them bursting with choice groceries. At the bottom of the second bag was a new pair of slippers and a shawl in a lovely peach colour. She held its softness to her cheek and then, pulling it round her, enveloped herself in its comforting warmth.

*

On the drive back to Silecroft, Charlotte was very quiet.

'Penny for them?' asked Izzy.

'I've been thinking about Mummy.'

'And?'

'I want to put it right. I can't imagine what it must be like living with shame for something you haven't done. What it must be like never being able to extinguish the stain, even after you've done time for a crime you didn't commit. I think being branded an ex-criminal is harder for her to bear than the brand that hot iron left on her face. And I've been thinking about baptism.'

'Baptism?' came the puzzled query.

'Yes, you know, like how Catholics believe baptism wipes away original sin – it's not your own sin – it's sort of inherited sin. I've been thinking it might not be too late. That there might be a baptism for Mummy.'

'You mean, prove her innocence? Perhaps we could talk to Mia – she's a human rights lawyer, quite junior, but she would be able to advise us on whether we might have any hope of an appeal. When George and I looked into it at the time, we were told there'd be no chance of an appeal unless we found compelling new evidence.'

'But there is, don't you see. I could tell them what I saw – and I'm thinking Auntie Jacky might agree to testify.'

'No, never. That would be admitting perjury. She would be risking prison!'

'I don't know – she feels very guilty. She wept when I told her about the prisoner assault and what they did to her face.'

'You really think she might testify?'

'She's terrified of going to prison but there must be grounds for mitigating circumstances. Surely the court would accept she perjured herself under duress. What's Mia like? Do you trust her?'

'I've never met her, but Rhianne met her at Christmas and liked her a lot. Theo talks about her all the time, and how smart she is. We could talk to Theo.'

'Yes, that's what we must do. Don't say anything to Mummy, I don't want to get her hopes up.'

*

They approached Theo. 'Yes, Mia would be a good person to talk to,' he declared. 'Human rights is her specialist area. She's only a junior but she knows her stuff. And don't worry, she'd understand it was confidential.'

'You won't say anything to Mummy, will you Theo, not until we know a bit more.'

'No need to worry on that score, Charlotte. This would mean everything to her. It would be a crushing disappointment if it didn't come off, so of course I'll keep my counsel.'

'Thanks.'

'Mia and I are very close. She's like the daughter I never had. If she thought it was important to me, she would give it her all. I know I'm biased, but she's very good at her job. She'll be a pretty hot-shot human rights barrister one day, mark my words. Come up to the attic this evening and we could Skype her. Beth doesn't need to know.'

*

'Three things,' pronounced Mia from the Skype screen. 'Firstly, we would have a very good chance of a non-custodial sentence for

Jacky. We could argue coercion based on compound marital abuse. Secondly, if Jacky and you *both* testify, I think we have a very good case to get the conviction quashed. And thirdly, if my nose is right, I'd say it sounds like there were some howling systematic failures in the original police investigation. This one just doesn't weigh right.'

'Weigh right?'

'Too many holes. Too many unanswered questions. Let me talk to James – he's my mentor at chambers – and I'll get back to you in a few days. It would help if we could get a peep at the original case files. Izzy, would you be willing to make an approach to the law firm that handled Beth's original case and see whether they would agree to work with us on this?'

'I'll contact Braithwaite and Braithwaite right away,' replied Izzy. 'I know Raymond very well. We kept him on as our own solicitor after Beth's trial. He's semi-retired now. His daughter is the senior practice partner and she's a chip off the old block. I'm sure they will still have all the files. I know Raymond was gutted they lost the case. He would want to help with any potential appeal.'

*

Izzy was right. Braithwaites', and Raymond in particular, were extremely keen to pull out all the stops for this one. They faxed copies of all the case notes to Mia's London chambers the next morning. She picked her way through them meticulously before taking them to her mentor. The more she read, the more confident she was of what his view was going to be.

James Henderson had been impressed with Mia from the day she first came for interview at his chambers and had volunteered to take her under his wing. Barely five feet, and probably not much more than seven stone, this petite figure with huge brown eyes and glossy dark hair, almost, but not quite, covering a disfigurement to her left temple, was an absolute firecracker. She had told him a little about her early life and how she came to England. It explained where the passion and grit came from and made him all the keener to help her get on. For experience, he had included her in his team on the recent case at Strasbourg. The prosecution had completely capitulated, mainly due to the forensic research Mia had done which had given James not one but two aces to play. Her work ethic, her preparation, her logical reasoning, were all first-rate. Best of all, she had 'the nose'. He'd taken on a lot of juniors who were robotically schooled in the finer points of law and would do tolerably well. Very few had 'the nose'. Mia had demonstrated that in spades in Strasbourg. She would go far.

'I've looked at those files you gave me, Mia,' he said to her in their mentoring session. 'Sad case. Give me your best analysis.'

'If I can get the perjurer to testify alongside the daughter, I think it's an open and shut case to get a conviction quash. I'm confident we could prove the perjurer lied under duress due to compound marital abuse, which I'm hoping will be enough to persuade her to break cover. The daughter is more than willing to testify but I would need to get an expert witness to testify as to the reliability of a seven-and-a-half-year-old's memory from thirty years ago.'

'And?' pressed James. 'What's your nose telling you?'

'My nose tells me this one stinks.'

James's eyes began to twinkle. *Atta girl*, he thought to himself but gave nothing away. 'Because…?'

'It's full of holes. I don't think the police did anything like enough to stress test the alibis. They didn't pay close enough attention to the medical reports from the hospital. Mrs Dagnall, as she was then, could not have sustained those injuries to the left side of her head if she had been driving. And they were too ready to accept the husband's forehead injury as being sustained in the alleged earlier pub fight, when it could just as easily have been caused by banging his head on the steering wheel. There's nothing on file either about the police interviewing neighbours to see if anyone saw the car pull off the drive and if they did, whether they saw who was driving – or indeed if anyone saw Mr Dagnall returning to the family home from the pub. It was a Saturday afternoon and it's not as if they lived on a remote farm, it was a housing estate. The police chose the lazy route. They took everything at face value, never stopped to work through a scenario where the mother was telling the truth. I don't think they even established strength of motive. They made out she was fleeing from an unhappy marriage. I don't buy it. Someone should have smelt a rat. She protested her innocence throughout, even at the parole boards which cost her two extra years.'

'Excellent analysis, Mia. I don't think you'll need me until the final push.'

'You mean you'll take the case?' she beamed excitedly.

'You bet I will.'

'And I can be your backroom lead?'

'Absolutely. None better. Go for the jugular, Mia. If you can get me proof of police incompetence, there'll be a whopping compensation pay out to boot.'

*

'I was shocked to see the state Auntie Jacky was living in,' confided Charlotte as she strolled along the beach with her mother, four sets of toes digging into the damp sand. Beth stiffened and quickened her gait, setting her face against the incoming breeze.

'I know she's your aunt, Charlotte, but she's nothing to me so why should I care what state she's living in. She did a very wicked thing. Perhaps she's getting the punishment she deserves.'

So far, Charlotte had seen little of the hard-nosed edge Theo had warned her about and was shocked and upset by the callousness of this response. 'She asked me to be sure to tell you she was sorry – real sorry – for—'

'For what? For stealing twelve years of my life! For cheating me of my motherhood! For abandoning me to prisoner abuse! Which bit is she sorry for?'

'She was abused too, Mummy. Controlled, abused, cowed. Can't you see that she didn't have a choice?'

'There's always a choice. She chose to save herself – that was her choice. It was cowardly.'

'Not everyone is as brave as you, Mummy.'

'It's not about being brave, it's about doing what's right—'

'Then, I am just as much to blame as her, just as cowardly. I *chose* to be mute.'

'You were a seven-year-old child for God's sake. She was a forty-year-old woman. I don't want to talk about it, Charlotte. I can't forgive her. However sorry she says she is; I can't forgive her.'

Bursting Bubbles

That evening, Rhianne and Eithan drove Charlotte over to meet Ciara. Izzy made an excuse that she needed an early night. Theo and Beth were amused by the thinly disguised ruse to give the two lovers some private time together in West Cottage.

'It was thoughtful of them,' said Theo placing a bottle of wine on the worktop in Beth's kitchen where she was trimming some broccoli, 'but they're wide of the mark, if they think we can't wait to jump into bed every moment that presents itself.'

'We were probably the same at their age,' she smiled. 'So, you've gone off me already, Theodore Kendrick.'

'I adore you more with every passing day,' he said, coming up behind her and putting his arms around her waist, 'and making love to you is fantastic, but playing house is divine too. Besides, I'm an old man – you've already had your wicked way with me once this afternoon. That rickety attic bed does my back in. Don't I get time off for good behaviour?'

'You're not old! You're two years younger than me and I consider myself in the prime of my life, thank you very much! Oh dear – is the bed rickety? Should I change it? Is it really bad for your back?'

Theo laughed heartily. 'You're so easy to play, Beth Brennan, it's like kids and candy. The bed is perfect. You should know I prefer firm to soft,' he said, not a little suggestively, and she threw a wet dishcloth at him.

'You beast! Forever sending me up. I never know when you're being serious.'

'That's half the fun.'

'Playing house? You said playing house.'

'Yes. Having a whole house to ourselves for an evening feels like playing house. Playing at being a proper couple.'

'I'm sorry it's so difficult at the moment, but Charlotte's only here for another week and then Izzy will be heading down to Cornwall to see Shelley and...' she suddenly stopped and turned to face him, broccoli still in hand. 'Is it play acting? Is that what we're doing, Theo? *Playing* at being a proper couple?'

'Don't be a goose, Beth. That's not what I meant, and you know it. I want to spend quality time with you doing ordinary things, like washing up and taking out the bins. Course I crave your body, it's a beautiful body, but I don't love you for your body – I love you for you. I love talking to you, debating with you, walking with you, laughing with you – yes even arguing with you. You can be infuriating and mesmerising and astonishing all at the same time. Course we're a proper couple, Beth.'

'I want those things too, Theo.'

'We need to talk about how we're going to manage when my book is finished. You have your business here. I have my practice clinic and my lecturing at the university. We're too old to do a weekend relationship...'

'I wish you wouldn't go on about how old we are. We're mid-fifties not mid-seventies. I don't want anything to change, Theo. I want it to be always like it is now, here together.'

'We both know that's not possible.'

'Why not? Why can't we continue as we are? We're happy, aren't we?'

'Beth,' he said, taking both her hands in his, 'we can't live in a bubble forever. I have duties and responsibilities. People depend on me. I can't just turn my back on them to follow some yellow brick road in Cumbria. I understand how important this business is to you – you've built it up from nothing. It's a phenomenal success but it's kept you closeted up here. You haven't seen anything of the world. I bet you haven't even got a passport. Well, you'll have to get one soon. Charlotte's itching for you to go out to Canada on a visit. You've talked about giving Rhianne more responsibility. Can't you see your way to sharing the management of the bakery with her just as you share the property rentals with Eithan so that you could spend chunks of time with me?'

'I can't! I can't!'

'Can't go to Canada?'

'No, can't be part of your life in Solihull or Birmingham or wherever it is you practise. I'd be an embarrassment to you, I'd... I'd—'

'You could never be an embarrassment to me, Beth.'

'Do I have to spell it out for you?' she said in frustration. 'I'M A CONVICTED CRIMINAL. It doesn't matter that I'm innocent. As far as the world's concerned I'm an ex-con. That smell never goes away.'

'So?'

'So! You're famous, Theo. People *know* you; they're *interested* in you. That first book of yours was seminal. It put PTSD on the map. It's had three editions already. You're quoted all over the world. Can you imagine what it would do to your profile, to your career, to be living with an ex-criminal?'

'Do you think I care what people think? I'm the arrogant prick, remember. To hell with what people think.'

'And my face! What do you think they'd make of this!' she shrieked, slapping the scar on her cheek.

'I don't care if you have a scar on both cheeks and a missing leg to boot. You're the woman I want to be with. Do you think I care a fuck what anyone thinks? God, Beth, you'd try the patience of a saint. I'm trying to tell you that I love you that I want to share my life with you. I want to marry you!'

'No! No! We can't. We can't.'

'Yes we can.'

'I *have* to stay here. You could come up whenever you can. There'll never be anyone else for me. I'll always be here for you, but I can't leave.'

'Are you going to hide away for the rest of your life?'

'Yes. Yes, that's exactly what I'm going to do. I can't live in your world, Theo. I'm safe here. And you're safer in your world if I stay here.'

'That's a load of bollocks! Don't pretend you're doing this for me. Don't insult me by offering me a cosy weekend concubine arrangement. You're a coward, Beth Brennan, a coward. I thought you were brave but underneath you're just a selfish coward,' he roared, 'and a callous bitch,' he added bitterly.

'A callous bitch?' she asked incredulously.

'Charlotte told me that you'd refused to forgive Jacky.'

'She had no right to—'

'She had *every* right. Jacky's as much her aunt as Izzy. They've forgiven her. They've forgiven *you*.'

'What do you mean forgiven *me*? I'm innocent, I didn't kill my own son. I didn't drive while drunk as a skunk, I didn't perjure myself in court. What have they to forgive *me* for?'

'And you say I'm the self-righteous, arrogant prick. Take a look in the mirror, Beth.'

'I... I... but I...'

'Izzy's forgiven you for shutting her out of your life for thirty years. Probably shutting her out for ever if I hadn't found her.'

'But it was for her own good, for her own safety.'

'So you keep saying. Whose choice was it to make – yours or hers? You're a thief, Beth, you stole her free will, you stole her right to make a choice. That's what she's forgiven you for – for being a choice thief. Charlotte too.'

'Charlotte?'

'Did you try to find her? Okay, maybe not the first few years but once you were on your feet, once you were a successful businesswoman you didn't try to find her.'

'She would have been twenty when I got out, had a life of her own by then. She was better off without me.'

'Whose choice was that to make? Yours or hers?' he yelled. 'And you're doing the same to me. Deciding what is and isn't good for my career. Stealing my right to determine my own happiness.'

With that, he marched out of the kitchen and was on his way to his attic room when he suddenly turned round and came back into the kitchen. Beth was crumpled over the chopping board. His heart lurched, but he ignored the urge to pull her into his arms.

'Just answer me one thing,' he shouted, jabbing his finger into the worktop. 'If your conviction was quashed, if you were proved innocent, would you marry me?'

'I could never get it quashed without new evidence,' she wailed. 'Even Charlotte coming forward wouldn't be enough – not that I'd ever want to put her through such an ordeal. A thirty-year-old memory of a seven-year-old girl won't stand up against two contemporarily sworn adult alibis.'

'Just answer the question, Beth,' he said hotly. 'If your conviction was quashed, would you marry me?'

'But it's a hypothetical—'

'Answer the question, damn it!'

'Yes. YES! I'd marry you! Are you satisfied now?'

'Quite satisfied. I'll hold you to it, Beth. You just accepted my proposal of marriage.'

'Hypothetically… it was hypothet—'

'Then we're hypothetically engaged. You'll need a hypothetical ring. Try this one on for size,' and he left a small box on the worktop before turning on his heels. This time he did take himself straight back to Middle Cottage attic.

*

Beth opened the box. The ring was exquisite. Tasteful, not flashy. Bruce had never given her an engagement ring, just a wedding band. They had to marry hastily, precipitated by her swelling belly.

A discreet registry office affair, overseen, shotgun-style, by her parents. Much as she wanted to, she resisted the temptation to try it on. She closed the lid gently and held the box to her lips. She would return it to him tomorrow.

*

Theo was furious with himself. He had wanted to get down on one knee, the full works, make it special for her. He looked at his watch. Mia would still be up.

'Hi Theo. This is a nice surprise. How are things?'

'What's your honest view about the chances of getting Beth's conviction quashed?'

'I'm fine Mia, thank you – how'd your case go?'

'Oh, I'm sorry, Mia. I didn't mean to be rude, I'm pretty distracted. How did your case go?'

'We won again. And the judge awarded compensation. Oh, Theo, it was amazing to be part of that team. James was fantastic. The atmosphere was electric. I felt ten feet tall.'

'That's something seeing as you only just scrape five,' he laughed.

'We can't all be towering goddesses like your Beth.'

'Seriously, though, Mia. That's brilliant.'

'Technically it wasn't *my* case. I was just the backroom junior doing all the research. But I was part of the team, that was the main thing – and I got to sit on the bench with them. It was exhilarating.'

'Wonderful, Mia. I'm so proud of you. I'm always proud of you.'

'You sound edgy. What's up?'

'I've sort of messed up with Beth.'

'Sort of? What does "sort of" mean?'

'I'd planned to propose to her.'

He chose to ignore the whistle that came back at him from his Skype screen and the accompanying banter. 'You don't let the grass grow under your feet – or should I say sand! Seriously Theo, isn't

233

this rather sudden? Are you certain it's what you want? You sure it's not some kind of delayed rebound?'

'Delayed rebound?'

'Josie died many years ago, but it could have been yesterday. It's like she's been frozen in time and it's only now you've come to terms with her loss. So, is it a rebound relationship? I like Beth, but you've only known her six months, Theo. She's a complicated, secretive woman. I wouldn't want you to get hurt – or her for that matter.'

'We've told each other everything about our past lives, there are no more secrets. This is the real deal for me. I love her, Mia. I didn't at first. I'm not sure I even liked her in the beginning. But once I got to know her, underneath that suit of ice she wears she's the most extraordinary, captivating – infuriating – woman. Everything is more joyful when I share it with her, more *colourful*: a book, a poem, a barefoot walk on the beach, fish and chips out of newspaper, a glass of wine, the ten o'clock news – anything and everything. She's a coloured lens in my grey world. I feel empty without her, Mia.'

'Okay, interrogation over, I believe you. I'm ecstatic for you, Theo. You said you'd planned to propose?'

'Ah, there's the rub. That's where I've messed up. Beth got all hung up about being an ex-con, said she couldn't share any part of my life unless it was tucked away in her bakery bubble. Said she'd be an embarrassment to me, damage my career. Wouldn't countenance seeing me anywhere except *chez elle*. She's as stubborn as a mule.'

'Takes one to know one, Theo! Don't you think you're being a bit Neanderthal about this? You can't expect her to give up everything she's built to trail after your coat tails.'

'Of course I wouldn't expect that! You should know me better, Mia. But I thought we could find a compromise where we split our time between the two locations. I want her to be a part of *my* world not just me be a part of *hers*.'

'Okay, I get it. So, are you going to tell me *how* you "sort of messed up"?'

'I backed her into a corner, into a hypothetical situation where her conviction was quashed and she wouldn't be an ex-con anymore, then demanded whether or not she would marry me.'

'*Demanded?*'

'She was so convinced it could never happen that she said yes.'

'So she *has* agreed to marry you.'

'Only hypothetically. It's all down to you, now Mia. You *have* to win that case. My future happiness depends on it.'

'No pressure then.'

'What's your honest assessment of our chances?'

'Of a conviction quash?'

'Yes, a conviction quash,' he repeated impatiently.

'Braithwaites' have sent me copies of everything they have on file. There are some other documents I want to access but won't have jurisdiction to request them until we formally apply for an appeal hearing. By "we", I mean Beth. She has to agree to initiate the action otherwise I can't act on her behalf. So sooner or later, someone's going to have to tell Beth what you three have been cooking up. Anyway, in answer to your question – if Jacky comes forward – ninety-five per cent. If not, I wouldn't rate our chances much more than forty.'

'Do you think Jacky will agree to testify?' he asked, rather crestfallen.

'We'll find out tomorrow. Charlotte and I are going to meet with her.'

'She won't testify if she thinks she'll go to prison.'

'Then it's up to me to persuade her I can get her a non-custodial sentence.'

'I'd better let you get some sleep, then.'

'Yes, early start. I'm driving up to Staffordshire. Never been to that part of the world. Izzy tells me it's stunning.'

'You need to get out more, Mia. For a girl who hails from Iraq and spends time in Strasbourg, it's about time you got to know a little more of this beautiful island you call home.'

'All in good time – and I'm not a girl anymore, you keep forgetting I'm a fully grown woman, old man.'

'*Mea culpa*, little one. I can still call you that can't I, *ma petite?*'

'Only you, no one else,' she whispered.

'Thanks for doing this. It means the world to me.'

'As if I hadn't been waiting my whole adult life to do something for you, Theo Kendrick. It's long overdue. Sleep tight, don't let the bugs bite.' And she signed out.

Theo smiled at his laptop screen long after it had kicked into saver mode.

*

Beth got up early next morning after a wretched night and was down in the bakery kitchen just after five. Rhianne was already there, having stepped into Beth's role for the duration of Charlotte's visit.

'Hi Beth, we weren't expecting you, is anything wrong? The Harrison's wedding cake was delivered on time. The other specialist orders are well in hand and the new temp is terrific.'

'No, no – everything is fine, Rhianne, you're doing great. I just thought I might as well come to work as Charlotte's gone with Izzy to Barlaston again. Sweep the cobwebs out of my brain.'

Rhianne was about to express surprise at Beth not wanting to seize the opportunity of a whole day with Theo but one glance at Hilda, who was shaking her head silently and putting her index finger to her mouth, cautioned her to keep her counsel.

When Theo did not appear for his usual coffee and croissant, Hilda shot Rhianne another knowing glance. At eleven o'clock Beth took off her apron and left the kitchen. She needed to find Theo. Their quarrel had left her miserable. She had churned it over and over in a sleepless frenzy until she could hide from the truth no longer. He was right. She was a selfish coward. She wanted to apologise, ask his forgiveness, ask if they could wipe last night clean and start over. She wanted – more than anything – she wanted him to take her in his arms and hold her. She knocked on his door a little timidly. Beth rarely did anything timidly but then that was in a world she had created where she was always in control. There was no answer. She shouted through the door, 'Theo, it's me. I came to apologise. I was wrong. Can we talk? Please can we talk.' Still no answer. She went down to the side street where he parked his car. It was gone.

Every hour she went out to see if his car was back, without success, until it grew dark. Dejectedly she locked up West Cottage and made her way upstairs to bed. Charlotte away, Izzy away, Theo gone. It felt eerily lonely. And yet, Beth had lived, nay craved, a life of solitude these past two decades, so why was it so hard to bear now? She put the ring box she had carried around all day under her pillow and lay on her bed fully clothed. Minutes later she was asleep from sheer exhaustion.

*

Theo had driven straight to Izzy's, and it was she who answered the door.

'Theo! Goodness, what are you doing here? I thought it couldn't be the estate agent. He's not due for another hour. We weren't expecting you. Come in. Mia and Charlotte are at Jacky's. I thought I ought to stay out of it. Too many cooks and all that. Besides, I don't think I'm Jacky's favourite person.' Noticing his dishevelled appearance, she added, 'Is anything wrong, Theo?'

Ignoring her question, he launched right into it. 'She's lived so long inside her head, I don't think she can live in the real world.'

'I assume we're talking Beth not Jacky here?'

'Sorry, yes.'

'Why don't I make us a pot of tea and you can tell me all about it.'

*

The estate agent had been and gone, delighted with his hot commission. He had at least three buyers in mind who would be fighting over it.

'Why don't you go and freshen up, Theo. There's plenty of hot water if you want a shower. You might want to come with me to pick up Mia and Charlotte,' she said tactfully.

Theo rubbed the stubble on his chin, realising he had not shaved that morning and shot her a grateful glance. When they arrived at Jacky's, it was Charlotte who answered the door – and she was beaming. It was a bit of a squeeze getting the five of them into the sitting room, especially with Jacky's bed in the corner but Charlotte and Izzy opted to sit on the bed, leaving the two-seater sofa for Mia and Theo. Jacky, seated in her armchair, was wearing the peach shawl and slippers and had a little more colour in her cheeks.

'What a pleasure to see you again, Mrs Dagnall. I'm in your debt. The address you gave me led me straight to Charlotte,' said Theo kindly, his eyes twinkling at her. It was the tone that had the female nursing staff at QE swooning and this frail lady was not too old to be touched by his charm.

'It's Jacky. Most folks call me Jacky,' she said, smiling a little shyly.

'Most folks call me Theo – Jacky,' he replied, not letting his eyes wander from her face and returning her shy smile with a gentle one.

Ever the professional, Mia got straight down to business.

'Theo, we are going to need you as an expert witness on two counts.'

'Two?'

'As a clinical psychologist – of some renown,' she added proudly, 'you can provide an expert view on one: PTSD and two: Elective mutism. Jacky has agreed to testify and has given me permission to requisition her medical records.'

Jacky bowed her head at this point, trying to hide her shame. Seeing her reaction, Theo reached out and squeezed her hand.

'You've nothing to be ashamed of, Jacky. He's the one who carries the shame.' She looked up at him gratefully and smiled weakly.

Mia was in full flow. 'With Jacky and Charlotte's testimony and you as an expert witness, Theo, we have an open and shut case for a conviction quash. With the medical records I'm confident I can get Jacky, at worst, a suspended sentence. Trust me, Jacky, you're never going to see the inside of a prison cell.'

'You can trust her, Jacky,' interceded Theo, 'she's the best. She was recently on a team that won a high-profile case at the European Court of Human Rights in Strasbourg.'

'That just leaves two pieces of the jigsaw to get into place,' continued Mia. 'One: We need Beth's agreement to lodge the appeal and for Braithwaites' and me to act on her behalf. Two: Once the appeal is lodged, I need to get access to additional papers, such as those that might have been overlooked by the prosecution, or not disclosed.'

'What kind of papers?' asked Theo.

'Medical notes from when Beth was taken to hospital after the accident and police files.'

'Police files?' asked Izzy, perplexed.

'Yes. I want to know how hard they tried to test the alibis. It sounds like they just accepted them without question. They didn't even interview Rob and Jacky separately to see how well the alibis tallied? Did they do house to house in the street where Bruce lived to see if anyone saw him? It was a Saturday afternoon, fair enough the car was in the garage so the family could have got into the car unseen, but did anyone see them drive out, see who was behind the wheel? Did they bother to check? Did they give any credence at all to the possibility Beth was telling the truth? And Charlotte! Charlotte was mute – she never confirmed her mother had been driving. They chose to assume it. I'd like sight of what got passed to CPS.'

'What's CPS?' asked Jacky nervously.

'It's Crown Prosecution Service, Jacky,' explained Theo.

'I'll be very interested to see what was in that CPS file. If there are glaring gaps in what was presented, if there were short cuts, we're into a whole different ball game.'

'Different, how?' asked Charlotte.

'Different as regards compensation. Beth will be entitled to a lot more if we prove police incompetence.'

'The compensation won't matter to her,' said Izzy, 'it's the conviction quash that means everything.'

'It matters to me,' replied Mia, passionately. 'It's a matter of principle. It's a matter of precedent. When human rights are trampled on, there has to be restitution.'

'I believe you,' whispered Charlotte to Theo, as they were getting up to leave.

'Believe me?'

'Yes. I believe you – she *IS* the best!'

'Thank you,' said Jacky, tearfully, as the five of them huddled by the front door.

'You're the one we have to thank,' replied Mia earnestly. 'You're the star of this show. A brave, courageous star. Without you we have no show.' And Theo smiled proudly to himself. His surrogate daughter was not just becoming a hot-shot lawyer; she was a pretty astute psychologist too.

*

Mia went back to London after breakfast next morning, via Braithwaites' where she left another long list of instructions. Izzy and Charlotte stayed on another day until the photographers had done their work and the estate agents had all they needed to market the property. Theo stayed too. He was in no hurry to get back. He was still furious with Beth. They drove to Silecroft in convoy.

'Keep a low profile for a few hours when we get back,' said Izzy to Theo. 'I want to talk to Beth alone. It's about time we had a twin sister heart to heart.'

'Don't worry. After what I said to her, I doubt she's in a hurry to see me.'

Beth greeted Izzy and Charlotte warmly when they piled into West Cottage later that afternoon. 'How did it go with the estate agent, Izzy?'

'Very smoothly. They think it will sell easily, and at a good price.'

'I need to Skype Zac,' said Charlotte, sticking to the pre-arrangement she'd agreed with Izzy.

'Don't you want tea and scones first?' asked Beth.

'No thanks, I've just enough time to catch him before he starts morning surgery. You and Izzy go ahead without me, I'll grab something later.'

Seated in West Cottage, scones and tea polished off, Beth asked anxiously, 'Theo's disappeared. I haven't seen him for a couple of days. You don't happen to know where he is do you?'

'I do,' came the cold response.

'Oh,' said Beth, a little surprised by the abruptness of the reply. 'It's just… it's just I wondered if he was alright.'

'What's it to you, Meg?'

'I don't understand?'

'What's Theo's wellbeing got to do with you? You don't own him. From what I hear you don't even want him, well except as a puppet on a string.'

'But that's absurd…'

'Is it?' came the steely interruption. 'Is it? He's not a plaything you can pull out of a drawer at will, like you do soldier Sid.'

Beth gasped at the callous reference to her dead son. This was a different Izzy. She'd never seen this hard side to her before. Izzy had always indulged her, soothed her, helped her.

'I don't understand…' she said again.

'You *choose* not to understand. It's not the same thing.'

Again, Beth gasped audibly.

'I get it, Meg. I get that you lived in your head when you were in prison. I get that it was a way of keeping something of yourself to yourself in an institution where your every breathing moment is owned by someone else. I get it that it was a survival tactic when you were first released. But I DON'T get that you kept it up for three decades! I DON'T get that you pushed us all away. I DON'T get that you stole my twin sister from me. You broke my heart. You had the power to mend it and you CHOSE not to.'

'I did it for you, I did it to keep you safe, I—'

Izzy shook her head violently, 'No! You did it for yourself. *You* ran away. *You* created this elaborate sanctuary. *You* dictated terms, Meg. I had no say in it.'

'Theo said you had forgiven me,' whispered Beth miserably.

'Of course I've forgiven you, because you're my sister and I love you. But it doesn't mean I like what you did. Just as I don't like what you're doing to Theo.'

'Theo? What about Theo?' she asked defensively.

'After George he's the best man I've ever known. What the hell are you playing at, Meg? How could you contemplate letting such a giant of a human being slip through your fingers? All because you won't compromise on your precious bubble. You'll never find a better man: he's intelligent, kind, nice looking – gorgeous voice…'

'Well you marry him then!' screeched Beth petulantly. She had meant to say that all she wanted was for Theo to forgive her and give her another chance. That she was ready to compromise, but her jealously got the better of her. 'You marry him! That way he can get a refund on damaged goods and have a shiny new one with no blemishes.'

'That was beneath you,' retorted Izzy icily and she got up to leave.

'Oh, please Izzy, wait. I'm so sorry. I didn't mean it. I don't know what came over me. It's like something in my head just flipped when I heard you talking about him like that.'

'You're not entitled to be jealous of a man you want as a plaything.'

'I don't want him as a plaything. More than anything I want to share my life with him…'

'But you want to control him. You want him on your terms. That's not love, it's possession.'

'But I *do* love him. I love him to distraction. I'm just so scared I'll shame him,' she said, tears flowing unchecked.

'There you go again, Meg. Isn't that for *him* to decide? He's a grown man in his fifties for God's sake. It's HIS choice.' Beth broke down at this point. 'I've made such a mess of everything, Izzy,' she wept. 'How do I make it right?'

Izzy resisted the urge to rush to comfort her. 'You could start by putting that ring he's given you on your finger and when you find him tell him you accept his proposal without any strings attached,' she said sternly.

'Where is he, Izzy?' she asked quietly. 'You know where he is don't you? Please tell me where he is.'

'By now he's probably up in Middle Cottage attic...'

Izzy didn't get to finish her sentence because Beth had already shot upstairs to retrieve the ring from under her pillow and was puffing up Middle Cottage stairs at breakneck speed. She was about to knock on his door when he opened it and she ran into his arms, breathing heavily.

'I heard someone coming and hoped it was you,' he said, hugging her close, feeling her heart pounding against his chest.

'Will you ask me again, Theo,' she pleaded, pushing the ring box into his hand. 'I'll live anywhere with you as long as I don't have to live without you. Will you ask me again... *please.*'

This time Theo made sure he got down on one knee. 'Beth Brennan, will you marry me and make me the happiest man alive?'

'Yes! Yes!' she squealed.

'Before or after the court case?'

'Court case – what court case?'

'Didn't Izzy tell you?'

'Tell me what?'

'Izzy wanted to be the one to tell you... She hasn't told you yet! You don't know and yet you agreed to marry me! No strings! What *did* Izzy say to you?'

Beth looked away sheepishly. 'She gave me a lecture on living in the real world. Made me see how blind and stupid I've been. But what's all this about a court case?'

'Jacky has agreed to testify. Charlotte is going to testify as well, and I am going to be an expert witness. Mia thinks we have a ninety-five per cent chance of getting your conviction quashed.'

*

An hour later when Theo had explained everything to Beth and they had freshened up, they came down to West Cottage kitchen where Izzy and Charlotte were already preparing supper. Beth went first to hug her daughter. 'Thank you,' she said excitedly and then, clinging to her twin sister, she whispered, 'One day, I hope to be half as wise as you.'

In the midst of the merriment Theo's mobile buzzed. It was Mia. 'Is now a good moment to ask Beth for permission to act for her?' she said.

'I think now would be the perfect moment.' And he handed his phone to Beth.

Grans and Grandmas

It was late June and more than two months since Charlotte had returned to Canada. Mia and Braithwaites' had been busy building their case. Mia wanted to leave no stone unturned, and James had been very helpful, especially with the warrants and subpoenas. Beth was in a high state of agitation about it and Theo was relieved that she would soon have the exciting distraction of meeting her grandchildren for the first time. He had reluctantly agreed to Beth's request that they wait until after the court case to get married. She wanted Charlotte and her grandchildren to be there. They were all coming over for the summer. Beth set the wedding date for Monday 9th August.

*

It was the morning of their due arrival. Beth was too excited to eat breakfast. She and Izzy sat by the window of the tea shop watching anxiously for a sighting of Theo's car. He had left for the airport after an early breakfast. There was nothing left to do. East Cottage maisonette had been cleaned from top to bottom and new beds installed. Beth had been baking madly – all sorts of delicacies and fancies she thought her teenage grandchildren might like. She got up to pace around and almost missed his car pulling up. The twin sisters ran out into the street to greet the visitors. Zac emerged from the front passenger seat, all six feet four inches of him. Somehow, Beth hadn't thought of a GP being tall and athletic. He had a rugged outdoor look about him, a full head of dark, wavy hair greying at the temples. Charlotte jumped out followed shyly by Jarrad, who had been squeezed between his mother and sister on the back seat. Anna glided through the other side door and announced herself with a toss of her long, dark glossy locks. They were all tall, Anna a match for her mother's six feet and Jarrad already outstripping both of them.

'You must be tired out after such a long journey. Your beds are made up if you need to sleep,' said Beth.

'You must be kidding,' said Anna. 'Who wants to sleep when there's so much to explore. I can smell the sea. Which way is the beach?'

'All in good time, Anna,' reprimanded Charlotte. 'Did you leave your manners in Beaumont? Your grandmother has waited all your lives to meet you.'

'Sorry, got a bit carried away,' said Anna, not the least sorrowfully. Then she looked at the two older women standing on the pavement. 'Which one of you is my grandmother?'

'That would be me,' said Beth stepping forward, not sure whether or not to hug this self-assured teenage tower, but she needn't have worried as Anna needed no prompting to give her a bear hug.

'What do I call you? Grandmother's a bit stuffy. Granny? Grandma? Nana?'

'What would you like to call me?'

'They all sound a bit old for you. You're much younger than my other grandmother. Can I call you Gran?'

'Perfect,' said Beth, already liking this spirited young lady. 'And you must be Jarrad,' she said, turning to her grandson.

'Pleased to meet you,' he replied offering her his hand. Beth made a show of shaking it, realising that hugging would need to come much later with this bashful, lanky giant. 'And what would *you* like to call me?'

He shrugged his bony shoulders. 'Same as her I suppose.'

'You don't have to call me the same as your sister if you don't want to. She's not your keeper.'

He shot her a shy grin. 'I like Grandma – it sounds very English.'

'Grandma it is,' she declared, beaming back at him.

Theo had been watching this little cameo with some amusement. *She'll have them eating out of her hand in no time – wait till they taste her cupcakes!*

Zac had been equally impressed by his mother-in-law's instant ability to get the measure of her grandchildren. 'That just leaves me. I'm Zac. It's an honour to meet you Mrs Brennan.' His handshake was firm and warm, and he accompanied it with a kiss on her cheek – being careful to avoid the scarred one.

'Beth, please,' she beamed up at him. 'Everyone calls me Beth, except Izzy – but that's a long story.'

'Pleased to meet you, Beth,' he repeated.

'This is your Great Aunt Izzy,' she said taking her sister's hand and pulling her forward. 'She's my twin if you hadn't already guessed.'

'Cool!' exclaimed Anna. And then mother and daughter were locked in a tight embrace, both of them blubbing. 'They're wonderful,' whispered Beth into Charlotte's hair. 'I never thought I would live to see this day.'

Then, just as quickly, she pulled away. 'Goodness, it's me who's forgetting my manners,' she said, wiping away her tears, 'keeping you standing in the street like this. Come on in, come in and I'll show you your maisonette. Lunch is waiting for you whenever you're ready and there's constant hot water if you want showers.'

Before heading indoors, she glanced quickly at Theo, her face radiant with happiness and nodded at him. He nodded back approvingly. They did not say anything; they did not need to.

*

The weeks flew by. Theo organised a three-day trip to London. He booked a hotel for them all. Beth insisted on paying. However, they fought over who paid for the theatre tickets and Theo won. 'If you think I'm taking my fiancée to her first West End theatre in forty years and letting her pay, you're off your head.'

'But there are seven of us, Theo!'

'Eight! Mia is going to join us. Even *she* gets evenings off occasionally. I'm allowed to treat my future step grandchildren aren't I, bossy mare?'

Izzy wanted in on the act too. 'And don't forget I want to treat my great niece and nephew. I'm buying the London Eye tickets, Madame Tussauds – and I want to take them to eat at Planet Hollywood. Oh, and we mustn't forget to get the timing right for the Changing of the Guard at Buckingham Palace. That's a spectacle they won't see in Canada.'

*

Anna was in seventh heaven. She loved the rich opulence and intimacy of the Regency theatre. 'If I'm going to be an actress, Mom, I'm going to need some serious singing and dancing lessons,' she said as she exited dreamily from the auditorium. 'I might even want to come to study at an English drama school. They're much better than anything we've got in Canada, you know.' She couldn't wait to Skype Rosie. Charlotte and Zac just smiled at each other. They were well used to their daughter's theatricals.

'She'll grow out of it,' said Zac. 'By next month it will all be about fashion and cat walks.'

*

Izzy was keen for them to spend a few days at Sycamore Lodge and for them to see a different part of England. Anna, who had already fallen in love with the opulent romance of the West End decided her great aunt lived in the kind of manor house to which she would like to become accustomed.

'And what have you liked best so far, Jarrad?' asked Beth, eager to ensure he was not entirely eclipsed by his pushy sister.

'I liked the shows and stuff, but my favourite was the Science Museum.'

*

Back in Silecroft there were plenty of walks on the beach and hikes up the fell to keep them occupied – and English TV programmes which the Adams teenagers could not get enough of. Izzy had insisted she stay with Rhianne, so that Beth and Theo had West Cottage to themselves.

'You could have Middle Cottage attic if you prefer,' suggested Beth.

'No,' replied Izzy, shaking her head. 'That garret will always be Theo's. I don't think anyone else should ever stay there again. Besides I'm only here for a little while to get to know my new relatives. I'll have to be back in Cornwall soon. I've been dying to tell you my news. Shelley is pregnant! I'm going to be a grandma too, Meg.'

'Oh my goodness! How wonderful. And I get to be a great aunt at last.'

*

'It's going to be so quiet when they go back,' sighed Beth as she lay nuzzled into Theo, having just shared Izzy's news with him.

'But more time for us,' he said, pulling her closer.

'Isn't it wonderful how well Zac and Eithan get on?'

'Hardly surprising, both being six foot four giants and crazy about basketball.'

'And Matt too, he fits effortlessly into that trio.'

'The girls have bonded instantly too.'

'Yes, I was surprised how well they get on. Rhianne is easy company, but Ciara can be a bit prickly at times and Mia is... well she's...'

'Nothing if not direct,' finished Theo. 'Charlotte's a credit to you, Beth. She can't have inherited all that grit and determination from her father.'

'I can't take credit for any of it,' she replied miserably. 'We've been separated for thirty years.'

'But she had you in her formative years, Beth, seven and a half years. She's never lost that. Anyway, *Grandma,* if you're going to have any chance of keeping up with these whippersnappers, you'll need your sleep.'

'There are other ways of keeping young,' she said, kissing him on the lips.

'I should have known you only wanted me for my body, Beth Brennan.'

'Don't flatter yourself old man.'

Questions and Answers

Mia was delighted with the progress they were making on the appeal case, which was to be heard on 14th July at Lancaster Crown Court. The jewel in her dossier crown was a cassette tape she had found amongst the box of papers Raymond Braithwaite gave her access to. He had made it on his first conversation with Beth when he had been appointed her solicitor to save him taking notes. It was old and a little crackly but perfectly audible. Mia made three copies, not wanting to overplay the original in case it conked out. She played a copy to James and suggested it could be used in court instead of putting Beth through the painful ordeal of having to recount the traumatic events of that day. James would merely need to get her to confirm its veracity from the witness box. It would be a powerful statement and have the added advantage of fending off allegations of memory contamination. James liked the strategy. He was already picturing the impact it would have.

*

As the court day drew nearer, Beth's joy in her daughter and grandchildren began to be overtaken by acute anxiety. Hearing the tape had brought the events of thirty years ago menacingly close.

The ghostly shadows that had dogged most of her adult life now tormented her more vividly.

'She's like an over-tightened piano wire,' said Theo to Zac. 'Is there anything we could give her to calm her nerves? It doesn't help that she gave up smoking about three months ago.'

'Is she using a patch?'

'Says she doesn't need it anymore. Only wore one for a month. She's a very stoic lady.'

'How much did she used to smoke?'

'I never knew for sure – it's a bit of a touchy subject between us – but I'm guessing fifteen a day since her late teens.'

'That's a long time, Theo. Glad she's given up. I can't prescribe for her, not over here. She'd have to go to her own GP but with that smoking history I think we should be doing whatever we can to reduce her stress levels.'

'I'll do my best to persuade her. Perhaps you could ask Charlotte to add a daughter's weight to the pleas. Beth can be unbelievably stubborn.'

*

Beth Brennan was having none of it. She insisted she would not have any chemicals dulling her brain when she was going to need her wits about her for the court hearing and told Theo in no uncertain terms to stop trying to control her. She did not want any fuss. The no-fuss approach extended to limiting the court party to the absolute minimum. Beth charged Rhianne with staying behind to run the bakery. Eithan must stay to keep an eye on Anna and Jarrad because Mia insisted Zac's testimony was needed and Beth flatly refused to have her grandchildren anywhere near the courtroom. Hilda begged to come. She wanted to stand shoulder to shoulder with Mrs B, in solidarity, as she had done these twenty years, but Beth would not hear of it. In the end, it was only Theo, Izzy, Charlotte and Zac who went to Lancaster. Mia and James checked into a hotel the day before the hearing. Mia had prepared a superb brief for him. He diligently went through it with her once more but there was little left for him to do. He did not even need to tweak the opening and closing statements she had written. She had exposed the jugular and handed him the knife. All he had to do was plunge it in.

*

Beth hardly slept a wink the night before the hearing, which meant Theo got precious little sleep either. As they were about to leave, panic set in. No matter how many times Mia had tried to reassure Beth that this was an open and shut case, she could not dispel a sense of doom. It had happened before so why could it not happen again? They had not believed her then. What if they still did not believe her? If she failed in this attempt, it would deepen the stain, not wash it away. She felt an uncontrollable urge to flee. Theo sensed it and held onto her more tightly. As he helped her into his car, he stopped to kiss her. 'Beth Brennan, you are not going to run from this. Today's the day you can finally cut the chains, banish the ghosts, re-write history. This is the last battle. You found a way to survive this war for thirty years. You're brave and you're strong. You can survive one more day.' She nodded nervously and squeezed his hand.

*

Beth had not ventured beyond Millom in twenty years. The bustle of Lancaster with its crowded streets and congested traffic was bewildering for her. She did not let go of Theo's hand as he guided her into the forum area of the Crown Court. Mia and James met them and escorted them to a meeting room where they waited to be called. When they were ushered into the courtroom, Beth shuddered. She had been in such a room before and it had ended with her being shipped off to prison. Compared to that day, the court felt eerily empty. There were a dozen or so spectators in the public gallery: local rag journalists, law students, habitual enthusiasts and odd nosy parkers. The jury benches were unoccupied; only the court clerk and usher were there to keep the judge company.

Mia, Raymond Braithwaite and his daughter, Julia, sat alongside James on the appellant bench with Beth next to them. The appellee bench was notably thin, a barrister and one junior. They had put out the B team, thought James. They were expecting to lose. They were resigned to taking a hit. He allowed himself a satisfied smile. They had no idea just how hard he was going to hit them. He stood to deliver his opening address.

'My Lord, this appeal will bring before the court unassailable evidence that a gross miscarriage of justice has occurred here. It is my intention to prove that two key witnesses for the prosecution lied on oath and provided false alibis that resulted in the wrongful arrest and imprisonment of Margaret Elizabeth Brennan, known then by her married name of Dagnall. I will be calling on eyewitness testimony from the surviving child in the car accident, Charlotte Rachel Adams née Dagnall, who was too traumatised to give evidence at the original trial. She will tell the court exactly what happened on that fateful day. It is also my intention to prove staggering police incompetence in the handling of the investigation.'

Judge Gillingham nodded and invited the appellee barrister, Mr Taylor, to give his opening address.

'My Lord, the case for the respondent will test the legitimacy of the new evidence. In particular, I will be questioning the cynical timing of this appeal, which follows the death of a man now being fitted up for this crime who can no longer defend himself and the earlier death of his brother, a key alibi provider. I intend to render unreliable any accusations of perjury from the original trial. I will also be robustly defending the actions of the police, who, given the strength of the alibis and the evidence available to them at the time, acted entirely properly and with due diligence.'

The judge nodded and invited James to call his first witness. 'I call Charlotte Rachel Adams.'

Charlotte stood up to her full six feet height, took the witness stand and was sworn in.

She said her name confidently, proudly without an ounce of nerves. She was determined to do this. She was determined to right a wrong that was, at least in part she felt, her doing.

'In your own words, take your time, Charlotte, could you tell the court what happened on the day your brother died in a family car accident.'

'We had been at Aunt Izzy and Uncle George's that morning.'

'We?'

'Mummy, me and my little brother Sid. We often went on a Saturday morning. Dad was usually doing up motors before he went to meet Uncle Rob at the pub. Aunt Izzy would pick us up in her car. She lived in a big rambling old house not very far away – somewhere in the country. I loved going there. Uncle George used to let me use his special paints and easel.'

'And how long were you there that day?'

'Aunt Izzy drove us home after lunch, like normal. Sid and I played in the garden. I heard a lot of shouting in the kitchen so I knew Daddy must be back. He called us in from the garden and told us to get our coats on, that Mummy had left something at Aunt Izzy's we had to go back for. He looked really angry.'

'Can you remember if your father had an injury to his forehead?'

'I don't recall any. I think I might have remembered because I might have thought that was why he was so angry, and he was always so particular about his looks. I think I would have remembered if his face was a mess. We all got in the car. Daddy in the front, us three in the back. Sid was in the middle between me and Mummy.'

'Where were you sitting, Charlotte?'

'I sat behind Daddy. It's where I always sat, 'cos Mummy had long legs. Sid wriggled into the front seat to pretend to drive like Daddy. Mummy pleaded with him to come back and begged Daddy to stop so she could get him into the back seat. Daddy took no notice. There was a lot of shouting and a horrible screeching noise. We swerved across the road and then we hit something.'

'Which way did the car swerve, Charlotte, can you remember?'

'I was thrown into Mummy on my left so we must have been swerving right. Sid was thrown forward and hit the dashboard. Daddy was wearing a driver's seat belt, so he was okay although I think he hit his head on the steering wheel.'

'You think, Charlotte?'

'I can't be sure. His head flopping forward is what I mainly remember. He pulled Sid off the dashboard and put his hand on his neck. I'm a nurse now so I know he must have been checking for a pulse. Then he turned to me and asked if I was hurt. I shook my head. I had landed on Mummy who'd been thrown into the passenger side door. She wasn't moving. He pulled her out and dragged her into the driving seat. He even fastened the driver seatbelt round her. That's when I noticed his head was bleeding.'

'Bleeding where, Charlotte?'

'Bleeding from his forehead.'

'And he definitely didn't have a bleeding forehead when he came back from the pub? When he spoke to you in the garden.'

'No, I would have noticed. It was quite a big cut and bleeding down the side of his face. I would definitely have noticed if he'd come home with that from the pub.'

'What happened next, Charlotte?'

'He told me to be brave, that he was going to phone for an ambulance because Sid was hurt. It would come very soon but it was important that I remember Mummy was driving. That he wasn't there, that it was just Mummy. I didn't understand. "But Mummy can't drive," I said. "Why do I have to remember she was driving? You were driving, Daddy." "No Charlotte," he insisted. "No! I was never here, do you understand? I was never here. I've been drinking so the police will put me in prison if they catch me. They'll go easy on Mummy. You have to be brave now, Charlotte. And remember Mummy was driving. I wasn't here." Then he legged it and I was left in the car crying. I got out to try and wake Mummy up. "Please wake up, Mummy," I said, "please wake up. Sid's hurt." That's when I saw the deer lying in the road. Our car must have only glanced it because it wasn't dead. It was lying bleeding in the road. It was bleating piteously. I felt so alone. I was terrified.'

'How long was it before the ambulance arrived?'

'I don't think it was long, but I had no sense of time, it was as if everything had been frozen. The police arrived first; they must have been nearer. The ambulance came very soon after.'

'Is there anything else you remember, Charlotte?'

'I remember Mummy moaning when the paramedics pulled her out of the driving seat so she must have been regaining consciousness. I remember them putting an oxygen mask on her and putting a blanket round me. I couldn't see what they were doing with Sid, but they worked on him all the way to the hospital. The ambulance was going even faster than Daddy and the siren was blaring. It was so scary.'

'What happened when you got to hospital?'

'They rushed Sid off somewhere. I stayed with Mummy. She had regained consciousness by then and we were being checked over by doctors. Then Daddy and Auntie Jacky arrived at the hospital. When the doctors had finished examining me, they took me to sit with Auntie Jacky. She held my hand all the time. Daddy went off somewhere with one of the doctors. When he came back, he was crying, I'd never seen Daddy cry before. *"Sid's dead,"* that's all he said. He just kept repeating it. *"Sid's dead."* Auntie Jacky hugged me close. I wanted to cry but nothing would come out, it felt like it had felt in the car, as if everything was frozen. Two ladies came to talk to me. One was a policewoman in uniform, I don't know about the other one – perhaps she was a social worker. They kept asking me what had happened, but I was too frightened to say anything and too mixed up, so I said nothing. Eventually I went back to Auntie Jacky's with Daddy.' Charlotte dropped her head to draw breath. 'Take your time, Charlotte. Take your time,' said James gently.

It was only at these last few words that Charlotte's fortitude faltered and the catch in her voice betrayed the tears she was trying to hold back. 'I didn't realise when I left the hospital that I would never see my mother again, not for thirty years.'

'Thank you, Charlotte. No further questions, my Lord.'

'Mr Taylor?' asked the judge, inclining his head towards the appellee barrister.

'Thank you, my Lord,' came the reply as Mr Taylor got to his feet. 'That's a very harrowing and remarkably detailed account for a seven-year-old to have remembered from thirty years ago. Do you seriously expect this court to believe you could have recalled that so clearly? It sounds like you have been coached and are reproducing a pat version of events as fed to you by your lawyers.'

'I'm telling you what happened as I remember it. It's branded on my memory. I even remember the smells and the sounds – the smells of the hospital, the sound of the deer bleating. Anyway, I had already told all this to Zac long before I ever came to England. Long before I ever met any English lawyers.'

'Zac?'

'Zac is my husband. I told him about my mutism before we got engaged. I didn't want him to marry me without knowing about my past or without knowing that my father was a criminal who had escaped justice.'

'I understand the police questioned you about the accident, but they couldn't get anything out of you. You *chose* not to speak, Mrs Adams. Elective mutism is what your medical records state. Elective suggests an element of choice. Perhaps you *chose* to be mute to protect your mother. Why should we assume it was to protect your father?'

'I wasn't trying to protect anyone. I was in shock. I was mute for a year. It wasn't until we got to Canada and put all of this behind us, that I gradually learned to talk again.'

'You can't have it both ways, Mrs Adams. You can't expect us to accept the veracity and clarity of your testimony as a seven-year-old and at the same time expect us to accept you were a seven-year-old so traumatised as to be unable to speak. Which Charlotte Dagnall are we talking about?'

'The Charlotte Dagnall who tells the truth. I have told you exactly what happened, exactly as I remember it and I remember it so well *because* it was traumatic.'

'It's very convenient, you coming forward now that your father is dead and can't defend himself?'

'I would have come forward long before now if I'd known the truth. My father lied to me. For years he lied to me. He said the police had gone easy on Mummy and she would be coming out to join us in Canada. I waited and waited. She never came. I thought she had abandoned us. It was only when I was going through his effects after his funeral that I found a note from Auntie Jacky and pieced together the truth. You can't imagine how I felt when I discovered Mummy had served twelve years in prison for a crime she didn't commit. Thirty years! He stole my mother from me for thirty years.'

'Your mother is a successful businesswoman by all accounts. Would your memory have been jogged by the prospect of a share of her wealth if you were reunited?'

'That's a loathsome and vile suggestion.'

'Answer the question, Mrs Adams, have you accepted any kind of incentive, monetary or otherwise, to testify today?'

'I have not,' she replied firmly. 'I am a wealthy woman in my own right.'

'No further questions, my Lord.' Charlotte returned to her seat, outraged. Mia had been busily making notes. Taylor was bound to challenge again with the same line of attack. She wrote a memo and passed it to Jacky to warn her to be fully prepared for such an ambush.

Theo was called next. He approached the stand with his habitual air of authority that regularly hacked off colleagues but delighted James.

'Could you state your qualifications please, Dr Kendrick,' invited James.

'BA, MSc, PhD, Fellow of The British Psychological Society and Visiting Professor at the University of Birmingham.'

'I have in my hand a copy of your book, *Understanding PTSD,* a world-leading text now in its third edition. You put PTSD on the map, Dr Kendrick. I think the court can accept that your credentials more than qualify you to give an expert opinion on human experience of trauma.' James made an open gesture of invitation to the respondent bench. Mr Taylor nodded and waved him on.

'In your expert opinion, Dr Kendrick, would a child of seven and a half be able to clearly remember the events of a traumatic experience that happened thirty years ago?'

'Undoubtedly. A child of seven and a half experiencing a trauma of that magnitude would either blank it out, what I call analgesic amnesia, or do the opposite, freeze frame it in all its horrific, sensual detail.'

'Sensual?'

'Yes. Victims may remember taste, smell, touch as well as sight and sound. It's why victims have such terrible nightmares. The nightmares are often a vivid reliving of some aspect of the trauma.'

'So in your view, is the account Mrs Adams just gave the court of an incident thirty years ago likely to be accurate?'

'Yes. It's entirely probable.'

'Moving on to elective mutism. Can you explain, in layman's terms please, the significance of it to this case.'

'Elective mutism is often linked to trauma. I have seen it many times when treating injured servicemen. Indeed, my latest PTSD case – a sapper wounded in Iraq – was electively mute for two months. In a child of seven and a half, bewilderment, fear, bereavement – remember the child had just lost her only sibling – and a sense of abandonment would compound the shut down.'

'It was almost a year before she recovered her speech. Is that normal, Dr Kendrick?'

'It is notoriously difficult to predict when, or indeed *if,* a patient recovers from this kind of trauma. The move to Canada undoubtedly helped because a completely new environment would remove many of the trauma triggers. In other circumstances the recovery of speech may have taken much longer.'

'Thank you, Dr Kendrick. No further questions.'

When Mr Taylor stood to cross examine, there was the slightest hint of a smirk on his lips. 'What is the nature of your relationship with the appellant, Dr Kendrick?'

'She is my fiancée. We are engaged to be married.'

The gallery, thinly populated as it was, suddenly hummed with interest.

'And you don't regard this personal relationship as in any way affecting the objectivity of your expert testimony?'

'Not in the slightest. I am a consummate professional. I am the top name in my field – at the pinnacle of my career. Why would I risk a world-leading reputation to deliver an inferior analysis? This is not a difficult judgement. A dozen clinical psychologists, infinitely less eminent in this field, would give you the same view.'

'Why, then are we not hearing from one of them – from a neutral expert with no emotional connection to the appellant?'

'Precisely because I *am* the best, Mr Taylor. This is an important case. Mr Henderson has fielded his A team,' he added pointedly.

James jumped up. 'My Lord, may I respectfully draw your attention to papers thirty-one and thirty-two: affidavit statements from two psychologists, unknown to Dr Kendrick or the appellant. They are on the list of standby witnesses to be called if required.'

'Do you wish either, or both of them, to appear, Mr Taylor?' queried the judge.

'No, my Lord. No further questions.'

Mia was inwardly beaming and for once in her life, Beth was thankful for Theo's arrogance.

Zac was called to the stand. It was a brief sortie.

'Dr Adams, did your then fiancée confide in you about the events she has just described to the court?' asked James.

'Yes. Seventeen years ago, it was exactly as she said, she wouldn't agree to marry me until she'd told me about her history, so I knew what I was letting myself in for. That's very Charlotte.'

'And what did she tell you?'

'She told me about the elective mutism first, that she'd been in Canada several months before she regained her speech. I'm a doctor, I knew there must have been some kind of trauma to bring that on, but it was still harrowing to hear about the car accident and the death of her brother. She was bitter about being abandoned by her mother – or so she thought at that time. She was particularly concerned for me to be aware her father was a criminal who had evaded justice by framing his wife. She was worried she was tainted by association and perhaps even culpable because of the elective mutism. She described the event exactly as she has done just now.'

'But she never spoke up about the truth of what she had witnessed, even when her speech came back, even when she reached adulthood?'

'She genuinely believed her father when he'd said the police had gone easy on her mother and that she would be coming out to join them in Canada. When she didn't come, Charlotte concluded her mother had abandoned them. As I said, she was bitter about it. By that point she had a new life. There was no point in stirring up a hornets' nest. Her mother was lost to her. Besides, she wasn't even sure if anyone would believe her.'

'Something must have changed?'

'It was after her father's funeral when she was clearing out his house and she found the note from her father's sister-in-law. She was beside herself when she found out the truth. I've never known her so angry. That's when she decided she wanted to try and find her mother and make things right. She had decided all this *before* Dr Kendrick found us.'

'Thank you, Dr Adams, no further questions.'

Mr Taylor stood to cross examine.

'Do you love your wife, Dr Adams?'

'Of course I love my wife. What kind of question is that?' answered Zac a little impatiently.

'Would you do anything for your wife?'

Zac immediately saw where the question was going. 'I would do anything for my wife provided it was legal, moral and ethical.'

'So, you wouldn't lie for her in a court of law?'

'Absolutely not.'

Jacky was up next. Mia felt a twinge of nerves. This was the pivotal testimony, and it was their weakest link. Jacky was brittle and fragile. A possible prison sentence was hanging over her. She might still crack under pressure.

She muttered her name nervously during the swearing in.

'Speak up, please Mrs Dagnall,' said the judge. 'Not all of us have the advantage of youthful ears,' he said, giving her a reassuring smile. It was all she needed. A few kind words to give her courage.

'You provided an alibi for the whereabouts of your brother-in-law, Mr Bruce Dagnall, at the time of the accident in which his son Sidney was killed. I have the court record in front of me and will read to you what you said under oath. *"Rob and Bruce arrived at our house together from the pub. Bruce had been in a fight. I cleaned him up. He had a cut to his forehead and the knuckles of his right hand were grazed. He was still with us watching the football with Rob when the police arrived to tell him about the car accident. It was a terrible shock for all of us."* Do you still stand by that testimony, Jacky?'

'No,' she said bitterly, 'it was a lie. It was all a pack of lies. Rob threatened me, you see.' She turned towards the judge as she added, 'He was handy with his fists, your honour... er... me Lord. He was always worst when he'd been drinking – or when I'd lost a baby. I lost five. Couldn't give him a child. It riled him sommat rotten. If truth be known, as close as they were, Rob was jealous of his brother. Bruce was five years younger, already had two kids and a bigger house – theirs was a posh semi with a garage and a garden. Ours was a terrace. Bruce did up motors in his spare time, you see, on top of his regular job at the Michelin so always had plenty of readies. You don't know what Rob was like. I was shit scared of him... excuse me your honour, er yer Lordship, it just came out.'

'It's alright, Jacky, just tell us in your own words, don't worry about how it comes out,' said James encouragingly.

'I didn't dare go against him, so I just said what he told me to say. I'm not proud of it. Rob kept telling me she'd get off lightly for a first offence – probation and a licence ban. I was utterly stunned when they gave her that sentence, but it was too late by then. If I'd changed my testimony I'd have gone to jail for perjury – that's if Rob didn't do me in first.' Again, she lifted her head up towards the judge as she added, 'I've lived with the shame of it for thirty years, your honour, er yer Lordship, and now that Rob's dead, I want to make it right.'

'You do realise the gravity of what you're saying, Jacky?' James urged her. 'You're admitting you perjured yourself in the original trial. That's a criminal offence. You can still be prosecuted. You might still go to prison.'

'I don't want to go to prison. Living with Rob was a prison sentence with no parole and now I'm free I wouldn't want to be locked up again, but I have to do what's right.'

'My Lord, documents eleven to seventeen have details of multiple injuries sustained over several years by Mrs Dagnall. May I draw your Lordship's attention to the GP references which state likely cause as domestic abuse, annotated with "patient unwilling to make a disclosure".'

The judge nodded.

'In your own words, Jacky, can you tell us what really happened,' said James, gently.

'It was a Saturday. They always met up at their local Saturday lunchtimes. Sometimes Bruce would come back with him and they would watch the footie together.'

'Did they come back together that day?'

'No, Rob came back on his tod and earlier than normal. He was in a foul mood. Said some fucker – excuse me again, me Lord – some fucker was putting it about that Bruce's Mrs was getting it off with a driving instructor. Said Bruce had gone ballistic and taken a swing at the guy. He'd missed and hit the wall, which is how he'd grazed his hand. The landlord threw them out. I knew to keep out of his way when he was riled like this so left him be and got on with some chores. It wasn't long after when the phone rang—'

'How long, Jacky?'

'Maybe half an hour, per'aps a bit more. Rob answered it. I could hear him on the phone. "Listen up, bro," he said, "get yourself off the road. I'll be there in ten minutes. Don't stray too far from the phone box but get yourself out of sight, understand?" Next thing I knew, Rob had picked up his car keys and was heading out the door. "Where are you going?" I asked him. "You're not gonna drive, Rob. You've had a skinful, surely you're not taking the car?" But I should have kept me trap shut 'cos he landed me one right across me mouth and told me to shut me face. He was only gone about twenty minutes. He brought Bruce back with him. Bruce was in a right state. He was shaking like a leaf. His face and right hand were bleeding, and he had a lump coming up on his forehead. I just assumed they were injuries from the pub fight. "Don't just stand there, gawping, woman," Rob said. "Get some hot water and the first aid kit. We need to clean him up." We all went into the kitchen. While I got the first aid kit out, Rob was going at Bruce something chronic. "Now you listen 'ere, little bro, and you listen good. No one saw you, you're sure?" Bruce nodded. "Right, so you're in the clear. This is how we'll play it. You came back with me from the pub – you got that head injury from the fight you were in. There were half a dozen blokes saw you throw that punch and saw the landlord kick us out. There's plenty witnessed us leave the pub together. We came back here, got it. Got it, Bruce!" he yelled at him. Bruce nodded. "You've gotta pull yourself together, mate. The cops won't be far behind us. When they don't find you at home, they'll soon track you down here. They *need* to find you here. Let the bitch take the heat, it's all her fault any which way you look at this. You've gotta appear normal, like nothing's happened other than being real mad from the fight you were in. You know nothing about the accident, got it, Bruce. Say it, *say* it, Bruce." He repeated it parrot fashion, "I came back with you from the pub. I got these injuries in the fight." Then Rob turned to me. He got hold of my wrist and twisted it like you do in Chinese burns. "And you," he said, "you keep your trap shut. Bruce came back from the pub with me. He's been here ever since. You cleaned him up after the fight.

Say it, say it!" He made me say it three times before he let go of my wrist, then told me to turn the box on.

'It all happened like he said it would. Rob had staged it well. Bruce was a bit calmer by the time the cops arrived about an hour later. The two brothers were sat watching the footie with a can of beer in their hands. Bruce didn't need to act. He was so shook up anyway that when they told him about the accident he conveniently fell apart. So, it was me who told the police Bruce had come back to ours from the pub and it was Rob who told them about the fight in the pub. They drove Bruce straight to the hospital. Me and Rob follered in a taxi. Bruce was with the doctors when we got there so we hung around the waiting room. When Bruce came in, I knew it was bad. He was white as a ghost and he was crying. I'd never known him cry before. "Sid's dead. Sidney's dead." He just kept repeating it over and over. We couldn't get anything else out of him, so Rob went to find out what had happened. He came back with the information that Sid had died on the operating table. He'd had a bleed on the brain they couldn't fix. Charlotte was unhurt but in shock and Margaret was being treated for concussion. It was like waking up in the middle of a nightmare. I had to hold it together for Charlotte's sake. We took her and Bruce back to ours. I felt bad that I hadn't gone to check on Margaret, but she and I weren't close. I tried to comfort the littl'un but she was in some sort of trance. Just sat there like a statue, not crying, not saying anything. Didn't even want a donut with a chocolate flake in. I never heard her speak again – not till she was a grown woman come back from Canada just recent.'

'Is there anything else, Jacky?'

Jacky looked down at her feet and twisted her hands nervously, then she turned her face to Beth. 'Just that I'm real sorry, Margaret, real sorry for all the pain I caused you, real sorry for being too weak to stand up to him.' She lowered her head and discreetly wiped her eyes.

'No more questions, my Lord.'

Jacky took a deep breath as Mr Taylor approached the witness stand. This was the part she was dreading.

'That's a very different account from the one you gave at the original trial, Mrs Dagnall. You either lied then or you are lying now. Either way you're clearly capable of lying through your teeth. Why should we believe a single word that comes out of your mouth?'

'I'm telling the truth now. Like I explained. I was too scared to before, but Rob's dead now.'

'It's very convenient, all these people dying who can't defend themselves. Your husband died two years ago. Why didn't you come forward then? Your conscience didn't prick you very hard, it would seem.'

'Margaret would have been out more than twenty years be then and I didn't know where she was or even if she was still alive. I just thought best let sleeping dogs lie. You can't put the spilt milk back in the bottle. It sat uneasy with me though. It's sat uneasy with me these thirty years.'

'You may still go to prison, Mrs Dagnall. Perjury carries a custodial sentence.'

'It's been explained to me that I might go to prison, but I have to do what's right. I don't think I'm long for this world, not with my dodgy ticker. I'd like to meet me maker with a clear conscience.'

'Has your husband left you in a perilous financial state?'

'If you mean did he leave me penniless? Yes. But I get by.'

'Margaret Brennan is a wealthy woman, your niece is not without means in her own right, have you been offered any incentive to perjure yourself?'

'I've been offered nowt and I don't expect nowt. Since I found out what they did to that poor woman in prison, to her face and the like, all I've wanted to do is put things right. Hoping's not the same as expecting. The only thing I'm hoping for is to be able to enjoy this bit of love that's come into me life for whatever time I have left.'

'No further questions, my Lord.'

Jacky shuffled out of the witness box with her head held high. She had done it! She had finally made it right. She had not let them down and she could look at herself in the mirror without shrinking.

'I call Margaret Elizabeth Brennan.' The words she had been dreading thundered into Beth's ears. Mia had walked her through everything, so she knew what to expect from James, but memories of hostile police interrogation and past barrister cross-examination still haunted her. No one had believed her then. They might not believe her, even now.

When the swearing in was done, James smiled at her encouragingly before his opening question.

'On the day in question were you driving the car in which your son, Sidney Ian Dagnall was killed?'

'I was not,' replied Beth. 'The only car I have ever driven is an instructor's car and that was only for three lessons.'

'You have protested your innocence for thirty years. Do you still believe yourself to have been imprisoned unjustly?'

'I do.'

'How did you get that scar on your face?'

'I was attacked by two inmates early in my prison sentence. They broke my arm in three places and branded my face with the sole of a hot iron. They said if I squealed on them they'd arrange the same face ironing for my daughter, Charlotte. They knew where she lived and where she went to school.'

'So, you suffered a vicious disfiguring attack and brutal threats to your daughter as well as a miscarriage of justice.'

'Objection, my Lord,' interjected Mr Taylor, 'a miscarriage of justice has not been proven.'

'Sustained,' agreed the judge. 'Keep your questions factual, Mr Henderson,' he warned.

'Yes, my Lord.' He turned back to Beth. 'Tell me what happened when you were arrested and interrogated.'

'I was treated for concussion. I wasn't seriously hurt but the police wouldn't let me leave the hospital and they wouldn't let me see my children. They seemed to think I had been driving the car and it was me that caused the accident. I kept telling them that Bruce was driving but they didn't believe me. They said they had several witnesses who put him elsewhere. It wasn't long after that they informed me Sid had died from his injuries. I begged to be able to see my dead son, but they flatly refused. I was formally charged with a list of offences including manslaughter and discharged into police custody.'

'So, you weren't allowed to see your dead son in the hospital. What about your daughter?'

'I was eventually granted bail on condition I had no contact with my daughter because of potential witness contamination. I didn't see my daughter again until she came back from Canada a few months ago.'

'Not even at your son's funeral?'

'I was not allowed to attend his funeral. His body was held in the mortuary until after the trial, until after they found me guilty. It was ruled there would be undue stress to the family to have the child's killer present at the funeral.'

James turned to face the judge. 'My Lord, as previously agreed in your chambers, I am going to play a cassette tape recording of the first briefing interview between the appellant and her then solicitor, Raymond Braithwaite, in which she describes in detail what happened on the day of the accident.'

'Objection, my Lord, th—' piped up Mr Taylor.

'Overruled,' snapped Judge Gillingham, before the hapless barrister could get another syllable out of his mouth. 'You were there when this was cleared in my chambers. Sit down!'

Theo sat up straighter and strained his ears. He knew of the existence of the tape and its importance to the case, but Beth would not let anyone other than the legal team listen to it. It was too shaming, she said. One airing in court would be harrowing enough. The tape was crackly and the sound quality poor, but the voices were audible. A man's first. Raymond Braithwaite, Theo assumed.

'25th March 1974: Interview with Margaret Dagnall, Stoke-on Trent police station.

Margaret, can you tell me what happened on Saturday. Take your time and tell me everything. Every little detail exactly as it unfolded. It's important I have as full a picture as possible so that I can build the best defence for you.'

Then Theo heard Beth's voice. The Liverpool accent was more pronounced and there was none of the huskiness that characterised the smoker's voice he was used to, but it was definitely Beth.

'You mean tell you exactly what Bruce said, even the swear words and everything?'
'Yes, everything.'
'Some of the things he said were disgusting.'
'It doesn't matter, Margaret, it's really important you tell me exactly what happened. You can stop at any time, and I can turn the tape off if you want me to.'

She must have nodded because there was no break in the tape, a short gap then he heard her again.

'Izzy drove me and the kids to her house as usual. Bruce was doing up a motor and then he was going to meet his brother at the pub at lunchtime. Izzy had surprised me with a present of some driving lessons. I've been wanting to learn to drive for ages, but Bruce won't hear of it. Izzy had thought it all out. How I could apply for a provisional licence and keep it at her house and how the instructor could pick me up from there so Bruce wouldn't know.'
'Why the secrecy? Surely, if the lessons were a present, Bruce couldn't object?'
'If he found out he would stop me going to Izzy's on a Saturday. He's very controlling, Mr Braithwaite. Very possessive.'
'Call me Raymond, please. Did you have a lesson on that day?'

'*Yes, it was my third. Izzy took us home after we'd all had lunch at hers. The kids were playing in the garden, and I was seeing to the laundry when Bruce came home from the pub. I could see straight away that he'd had a skinful. He started raving at me like a lunatic. "You deceitful little bitch! You think you're so clever, you and that fucking twin of yours! Well, you've been rumbled. Pete Griffin saw you. Came up to me in the pub, all cocky. Said that I must be letting you learn to drive now. I told him he must have had one too many, that my missus ain't ever driving — I put her straight on that. He said he saw you bold as fucking brass. You were behind the wheel at the Trent Vale lights. Said he knew for definite it was you alright — said you're a looker. I told him it would have been your twin sister, you're as alike as two peas in a pod. Told me I was wrong. Couldn't have been your twin — she's already a driver ain't she! So why would she be sitting alongside an instructor in a BSM Learner car? It was you wasn't it? You fucking deceitful little bitch. It was you!"*

'*I said I could explain. "Well, how about starting with how you paid for the lessons. Did you spread your legs for the bastard or just give him a blow job? What's the going rate for a driving lesson?" I told him not to be so disgusting. How could he think such a thing! I've never been with anyone but him — EVER. He knew that.*

'*He said he knew no such thing. I told him Izzy and George paid for the lessons. A present. That they look after the kids for me while I have a lesson on a Saturday morning. I said it would be a good thing for me to learn to drive, I'll be able to help out more, it'll open all sorts of doors. "Open all sorts of zips you mean, you dirty bitch," he said. Don't you think I know what you'll get up to if you can swan around in a car while I'm at work. Well, there'll be no more driving lessons."*

'*I explained I've only had three and Izzy has paid for twelve. "More fool her," he said. "Fetch me your provisional licence, that's gonna be burnt for a start."*

'I told him I couldn't fetch it. He told me not to defy him and threatened me with more than a slap around the mouth if I did. I explained it isn't in the house. It's at Izzy's. I keep it there 'cos the instructor always picks me up from there. "You sneaky, ungrateful bitch," he said. "Might have known that fucking twin of yours would be in on it. How many lessons does a threesome buy?"

'I told him he was being revolting, but he said we were going over to get that licence right now and burn it, and that he was going to sort out what he called my "devious twin and her four-eyed dummy of a husband". He said there would be no more Saturday visits to Barlaston from now on. I begged him not to go. I promised to stop the lessons and said I would get Izzy to bring it over the next day. He told me to get into the car right away, and he went to call the kids in from the garden.

'It's not much above fifteen minutes to Izzy's house, but I was still scared witless. Bruce had been drinking and he was red-hot angry. I sat in the back of the car behind the passenger seat, Charlotte behind the driver seat and Sid between the two of us. I was so distracted, so worried Bruce might lay one on George that I wasn't paying enough attention. Sid wriggled between us into the front seat. He wanted to drive like his daddy. "Come back to Mummy, Sid, quickly," I said. "Good boy, come back to Mummy." But he wouldn't. I asked Bruce to stop the car so I could get Sid into the back seat. It was too dangerous for him in the front.

'He wouldn't stop. "So, you don't trust my driving now, you faithless bitch," he said. "Not as good as BSM lover-boy? I'll show you what real driving is." And instead of slowing or stopping, he put his foot down. He was going far too fast. I was petrified. I begged him to slow down.

'Once you get onto the rural lanes, you have to be on the lookout for the odd deer straying from the Wedgwood parkland. There are road signs up about it. It's one of the first things I learnt from my instructor. And one did stray out onto *the road. We could see it ahead of us. Bruce slammed on his brakes. We skidded across the road, but he still struck the deer. I must have hit my head on the side window and knocked myself out because the next thing I knew, I was being hauled out from behind the steering wheel by a paramedic. I had no idea how I got there. Charlotte was sobbing at the side of the car. I couldn't see Sid anywhere until they put me in the ambulance when I could see the paramedics were working on him. Bruce was nowhere in sight.*

'When I got to the hospital, I kept asking after Sid and Charlotte and Bruce, but they wouldn't let me see them, said they were being attended to. The medics treated me for concussion and a head wound but wouldn't discharge me and refused to let me discharge myself because the police wanted to interview me. Two officers came to speak to me, a man and a woman. It was the male officer who asked all the questions. I didn't understand why he was asking me about my driving licence and my insurance. I told him I had a provisional licence, but I wasn't driving. I'd only had three lessons on an instructor's car.

'He asked me why then did they find me unconscious at the wheel? I replied that I don't know how I got there, somebody must have put me there. Bruce must have put me there. Bruce was driving. He was driving like a maniac that's how we came to hit the deer. "Your husband wasn't driving," he said. "He wasn't anywhere near the scene. He went back to his brother's from the pub. His story checks out, we've taken statements from his brother and sister-in-law and the pub landlord. You're going to have to come up with a better fairy tale than that Mrs Dagnall." That was when he arrested me on suspicion of dangerous driving and driving without licence or insurance. Not long after the two of them came back again. It was the male officer again who spoke. "We'll be adding manslaughter to the charge sheet, Mrs Dagnall," he said. "I'm sorry to inform you that your son has just died from his injuries."

'It was like being hit by a tidal wave. I screamed and screamed. I begged them to let me see Sidney. Begged them to let me see Charlotte.'

There was a gap in the tape and then Theo heard Raymond's voice again.

'And did they, Margaret? Did they let you see them?'

Theo could hear that Beth was sobbing now.

'No. They... they... they handcuffed me to the bed. Said I was a flight risk. I was discharged into police custody. They questioned me over and over again. The same questions. I keep telling them I wasn't driving, that it was Bruce. But they don't believe me. I keep telling them to ask Charlotte. She was there. She knew who was driving. I don't understand why I'm still here, in this police cell. I haven't done anything wrong. Surely, they know the truth by now? Will you be able to get me out of here, Raymond? When will I be able to see Charlotte? When—'

James turned off the cassette. While the tape had been playing, Beth had looked increasingly anguished and agitated. Beads of sweat had formed on her brow and her fists were balling. Theo had seen it straight away and James had not missed it either.

'I have only two short questions for you, Beth. Firstly, is that you speaking on the tape?'

'Yes,' she answered, hardly above a whisper.

'And secondly, is it an accurate account of what happened?'

'Yes, it's the truth. The same truth I've told all along.'

'Thank you, Beth. No more questions, my Lord.'

'Mr Taylor?' said the judge.

'No questions, my Lord.'

Theo was surprised and relieved that Beth would be spared cross-examination, but James was not surprised. He would have done the same in their shoes. No point drawing undue attention to issues that were going to come up in the dissection of the incompetent police investigation. They knew the case was lost. It was a damage limitation exercise for them, and they could not afford to fan the flames of sentiment or raise the emotional temperature. Beth stepped down from the witness box a little unsteadily and James helped her back to her seat. The judge looked at the clock and decided they would take a lunch recess. James felt more than satisfied with proceedings. The foundations were in place now. Surely the miscarriage of justice was assured. The afternoon session would focus on police negligence.

*

Theo could see that Beth looked spent so declined to join the rest of the group for lunch in the court café and took her back to their allocated meeting room where they could be alone.

'Charlotte is going to bring us a sandwich. We've got this room to ourselves now so you can get some rest. You look spent, Beth.'

'I'm not hungry,' she said lamely. 'I feel naked, Theo. I feel like all the grubbiness of my life is being pawed over by strangers. It's shaming.'

Theo took her in his arms. 'Theirs is the shame, not yours, Beth. This miscarriage of justice is shameful. You've been pure and truthful throughout.'

'But I'm not pure and truthful. What about all the lies I made up about Sid? If they knew about that they would say it proved I was a fantasist. They always claimed my testimony was a fairy tale. It would be like all their Christmases coming at once for them, they'd say I was a serial fantasist.'

'Please stop worrying, Beth. They're not to know about any of that. And even if they did it can be explained away. It's going swimmingly, darling, and the killer punches will come this afternoon. You're going to be exonerated, Beth. Trust me, believe me, you're going to be exonerated.'

When Charlotte arrived with food and drink, Beth was sobbing quietly against Theo's chest, so she deposited it on the table and exited discreetly.

*

The afternoon session began promptly at two o'clock. 'I call Gary Bernard Turnbull,' boomed James.

Gary Turnbull took the stand impatiently. He would much rather be on the golf course than answering questions about a case from thirty years ago. When asked, he gave his occupation as retired detective inspector.

'Mr Turnbull, you were the detective sergeant who took charge of this case, is that correct?'

'Yes, that's correct.'

'And you were assisted by a WPC Baldwin?'

'If you say so, I can't remember her name. She only lasted a few months on the force. Didn't have the stomach for the job as I recall.'

'Have you familiarised yourself with the case or would you like me to go through it with you?'

'I got the station to dig out the notes for me, so no need. It's thirty years ago but it's not one you forget easily.'

'Oh, why would that be?'

'Well, because a child died. You tend to remember cases where a child dies and because the mother refused to confess. Denied it over hill and down dale. Bold as brass she denied it all, even though we had indisputable evidence. You tend to remember the stubborn ones.'

'Indisputable evidence?'

'She was found at the wheel, was even strapped in with the seat belt. That's what saved her. Shame belts hadn't been fitted in the other seats as it would have saved the littl'un but it wasn't compulsory in those days. Open and shut case. No other adult there, just the mother and the two kids – and as I said she was in the driving seat.'

'So, it was you making all the running, doing all the suspect interviews?'

'The WPC was a waste of space, so draw your own conclusions. The gaffer, DI Kenyon, may he rest in peace, was technically overseeing it. But this was small beer – a driving conviction – so he left it to me.'

'Small beer, Mr Turnbull. An interesting assessment.'

'It was an open and shut case. There was no other credible suspect. She kept saying it was the husband, but we checked him out. He had cast-iron alibis that put him elsewhere.'

'Cast-iron?'

'He'd been in the Plough with his brother. Apparently, they always went to the pub together Saturday lunchtime. The landlord remembered them being there because he'd thrown them out for fighting, which explained Bruce Dagnall's injuries. They left together and we caught up with them together at his brother's house.'

'And what time did they leave together?'

Gary Turnbull flicked through his notes before answering. 'The landlord didn't give a specific time.'

'I see, and you didn't push him for a specific time?'

'I wanted to find the husband first. When we found him at his brother's house watching the footie and both the brother and the brother's wife swore blind he'd come back there from the pub, I didn't see there was any need.'

'I see. And did you take statements from the brother and his wife together or separately?'

'Well, together, of course.'

'I see. So, you never thought to stress test their alibis?'

'What for? It was obvious she'd done it and was trying to fit the husband up for it.'

'And it never occurred to you it might be the other way round?'

'Why would it? The evidence was all there. It was an open and shut case. Even the little girl that was in the car didn't speak up for her. The woman had clearly concocted the whole fairy tale.'

'So, you didn't, at any point, work through a scenario – check out the possibilities – that the husband had been driving and fled the scene of the accident and got his brother and sister-in-law to provide false alibis for him.'

'No. That didn't fit with the evidence.'

'No further questions, my Lord.'

'Mr Taylor?' invited the judge.

'How long did you serve in the police force, Mr Turnbull?'

'Thirty-five years.'

'In thirty-five years, was the quality of your work ever called into question?'

'Never. Kenzy – er DI Kenyon – was always pleased with my work. Never had any complaints. Was promoted to DI meself not long after this case, actually.'

'Thank you, Mr Turnbull. No further questions.'

'I call Mrs Wendy McPherson,' announced James. A middle-aged woman in a smart navy suit and silk blouse was escorted into the courtroom and took the stand. She gave her occupation as Principal Social Worker. She was James' Trojan horse. Taylor would not have realised the significance when they saw her name and occupation listed on the witness sheet. He was amazed that Mia had managed to track her down but then she was quite exceptional, this little firecracker he had taken under his wing.

'Mrs McPherson, I understand your first career was in the police force and that you were the WPC on this case, WPC Baldwin as you were then known.' Mr Taylor's head jerked up and an anguished look spread across his face as his brain started to compute what might be about to unfold.

'Can you tell us what you remember about this case?'

'I remember feeling dismayed by the whole thing. I was there at the hospital. I sat in on all the interviews with Margaret Dagnall. I sat in on the statements provided by Rob and Jacky Dagnall. Jacky looked scared stiff to me, and I didn't think it was just because she was in a police station giving a formal statement. It smelt wrong. I wanted to talk to Jacky alone, but Sergeant Turnbull wouldn't permit it. I kept telling him that I thought the suspect was telling the truth and shouldn't we be following up some alternative lines of enquiry? He insisted it was an open and shut case and we didn't have the resources for wild goose chases. So, I did some digging on my own time. I couldn't get to see Jacky alone, but I did call up her medical records and that's where I found the tell-tale evidence of probable domestic abuse. I took my findings to Sergeant Turnbull. He balled me out. Said I had no right to take matters into my own hands and "you women are all the same, reading domestic abuse into every little slap". I could see I wasn't going to get anywhere with him, so I went to DI Kenyon. He didn't ball me out, but I could see he was furious with me for going over Turnbull's head and bringing this to him. The next day I was told I was going to be transferred, something to do with a breakdown in the relationship with my sergeant. I was so disgusted I resigned on the spot. I left the police force and retrained as a social worker.'

'No further questions, my Lord.'

'Mr Taylor?' asked Judge Gillingham.

Mr Taylor stood up slowly. He needed time to think through how he would handle this.

'I'm surprised you remember this so vividly from thirty years ago.'

'It was a scarring experience. Of course I remember it. It was the case that finished my career in the police force. It's not something you forget in a hurry.'

'But surely you wouldn't have remembered the names of alibi witnesses. You called them Rob and Jacky.'

'No, I didn't remember their first names. I remember her face and how frightened she looked, and I remember the suspect Margaret Dagnall – I couldn't forget her name, poor woman. Mr Henderson's colleague gave me a copy of the court report from the original trial so that's how I recalled their full names.'

'So, Mr Henderson's team spoon fed you information. It sounds to me like you've been coached, Mrs McPherson. Have you been told what to say here this afternoon?'

'I have not. When I read the court report and saw that she had been sentenced to eighteen years, I was sickened. I volunteered to testify today. I volunteered to share what I know. I volunteered to try and right a wrong from thirty years ago. I didn't need help remembering the substance of what went on, just small details like first names. I've told the truth exactly as I remember it. I have not been coached.'

'As you remember it, Mrs McPherson, and we all know how unreliable our memory can be from thirty years ago. No further question, my Lord.' It was the best he could do, but he knew an additional nail had just been driven into the coffin of this hapless case, which he sorely wished he could have avoided taking.

'I call Mr Farrukh Ahmad,' announced James. On swearing in, Mr Ahmad gave his occupation as consultant pathologist with an impressive array of qualifications.

'Would you read out the description of the injuries sustained by Margaret Dagnall on 23rd March 1974 from the hospital records we requisitioned from the police archive files.'

'Injury to the left temple consistent with a blow to the head. Initial period of unconsciousness reported. Minor epidural hematoma present. Treated for concussion, wound dressed. No other injuries sustained. Discharge not recommended until epidural hematoma has healed,' obliged Mr Ahmad.

'What does that mean in layman's terms?'

'It means she hit or was hit by something resulting in a blow to her left temple which rendered her unconscious. An epidural hematoma is a minor bleed on the brain that is not life threatening and generally heals itself very quickly.'

'In your expert opinion, is it possible that the injury was consistent with the patient hitting her left temple on a car side window?'

'Entirely possible.'

'If you are driving a car, wearing a seat belt and the car hits an obstacle, could you sustain an injury to the left side of the head?'

'If it was a right-hand drive car that would be highly unlikely. It would be much more likely that the head would be thrown forward and hit the steering wheel.'

'Thank you, Dr Ahmad. No further questions.'

Mr Taylor got to his feet. '"*Entirely possible*", "*more likely*", not exactly cast-iron conclusions. It leaves room for an element of doubt wouldn't you agree, Mr Ahmad?'

'My job is to give my best judgement on the evidence provided. On the basis of that I have concluded that it is highly unlikely the patient could have sustained that injury – bearing in mind there were no other injuries reported to other parts of the face – from behind the driver's wheel. That is my expert opinion.'

'No further questions, my Lord.' Mr Taylor had gambled and lost and was regretting taking up the cross-examination opportunity.

'I call Assistant Commissioner Barbara Pointer,' declared James. A stern woman in her mid-forties entered the courtroom. Unlike Gary Turnbull, it had not needed a subpoena to bring her here. She was smart enough to know she was expected to represent the force, warts and all, and it was better to do so willingly rather than under duress. This was the last card James had to play and he was certainly going to relish it. He got straight down to business.

'The senior officers who oversaw the original case are unfortunately deceased and I appreciate this is neither of your making nor happened on your watch. I imagine you would still have been at school when this miscarriage of justice occurred,' he said gallantly.

'*Alleged* miscarriage,' she interjected sourly.

James smiled inwardly. He enjoyed a spirited combatant. 'But you are the senior officer in charge of serious crime, and that brings with it responsibilities for past events as well as present.'

'I don't need a lecture from a barrister on my responsibilities,' she replied coldly. 'Sitting public servants, including prime ministers, understand it comes with the territory.'

'Thank you for the eloquent clarification,' said James. 'You're an experienced detective with an exemplary record and a reputation for thoroughness and fairness. You're a sought-after speaker on detective training courses. As such, would you have been satisfied with the detective work that was undertaken if it had been on your watch?'

'Objection, my Lord,' yelled Mr Taylor. 'Assistant Commissioner Pointer cannot possibly be expected to speculate on a hypothetical scenario.'

'Where is your line of questioning going, Mr Henderson?' asked the judge.

'I want to establish that the case passed to the CPS had serious omissions which, had they been included, would have given rise to sufficient doubt and the CPS would have thrown it out.'

'Objection overruled.'

'Let me put this to you slightly differently,' said James. 'Having studied the archive notes of this case, was it a model of good practice?'

'No, I can't say that it was, but you have to consider this in the context of the times and the resource constraints that this station was working under.'

'Would you have regarded it as an open and shut case if you'd been in charge?'

'I can see how it might present as such, but I would have wanted to stress test the alibis in the light of a credible alternative.'

'Credible alternative?'

'That the prime suspect may have been telling the truth. I would have wanted neighbours to be interviewed also. They may have seen or heard something critical.'

'Not the police's finest hour then?'

'We've had many fine hours and we are a very fine force. It's important we acknowledge when we fall short of the mark. That's the only way we can continue to improve. Irrespective of the outcome of this hearing, I will be authorising an historical study of this case to ensure lessons are learned and best practice fostered.'

She had been very careful and canny in her answers, but James had squeezed out enough for his purposes. 'No further questions my Lord.'

'Mr Taylor?'

'No questions my Lord,' came the hasty reply. He knew when to cut his losses.

'I have no further witnesses to call, my Lord,' said James.

'In that case let's move to your summing up, Mr Henderson.'

'There have been a lot of glib references to thirty years in this hearing, as if we might be talking of thirty days or thirty hours. It's an exceptionally long time. We're talking a generation. Thirty years ago, a computer would have taken up the height and width of a whole wall of this courtroom with a total RAM of sixteen kilobytes. Today it would fit on a tea tray with a RAM of five hundred and twelve megabytes, thousands and thousands of times more powerful. Yes, thirty years is an exceptionally long time. In 1930 it was half the average life expectancy in the UK. For thirty years Beth Brennan has lived with this miscarriage of justice, lived with its stain, lived in its shadow, cheated of her motherhood, of her grandmotherhood. Twelve of those years were served behind bars, robbed of her freedom, her youth, her hopes of a teaching career. Moreover, she was incarcerated for those last two years because she continued to protest her innocence and was denied parole, not once but twice. This whole tragic affair, this travesty of British justice need not have happened. The incompetence and negligence of the police investigation is staggering. I move that this conviction be quashed, and appropriate compensation awarded to the petitioner.'

Mr Taylor got wearily to his feet. He must try and fashion a rousing closure from the ashes of this case, and there was no hope of a phoenix rising to his rescue. 'What is staggering, my Lord, is the cynical timing of this appeal following the death of a man who cannot defend himself. The appeal hinges on the testimony of a woman who is a self-avowed perjurer and on the convenient death of the other key alibi provider. Are we really expected to believe that a woman who left this country thirty years ago as a child of eight and made a life for herself in another continent could remember events so vividly as she recounted today? No, my Lord, the timing of this appeal has more to do with the recent betrothal of Dr Kendrick to the appellant and his desire to eradicate any whiff of scandal surrounding his future bride and her criminal past. It's Dr Kendrick who has been driving this. He was the first to speak to Jacqueline Dagnall. It was he who crossed the Atlantic in search of Charlotte Adams. I contend this has been an elaborate spectacle to preserve his own reputation at the expense of a dead man who cannot defend himself. With regard to the allegations of police incompetence, I would urge you to consider the facts as they presented at the time. The testimony of three alibis, the discovery of Margaret Dagnall at the wheel of the car were all pointing one way. Sergeant Turnbull acted entirely properly. In the circumstances, it was not unreasonable to pursue a single line of enquiry which, I hasten to point out, was ultimately upheld unanimously by a jury. This was a safe conviction which should stand.'

Mr Taylor sat down, and Judge Gillingham addressed the assembled group. 'We will reconvene in the morning at ten when I have had time to consider all the evidence presented today.'

'All rise,' said the court clerk.

James and Mia were disappointed the judge was not prepared to give a judgement that day. It was only just four o'clock and it could all have been done and dusted by five. Now, it would be another long night and agonising wait for Beth. Nonetheless, James was mightily pleased with how it had gone and exceedingly pleased with his talented junior.

Deliverance

Beth arrived at court with Theo next morning after another tense night. Theo's phone had been pinging away on the journey and he was too focused on shepherding his fiancée through the bustling streets of Lancaster to let go of her hand and pick up. So he missed the warning call from Mia and was unprepared for what awaited them in front of the court house. Crowds had gathered outside the entrance. Photographers and journalists were buffeting each other to get the best vantage point. There was shouting and chanting and waving of placards from the assembled multitude – mainly women. Beth caught sight of some of the placards as Theo rushed her into the building, shielding her from the volley of flash guns firing off all around.

Angela Channing is INNOCENT
Free Donna Anthony
Mothers *not Murderers*

'I don't understand,' wailed Beth anxiously, when they were safely inside the foyer. 'Where have they all come from? What are they doing here?'

It was Mia who answered. 'I tried to tip you off, Theo, but you weren't picking up. Since the Sally Clark case, lots of support groups have sprung up. Word must have gone viral overnight that there was about to be a verdict announced on another motherhood miscarriage of justice. The public gallery is already packed. The nationals have got wind of it. They're out in force too. Isn't it wonderful!' Mia was clearly relishing the attention the case was getting but Theo signalled to her to cool it. He could feel the tension in Beth's arm. Mia's dream scenario was Beth's worst nightmare.

*

Mia was right. The public gallery was already packed when they entered the courtroom and there were two familiar faces beaming at Beth when she entered. James had got clearance for Hilda and Rhianne to be admitted inside the courtroom. Beth acknowledged them silently, the tiniest trace of a nervous smile escaping from her lips.

'You didn't really think you were going to keep them away, not after Izzy gave them an update on how well it had all gone yesterday,' whispered Theo in her ear. 'And before you ask, Anna and Jarrad are fine – Eithan stayed home to keep an eye on them.'

The judge was late. Beth's nerves got tauter and tauter. Even James was beginning to feel uneasy. Surely this was an open and shut case. It had surprised him that the verdict was not given yesterday so what could be keeping him now? No one could lean on this judge, could they? He had a reputation for uncompromising fairness.

At twenty-past ten the court was asked to stand, and Judge Gillingham took his seat. His clerk need not have pre-warned him about the packed public gallery and media interest. His trained eye had the measure of the scene in seconds. It would not influence him. He was too long in the tooth to be affected by flattery, praise, bribery or gallery barracking. His trained eye had also taken in a salient fact his clerk had omitted to mention. The spectators were almost entirely female. Grannies, mothers, pregnant women. He was looking at a multi-ethnic sea of motherhood. He waited until everyone was seated and then waited a little longer until there was perfect silence, so it was clear just whose courtroom it was and who was in charge. Then he began.

'It is an inescapable and sobering fact that a small number of mothers do abuse, harm and even murder their children…'

Mia took an intake of breath and James sat up straighter in his seat. This was not what they were expecting. Surely to God he was not going to uphold the conviction.

'… But this is such a tiny percentage compared to the vast majority of mothers who love, care and nurture their children,' continued the judge. 'In the face of this overwhelming statistic, I am at a loss to understand how a young woman could have been so ineffably abused by our justice system. Her protestations of innocence were ignored. At no point did the investigating officer explore the possibility she might be telling the truth, explore the possibility that she could have been framed. There was a credible alternative to be worked through, checked out. Lazy policing led to it being spectacularly overlooked. The real culprit was never interrogated, the alibis were never stress tested, neighbourhood interviews were not conducted, crucial photographic evidence from the crash scene was not examined and medical reports on the injury sustained by Margaret Dagnall were not considered. There was insufficient challenge from senior officers, too ready to accept a seemingly open and shut case. Stretched resource is never an excuse when an individual's liberty is at stake. And what have been the consequences of this catalogue of incompetence? A young mother was denied decent, customary bereavement practice, not even the opportunity to hold her dead son before he was taken to the mortuary, nor attend his funeral. She was further denied the joy of motherhood with her only surviving child. Imprisoned for ten years during which time she was subjected to a horrific and disfiguring attack by inmates. She endured a further two years of incarceration because she continued to protest her innocence at parole boards. Before us sits a woman whose life has been needlessly, shockingly blighted. This has been a colossal miscarriage of justice from which lessons *must* be learned. In my twenty-seven years on this bench, I have never felt so ashamed of the justice system I serve, nor more sorry for the human misery it has inflicted. Jacqueline Dagnall,' he said turning to Jacky who was sitting nervously tugging at her shawl. 'What you did was very wrong, but I accept that it was under duress. You have already suffered much in your life, and my recommendation is that no further action is pursued against you.' Mia heaved a sigh of relief. No CPS would be willing to go against such a recommendation, especially given the drubbing the police were getting here. Jacky burst into tears, muttering her thanks and beaming at the judge through watery eyes.

'Beth Brennan, as you now like to be called,' he continued, training his eyes on the woman sitting woodenly between Mia and James. 'Your conviction is quashed. I offer heartfelt apologies on behalf of the justice system that has failed you so abjectly. Costs are awarded.' The murmurings of appreciation that had begun to build in the gallery were quickly hushed by the banging of the judge's gavel. 'I *will* have silence in my court, or I will clear the room.'

He waited until all the whisperings were spent, keeping his piercing eyes on the faces in the gallery. And then he waited an extra ten seconds before picking up again.

'I have deliberated long and hard over the question of compensation...' There were a few more hushed murmurings from the gallery. The judge reached for his gavel but needed only to raise it a couple of inches before complete silence was restored. 'For the twelve years of incarceration, the destruction of a young life, the theft of motherhood and the stigma of disfigurement and criminalisation, compensation of £1.2 million is awarded.'

No judge's gavel could have held back the communal gasp that swept the court. Mia and James jumped to their feet. It was the largest sum ever awarded in such a case. The clerk, understanding the status quo could not be maintained much longer, acted quickly. 'All rise.' Those in the gallery who were not already on their feet stood to attention and Judge Gillingham managed a dignified exit ahead of the spectacles of jubilation which followed. There was hooting, hugging and cheering from the gallery, a Mexican wave of flash bulbs swept around the room. Rhianne and Hilda clung to each other with wet cheeks. Theo and Charlotte pushed their way out of the second row to get to Beth still flanked between Mia and James at the front. But it was Zac who got there first. He had been watching Beth studiously from a few rows back. He had seen her stiffen and the good side of her face droop. He hand-sprung over the bench that lay in his path, his long legs racing to the front of the courtroom. 'Someone call an ambulance NOW,' he yelled, reaching Beth just in time to catch her as she keeled over. 'She's having a stroke.' As she slumped into his arms, the toy soldier rolled out from her fisted hand. Izzy spotted it and rescued the little wooden figure from trampling feet.

James dialled 999 on his mobile. There were screams from the gallery. The clerk reappeared to see what the commotion was all about.

'She's crashing, Charlotte,' shouted Zac, 'see if you can find a defib – and get those people out of here!' Then, calmly, he began to administer CPR.

Charlotte ran to the clerk. 'Is there a defibrillator here?'

'Yes, it's in the foyer. I will show you.'

'And can you clear the courtroom please.'

'Has someone called an ambulance?' asked the clerk.

'Yes, one is on its way.'

Charlotte rushed back to Zac with the defibrillator. Theo looked on anxiously as husband and wife put the machine to work. By the time the ambulance arrived, not many minutes later, they had stabilised her.

'She'll need oxygen,' said Zac to the paramedics as they lifted her onto a stretcher.

'We'll take it from here, sir. Don't worry, the hospital is very close by.'

*

It had all happened too quickly for them to take it in. Jacky could not stop shaking. 'It should have been me, not her,' she moaned. 'I'm older. I'm the one with the dodgy ticker. I deserved it more than her.' Izzy held her hand and comforted her. 'Shh, now, Jacky. She's going to be alright. She's in the best place. Zac got to her in time. We have much to be thankful for.' Hilda and Rhianne still clung to each other, sorrow replacing their recent tears of joy. Mia was holding on to Theo, who was too shell-shocked to respond to anyone. James and the Braithwaites, outsiders in these intimate scenes, watched it unfold before them like some Greek tragedy in suspended time.

*

'Will she recover?' asked Theo of the consultant in charge of Beth's case.

'It was a significant stroke that has affected her right side and her speech. I expect the speech to come back eventually, but it will be some time before she is intelligible. We will arrange for speech therapy. In time, she will regain the use of her leg. For now, she will need a walking aid and some intensive physio. I understand she is ambidextrous, which is very fortunate as she will have little, if any, functionality in the affected arm. But in answer to your question, yes, she will recover. It's weakened her heart of course, so there is always the risk of a further stroke, but she has every chance of making a good recovery. The smoking history was the main cause, but stress was the trigger, so I don't need to tell you, Dr Kendrick, that she needs as stress-free an environment as possible going forward.'

'And her brain?'

'It's unaffected, almost certainly down to the swift action taken by Dr Adams. He preserved her brain – and probably her life.'

'Yes, he was amazing,' agreed Theo.

*

In the week that Beth was in hospital, life returned to a semblance of normality. Rhianne and Hilda kept the bakery going. Much as they hated leaving her, Theo had said it was the biggest contribution they could make to her recovery – for Beth to know her customers were not being let down and that the business continued to thrive. 'Stress-free, that's what the doctors ordered, remember, stress-free,' he had urged them. Anna and Jarrad visited their grandmother in hospital three times, Jarrad was fascinated by all the machines in the specialist unit and wanted to understand more about how defibrillators worked. Anna, once she knew Gran was safely on her way to recovery, basked in the glorious drama of her father playing the hero, which she could not wait to recount to Rosie. Raymond came a couple of times, once on his own account and once at Beth's request.

*

Theo knew it was not feasible for Beth to pick up again at the bakery and he was surprised at how readily she had accepted the passing of the baton to Rhianne. Life would take on a new rhythm, a new routine and Theo embraced it. The prospect of sharing his remaining years with Beth, however restricted they might be, filled him with indescribable joy. 'You have to make good on your promise to marry me now the court case is over,' Theo reminded her.

Beth's speech was improving but still not intelligible, so he waited as she wrote her response on a notepad. 'Are you really, really sure? I'm going to be a drag on you. I'll hold you back. Before it was about my criminal record. Now it's about my disability.'

'For pity's sake, Beth. We've been through this a thousand times. I consider myself the luckiest man alive. I nearly lost you, do you think I care if you walk with a stick and talk a bit funny? And I'm not after your money, in case that crossed your mind. I've asked Mia to draw up a pre-nup for me to sign away any rights to your compensation package should you die before me.'

'As if that would ever have crossed my mind, you idiotic

Neanderthal. p.s. I love you. p.p.s. – no need anyway I've already given the money away. Raymond has the details, he'll fill you in.'

'What is it with you women and Neanderthals. That's just the sort of thing Mia would say. So, it's settled then?'

In answer, she put the notepad down and nodded. Her eyes were shining, a shy smile unfurling crookedly from her mouth – which he promptly kissed.

'You just have to talk to Izzy about your bridal dress. She has excellent taste, and she is your identical size after all, so can shop for you.'

*

Beth was due to be discharged the next day. She had been fitted with a walking aid and given a schedule of appointments for physio and speech therapy. Anna had to have a new dress too of course, so accompanied Izzy on her hunt for a suitable bridal dress. 'It's romantic, isn't it, Great Aunt Izzy? The oldies can surprise you sometimes.'

'Not so much of the oldies, if you don't mind.'

Izzy selected a tasteful dress, floaty and feminine in a soft blue, and Anna chose a racy crimson red number. Izzy left Anna arguing with her mother about the protocol of attending her grandmother's wedding in a strappy, low-cut number, and set off to the hospital, excited to show Beth the dress she had picked out for her. If she hurried, she would get there before Theo with enough time to model the dress for Beth and get it hidden away before the groom-to-be turned up.

*

As she approached the ward, Izzy could hear the sound of alarm buzzers ringing. Her eyes were drawn to the red flashing light above her sister's bay. Izzy started to run. 'What's happening?' she asked as she hastened her step.

'You can't go in there, I'm afraid,' said a nurse, putting her arm across to bar Izzy's path. 'We're dealing with an emergency, just now.'

'Is it my sister? Please tell me. Beth Brennan, my sister – is it Beth?'

'We're doing everything we can for her, please go to the waiting room.'

'But what's happened? What's happened?'

'Please go to the waiting room. Someone will come for you. You need to let us do our job.'

Izzy made her way to the waiting room and called Theo.

'Hi Izzy, I trust you've found a dazzling dress for my beautiful bride,' came the breezy reply.

'Theo, something's happened. They won't let me see her and there are medics in there with her and flashing lights and buzzers.'

'I'm thirty minutes away – I'll be there in twenty. Ring Charlotte.'

'Yes, of course. Oh, do drive carefully Theo.'

Charlotte and Zac joined Izzy five minutes before Theo got there. The four anxious relatives waited two hours before a doctor came with news of his patient.

'Are you relatives of Beth Brennan?'

'Yes,' responded Theo authoritatively, 'I'm her fiancé. What's taken so long? Is Beth alright?'

'Beth had a second stroke. This one was bigger than the first. We've moved her to intensive care. She needed a ventilator and close monitoring. We've been running tests to check for brain activity.'

'And?' asked Theo nervously.

'So far we can't detect any. But we'll check again in the morning in case there is a delayed response. But I have to prepare you for the possibility that the damage may be permanent.'

'Is she in pain?' asked Charlotte.

'No, she's sedated, and the machines are keeping her organs going. She's peaceful. I'm sorry I couldn't bring you better news.

Our records show next of kin to be a daughter, a Mrs Charlotte Adams. Are you Mrs Adams?' he asked of Charlotte.

Before she could answer, Theo butted in, 'I'm her fiancé. We were due to be married in two weeks' time. You can address your questions to me.'

'I'm sorry, sir, but in these circumstances, we are required to work with the legal next of kin regarding any decisions that might need to be made. It's hospital protocol – and it's the law,' he added, noting how distressed Theo had become. 'Why don't you all try and get some rest. There's nothing more you can do tonight. Come back mid-morning, we should have a clearer picture by then.'

Izzy put her hand on Theo's arm. 'It's alright, Theo. No one is going to make any decisions without talking to you first. We may be worrying unduly. All might be well come morning. The best thing you can do now for Beth is get a good night's sleep. Come back with us. We need to support each other through this.'

Theo nodded weakly. His mind was a blur. Izzy's calm was an oasis of sense he clung to gratefully. Charlotte cast a quick glance at Zac. It was going to be a long night and neither held out much hope for a morning miracle.

*

The troubled four duly returned to the hospital next morning and sat in silence waiting for the consultant to bring them news. It came at a few minutes past eleven. Charlotte and Zac were expecting it, Izzy had privately resigned herself to it, but Theo took it like a man flattened by an articulated lorry. The news confirmed that Beth was brain dead. She was only being kept alive by machines.

'Can we see her please?' asked Izzy.

'Yes, of course,' agreed the consultant. 'She's hooked up to a lot of tubes and wires and there's a nurse in attendance so no more than two at her bedside at once please.'

'You and Theo go first,' offered Charlotte.

The room was brightly lit. The busy hum and click of machines seemed eerily at odds with the lifeless form lying on the bed. Izzy wept silently. Twins needed no words. The very air between them was enough. She kissed her fingertip and placed it briefly on her own and then on Beth's heart and held it there, unable to stem the tears streaming down her face. Then she left the room to afford Theo some privacy. He stared at the array of wires attached to numerous contraptions and then at Beth's face with the ventilator tube taped to her mouth. Her scar seemed oddly innocuous amid the ugliness of the beeping machines. It helped him recover his equilibrium. He took her hand in his. 'You win, Beth Brennan. You never did make an honest man of me. You shot down every missile life has thrown at you. You just ran out of road.' He kissed her on the forehead, tenderly stroked the scar on her cheek and sat with her until he could banish the machine-shackled image from his head and replace it with her animated eyes, one exuberant pink cheek and a set of liberated toes squelching in the sand.

Charlotte and Zac went in next. By the time the young couple returned to the waiting room, Theo was prepared. He knew what was coming.

'We need to talk about Mummy,' began Charlotte hesitantly. 'The medics are asking me, as next of kin, whether I want to switch the machines off.'

'She's lived in one prison or another ever since her marriage to Bruce,' said Izzy. 'We can't condemn her to another. It would be beyond cruel.'

'I agree,' said Charlotte quietly. 'Theo? A few more days and you'd have been next of kin. You must have your say.'

There was a catch in his voice, but his words did not falter. 'More than anything I want to set her free.'

'So, it's settled then?' asked Charlotte, a little less hesitantly.

Silent nods were all the answer she got or needed.

*

Mia worked hard to keep the media at bay so the family could have a private funeral. After the scare of the first stroke, Beth had tied everything up in a detailed will she had dictated on her notepad to Raymond. Briar Cottage went to the McArthurs, who also inherited the bakery business and the three terraced cottages on condition that Middle Cottage attic was made available for Theo's exclusive use for the remainder of his life. Of the two other rental cottages, one went to Izzy, the other to Charlotte so they would always have holiday homes to enjoy with their families. Charlotte also inherited the sizeable portfolio of investments Beth had built up over the years. The £1.2million compensation package did not feature in the will because Beth had already given it away before she died. Raymond had managed that for her too. Half went in trust for her two grandchildren and half to the children's hospice in Millom which Beth had been actively supporting for nigh on twenty years. Hilda was the only other beneficiary – Mrs B left her a lump sum to go with the pension provision she had already made for her. There was one other legacy, a tiny wooden figure housed in a small velvet pouch with a hand-written note.

I leave my most precious possession to Theodore Alistair Kendrick. The best of men, whose best is yet to come.

*

Rhianne put on a splendid wake at the bakery tea shop. Eager promises were made to reunite once a year at their holiday homes before farewells were made and guests departed. Izzy took a last walk along the beach with Theo. 'I'll be based in Cornwall most of the time,' said Izzy. 'Shelley is going to need all the help she can get once the baby arrives. You know you'll be welcome anytime.'

'I know, Izzy, thank you. No need to worry about me. Between you, Mia, Rhianne and Charlotte, I'm awash with invitations.'

'But I do worry, Theo.'

'Why? Because you think I'll pull the drawbridge up for another twenty years?'

'Well, I…'

'Look, Izzy, I'm not going to sully Beth's memory with indulgent self-pity. I'm a lucky guy. I've loved and lost twice. That's once more than many and twice more than some. I cherish the time I had with Beth. I miss her like crazy but I'm not going to waste whatever years I have left. She said the best of me was yet to come and I intend to honour her faith in me.'

'Are you going to pick up your clinic work again? The new book is finished, isn't it?'

'Yes. And yes, I will go back to my clinic work eventually, but not until I've done some more training. Beth maintained there was a dimension missing from my PTSD work and she was right. I haven't paid enough attention to the impact of grief. It's made me reflect on the loved ones we've lost and how differently we've all grieved.'

'I suppose we each have to find our own way to deal with pain,' she responded.

'Mia reacted with hot anger until it burned itself out. Beth created a fantasy world and sealed it in with an armour of ice. Eithan shut down completely. I wore it like a hair shirt. But you, Izzy, you seem to have navigated your sea of grief more sanguinely than the rest of us.'

'I accepted it as a fair price for the love I had with George. You might say we've shaken hands, grief and I.'

'I'm not ready to shake hands with grief just yet, Izzy, but I'll get there. In time, I'll get there.'

'Beth would be proud of you. It's what she would have wanted.'

'The BBC have approached me about a Radio 4 series featuring some of my case studies.'

'Sounds like you're going to be pretty busy in the coming months.'

'I plan to be. The training and the BBC will have to wait. I have another book to write first. About one more soldier.'

'Eithan?'

Theo shook his head. 'I'm pitching that one to the BBC to be included in the radio series...'

'You're going to tell Beth's story!!' she interrupted excitedly.

Theo nodded. 'The world has to know what happened, Izzy. Yes, I'm determined to tell Beth's story.'

'Is that what you'll call it, *Beth's Story?... Soldier Beth?*'

Theo shook his head again and pulled out a little wooden figure from a pouch he kept in his pocket. He held it out on the palm of his hand. 'I'm going to write *Toy Soldier*.'